REBEL KING
BOOK TWO
The Hardships

The Har'ships

CHRONICLES OF ROBERT DE BRUS, KING OF SCOTS

A NOVEL

CHARLES RANDOLPH BRUCE
AND
CAROLYN HALE BRUCE

BRUCE

Cover design and illustration and interior character drawings
by Charles Randolph Bruce

Dedication

•

To those men and women
who served,
who are serving
and who will serve
to keep us free.

"People who are willing to give up freedom for the sake of
short term security, deserve neither freedom nor security."
- Benjamin Franklin,
Historical Review of Pennsylvania, 1759

Map of events 1306 - 1307

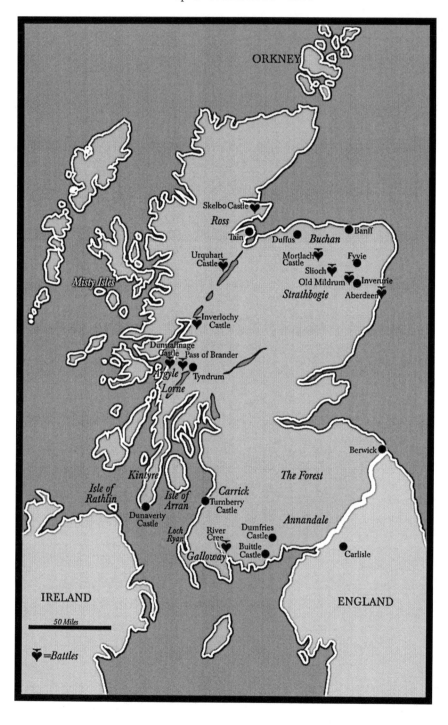

ORKNEY

Skelbo Castle

Ross

Tain   Duffus   *Buchan*   Banff

Urquhart
Castle   Mortlach   Fyvie
                    Castle
                         Slioch
                    Old Mildrum   Inverurie
                                   Aberdeen
                    Strathbogie

Inverlochy
Castle

Dunstaffnage   Pass of Brander
Castle
Argyle   Tyndrum
Lorne

Berwick

Kintyre   *The Forest*

Isle of   *Isle of*   *Carrick*
Rathlin   *Arran*   Turnberry
                         Castle
Dunaverty   *Annandale*
Castle   Loch
              Ryan   River   Dumfries
                      Cree   Castle
                              Buittle   Carlisle
              Galloway   Castle

IRELAND   ENGLAND

50 Miles

♥ =*Battles*

List of Character Illustrations

Andrew Stewart

August 10th 1307
Galloway in the South of Scotland

The morning sun had not yet risen over the craggy mountain, but the sky was well lit above the small, fog-laced haugh. Birds greeted the king and his squire with songs and cries of warning as the two made their way through a thicket toward the river. Crystal clear, the river was fed by numerous small creeks that flowed out of the distant gray-blue mountains, and a large spring that bubbled up a short distance away.

At the edge of the sparse tree line King Robert de Brus paused, warily observing the scene and abandoning his usual proprietary admiration of the beautiful heather-garbed valley floor. Seldom was he able to relax his guard.

Seeing naught around him but the peaceful river valley, the king and his squire cautiously picked their way down the rock-strewn incline to the river's edge, pausing there to survey their surroundings once again. All was quiet.

Robert removed his armor and clothing and handed it to the squire, then squatted and dipped his large hands into the cold water, scooping up their fill. Splashing it onto his naked torso, he shivered from the shock.

"Ah-h-h!" he cheerily growled. "Andrew! Ye had best come take advantage of this fine, cold water, Lad," he yelled to his squire as he repeated the cleansing. The king had slung his huge sword belt around his neck, and the point brushed the mud somewhere behind him as the sheathed blade pushed between his hunkered legs. Dipping into the torrent again, he wet his face and auburn beard, and again to drench his long locks of fairly auburn hair. Then, with experience of a man who has long lived with his enemies about him, his senses perked up at the sound of crackling tree branches, but he calmly continued his ablutions, his wary eyes furtively glancing hither and thither.

Andrew Stewart, the thirteen-year-old squire accompanying him to the stream, stood an easy ten paces behind the king, holding the royal raiment of rough-made clothes. The king's chain mail hauberk and his chest and back armor, leather and metal plates, having accumulated quite a number of dents from battles against the English in the previous several months, lay on the ground nearby. The youth was unaware of the sounds his king had noticed, and continued to enjoy his adolescent's daydream as he watched lazy puff clouds catch the gold and orange colors of the early sun.

King Robert arose from his washing, his eyes scanning the landscape as he turned toward Andrew. He motioned for his bloodstained garment and his saffron tabard, sewn for him with the red lion rampant upon it by a proud peasant woman before the battle of Loudoun. The wounds he received there were minor and long since healed, leaving behind but faint linear white scars.

After the bloodletting on Loudoun Plain, Robert had lost no time in consolidating his precarious claim to Scotland's throne. Among his enemies he counted not only the well-trained and well-armed English troops, but many of the Scottish nobility as well. Scots opposed to de Brus considered him a usurper of the throne who murdered John "The Red" Comyn, his nearest competitor, and brazenly, some said, crowned himself.

Furthermore, there was a faction of the Scots opposition who yet contended that the rightful throne belonged to John de Balliol. Indeed, de Balliol had been ceremoniously crowned at Scone, but shortly abdicated under duress from Edward I, who contemptuously tore the royal emblems from the Scot's tabard and left him forever shamed before his people. He was then imprisoned in England, eventually being released to retire to a life of comfort and prestige, if not power, on the continent.

Thus, as Robert stood naked and dripping wet on the edge of the brightly sparkling stream, he had a long roster of enemies to choose from, were he to hazard a guess as to whom it was now approaching with possibly murderous intent.

"Quietly look beyond me Lad and see if ye ken the likes of them sneakin' up on us," said Robert quietly as Andrew came to him and handed him his linen shirt.

Andrew scrutinized the area carefully as the king turned his back to the direction of the sounds and quickly dried his hands and face on the cloth.

"What d'ye see?" whispered the king as he took the scabbard belt from around his neck and handed it to the boy.

"On the edge of the wood," said Andrew softly, "a bush yonder is shakin.' Aye, I can see folks a'hidin' there!" he whispered as a tingle of fear and excitement traversed his spine and puckered his buttocks.

Water dripped from Robert's hair onto his shirt as he looked at it. "Might have to wash the bugs out of this one day soon," he smiled and slipped the louse-ridden garment over his head.

Andrew, however, didn't notice the king's smile. His wide eyes were on the thicket beyond. "They're a'comin', Sire!" he whispered urgently to Robert.

"How many?" asked Robert, still not turning.

"Three's all I see, one old, two young, walkin' fast this way!" relayed the youth, briefly. "Losels by the look of 'em," he added.

"Where's yer bow, Lad?" asked the king as he calmly reached for his sword.

"By yonder tree... but I hain't got but the one arrow," said Andrew, glancing toward the bow.

"Aim straight for one of 'em's head so they don't see it comin'. Hie!" said Robert, and he turned to face the assassins. Andrew ran for the tree and stood behind it while retrieving his weapon.

The three men suddenly stopped at seeing the enormous knight standing less than twenty paces before them.

"Ye men need not die this morn," said Robert in a strong voice as he calmly drew his sword from its sheath.

The older man looked at his two companions, flanking him with their swords and daggers at the ready! "Ye ones be with me still?" asked the man, though his throat had gone suddenly dry and his armpits tingled as he began to sweat in the crisply cool air.

"Aye, Da," they both answered in unison.

"Land we've been promised, and 'tis land we need," added one of the sons, stiffening the resolve of the other two even further.

"Then let's be at the deed!" cried the man, and the three charged the king and his squire.

Andrew swiftly nocked the single arrow, and drawing it full back, loosed it on the young man then leading the charge and thus closest to the king. Trying to discern if they would cease their run, Robert watched as the shaft reached its target and the youth fell dead at the running feet of his father, but the father and his remaining son slowed not at all. His face set in a mask of resolve, Robert at last dropped the blade's scabbard and held the mighty sword with both hands, ready for the fight.

Andrew stood well back, for he had seen the damage levied by the large sword in the hands of his king and he wanted not to be an accidental victim of the blade.

The younger runner came headlong at Robert and swung a first, too-broad arc with his sword, momentarily losing his balance. Robert easily sidestepped the son's blow, but the father swung a wild, glancing blow from the other side, carving a shallow slice from Robert's shoulder.

"Enough, fools!" shouted Robert, but the attackers heeded him not. Thinking the wound had rendered him weaker, they came toward the king in even greater excitement. Robert needed only a single slash of his sword at neck level to silence both father and son.

The young man died almost instantly; the father lingered momentarily. Robert stood over him in his death faint and asked, "Who sent ye to take my life?"

The man saw his son lying dead beside him. He tried to rise on one elbow, but simply made the blood rush more quickly from his gaping wound.

"Ye are dead, ol' man. Who sent ye?" repeated Robert.

"Yonder son... dead?" gurgled the man.

"Aye," replied Robert, "as dead as ye will be in a moment more."

The man rested his head again on the heath as tears of brief mourning for his two sons welled in his eyes and followed the furrows at the corners of his aged brow to disappear into the hairs of his beard.

"*Who* sent ye!?" Robert repeated again, knowing time was quickly running out. "And what is meed for such murder?"

"'Twas..." the tough old man sputtered and coughed, "... *Umfraville*... promised a croft... 'pon yer head..." Then he exhaled a long, rasping groan and was dead, sinking heavily into the sparse heather.

The man they intended to assassinate stood sorrowfully over the three churls and heaved a great sigh as Andrew left his hiding place and rejoined his lord. Standing silent, the hunted monarch looked about, searching for possible additional assassins. Seeing none, he turned back to the carnage and shook his head in frustration. After a moment a scream erupted from his troubled heart. "FATHER IN HEAVEN!" he yelled to the sky, and his voice dropped to a mere whisper. "Why is my country devouring itself alive?"

Andrew stood near and kept watch while his wounded king said a silent prayer. When Robert again turned toward his squire, his eyes were welled up with tears for the Scots peasants, turned to assassins by the promises of his enemy.

Ingram de Umfraville

AUGUST 23RDRD 1307
CASTLE BUTTLE IN GALLOWAY

Ingram de Umfraville, having played the fool's handmaiden to the amusement of all at Loudoun Plain, was most determined to wreak revenge on Robert de Brus by any means at his imagination, fair or foul. Thus, he and two of his most trusted captains traveled to Castle Buittle, that imposing pile of no particular beauty belonging to the family of deposed King John de Balliol, and now temporarily occupied by Dungal Macdouall, Lord of Galloway. Macdouall sought shelter there but recently, for his own lands were often raided by the growing army of Brus.

The three arrived at Buittle in the late afternoon and were immediately ushered into the great hall. There they were presented with libations of the choicest wine Macdouall could offer from the former King's middling wine cellar.

"My Lord, Sir Dungal, will be with ye presently," said the steward of the castle, and he placed the wine and four ornate gold quaichs before the honored guests.

"We'll have our leisure 'til he shows himself," replied Sir Ingram as the travelers sat wearily on the bench seat in front of the large oak table. The servant poured each of three shallow, two-handled cups full with the wine and left the dripping pitcher for their further imbibing.

Bowing respectfully, the steward withdrew from the great hall and went directly to Lord Dungal in his solar.

"What make ye of that lot?" asked the fearful Dungal, sitting among rumpled bedcovers.

"They strike me as bein' peaceable 'nough, Milord," replied the steward, approaching the visibly trembling nobleman. "Air ye cold, Milord?" he asked, drawing nearer. It was then that he noticed sweat glistening on the wrinkled forehead of his present lord. "Ye appear not well, Milord. Have ye a fever?"

Ignoring the servant's concern, Sir Dungal said not a word in response but arose, and leaving a trail of coverings on the floor, staggered his way to the wall his solar held in common with the great hall. Silently, he opened a small, hinged door at eye level to reveal a five-inch hole that allowed him to look down on the unsuspecting guests below. The visibility was poor in the dimly lit hall and he cupped his hands around the hole in an effort to see his visitors better.

"One day, I shall figure a way to know also their words and not just their loud laughs," complained Dungal to himself when he couldn't hear the men's conversation well enough to understand, and he closed the spy hole softly. Somehow, he knew they plotted with The Brus against him, but so clever were they about it that he had not yet unraveled the fabric of the deception to know how it was woven.

In a way, he felt sorry for de Umfraville, for he was undoubtedly under the hellish spell of Brus and therefore not responsible for his evil treachery. He gnawed nervously at his fingernails and gazed glassy-eyed into the nothingness of a dark corner, where he alone saw images of evils being perpetrated upon him and his. The steward had learned better than to stir him when he stared thus.

"Piss pot!" barked Dungal as he suddenly turned toward the steward with pretended angry eyes to mask the mortal fear he imagined for his personal safety and well-being. "Never mind!" he shook his head and waved his hand to negate his previous order. "'Tis foul of content and smell and needs to be emptied. Tend to it!" With that, he wheeled about and rushed to the garderobe off the solar to relieve himself. So nervous was he that he was well wet before he managed to unleash his fastenings, but as soon as he did so, he let fly a yellow arch toward the garderobe seat, some four feet away. More urine splattered about than ever made the opening, and he cursed loudly all the while, saying that he and his privy were both awash in it.

The steward hastened to remove the sloshing chamber pot from under the bed and take it out of the solar to have it emptied and cleaned, thus to escape the approaching madness. He wanted to be well away before the lord of the castle called him to clean up the amber mess, but the loud voice of his lord was soon issuing other instructions for him from within the small adjoining chamber.

"Have a few of them slave women feed up supper to our 'company'," ordered Lord Macdouall, adding, "Make sure they have the brass to show some tit and keep them men's wits from the fact of my absence! And don't send none of them scrawny wenches that look half starved, neither. Be sure they have tits that a man could fill his hands with and then some." He gestured with one hand by clutching an imaginary breast on his own chest.

"Aye, Milord," returned the steward with a bow.

The last of the urine dribbled and fell on Dungal's feet, and his penis received a terse, useless wriggle as he tucked it back into his already soggy leggings.

"Send for wardrobe!" again ordered Dungal as the steward opened the door to the solar.

"Aye, Milord," replied the servant as he turned and gladly closed the door behind him.

Within the span of an hour and a quarter Lord Dungal finally made his entrance, loudly shoving the huge door to the great hall wide open. "Greetin's to the lot of ye!" he shouted at the top of his wind.

Well watered and flushed red with their pleasure from the women's beguiling, the startled trio of visitors jumped to their feet ready for a fight until they realized the sudden clamor was but Lord Dungal's arrival. They bowed appropriately as the lord approached the table. He was outgoing and lightheartedly gay in his demeanor, and the nearby steward wondered if this were the same man he had left in such a disagreeable state but a short while before.

"How be yer constitution, Sir Ingram?" asked Dungal while striding toward the three bowing men.

"Passin' well, thank ye for inquirin', Milord!" replied the surprised Umfraville, standing erect to greet the lord of the castle with equal eyes. "And how fares yerself?"

"Tough as a mighty oak," said Dungal, grinning as he flexed his biceps and held his arms over his head comparable to a tree before he grandiloquently swished his cape over his shoulders and sat in his large chair across the table from the three men.

"More wine… and a joint of meat!" he ordered, and the women sent to entertain Umfraville's band hastily retreated into the kitchen, their spells successfully cast.

"The maidservants in yer keep purely know how to capture a man's attention," said a lusting Umfraville, his eyes roaming the kitchen doorway looking for one maid in particular.

"Peel yer orbs, Ingram! If ye stare hard enough, ye may see through the stone and hail yer lass," replied Lord Dungal accompanied by a heavy belly laugh that echoed sharply in the great hall. The three visitors returned the laugh and the meeting commenced on friendly ground.

"What brings ye three to Buittle?" asked Dungal, picking up the pitcher of wine and pouring himself a quaich full to the brim.

"To the point...," said Ingram, his voice suddenly laced with anger, "that damned whoreson usurper!"

"Aye," returned Dungal blackly, "Robert de Brus of the evil spells and evil deeds."

"The same, Milord," replied Sir Ingram, quaffing his wine.

"He has been here in Galloway, raidin' the locals..." said Dungal through a swallow of wine, "...stealin' kine to feed his paltry army of nobodies. Most poor crofters have run off south to Inglewood Forest with their livestock, tryin' to hold on to what they can." He grew quiet for but a moment before adding loudly, "And I myself have sent my entire family to lands of my holdin' across the border and out of reach of The Brus' devilish trickery!"

"Are we not Scotsmen to the blood and bone of our bein's?" asked Umfraville, dramatically placing his hand on his chest. His host knitted his brows together in questioning manner, but made no reply. "Well, if we *are*," Ingram persevered, "for the sake of our beloved Scotland we *must* rid oursel's of this Robert de Brus who professes himself king!"

Dungal nodded and faintly smiled in agreement.

"Did he not coldly murder my kinsman to eliminate opposition to The Brus' royal ambitions? He, himself, has ne'er so much as denied it! As Scots we must see that he is appropriately executed for *that* crime, if no other, though God knows he has been wanton in his slaughter, and in the depravity of his deeds against the Scots people!" None could hold a candle to de Umfraville once he began his orations in earnest.

"And the English!" his eyes widened, his brows arched, and he paused to achieve the desired foreboding. "What will become of Scotland once young King Edward returns to avenge the butchery de Brus has wrought upon the English? We will all be held responsible for the madness of the man, if we permit him to roam the countryside gathering his 'army' and acting in the name of Scotland! Aye! We shall one day find our own heads looking down from o'er the gates of our cities, placed there by the hand of Edward de Caernarvon!"

Sir Ingram was well into his diatribe when the door opened to the kitchen and servants entered carrying steaming trenchers of meats and breads and puddings. However, the meats were served, not by the maidservants who had previously served them and held the visitors' rapt attentions with sexual artifice, but by homely kitchen lads who simply laid the food upon the table and left the men to serve themselves. Sir Ingram frowned and grew quite sullen from twice-felt disappointment.

Lord Macdouall waved the steward to his side and instructed him to fetch Gavin, his most trusted friend and bodyguard, and Sir Patrick Macquillen, to join them for the meal. "We have plannin' to be about," said Dungal, turning back to the table. At that moment he noticed Umfraville's facial comportment and grinned knowingly.

Caught, Umfraville lied, referring to the absent maidservants, saying, "Ach! 'Tis nothin' to me!" Though he gazed from beneath knitted eyebrows, he feigned boredom of a sort.

"Ye'll see them directly," said Dungal with a sly smile, "as this meet is concluded," then added almost sweetly, "I promise."

"And if this meet goes not to yer likin'?" asked one of Umfraville's captains, not wishing to be left wanting.

"Let us not dwell on the misfortunes that might befall us, but on how we can rid oursel's of this scourge that infects our blessed Scotland," offered Lord Macdouall with a broad, if not very reassuring grin.

"Aye," agreed Ingram dourly, putting aside his libido and his orator's arrogance in favor of his lust for revenge on de Brus. His two captains hesitated to voice agreement, being busy eating. Umfraville kicked at their shinbones and elicited an immediate understanding.

"Aye," said the one captain, followed by a quick grunt of agreement by the other, caught with his mouth full to overflowing. Dungal smiled.

Sir Patrick arrived at the table momentarily and seated himself to Dungal's left as the lord said to Umfraville, "Ye recollect Sir Patrick, from Kintyre?"

"Aye," replied Umfraville with a sniff, "yer 'patriot.'"

"Patriot for sure!" retorted Dungal, taking offense. "'Twas him told me when them Bruses were a'comin' to get my hide!" Softening his attitude to preserve the mood of the meeting, he added more pleasantly, "But, we fully tricked them villains."

Patrick smiled fleetingly, uncomfortable at the discussion, and wondered if there would ever be another event in his life to eclipse his treachery against his kin for the sake of attaining power quickly.

When the English caught his uncle, then Lord of Kintyre, invading Galloway with two brothers of Robert de Brus and an army of four hundred Irish conscripts, Sir Patrick assumed that he would be well rewarded by the old King Edward for his part in betraying the plot. At his uncle's demise, he had expected to become the new Lord of Kintyre, but King Edward was now dead; King Edward the younger had retreated to England. Thus, Patrick's plan seemingly had dwindled to the mere table braggings of a madman.

The goliath called Gavin, as crude in manner and appearance as he was large, arrived in the hall. He took the seat to the right of Dungal, and with no greetings to anyone, pulled his dagger from its sheath and drove it deep into the joint of meat before him, cut a large portion and began eating. No one challenged him, not even Lord Macdouall.

"A drink," proposed Dungal with his wine cup held high, "to the lucky bastard who kills the one callin' *hisself...* King of Scots!"

With enthusiastic "Ayes" all around, the six men held cups high and drank deep to the death of the vengeful and often lethal King Robert. They then unceremoniously continued their repast, all except Lord Macdouall. He sat calmly watching each man in his turn through cold, emotionless eyes. He swilled the dregs from his cup and again wrapped himself in his mantle of affability.

"Now then! What wit have ye to propose for a plan, Sir Ingram?" asked Dungal, slamming down his cup and wiping grease and wine from his mouth onto his velvet sleeve.

"Milord," Umfraville said with his mouth full, and held his hand up to beg a pause while he quickly washed down his food with a swig from his goblet. When he again spoke, he said, "Sir Dungal, the English still have a strong interest in Scotland, despite the death of old King Edward. Now, we must simply dance to the music of a different tune."

"How so, Sir?" interjected Patrick, who had a deep interest in the new English king. After all, only the king could appoint him Lord of Kintyre, per his original plan.

Umfraville looked at Sir Patrick and sniggered derisively before he began to speak. "Young Edward is somewhat..." he paused and made circles in the air with his hand before adding, "...swallowed up in the return of his..." Umfraville paused again and smiled, "...friend, Piers Gaveston, but, the nobility surroundin' the crown have no interest in Gaveston's return, and in fact, are beginnin' to oppose such openly."

"Aye, but how is this to further the elimination of The Brus?" impatiently asked Dungal through a half-chewed chunk of meat. He cared not a whit for the young king or his foibles.

"'Tis thus, Milord Dungal," Umfraville explained patiently, "despite his self-made troubles in England, Edward would be loath give up the idea of maintaining suzerainty over Scotland. 'Twould not reflect well on him otherwise, especially since his father was so very ardent in his desire to preserve it."

"I have already given oath to young Edward," said Macdouall, shaking his head negatively.

"As have I," returned Umfraville, "but, we have appetites of our own... and have not yet laid forth a plan that would satisfy all."

"Ye think ye'll get English troops... beyond those that garrison the castles here'bouts... to pursue Brus?" asked Patrick, propping himself on his elbows and all but pushing his body across the table with renewed interest.

"Twixt Ayr and Bothwell are more than two thousand well-trained knights, who still smart from clashes with Brus," replied Umfraville. "They'd be willin' and formidable fighters... if they were but turned to our command!"

Gavin, for the first time since having sat at the table, looked up from his food and grunted an approval, punctuated with the waving of a fowl's leg bone in Umfraville's direction.

"Well, Gavin is for it," laughed Dungal, soliciting an additional mild laugh all around. Gavin continued to eat noisily.

"How do we manage to get these troops?" asked Patrick, trying to reform the conversation more to his liking. "Hain't Aymer de Valence yet Warden of Scotland? And as such, don't he have these troops for his own use?"

"Lord Valence is gettin' old, and soft," frowned Umfraville, somewhat disconcerted. "Don't forget, 'twas he that gave up the field at Loudoun, right when I had beaten Brus' gang of common scum. After my array had taken the batterin' in the first vanguard assault, 'his Lordship' just strolled off back to Bothwell as if he were takin' a leisure jaunt through the countryside!"

"Hah!" came a derisive whoop from Dungal's right. All grew silent and paused in their eating, turning their eyes toward Umfraville.

"Ye spoke, Sir?" Umfraville confronted the scoffer.

"I heerd ye was tricked into runnin' yer fine knights into ditches," interjected Gavin with the satisfied smile of one completing a verbal coup. He hadn't even looked up.

Umfraville, already flushed red from throat to ears, jumped to his feet and drew his broadsword, and would have leapt across the table at Gavin had it not been for his two captains, who, with cooler heads, grabbed his arms and held him from the task.

"Let's not spill good Scots blood fightin' amongst oursel's!" suggested Patrick, who again tried to bring the conversation back to its original intent. "Ye have not traveled this far to die needlessly."

"Leash yer mutt, Macdouall!" threatened Umfraville, "else I'll have him skewered 'pon my blade!"

Dungal smiled and paused, his mind reeling with the consequences of various scenarios, then signaled Gavin to mind his eating and stay out of the politics. Gavin, who had ignored Umfraville's outburst, only grunted as he got a chunk of bread from the loaf and continued to eat.

"Now, return to the parley," coaxed Dungal, who had remained comfortably seated all the while.

Umfraville laid his sword on the table for quick access, and he and his captains returned to their bench seat.

"What say ye that we be at doin'?" asked Patrick, seemingly willing to undertake any deed that might draw the attentions of young King Edward and thus benefit his own ambitions.

"I shall go to London and seek an audience with the king!" declared Umfraville.

"And how will that run the Brus rabble out of Galloway?" asked Dungal, who had but a myopically provincial view.

"Only he can put de Valence's troops to our purpose, Milord! Brus will pluck us out, one by one, if we are not amassed against him in great numbers," declared Umfraville soberly and cast a glaring look at Gavin, who ignored him completely and tended to naught but his belly.

"Aye," agreed Lord Dungal reluctantly, "'Twill be civil war, but if it be war Brus wants, 'tis war he shall get!" And they drank again to their success against the evil lurking upon their land.

Later that night, Lord Dungal saw to his promise of sending several bosomy women to the beds of his guests, but retired to his own bed alone, for he trusted neither slave nor friend. He slept fitfully for a short while, soon awakening in a cold sweat from a nightmare depicting for him his own death by headsman's axe. He could feel the axe cutting through his neck ever so slowly, and was saved into wakefulness only by the tingling of the death swoon.

"My God! My God, save me!" he shrieked in his delirium. In his mind's eye he could see Robert The Brus again on the moon-drenched riverbank, eyes red aglow, and the gleaming broadsword ushering all Macdouall's brave knights to their deaths. A guard's loud knock on the door brought him to his feet, fully realizing the gravity of his vision.

"Ye a'right, Milord?" questioned the calm voice.

"Aye!" shouted Dungal angrily through the closed door. He returned to lie again upon his bed, where he mopped the sweat from his face with the light blanket and threw it onto the floor. "Damn rag's too hot for the night," he said half aloud, then settled to await a more peaceful sleep.

As he lay trying to force himself into oblivious rest it seemed an eternity passed, yet sleep did not come and Dungal became fretful. Knotting himself at the top of his bed, he covered his body, head and toes, with the retrieved blanket.

"Macquillen's doin's, it is!" Dungal gasped wide-eyed as the thought first struck. And after it took root in his mystified mind, he mumbled it over and over while twisting the hairs of his beard. Finally, his revelation grew to full bloom and his thoughts traveled a path of, what was to him, perfect logic. "'Twas he... that brought those two brothers of Robert Brus to my land and... tricked me into doin' the murder of them... and his uncle! 'Tis he has come twixt me and the Lord God Almighty, that I've been abandoned to suffer the ire of The Brus, who hunts me, e'en to this very moment," his voice trailed off to a whine.

Dungal's eyes rolled and strained to see in the black night. He suddenly jumped to his feet and rushed frantically to the window, peering into the partially moonlit darkness toward the north wall. "Robert's a'comin' o'er yon curtain... I ken his flaming hot breath rushin' out 'pon me!" he cried, writhing in the imagined pain of being scorched. "Oh God! Save me from Patrick Macquillen's evil grasp! Include me not as a partner in his low, selfish crime against thee!"

Dungal sunk to the floor in a fit of fearful tears and sobbed there for near an hour before he ceased sobbing and stared unfeeling at the far wall. There, his crippled mind formed images of the devilish tortures that he faced as long as he held Sir Patrick in favor... and that one yet slept under Dungal's roof only a short walk from the very spot whereon he sat.

It was then that Lord Macdouall came to the notion that Sir Patrick must leave.

Dressed in his sleep shirt and nothing more, Dungal, in his great strength, threw open the large oak door to the solar. The two guards straightened themselves hastily at the suddenness of his appearance, but he paid them no care as he tottered down the corridor toward the sleeping chamber of Patrick Macquillen, and there hammered heavily on the door.

"Awaken, ye baseborn lout! 'Tis the lord of the castle!" screamed Dungal, all the while pounding his hefty fist against the oak.

Quickly the door opened and the glow of Patrick's candle lamp was all Dungal could see.

"Ye need leave this place... NOW!" screamed Dungal.

At first, Sir Patrick was dumbfounded. "Milord, what is the danger? Are we attacked?"

"Nay," Macdouall responded with a negative motion of his great head. "We are not attacked. *Ye* are the danger! Ye and the evil schemes that ye have brought to my door and to my soul! Ye have damned me to suffer the fires of hell for all eternity!" He was again on the verge of tears.

The awakened knight who was the object of such biting rhetoric stood agape and watched the actions of the distraught giant standing in his doorway. Being at a loss as to the meaning of the man's rantings, he concluded that Lord Macdouall had been too long in his cups. A pleasant smile graced his face as he said, "Yer wine's soaked to yer head, Milord. We shall together laugh about this incident on the morrow," and he turned to close the door, thus dismissing the one intruding upon his rest.

"Shut not this door against *my* hand!" cried Dungal as he pushed his emotion-wracked person into Patrick's room.

Too late, Patrick grew fearful, and rushed to withdraw his dagger from beneath his pillow. The flash of the blade in the lantern's light was all the provocation Dungal needed in his delirium. His warrior instincts took control and the dagger was slapped to the floor before Patrick could get off a single strike with its well-honed edge.

In a single beat of Patrick's startled heart, Dungal's large hands closed on the younger man's throat and swiftly pushed him backward onto the bed. Though Patrick flailed at the madman's face and arms and thrashed about and tried to kick the massive body away, the grip around his throat held tight.

The commotion had awakened Patrick's companion, and recognizing that murder was afoot, she began to scream at the top of her power as the life breath of Sir Patrick Macquillen was being squeezed from his body. The two guards standing night watch rushed into the room, but finding the lord in no peril, made no move to stop him. Instead, they watched as he completed his act. They then quietly stepped out of the room and returned to their posts.

The rag-doll in his iron grip at last dead, Lord Macdouall felt an immense weight had been lifted from his very soul. He then dropped the knight and looked down upon the body with calm demeanor, though the bedclothes had caught fire from the tumbled lantern.

The woman in the bed had ceased to scream and had instead drawn back into the shadows, fearing that she might be next. Now, however, seeing the face of Lord Macdouall in the mounting flames, she realized he had accomplished all he had set wit to do. Swiftly and quietly, she rose up to seize the washstand's basin of water and throw its contents onto the fire. Successful in putting out the flames, though the cloths yet smoldered, she dragged the remnants off the bed and put them upon the hearth, rendering them harmless. Turning about again, she saw by the moon's light that there was none in the room with her but the dead Sir Patrick.

Dungal returned to the solar, where he slept as he had not for the past three months. His demons lay in repose, peacefully at his side.

AUGUST 26TH 1307
GALLOWAY, SOME MILES EAST OF CASTLE BUITTLE

Fergus, a lanky Scot of nearly six feet in height, had miraculously survived the English Swan Knights' rampage in Annandale late in the summer of 1306. The Swan Knights were highbred young men turned to merciless pillaging, rape, and murder under the command of Edward de Caernarvon, then Prince of Wales. Edward had been under terrible duress by his father, King Edward, and seemed to take particular delight and relief of his frustrations in massacring Scottish peasantry with his elite force.

Fergus would forever carry a long scar across his back where one of the Swan Knights had ridden him down as he tried to escape. The mercifully superficial blow fainted him and the knights took him for dead; when he came to himself, his kin and his neighbors lay dead all about him. He lived, but would not have without the help of the only other survivor, an old man who had hidden in the copse at the top of the hill above their village and escaped the English butchery. He, too, was now dead.

"This one 'ppears to be goodly eats," a smiling Fergus said through the puffy cloud of dust he made smacking a longhaired ruddy beef cow on the rump.

"I'd fetch 'bout a three-pound hunk from right there," fantasized Cuthbert, and his mouth watered as he placed his thumbs and fingers in a circle to frame a particular portion of the beast's side. Cuthbert couldn't resist actually biting the hairy skin. The cow stopped chewing and turned her head to view the two men, almost seeming to know the content of their conversation and the bite, but then, as if she really didn't care, she returned to munching the green grass of the gently sloping countryside of Galloway.

That afternoon there were fifty-three similar bovines amassed on the hill, taken from various farms around the area by King Robert's army, which numbered about five hundred hungry warriors. Farmers in sympathy with the rebellion were promised payment by the Scottish crown at a later time. However, many were the beeves that were confiscated from Robert's enemies at sword point or death.

Cuthbert and Fergus, along with ten of their fellows, had been given the order to tend to the commandeered herd morning, noon, and night, but it was a chore they performed with the pleasure of hungry men who now would eat well for a while.

Higher on the hill King Robert lay asleep on the grass. He was on his back, his broadsword across the saffron tabard with the red lion, now worn on his chest always save when he washed. His hand, which had no doubt held the great sword's handle as he drifted off to sleep, had slipped at the behest of gravity and hung peacefully in mid-movement waiting for its master to return life to it.

The king's keen senses were disturbed not at all when his nephew Sir Thomas Randolph came to his side and sat, his legs flat out on the ground facing down the hill. Robert's weariness from the last months of battles, living in the wild, and constant pining for his captured queen, had drained much of his reserve energies. He found himself tired almost continually, and exhausted, often.

Captured by Aymer de Valence, Earl of Pembroke, along with Robert de Brus' brother-in-law Christopher Seton, Thomas Randolph had only recently returned to fight alongside his kin in the struggle for Scottish freedom from England. For many months he had half-heartedly lent his considerable warring skills to the efforts of Lord Pembroke, charged by the late King Edward with the task of annihilating Robert de Brus and all his supporters. Thomas, a man the earl knew well and liked and understood, had been given the choice of following Seton to the gallows, or pledging his support to England. Faced with his own impending demise, Thomas chose the latter. He had borne the hateful pledge of fealty as long as he could, but at the battle of Loudoun Hill, he turned his back on Pembroke and England, and rode calmly across the bloody field to rejoin the valorous, though greatly outnumbered Scots.

Loudoun had been a resounding victory for the Scots, but an even greater loss for the English. Not long after, King Edward, quite old and ill, determined that he would personally lead his army to rid the isle of the cursed Brus once and for all. He pressed forward, draining his little remaining life reserves until he could go no farther. Finally, he died after leaving his son with the mandate to complete the mission. However, being neither the king nor the soldier that his father had been, King Edward the younger soon withdrew from north of the border to tend other interests, leaving the Scots king to deal with his enemies at home.

Thomas withdrew a small whetstone from his rabbit-fur pouch and spat on it. He then unsheathed his dagger and began to hone a fine new edge to the blade.

At last Robert breathed a great sigh as if to bid farewell to his peaceful respite, and awoke too see Thomas sitting beside him. He smiled and sat up, stretching arms and shoulders to loosen their tension.

"See any naked dancin' women in yer dreams?" snickered Thomas without pause to his task.

"Nary one danced, Sir," returned Robert with a grin, adding, "Good to have ye back, Nephew!"

"'Tis good to be home, My King," replied Randolph in almost a whisper.

"We've got no home, save where we lay our heads at night," warned the king in a melancholy tone.

"Hain't my worry," Thomas paused his honing and ran his thumb over the blade to check his progress, then continued his task and his thought. "One day soon, we'll have castle fires a'plenty to keep our feet warm, and a regular woman to take to bed."

"Ye're not suggestin' that ye aim to take a wife, are ye?" asked Robert accompanying his query with a finger poke in Thomas' ribs.

Thomas jumped and smiled, "Ye think I'd not be fittin' for takin' a wife, Uncle?"

"Well, 'tis certain ye must be some satisfyin' to them," said Robert, "ye've got them whirrin' 'round ye all the while."

"Let's run the English out of Scotland first, then talk of home and hearth and the pleasures of it," grinned Thomas.

"Aye," agreed Robert, nodding, "and that we will do this winter."

"Winter?" questioned Thomas, "That's no time for campaignin'!"

"'Tis our *only* time," replied the king, grimly. "Whilst the English are distracted and lie comfortable in their warm beds, *we* will reclaim Scotland."

"Humph!" replied Thomas gruffly, knowing that only the very toughest would see the spring, if any of them would at all.

"Humph! indeed," agreed Robert, knowing and agreeing with Thomas' doubts. Sitting quietly while Thomas worked his blade against the stone, both men espied twenty-year-old James "The Black" Douglas, walking up the hill in their direction.

"Here comes "black" trouble!" teased Thomas loud enough for James to hear him.

James smiled at the jest, and as he reached the two, stood before his king and fidgeted with his broadsword in a nervous sort of way, and it was obvious he had climbed the hill with a purpose.

"What bothers ye this fine day, Sir James?" prompted the king after observing the nervousness of the man for a seemingly interminable stretch without a word.

"Sire," he started, "uh... My King... uh..."

Thomas started to giggle.

"Keep yer peace, Randolph!" cautioned James, flushing red.

"Speak yer mind, son" encouraged Robert, who was but twelve years senior to the young knight. He changed his sitting position, folding his legs and tucking each foot under the opposite thigh. "Say what ye will."

"My king," again started James, "...Sire, 'tis Douglasdale!" he finally blurted.

"Ye want to return to yer ancestral home with laurel encirclin' yer head?" asked the king trying to help.

"Nay, Sire, it be not my own glory that I seek. 'Tis my ancestral home, aye," said James, finishing his statement between clenched teeth, "but I want most to deny it to the English, my enemy, who now occupy it."

"I understand yer plight," said Robert sympathetically, "but it may not be the best thing for us that we take Castle Douglas, Jamey. Our army has done right well, strikin' sudden and gettin' fast out. Layin' siege and capturin' that tower fortress requires more men and provisions than we now have, or likely will have, any time soon."

Sir James sank to his knees at the feet of the king and looked at him straight eye-to-eye and explained, "Sire, I want not for ye to risk yer hard won army to fight my cause."

"Then what?" asked Robert as Thomas returned to sharpening his dagger. "Our causes must match, or we will win only revenge battles, and yet lose the war."

"Sire, give me but twenty men of my own pickin,' and I will deliver Douglasdale and all of the surroundin' countryside to yer peace," challenged Douglas.

"But ye did such only months ago, James. The folk there now quake at the mere whisper of yer name," returned the king.

"Aye, but I hear, from them that I trust, that Sir Robert de Clifford has rebuilt all that we laid waste to, so's it's again as good as ere it was," argued James.

Robert sat in thought for a lengthy period, then said, "Twenty men?"

"Aye," smiled Black Douglas, "twenty men... and I promise the deed will be done to a proper conclusion this time, or I shall die in the attempt of it."

Robert straightened his back and repositioned the broadsword in his lap as he mused the ramifications. "I want ye to take Douglasdale, village, fields, and castle," he said, pointing in the general direction of the area in front of him as he sat facing north. Then the king swung his arm across to the right and to the southeast and said, "And with the recruits ye'll gather, I want ye to bring all of this land under my peace, to the edge of England!"

James was quiet for a moment, his piercing eyes gazed at Robert from beneath a furrowed brow. This was more than he had bargained for, and with only twenty men at the start! Suddenly, he was encouraged with the venture, and it manifested in a broad smile through his thin black beard. "Ye've a bargain, My King!"

"Then so have ye," returned the king.

"The English in Douglasdale shall pay dearly for takin' my father's life in London's Tower!" swore James Douglas.

"Jamie, ye must see that we win the war," reminded Robert.

"Aye, My King," said Douglas as he reached for Robert's hand to kiss it, but the king withdrew it from him.

"Ye need not perform those acts of faithfulness in the field, young Douglas. And furthermore, when I am seated firmly on the throne of Scotland, I, indeed, will kneel and kiss *yer* hand."

James knew not what to think of his king's statement and so chose to say naught, but the king knew and meant exactly what he had said.

"Tell my brother Edward of yer goin,' and that he's to get ye the horses and the men and victuals ye require," instructed the king.

James stood and graciously bowed before the king, "Ye will allow me at least a symbol of my gratitude with this humble bow."

Robert smiled and shooed him away, saying, "Aye Lad, be about yer business, now."

"Ye put a lot on the shoulders of such a young lad, Robert," said Thomas as they watched James Douglas striding down the hill as if he were king of all he viewed. His dark physical appearance, as well as his youth, spirit, and demeanor was so reminiscent of the king's youngest brother, Nigel de Brus, that it fair brought tears to both men's eyes.

"A man knows not the strength of his sinews 'til they are drawn out to their limit," philosophized Robert, somberly.

"Ah, but when they break, they are of little use," gainsaid Thomas.

"We'll see," replied the king.

Within half an hour young James Douglas, Scottish knight, and his twenty men rode out of the camp toward Douglasdale. James nodded his bare head toward Robert in salute as he led his column toward the northern territory. Robert watched until the last of the entourage disappeared in the undulating hills.

As the sun was beginning to set on the beautiful day, Edward Brus and Robert Boyd brought beef in gravy and hot bread up the hill for themselves and for the king and Thomas, who remained sitting, talking about old times and new beginnings.

"Ye men hungry?" asked Edward, handing steaming bowls to the two roosting men.

The bowls were eagerly accepted and the four delighted in the eating.

"We gatherin' up more cattle?" asked Sir Robert Boyd, the large, well-proportioned man who looked more than his length of less than six feet. He was the last man to have escaped the English at the fall of Kildrummy Castle. Nigel de Brus, wounded in the hand-to-hand combat within the castle's courtyard, had refused to leave with Boyd, knowing that his severe injuries would slow his able-bodied friend and assure them both of capture and certain death.

"We can handle no more," replied the king.

"Where are we headed?" asked Edward between bites of the hot beef.

"North," answered Robert.

"Where north?" pushed Edward, wanting more specific information.

"To the earldom of Buchan," said the king.

Edward raised his head from his supper and a trickle of gravy followed the curve of his lip and rested in the hair of his beard. The others paused, too and looked at Robert with surprised eyes. "We're goin' against the likes of Lord John!?" asked Edward after pushing his mouthful into the pocket of his cheek.

"He is a Comyn, is he not?" returned the king, continuing to eat.

"He is..." said Edward, "and with an army of many more than the likes of ours!"

"Stretchin' sinews again, Robert?" smiled Thomas.

"If we can stretch 'em for young Douglas, we can stretch 'em for the rest of us," returned the king without further comment.

Edward and Robert Boyd looked at each other through squinted eyes, their brows frowning in puzzlement at the meaning of Thomas' question and Robert's answer.

"Ne'er mind our babble," said Robert with a smile.

• •

Next morning the camp was awake early on orders of King Robert. The army was leaving the land of Galloway for the north.

"Are we a'goin'a be in charge of the herd?" asked Fergus.

"King said so," replied Cuthbert, impressed that they had been named to command the herders, "so tell all them underlin's of ours to cut a stout switch for themsel'es, to keep the kine in a bunch." As Fergus ran off to convey the order, Cuthbert gathered up his paltry possessions and stuffed them into his pouch. Then, slinging the pouch strap over his head, he pushed one arm through the loop and settled the pouch snugly under his arm before marching off toward the herd.

King Robert, shielding his eyes from the glare of the early sun, puzzled how long it would take for their nearly five hundred men to consume the fifty head of cattle as he glanced down the hill at the herd. It was about then that Edward emerged from his tent, his eyes bleary from too much camp-made ale from the night before. He dropped to his knees in the dew-soaked pasture grass and ran his tongue along the blades, sucking up as much of the moisture as his dehydrated body could. Then he began to disgorge the foul poison he had so willingly drunk.

Robert twisted his face at the stench, then turned to Boyd. "He'll not be worth a tinker's dam 'til mid-day!" said the king, disappointed at his brother's irresponsible deportment. "He knew we were to leave today."

"Aye, My King," Boyd defended Edward, "and he knew there would probably be no more of the ale for heavy drinkin,' too."

King Robert looked at the puking drunkard and turned his face away. To Boyd he said, "Get his tent struck and see to him 'til he's purged his guts!" He then turned down the hill toward his awaiting army.

The two wains that the Scots scroungers had commandeered from nearby farms were abandoned in favor of pack animals to haul everything, including grains and other staple provisions, cooking utensils, medicines, weapons, armor and tents. Even the beef cattle were burdened like pack animals. The army of King Robert de Brus traveled as mobile as could be imagined.

Robert climbed aboard his huge warhorse and looked about at his accumulated band. Almost to a man, they were looking to him for the signal to begin. At last, he took out his broadsword, swung it around his head, and let go a loud war cry. With a nudging kick at his mount, he then began the trek northward to Buchan with his band of most unlikely warriors in tow.

The unseasonable chill in the morning air was a mere hint of what lay ahead with the coming of winter.

King Edward II of England

SEPTEMBER 8TH 1307
CASTLE WESTMINSTER IN LONDON

King Edward II, a man of just twenty-three years, had been king only since his father's death in July; hardly long enough for him to have extinguished a honeymoon period with his earls, lords, and barons, and yet, he was in trouble. He had not the wiliness of his father with which to accomplish necessary deeds and gain his own desires, but he had much that was not easily accepted by his nobles.

His illustrious father had even had the cunning to coerce him, who had no interest in such, into taking a personal role in the war against Scotland by placing him at the head of an army of three hundred elite knights. Then Prince of Wales, Edward and his knights were sworn just the previous year at a bizarre ceremony centered on a feast of swans. He and his so-called "Swan Knights" had then utterly ravaged southern Scotland, and with Aymer de Valence, had taken Kildrummy Castle from the defending Scots commanded by Nigel de Brus.

It was this Edward who took nineteen-year-old Nigel to Berwick, and though he was gravely wounded and nearly dead already, subjected him to a mock trial and an execution in the manner Edward I had created for the very worst of his enemies. Like William Wallace, Nigel was hanged until half dead, revived, disemboweled while conscious, decapitated, and quartered. His boyish head was then displayed on a pike above the Castle gate as a warning to any who might choose to follow in his footsteps.

Now, a year later, almost to the day, since Kildrummy's fall, young King Edward burst through the huge carved oak doors of his private chambers as his steward, Hetherington, spoke in a loud voice behind him. "The king retires to contemplate your... requests!" the steward said as the king slammed the heavy doors against the horde of angry voices in the adjoining hall. The quiet was almost deafening as he flung himself into a large, sumptuously cushioned chair, positioned to overlook the magnificent view of the city and the river.

"Damn! Damn! Damned bastards!," he muttered aloud to himself. "Who in hell do they think they are... demanding this... demanding that..." His flushed face was the very picture of a spoiled child, protruding lower lip and all.

He stared through the windowpane, absentmindedly playing with his jeweled dagger by stabbing at the gold-embroidered velvet cushion between his legs. "Father told me not that being king was so poor," he lamented. "I *wanted* him dead, but now..." He paused, for what he thought next, he had dared not admit, even to himself. He was saved from his deadly thought by the entrance of his steward.

"Go away!" demanded the king, still pouting.

"My Lord King," insisted Hetherington, "you must hear me out!"

Edward knew Hetherington was totally devoted to him, and if there were any in his court to be trusted to speak in his best interest, it would be he. Therefore the king tolerated the intrusion. "Speak!" said he curtly while pushing the dagger deep into the cushion beneath his crotch.

"The Earl of Ulster has arrived and seeks an audience!" announced Hetherington in a voice that was almost a whisper as he came to the chair where sat the king.

Edward frowned, at first failing to grasp the importance of the request, but his demeanor suddenly changed and he smiled, never taking his eyes from the scene in front of him. "Show him in," ordered the king, and the steward bowed and withdrew.

Lord Richard "The Red" de Burgh, earl of Ulster in the north of Ireland, had been one of the closest of lieutenants to King Edward I, and was among England's primary military planners for the continuing war against the French. He had now purposefully returned to England, to talk to the son of his old friend, the late king. He was a tall, solidly built man nearing his half-century mark, the years having taken their toll on his weathered face and graying red hair, but his full mature strength still remained within his command.

The earl paused and bowed as he approached the slouching figure, although the king remained with his back to the room.

"I thought you in France, Milord Earl," started the king. "Did I send for you?"

"Nay, Sire. Ye sent for me not," said Richard. "but I am here, nonetheless... upon my own mission."

Edward stood and faced the earl, who felt somewhat obligated to bow once more, for he knew the king had not witnessed his first attempt at courtly gestures.

The king propped a casual elbow on the back of the abused chair and watched the dagger swinging precariously between his thumb and index finger. "How can you be of service to me, here?" questioned the king after a long awkward pause. "Your duty lies at the head of my army in France."

"As ye may be aware, My King," said Richard, "I was of invaluable service to yer father, God rest his noble soul, for many a year."

"I may be... so aware, Lord de Burgh, but why this bold boast?" Young Edward looked at the Irish earl and slyly smiled, thinking to draw the old man into an inescapable trap without especially realizing why.

Richard paused. He had rehearsed the line over in his mind, never truly believing he would go through with his proposal, for he thought the new king to be a whelp and a coward. For those reasons he trusted him not a jot, but he continued nevertheless, saying, "Because I came to swear fealty to ye, as well, Sire."

"Oh?" said the king in a somewhat suspicious voice, "Fealty, to me?!"

"Aye," agreed Richard, "for a price."

Edward smiled and quietly chuckled to himself, *Now, the fat is in the fire.* He was pleased for finally unraveling what had been a conundrum only to him.

Richard looked at Edward as if he were witnessing a jester juggling invisible balls in the air.

"Would this have... anything to do, My Lord," he knew well the answer to the coming question, "...with the certainty that I have your daughter locked away, and that she remains but a hair's breadth from my pleasure?" gloated Edward.

Richard remained calm to view, but his mind scorched red with anger. "I have come to plead for her safety in trade for my allegiance, Sire," he said at last.

Edward deliberately turned his back to the earl as he continued to ravage the upholstery of the chair by ripping the back, bottom to top, with a keen-eyed smile that sent chills throughout the earl's body.

"Your daughter, My Dear Earl," softly began King Edward, but his voice soon grew to a crescendo, "is the wife of my sworn enemy... your son-in-law Robert de Brus, who *thinks* himself King of Scots!"

"My concern is for my daughter, and her alone," said Richard calmly and resolutely, "not for the survival of her husband."

"And if I were to pit the two of you in the field?" questioned the king.

"If we have a bargain in the regard of my daughter's safety, then my loyalty would be with ye, Sire," offered Richard, who remained standing staunchly as the king turned the large, mangled chair toward his guest and lounged unceremoniously into it.

"And if I should not guarantee her safety?" further goaded the king, flexing his newly acquired power.

"Then, Edward Plantagenet, ye will ne'er hold any Irish to yer cause," warned Richard in the firmest tone of voice.

Edward jumped to his feet at the calm affront, the dagger still in his hand and his eyes ablaze as he slowly approached the much larger, older warrior.

The dagger glinted in the late afternoon sun that streamed through a westerly window. The earl watched the king's every movement with distrusting expectations. His hand instinctively went for the hilt of his sword as he took a full step backward.

Edward stopped his advance and smiled. "You fear your king, Sir?" he asked almost casually.

"I fear no man, Sire," returned Lord de Burgh. "Of what value would I be as a soldier if I cowered before an implied threat... even at the hand of my sovereign?"

The king looked coldly at the stalwart earl and contemplated what might be the product of putting the impudent soldier in his place. Unfortunately, with the war in France, he needed the earl and his tough Irish army, at least for now. That decided, Edward smiled disarmingly and said, "The guarantee is yours... for your oath. Elizabeth de Burgh, the so-called 'Queen of Scots,' shall not be harmed for so long as you live... and your fealty is mine."

"And Robert's child, Sire?" asked Richard, pushing to achieve the most possible from the agreement.

"We make not war on children... Milord... but she *shall* remain in the nunnery... 'til we rid Scotland of its scourge," said the king, and he exited the room.

Bowing respectfully as the king withdrew, the earl was left standing alone. He was satisfied that he had accomplished his primary task, at least temporarily, but uncertain of the English monarch's pledge should troubled times bear heavily on the throne.

Thomas Dickson

September 12th 1307
Douglasdale in Scotland

Thomas Dickson's ancient and gnarled cane supported his heavy body as he slowly limped down the rutted cart path toward Saint Bride's Abbey in Douglasdale. He paused and leaned against the low stone wall surrounding the front of the abbey kirk to take a deep, labored breath before continuing to the door.

It was his habit of long standing to make a pilgrimage to the small church for prayers every evening, though he was very late in doing so this night. Usually, he would be well gone from the abbey by sundown, and he would at this hour be home and eating his solitary supper, but it was of little consequence to him that he traveled the path after dark. He had walked it as man and boy, and fair knew every pebble along his way.

Thomas' poorly clothed frame belied his erstwhile important position as steward of Castle Douglas under Sir William Douglas, late lord of the surrounding bountiful lands. Sir William, father of James "The Black" Douglas, had met his foul demise some seven years past at the hands of the English in London's tower for his part in the failed rebellion led by William Wallace.

Even in the forest kirk's darkness Thomas could see the yard's stand of grave markers, illuminated this cold night by the bright autumn moon, already high above him. A shiver cut through his body as the wind blew leafless tree branches to and fro, giving the stones and weathered boards the eerie appearance of being alive.

Unexpectedly sudden was a deep voice that emanated from one of the gravestones, seeming to beckon him to his own resting place. "Come forth, Thomas! it said.

Thomas fell a full step backwards from fear, and had he not held fast to the long stick in his withered fingers, he would have tumbled to the dry, leaf-strewn grass.

James Douglas arose like a specter from his hiding place behind one of the nearby stones. Old Thomas, the blood having rushed from his head, nevertheless forced himself to meet this apparition as he peered into the dark, moving shadows.

Young James giggled.

"Ye know me not, Thomas Dickson?" questioned James. "'Tis I!"

"Ye!?" said Thomas in great relief and excitement, recognizing the man by his voice, for he yet stood in shadow.

"Aye," smiled James as he stepped over the wall and approached his father's former servant, placing his hands upon the old man's shoulders in genuine affection.

"Milord! I am pleased that ye yet live! What brings about yer returnin' to this quarter?" asked Dickson with a wide, nearly toothless grin.

"Yon keep," said James and he pointed down the road toward Castle Douglas, alight in the cold windy night with merry watch fires and warm hearths.

Thomas sighed and blinked as he gazed into the wind toward the great, moonlit tower atop the centuries old motte. Rising nearly straight up a full four stories above the motte, the tower's total height was elevated to nearly a hundred feet above the surrounding low, undulating hills. The stone exterior of the building was pierced only by the forward and rear portals and a handful of loopholes, or arrow ports, on each side.

That seat of strength and honor in Douglasdale had once been all but the whole world to Dickson, thus when he turned again toward the fresh-faced knight, he was obviously uncomfortable and at last said, "Lord Douglas…" He began, and then stopped to begin again, instead speaking from his heart to the boy he had known.

"Jamie lad, when ye retook yer family home and left Robert Clifford's garrison without their heads, ye thought it would put off Clifford and his ilk from returnin.' Aye, we all did. Even when ye left yer castle standin' empty, we thought we were safe from the bastard… but leavin' the place open for them damned dog-tailed English to return…" he shook his grayed head, "…well, they made sure that all of us remainin' here'bouts caught hell for it. We're still catchin' hell for it!"

"So I heard, Dickson," the younger man's demeanor was grave. "I have come to balance the scale with the English for the cruelty laid upon the heads of the people of Douglasdale. And when I'm done this time, Thomas, they'll not be eager to return to Castle Douglas," vowed James. "At the very mention of the name 'Black Douglas,' they will soon know a fear like no man e'er has known. I swear it to ye, Old Friend."

"Oh, the English for certain have great fears of yer returnin,' Young Douglas," said Thomas, "but so do the likes of us who live in the village!"

James again frowned and Thomas grew somewhat afraid of the unpredictable fellow.

"D'ye want always to be a country of slaves, man?" asked James gruffly.

Thomas looked at Sir James a full moment without knowing a word to speak.

James finally gave a low whistle across the small cemetery, which proved replete with his stealthy footed highlanders, as each headstone seemed to produce one from its core.

This time Thomas was not intimidated by the ghostly shapes suddenly appearing amongst the gravestones. He simply asked, "How many have ye to take the castle?"

"Twenty," replied James with a certain pride, having grown used to doing much with little. However, the old steward groaned in dismay.

"Arrgh! 'Twon't take but a minute ere ye'll all be kilt!" exclaimed the old man waving his arms. He then turned to leave, shaking his head and not wanting to be any part of such a predictable failure.

Before he had gone ten paces, James asked, "Ye'll not get us help from the village, then?" The freedom fighters formed in a pack behind their dark-haired leader.

Thomas turned and looked James in the eye, tears streaming from his own as he said in a quavering voice, "As brave and fearless as yer father was, he would ne'er have tried this trick with such a triflin' small bunch."

"But, ye know not the trick I plan, Sir Thomas!" boasted James, trying to assure his old friend that he had indeed a clever plan up his sleeve.

Thomas rubbed the gray whiskers on his chin and wiped the tears from his cheeks as he thought, at last replying, "Ye air still with Robert de Brus?"

"Aye," answered James.

"Then for the sake of the honor of King Robert and yer father, I'll share yer return with some. If they decide... on their own... to join ye, then I'll be back direc'ly and we will all talk of yer scheme. If I fail to return by moonset..." he paused and looked at the knot of steadfast warriors, "...either I could find no one, or I am caught by the English. Whichever, ye had best be gone from this place afore cock-crow... and

Godspeed to ye, James Douglas." He nodded and doffed his tattered hat but slightly, turned and slowly shuffled back toward the tavern without another word.

He thought there were sure to be a few stout lads and rowdy drinkers willing to take on the English, even when led by a revenge-crazed youth certain to meet an early death from pure foolishness.

James led his men into the darkness of the kirk's refuge, for the cold night breezes chattered their teeth when they stood in wait outdoors for too long a time.

Thomas soon pushed open the well-abused door to the village's only tavern. Candles flickered on the few tables, prompting the old man to close the door quickly before the wan lights blew out and he incurred the wrath of the denizens.

Against one wall leant the large and balding tavern keeper, posted protectively before a long table upon which stood several glass bottles and crockery jars containing the tavern's limited selection of wines and hard cider.

The keeper fooled no one with the fancy glass bottles. Their contents had long ago been sold and they refilled with wines of much less quality, purchased from Irish smugglers for a paltry price. But, on a night like this a mulled wine appealed to some, and so the tavern keeper kept it in sight.

Solidly braced on the end of the table was a small barrel of poor quality ale, brewed on the premises by the keeper's wife. For all its homeliness, the humble ale was by far the preferred cup of the locals, and there were no "foreigners" out on such a night in Douglasdale.

Thomas Dickson crossed the straw covered dirt floor to the fireplace and flung back his cloak to allow the heat to penetrate faster to his shivering core. He stretched his bony fingers wide apart and held them closer to the heat, absorbing as much warmth as he could while glancing about the room at the mostly dour faces above the ale tankards.

One of the patrons, a rangy man named Cam, stumbled up groggily to the tavern keeper and held out his cup for a refill.

"Ye've had a'plenty, Sheepherder," said the keeper with disdain. He could always tell the shepherds by their smell, having been one himself for most of his early years. His dislike of those who now tended the flocks, his wife said, showed he had "got above his raisin'."

"One more, I beg... then I'm on me way, for the night," pleaded Cam hopefully, his eyebrows raised as high as he could lift them in an attempt to look less drunk.

"Ye have coin?" asked the keeper without moving a hair.

"Nary a pence, have I left," said the man in true regret, adding hastily, "but, but, but, me ma has a pence she earned at the fair in Lanark this very day, and I glad will be to bring it to ye on the morrow."

The keeper looked dubiously upon the poor sheepman's gall and said mockingly, "Then 'on the morrow' is when ye drink. Be off with ye!" and he swung his great arm in Cam's direction to shoo him away, which effort was quickly rewarded.

Cam scratched his grizzled neck stubble and returned slowly to the table near the fireplace with his empty tankard. Sadly, he set the vessel on the table and lowered his haunches onto a stool, leaned over the table, and hid his face in the crook of his arm.

Thomas, having chosen a likely bunch to approach on Black Douglas' behalf, hobbled near to a table of six men who were drinking ale and loudly telling each other stories that none believed, though all enjoyed.

He drew a three-legged stool up to the table and sat on it, watching their faces as they continued their yarn-spinning. None of the drinkers paid him mind until Thomas eventually decided to tap his cane softly on the edge of the table, hoping to gain their notice without arousing the attention of others nearby.

"Ye want somethin,' Ol' Man?" asked the sleepy-eyed drinker nearest to Thomas. The others turned to see what story the old stranger would tell for their amusement.

Having the focus of the table, he waved his hands toward himself to indicate he wanted not to speak loudly. The curious men's heads pushed toward the center of the table as Thomas whispered, "The Black Douglas is a'waitin' at the kirk to be joined by the men of Douglasdale… to run the English out of his castle. This time for good!"

Every man sitting at that table loudly burst out with raucous laughter. The others in the tavern thought it was just another tale being told to entertain, and paid them no heed whatever. Having met with hilarity rather than anger and ill treatment, Thomas felt himself fortunate. He smiled at them before rising with the help of his walking stick and moved on to the table of his second choice.

Suddenly not as drunk as he had been prior to having overheard the whispered news of Douglas' return, Cam now wondered how much the English would pay for the knowing of such. He sipped the last drop off the rim of his cup and quietly stood and slipped out the door. Only the tavern keeper noted his departure, and he with a sense of "good riddance" at that.

Within another hour Thomas returned to the meeting place with but three men gleaned from their tavern stools. They bore the look of men who were capable of warring and enduring hardship, and at the moment being well filled with the tavern's bad ale, they were damned willing to fight.

Especially the English.

"The rest catchin' up, soon?" asked James as he rushed out to the lane to greet his new recruits.

"This be the lot," replied Thomas quietly. "The local men are not much roused 'bout yer doin's, Sir James."

Douglas was silent. Disappointment filled his heart when he realized there would be no help forthcoming from the villagers, but he determined to mount his plan anyway. He said nothing but returned to his men inside the kirk. Thomas Dickson and the three newcomers followed.

The warriors stood about him in the vestibule as James began to assign each man a task toward fulfillment of his plan, while just a short distance away, his efforts had already been betrayed.

Cam the shepherd had received a silver shilling for his treasonable news, upon which he returned to the now welcoming grin of the tavern keeper. The keeper would soon possess the coin of treachery, and Cam would have the several pots of ale that he craved.

His action meant no more to him than that.

Now, from the edge of the stand of trees across the field from the kirk, a contingent of twenty horsed English knights and a like number of squires and foot soldiers watched the Scots reenter the stone church. The alerted English had arrived before Thomas Dickson returned, and stood waiting in full battle armor to spring their trap on the unwary Scots.

The Black Douglas chose not to place pickets around the kirk, for he needed every one of his men to know the plan. Besides, it was late; the sleeping English could not yet know he was there.

As the Scots closed the door behind them, the captain of the English contingent quietly unsheathed his broadsword and with his spurs, gently nudged his horse forward toward the kirk, followed closely by his knights. The others followed on easy feet, deftly navigating the up-thrust stones and timbers of the burial ground until they reached the doors of the dark sanctuary.

With no warning the doors burst open in front of the plotting Scots, who instinctively fell back into the nave, and the horsed English knights poured in upon them with blades flashing nearly to the rafters in the cold moonlight spilling through the arched windows.

Douglas drew his sword as soon as the doors swung out, and took his stand as the others in the Scots clique backed up to produce their weapons and assess their predicament.

"On them, lads!" exhorted Douglas and he cursed loudly as he looked up to see the helmeted head of a huge knight, his sword raised and ready to be brought down heavily on Douglas' bare locks. The Scot instantly fell flat to the stone floor, leaving the English sword slicing through empty air.

Dropping his own blade, and without thinking, James encompassed the horse's front legs within his brawny arms, holding on as tightly as possible. The horse, thus hobbled, reared up in panic and dealt his rider's helmeted skull a sharp blow against the broad oak beam above them, toppling the knight to the floor, unconscious.

Flung into the air by the horse's rearing, James landed atop several English squires, who collapsed in a pile. His fall thus broken, he quickly pulled his dagger and thrust it into the unmounted knight's helmet visor before the knight regained his wits. The wretched fellow's last scream was mercifully short, and James turned quickly, retrieving his sword in time to dispatch another man.

Riderless and uncontrollable, the kicking and stamping horse was more of a hazard than a half-dozen men, to Scots and Englishmen alike, and it was consequently necessary to kill him. An English pikeman accomplished the feat at the order of his captain.

The small company of highlanders were skilled and experienced warriors, and at first, held their ground well, but the number against them was soon overwhelming. There was no room in the small church even to catch one's breath safely with all the horses and men still battling wildly.

Douglas found himself surrounded by English squires and foot soldiers. Two-handed, he swung his sword in a wide swath and slew or wounded several minimally armored men in a single stroke. After that, the English pressed him less tightly. He, however, afforded them no respite, attacking at every opportunity.

The monks of the abbey, preparing to retire for the night, heard the calamitous noise from the church and soon hastened to see its cause.

The first brother to arrive opened a side door, his six companions close behind. His timing placed him squarely in the open doorway just as one of the highlanders separated an Englishman's head from his body, and a generous splattering of blood crossed the partially opened doors and the startled monk's face. He blinked with surprised horror and quickly pushed backward against his fellow monks, forcing them back through the portal. Slamming the door tight shut, all seven monks shouldered their weight hard against it.

Thomas Dickson had no weapon save a dagger that his creaky fingers never managed to release from its scabbard. The faithful old steward was suddenly slashed across his belly and staggered backward against the wall.

Holding his wound together, he stood at the edge of the fight trying to maintain consciousness. Suddenly, his wits came back sharply on the futility of the skirmish, and the servant of William Douglas knew that if The Black Douglas' men did not escape they would all die, then and there.

With all his remaining strength he pulled a cloth from the alter and wrapped it tightly around himself to hold his gaping wound together, and hurried as fast as he could, limping toward the back of the kirk screaming, "Ye men of Brus follow me! – Follow me!"

The highlanders broke and followed Thomas outside through a rear door and into the cloistered garden of the abbey, surrounded by a high wall.

"Ye three stand with me!" ordered Douglas, and three highlanders joined him to form a rear guard and face down the remaining English force.

More than half the English who had come for them remained inside the vestibule and nave, either dead or gravely wounded, many accidentally at the hands of their own comrades or horses in the cramped interior of the church, but they who could yet wield a weapon tried to follow the fleeing Scots.

The narrow width of the door restricted the pursuers' ability to reach the retreating Scots in numbers of more than one or two at a time, and the horsed knights could not get to them at all. As a result, any English soldiers of foot who passed through the portal died on the four Scots' sword blades.

Old Thomas Dickson held his abdomen together long enough to show the escaping highlanders the small hidden door opening out the rear of the cloister at a spot not far from where their horses were tethered. His strength spent, he slowly sank to his knees by the opening as one by one they slipped through.

Sir James and the rear guard managed to shut the door to the vestibule just long enough to make their escape through the walled cloister. By the time the English broke out and found the small door in the rear wall, only the lifeless body of Sir William Douglas' loyal steward remained.

Inside the small anteroom where the fearful, gray-clad monks huddled against the heavy wooden doors they yet strained to hold closed, only the screams of agony and the groans of dying men attacked them. They had heard the light horses of the Scots riding away from the rear of the cloister garden, and the heavy English warhorses clattering out of the building and hastening away in chase.

It was some time before they regained enough courage to open the door and peer into the inky blackness of their sanctuary, where none wished to tread without light.

One of the brothers retrieved several lit candles, which they held aloft as they set tremulous foot into the room, their hearts pounding. All made the sign of the cross upon themselves and prayed for God's mercy as they saw the carnage laying about in a sea of red.

There were two of the three tavern volunteers, two of Douglas' highlanders, and three English knights and twelve squires and foot, all dead or near death. The timid brothers recovered their wits enough to begin separating the dead from the dying and to minister to each according to his needs.

It was the next morning before they found the remains of poor Thomas Dickson and gave him a decent burial, complete with requiem mass sung the next time a priest became available for the service in such an insignificant abbey.

If not for his valor, James Douglas and the others knew, the Scots' invasion of Douglasdale would have been squelched at the outset.

· ·

Toward morning, as faint first light shone, Captain John Thruswall peered from the lower battlements of Castle Douglas into the still dark landscape. Across a wide, steep-sided ditch, thirty feet deep and completely encircling the base of the motte, the castle's commander could see little of what lay beyond. Even the bailey was inky black except where cooking fires glowed in several hovels.

He shivered as he thought of the hordes of Scots that might, at that moment, be crawling through the darkness toward him. Slowly he turned to look up the motte toward the keep. He even thought of retreating from the crenellated wall along which he paced and climbing the long stairs to the keep. For sure, he would be safer there than on the wall overlooking the ditch, but with jaw set, he regained his nerve and strode off instead to make sure that the heavy oaken gate and portcullis were both in place, and the drawbridge was lifted.

"Keep a keen eye!" he ordered in a gruff voice to the sentry as he passed. The captain was a large man, in height as well as girth. He had volunteered to accept this post, while all others feigned excuses to Lord Clifford on account of The Black Douglas' threats of death to all who would make so bold as to inhabit the Douglases' ancestral home.

"Aye, Cap'n," replied the castle guard, a Scot of less than twenty years whose name was James de Burkville.

"They're a wily and wicked bunch," continued Thruswall, "and escaped knight and foot who went for them in the kirk night last."

Burkville nodded and repeated his obsequious say. He then continued his assigned portion of the parapet to the point where he would meet with Henry Symonds, another Scot, of about thirty-five years, who also stood guard in the slowly gathering light.

Thruswall watched the pair in contempt. He wondered how the English could fear such slovenly and pitiably inept warriors as they. How could the Scottish rebels ever get such a band of worthless soldiery as these to presume to attack a well entrenched and fortified English command as this? It was not possible.

Yet, having been informed that The Black Douglas was roaming free in the neighborhood, he feared Douglas greatly for his cunning. He felt assured that Douglas would not attack outright, but would use some sort of trickery or subterfuge to try to enter and take Castle Douglas.

As Thruswall approached the gatehouse the two Scots lookouts drew near each other on the wall walk.

"Cap'n wants us to look alive. I hear it's for the likes of Black Douglas," said James de Burkville quietly. He looked over the wall into the ditch and across toward the bailey, watching for any Douglas men.

"Scared to shivers, is he?" commented Henry with contempt as he followed suit, or feigned doing so.

"Aye," laughed James trying to keep his amusement from the captain's ears.

"Aye, indeed," snickered Symonds as he turned to patrol his quarter.

Burkville turned and walked back to the gatehouse tower where Captain Thruswall stood, nervously shifting his weight from one foot to the other, waiting for... he knew not what.

The English officer began walking continually along the fortification, looking for the Douglas men to scale one side or the other in the pre-dawn blackness, or a sudden attack of fire arrows to come streaking onto the wooden roof of the tower itself!

As the weak dawn light shone through the morning's haze and filtered evenly on field and village, the captain began to relax, to feel more in control of his surroundings. Soon a vassal brought hot broth for the men on watch, and the captain welcomed the warmth. The sun at last topped the trees on the hill, and as he stood facing it and sipping his broth, he felt how tired he was after the tense night.

But wait, what was that he heard? He stopped all movement, straining to identify a distant sound. Bells, perhaps? He heard a variety of small, tinkling bells it seemed, but from where?

He strode briskly around the wall walk, peering into the half-light at the edge of the forest to see if men were sneaking out to attack, though in truth, the noise he heard sounded very different from armor's clanking ring. This was high pitched and thin metal ringing, not the heavy clamor of weaponry.

"Somethin's a'comin' down the road!" shouted Henry Symonds, and the captain ran to the man's side. "Off there, Cap'n," the man pointed to a column moving slowly upon the lea toward the castle. There were people and a variety of farm animals, from what they could see.

They all waited patiently until the small procession got closer and they could better identify the approaching travelers.

Henry stretched his body out over the wall edge and strained to see down the road, "Just some farm women, and a few boys," he reported to the captain, as he again stood erect.

"Headin' to the last day of Lanark Fair, I reckon," said Burkville.

"Victuals?" questioned John Thruswall.

"A reasonable guess, Sire," Henry replied, "looks like they're a'drivin' geese, or maybe shoats, to market... Must be shoats, I don't hear no geese a'honkin.'"

Sir John carefully watched the approaching procession. There were shoats, or young pigs, being kept on the road with sticks wielded by several youths, apparently about the age of squires, and there were women leading horses bearing huge sacks of grain on their backs. He also heard chickens cackling in the mix.

His stomach growled in sympathy with his eyes. "Roast piglet... dripping with juices, and grain... to make hot bread," he thought aloud, "What a boon!"

James realized the captain's plan and cautioned, "Cap'n, most locals know of our scarcity of stores and steer a wide path from the castle when they're a'carryin' foodstuffs."

"Perhaps these wenches are not locals!" barked the captain, not wanting to believe anything that might interfere with the filling of his hungry stomach. "Perhaps they don't know our right and ability to confiscate their excess provisions! And they *are* excess by the very nature of being taken to sell at the fair!" the Englishman reasoned.

"Aye, perhaps so, Cap'n" said Burkville coolly as he turned to view the procession.

"Ye'll be the last man in my command to eat, I swear!" the captain said through set jaw as he pushed Burkville aside and shouted to the caravan beyond the bailey. "Halt, ye there ... in the name of King Edward the Second of England!"

The travelers on the road with their beasts of burden dutifully obeyed. The swineherds were a little slower to react, as they had to control the unruly piglets.

"If they move from that spot shoot them, starting with the frontmost!" commanded the captain, loudly,, and turning on his heel, made for the stairway.

"But, how can I when I have neither bow nor bolt, Cap'n?" called Burkville after him, freezing him in mid-stride.

Thruswall turned, his ire flushing his cheeks bright red as he again faced the Scotsman. "Then send for the archers, imbecile!" he screamed, his anger nearly overtaking his hunger. He walked to the soldier and put his face into the smaller man's breath and said quietly but fiercely, "If they leave before I get down there, I'll have ye drawn and quartered, ye misbegotten son of a whore!" He started to turn away, but looked back at the guard with one more insult, sneering, "But then, all Scots women are whores, are they not?"

The rebellious Scot wisely held his tongue this time, but smiled to himself at having riled the officer once again. Captain Thruswall made for the gatehouse stairway and ran down to ground level, all the while screaming curses and insults at the entire Scots population and calling for the drawbridge to be lowered and the gate to be opened.

James leant over the wall to witness the captain taking bread grains from the mostly defenseless women. The caravan stood motionless on the road while the captain gathered a contingent of partially armored knights, squires, and vassals in the bailey to confront the travelers. He then mounted his horse to lead his procession out of the palisaded bailey toward the roadway.

Within several minutes the bailey gate swung open and the helmetless captain rode ceremoniously out, leading his entourage to take possession of the sacks of grain, the shoats, and the chickens.

Henry Symonds joined James to watch. "Think they'll take them horses too?" he questioned as he spat over the wall.

"Hope they do. Horse meat be pleasin' to my tongue," replied James with eyebrows raised. "And they'd go a long way toward proper feedin' a garrison. Not like them chickens and wee piggies... a man could eat a whole one o' them and still starve to death."

All but two squires remained in the rear as Thruswall rode purposefully to the front of the caravan and dismounted his unarmored horse. He would confront the female leader of the procession face-to-face.

As he strode forward, he noticed that she was right broad in shoulder and had large and calloused hands for a woman. Obviously, he beheld a simple farmwoman who had worked hard all her life, and judging by her size, had always had enough, if not more than plenty to eat.

"We'll be taking these chattels in the name of the king," said Thruswall in as authoritative a manner and voice as he could muster to hold any resistance to a minimum.

The woman to whom he was stating his intentions but stood with her fully hooded head yet bowed in apparent servitude.

Thruswall, angered that the woman failed to answer her betters, roughly grabbed her hood and flung it back off her face. What greeted him was a bearded and grinning visage, with black hair and fierce but amused eyes. "My God in heaven!... it's a bearded woman!" he uttered, his eyes wide and his mouth agape in startled surprise.

Sir James Douglas, the "bearded woman," giggled and smiled gleefully as the hood was taken from his face, for his ruse had foxed and now completely dumbfounded the captain. Douglas' unsheathed broadsword, hidden in the folds of the long dress and surcoat he wore, was quickly drawn and pointed at the flummoxed captain, who promptly fell back against his horse's legs.

The Douglas highlanders immediately threw off the sacks of grass they had flung across the saddles and quickly mounted their steeds to rush headlong into the English king's would-be highwaymen.

Their ploy had worked completely.

Douglas was on Thruswall before either sword or dagger was drawn by the frightened, prostrate man. With the captain's head bare and unprotected, it was simple instinct for James to draw the foible of his sword across the top of Thruswall's chest armor. Blood ran profusely from his throat, flowing scarlet across his useless breastplate.

From the safety of the wall the two Scots guards were aghast.

"Good God A'mighty!" muttered James, stunned and breathless. "Them hain't women...!"

"'Tis the Douglas!" assumed Henry Symonds, and suddenly realizing the fearful danger the entire castle was now in began to scream in panic, "THE DOUGLAS! THE DOUGLAS!"

James Burkville ran to the edge of the wall walk and shouted to those in the bailey and guarding the bridge and gatehouse, "Make fast the gate! Drop the portcullis! We're under attack!"

Since his last campaign through Douglasdale, the mere mention of Douglas' name struck pure terror into the stoutest hearts within the castle, English or Scot. Not a thought was given to those remaining outside when the soldiers ran from the bailey across the bridge and into the tower, slammed the massive gate tight shut, and dropped the great wooden beam into its heavy iron brackets. Running through the gate tunnel, they barely beat the portcullis as it dropped and struck the ground with a resounding thud.

Only then did the wall guards sense their own safety and return their attention to the last of their forsaken comrades, who, unable to flee, quickly fell to the swords and daggers of Douglas' men.

Shed of his female garb and mounted on his own horse, Sir James looked around for more of the enemy, as did his men, but no others came forth from the castle. They then realized the skirmish was won and a chorus of cheering voices went up from the roadway.

However, the castle, now tightly sealed against them, remained to be taken.

The two Scottish guards stood watching the gruesome spectacle and in their hearts wanted to cheer with the renegade band, but, afraid of what the attacking Scots or vengeful English defenders might do with them, they dared not. Thus they timorously waited with the castle-bound English and tried to make themselves inconspicuous.

Below them, three of the highland warriors went to James Douglas. "What would ye have us do now, Sir James?" asked one.

Douglas, now the invader trying to capture his own home, turned and inspected the castle in hopes that a way to do so would be forthcoming, but the castle was well secured and the parapet was coming alive with its garrison, a number far greater than his command.

He motioned to the bodies on the road, all of them English. "Take weapons and anything else of use from them. They need such no longer," said Douglas, dismounting and walking through the slaughter.

The three men dutifully hunkered down and began to strip the armor and weapons from the bodies and check their pouches for coin.

Sir James found a comfortable seat on the shoulder of a dead horse, propped his elbows on his knees and planted his head into his upturned palms.

The helpless men in the castle began jeering at the small band of rebels, but none wanted to open the gate and come out after them.

As James sat in thought he looked upon the body of Captain Thruswall, only a few paces from his feet. The flushed color was gone from the immobile face and his eyes were set in a half-closed stare as the wind played with the curls on his brow.

Against the dark blue velvet of the dead man's sleeve, the brownish-white corner of a parchment extended from the edge of his left gauntlet, and James, thinking it might be orders or instructions from the captain's superiors, directed a soldier to bring him the missive.

The Scottish commander unfolded the letter and read it. It was not an official document, but a very personal one. He read it anyway since it came from a lady and was scented with a sweet bouquet that stirred memories of other ladies he had known as a half-grown lad within the very walls he now sat beneath.

Amid the laughs of his own victorious men, and the jeering of the English within the castle, James grew silent and dour.

"These English were right well paid, Milord, else they had no place to spend their weal," said one of his men, grinning with the exhilaration of being victorious and wealthy. He shook a pouch filled with coins in front of James' face.

James pushed the small leather bag away and looked sadly at the supine captain, now stripped down to his linens. With a pat he indicated a spot beside him on the ribs of the horse as an invitation for the Scottish warrior to sit. He did, and waited patiently for James to speak.

"Now, there's a man," James finally said, nodding toward the dead man, "who was a suitor for the affections of a lady back in England."

"How ye reckon, Sire?" questioned his companion, looking at Thruswall's corpse with greater interest.

James offered the letter for his companion to read.

"I hain't ne'er learnt to read," said the lad matter-of-factly.

James nodded his head and related, "Says here that she who sent him this letter was willin' to give her hand and duty in marriage, if he would but first serve a year as commander of Castle Douglas." He exhaled a long, sympathetic sigh and added, "'Tis obvious he agreed to her demand for here he is."

"Reckon so," concluded the youth, somberly.

Douglas scratched his thin black beard and said, "Damn shame...

only one more season to go... and she would have been very happy, or very furious."

"I fail to see yer meanin'," the soldier looked puzzled.

"'Tis simple, Lad... by makin' such obligation a part of her acceptin' him to her marriage bed... either she wanted to find out the depth of his grit, or she thought to get rid of him. Either way, she won something, but... I think I know which way she thought it would be resolved. Says here that the English think this castle is the most dangerous to occupy in all Scotland," explained James.

The lad nodded and James looked again upon the dead captain. "She ne'er loved ye, Laddie, and now she's free to take another." He folded the captain's letter and sat quietly in thought for more than a few minutes, until the soldier at his side felt compelled to speak.

"What be the plan to take back yer castle, Sir James?" asked the youth deferentially.

"With this letter," replied the Scottish commander, noticing that he had stained it with the slain man's blood.

"Aye?" was all the high lander replied, thinking his lord had gone witless.

"Aye!" replied James, and he arose, looking at the stalwart men he had led to this spot. Ordering them to wait where they stood, and with his sword in one hand and the letter in the other, he walked the short path through the bailey toward the bridge gate.

"Milord!" warned one of the highlanders, "Ye're in range of their archers!"

Sir James Douglas kept walking. One feisty archer on the battlement loosed an arrow that whizzed past his leg and with a thud, half buried itself harmlessly in the dirt. Fearlessly, James kept walking and holding the letter high in the air.

The garrison on the wall walk were stilled from further action, becoming ever more fearful as James Douglas came so boldly toward them with naught more than a bit of paper to serve as his shield.

James stopped when he was easily within earshot of the men gathered on the wall across the ditch from him. His small band of highlanders lined the roadway parallel to the castle, unable to do more than pray their leader knew what he was about.

"Ye men in my castle!" he shouted holding the bloodied paper in the air so that all on the wall could see. They had good reason to listen. "This letter," he continued when he had their full attention, "was taken from the body of yer captain, yonder." He turned and looked at the man he had just killed.

There were mixed murmurs on the wall until Douglas again started to speak. "Ye are now leaderless... and near to starvin' behind the gates of *my* ancestral home. Yer 'King Edward the Lesser' has abandoned ye, has he not? How long is it since he last sent ye victuals and other stores, I ask? And how long ere ye shall receive such again?" James stood silently and allowed the men to mull over his words before he spoke again, this time allowing his anger to emerge. "Will ye lay down yer lives for a King who no longer e'en feeds ye?" Again, he paused, pacing a few steps, turning, and pacing back.

"I ask ye... d'ye think that I... and the army of King Robert de Brus... have not the means... and the will... to raze these walls asunder and kill e'er livin' soul within?" he shouted and gestured toward the wall on which his audience stood.

"I, Sir James Douglas, master of the castle ye abide in... offer ye a choice... but only this once! Yer choice is ... twixt peace... or death! Ye open the gates... leave this place... and ye go in peace to yer women. Think of yer poor captain, yonder... ne'er to see his sweet love anew!" Another pause.

"Suffer yon gate to remain shut against me... and I swear that each of ye will die... and slowly... cursing the mother that bore ye," spoke James, and there was no doubt of his truth among the men on the parapet. Motionless, they stared at him with a mixture of admiration and abject fear.

Having made his point, the knight turned, picked up a stick from beneath a tree, and stuck it in the ground so that a shadow fell on a relatively smooth spot on the ground. He then took out his sword and struck a line in the dirt very close to where the shadow marked the moment.

"In a short while," he shouted then, "the sun shall mark the end of yer time to decide. Life?... or death. Which way ye choose... it must be for the lot of ye. All live... or all die." With that he turned his back on the armed garrison and walked back the way he had come.

Sir James, the eighteen highlanders, and the surviving tavern conscript stood on the road for about half the shadow's distance to the mark, talking quietly amongst themselves. With their newfound coinage, a few wagered on the decision the holed garrison would make. Others ate oats their dead foes had been hoarding in their privy pouches, saved for the day when the castle's rations were completely gone.

Afore long, he estimated the amount of passed time and walked back to the sun clock he had made with the stick. The shadow grew frightfully close to the streak in the dirt, and James soberly withdrew his sword from its scabbard as the last few grains of soil were being covered by darkness. It mattered not to him that he had little chance of carrying out his threat until the whole garrison was starved into submission.

Then he heard a loud noise at the bridge gate, and a voice from the parapet quickly shouted, "We choose to live, Milord!"

The massive doors of the gate opened slowly, as a few members in the garrison were suspicious of Douglas' penchant for trickery. James' men remained where they stood on the road, however, and gave no evidence of chicanery, though they were prepared in case the English did so.

The abandoning forces opened the gate, cautiously crossed the bridge to the bailey, and filed quietly, if uneasily, past the comparatively few highlanders and looked soberly upon the bodies of their dead captain and comrades. Some were obviously pacifying the tempers of others who wanted to break their chivalrous word and attack the Scots as they passed. Several took the opportunity to spit on the body of the unpopular captain.

James had ordered that each man be given a sum of coin for his travels, a kindness the departing soldiers had not expected from the fierce Scottish leader, but more than a patronizing gesture, it was meant to discourage possible malcontents from doubling back later for an unpleasant surprise visit.

By their own design, James de Burkville and Henry Symonds were the last to leave Castle Douglas. Together, they anxiously approached its owner. They had removed the caps and doublets that bore the colors of King Edward and donned plainer garb before coming before Douglas. Awkwardly, they bowed more or less in unison.

"What be yer notion," Douglas barked crossly at the two. They had been pointed out as traitors by departing English.

"Ye a'wantin' more men for the cause of King Robert, Yer Lordship?" asked Burkville timorously.

"Aye," replied James coolly. "But we need *men*... not cowards who sell out their land for an English tuppence," he insulted them and walked away. He would have enjoyed cutting the heads from their shoulders had the garrison not surrendered in unison. He had given his word that they would thus live, though he found himself tempted.

"Sire, ye know not how it was here when ye left before," Symonds said brashly. "Me lads were goin' hungry, me mother, too!" He increased the strength of his voice to make Sir James hear as he walked further away. "Me wife died tryin' to nurse our wee-est when she had little to eat for her own self, and when she died, the baby went soon after..."

His friend tried to make him stop before they both wound up without heads, but Henry wouldn't let James walk away in peace, following after him, haranguing him all the while.

"'Tis one thing to go hungry, yerself... but, have ye e'er seen anybody ye cared about starve to *death*, Black Douglas? It fair tears the bowels out of ye, and all the time ye're knowin' that yer ma and yer wee ones will soon be too starved to eat, even if ye had food..." He slowed his pace and then stopped, but James kept going.

"I know, now, why they call ye 'Black' Douglas!" he yelled, tears streaming down his weathered cheeks. "'Tis yer heart that's black, ye bastard!"

Sir James Douglas stopped walking. Drawing his broadsword he spun around and started back toward the Scot, now standing alone on the road. No one else moved. James lifted his sword as he approached the man, taking it above his head with two hands.

The weeping Scot waited, hate burning in his gaze like hellfire, and he drew himself up to his tallest to await the fatal blow.

James stopped at sword's length and brought the blade down with all his might, just short of the steadfast Scot. The blade sank itself the length of a man's forearm into the soil, and James trembled with the rage he felt at being talked to so. Both men stood looking at each other with equal ire.

"Ye will *not*... make me break... my word!" yelled James, finally, still shaking.

"I care naught for yer word... nor my own life!" retorted Symonds, "when me babes are chewin' bark from the trees to live! And that's what was happenin' when ye left Douglasdale on its own to meet the English army... *Lord* Douglas!"

James stood riveted, watching closely Symonds' eyes as he told of the horror the people of Douglasdale suffered.

"They took all... *all* the food from us that they could find, and then waited for us to die from hunger... as many did. And the children's bellies began to swell with their emptiness, and the old folks withered. And I and me friend. Burkville, came to the castle and begged to be allowed to rebuild and guard it, that our folk might live!" The tired and drained man held his ground and challenged Douglas, "If that be treason... 'tis no more so than what ye done to us when ye ran off!" He wiped his eyes and nose with his sleeve, his piece said, his rage spent.

The Black Douglas, too, felt suddenly tired and dropped his head to his chest. He still trembled, his hands locked on the great sword. After a moment, he gave a tug and found that the blade was stuck tighter than his exhausted arms could easily pull free. With a grunt and a sudden jerk, he pulled it from its viscid seat and stood looking at it. The proud blade, heretofore always honorably wielded, was smeared in soil and thick Scottish clay.

James found it heavy, and rested the point on the road while he looked at the faces of the Scots soldiers he knew so well. Their faces were grim, and he knew that they were in great sympathy with the former collaborator. They, too had suffered great losses within their own families at the hands of the English and knew well the man's anguish.

He heaved a great sigh and looked again at the broadsword's blade. He picked it up and stepped to where the Henry Symonds stood, still unmoving.

"Ye're a brave man," James said wearily. "Many's the armed English knight who has broke and run from the sight of this broadsword raised against him. And ye were unarmed."

Henry's expression did not alter as he said, "Dyin' proper is easy. 'Tis livin' proper that is the hard thing..." adding sarcastically, "...Me Lord."

James looked at him and nodded. He understood that he was being challenged to do the proper, hard thing.

"In answer to yer friend's question a while ago, I am in need of brave men to serve with me against the English." He looked at the man's face, still unchanged.

"Me friend and me would find it proud to join yer bunch," said Burkville as he drew nearer to his friend.

"Ye get one chance only, and if either of ye show cowardice or aid the English in any way, I'll have ye both kilt."

"Aye, Milord, we understand."

The leader of the Scots looked up at the castle in which he had played as a child, in which his forebears had lived and died. He then turned back to his two new recruits.

"Any more hidin' out in the keep?" he asked.

"Nay, nary 'nother," said Symonds.

"This is what I would have ye do, in the name of King Robert," said James.

"Aye?" said de Burkville. Symonds remained silent until his friend poked him with an elbow. It was plain he still held no love for Douglas, but he also agreed.

"Set fire to all the timbers inside the tower," James ordered. "I want it all burnt."

"But, there'll be naught left save the walls," observed Symonds in surprise.

"And when there's naught left save the walls, tear them down, too," said Douglas.

"Tear down yer da's house?" asked Burkville dubiously.

"The bastards will ne'er again use it to enslave... or starve... Scots." James had tears in his eyes as he motioned with his head toward the castle for the blaze to be set. He signaled for the other soldiers to help, and within half an hour, thick black smoke billowed out of the top floors of the keep. Then the next floor down, and then the ground floor emanated smoke and flames. Soon, every thatched roof and board fence within the bailey were being consumed in a roaring blaze, the flames finally engulfing everything that would burn.

James Douglas stood off in the field across the road and watched his hereditary home being reduced to cinders by the searing heat. When the fires burned themselves out and the walls yet standing cooled, every stone that yet stood one upon another he would have knocked down, until Castle Douglas was leveled to the ground.

Richard de Burgh
Earl of Ulster in Ireland

OCTOBER 23RD 1307
THE ROYAL MANOR HOUSE
BURSTWICK-IN-HOLDERNESS IN ENGLAND

Elizabeth de Burgh, the wife of King Robert, had been under house arrest in an old and decrepit royal lodge since being caught attempting an escape to the Orkney Islands more than a year earlier. She, Robert's daughter Marjorie (by his first wife, Isabel de Mar), his sisters Mary Campbell and Christian Seton, and the Countess of Buchan, Isabel McDuff, had all been captured and sentenced to incarceration under diverse and harsh conditions in various parts of England by King Edward I.

Elizabeth's father, Richard de Burgh, arrived at the site of her imprisonment to meet with her for the first time since her arrest.

He sat pensively awaiting Elizabeth in a small, musty-smelling room at the front of the ancient lodge. It was certain that little attention had been paid the upkeep of this estate for many years. Even the grounds were overgrown and wild. His mind removed him from the gloom in which he sat and placed him in a long ago garden with his wife and children, strolling to the water's edge along a manicured path bordered with roses he could almost smell.

The latch being lifted instantly brought his thoughts back to the present.

As the queen was ushered into the meeting room, the old soldier rose to greet her. Seeing him she stopped. He bowed with suitable grace to the Queen of Scotland.

"Father," said Elizabeth coldly, and with mild surprise at seeing him.

"Ye've not a kind word for yer ol' Da?' asked Richard de Burgh as he crossed the small receiving room to be nearer his daughter.

Elizabeth frowned a bit, her mouth pursed to speak, then relaxed again as she thought better of it.

"I have seen the king," offered Richard as an opening to the uncomfortable, even awkward, situation.

"Which king," she shot back at him, "yer king, or my king?" His daughter turned her back to him and walked to a nearby chair, where she stiffly sat.

"King Edward, whose hospitality ye currently enjoy," he said cautiously, not wanting any word of his to be unfavorably reported to Edward, lest he endanger her.

"'Yer king,'" she commented, "...not mine."

Elizabeth, smiling and looking around the stuffy quarter, sarcastically barbed, "'Tis sweet to have a cushioned chair to sit upon, for I've ne'er before been allowed in this room, nor offered a cushion, ere this minute."

Her father drew a similar chair to her side, and adjusting his broadsword, sat.

"And what does 'yer king' say?" snipped Elizabeth, not actually looking at him. "I heard the *old* bastard passed on to his glory. No doubt he sits by Hell's throne, offerin' instruction to the Prince of Darkness. Aye, ol' Lucifer must be learnin' quite a bit from Edward Plantagenet." She looked at her father sitting tight-lipped at her side.

As he made no comment, she went on.

"No doubt the new little tyrant is runnin' about with crown and trews askew, under great pretense of command and resplendence... killin' Scots hither and thither, thinkin' duty – duty - duty!" she said with emphasis, her mood unaltered.

"I fear the king has more abidin' matters, else he *would* be killin' ev'ry Scot in his midst," replied her father in muted tones.

"When next ye two are in yer cups, tell 'yer king,'" started Elizabeth, "that yer daughter, the Queen of Scots, has neither a decent wrap nor dress to wear, nor a bed with boards, head or foot. And as for those ladies-in-waitin', his father foisted upon me... well chosen as instruments of torture they were, for neither has wit nor wiles, but both bemoan their ails to me the live-long day without cease!"

Her father leaned close to her ear so the guard at the door could not hear and whispered, "Robert yet lives and roams free."

Silence lay between them.

As his meaning finally took hold in her heart, great tears welled in her eyes. This was the first bit of news she had received of her beloved husband since being brought to this horrid place. Her head fell into her trembling hands, where she held little more than a rag for a handkerchief, and it was soon soaked with silent tears of relief. "My dear God, my dear God... thank ye, thank ye, thank ye," she whispered repeatedly.

Richard placed his hand on her shoulder and patted it gently. It was several minutes before Elizabeth was able to compose herself. With a wet face she looked at her father, smiled, and said, "And ye said he would be but a 'summer king'!" She held her head high, as should a proud queen, adding, "He has thus far reigned most of eighteen months!"

"I cherish my ineptness at predictin', My Daughter," smiled Richard as he scooted his chair closer. The guard was roused by the noise of the chair on the flagstone floor, but seeing nothing untoward, turned round, again.

"He knows not if ye yet live?" asked Richard.

She shrugged, not knowing the answer.

"Can ye get a letter to him, Father? Is he winnin' our war? Has... he been wounded?" asked Elizabeth in hushed and excited tones, though fearful of the answers.

"He is not winnin'... but, last I heard he's not been wounded. Neither has he yet lost," relayed Richard.

Elizabeth looked into the kindly, smiling face of her father. How could she have treated him so coolly on his arrival? She mused for a moment as she again allowed herself to feel a daughter's fondness for her father, then reached across the arm of the chair and hugged him tenderly. A reserved man in the ways of open displays of affection, he clumsily returned her hug.

Elizabeth sat back in her chair, happy for the first time since her capture, but suddenly becoming fearful as her analytical intellect overcame her joyous emotions.

"I changed my mind about the letter," she said with a quality of urgency.

"Just when I thought I had a plan to get one through to him," whispered Richard with a smile.

"He might try to reach me," said Elizabeth shaking her head negatively, "and that would certainly be disastrous!"

"Ye will not be harmed, on that I have the word of the king," assured

Richard.

"Aye... and ye can trust his word... about as far as ye can throw him, and that's worth naught," she returned dryly, echoing his own fears. "But worry not for me, Father."

"Watch how they handle ye, My Dear," Richard cautioned. "If I should die, and Robert is losin,' ye will be in gravest danger."

"And if my Robert shall win?"

He cocked his head to one side, his eyebrows raised as he considered her query. "Then, a bargainin' piece ye'll be, and they will nurture ye mindfully," he whispered.

Knowing that her father had made a bargain of his own to ensure her safety, she took his great hand in hers and asked, "What price have ye paid for this cruel pact, Father?"

"Nothin' of consequence. Only what I was willin' to do anyhow," he replied, and kissed her hand tenderly.

Their chat went on for another few moments before Elizabeth asked, "Have ye any news of young Marjorie?"

"Well cared for in a nunnery here'bouts... naught more could I learn," he replied.

"And my sisters-in-law?"

"Still alive," he said, but she knew there was more to tell when he cast his eyes to the toe of his boot.

"And how do they fare?" she asked with a frown, not wanting to be spared troubling news.

He hesitated, trying to find the words that would be the most comforting to her, finally realizing the truth was best between them.

"The one married to the Campbell lives in a cage made of sticks hanging on a wall outside the keep at Roxburgh. Only the privy offers refuge from the cold and the curiosity of the rabble within the castle."

"He carried out his sentence!" cried Elizabeth, crossing her arms and clutching her shoulders to keep her heart from bursting. "I could not imagine that even he would be so cruel to poor little Mary. And her sister, Christian...?"

"A nunnery. Her life there is austere, but she lives within walls, at least."

"And that bright young wisp of a girl, Isabel... Countess of Buchan ere she ran off with her husband's warhorses..." Elizabeth paused and smiled to herself, remembering Isabel's arrival at the manor house with all those fine animals on the morn after Robert's coronation. So plucky she was, with her weapons and her armor, and yet so beautiful.

"I fear she suffers the same fate as Mary Campbell, though at Berwick, not Roxburgh," he said.

"Merciful Jesus, will their torture ne'er end?!" she cried, burying her face into her hands once more.

Overhearing, the guard turned toward them again and smiled to himself.

It was several moments more before Elizabeth recovered. Lord Richard stood and warmed himself before the fire as their meeting drew to an end.

Richard eyed Elizabeth from head to toe, capturing an image within his mind and heart that he might remember how she now looked, once they parted. He was sure that Robert would want to know every detail of her beauty, presuming he could locate the fugitive king.

Elizabeth smiled, for she knew he was taking her with him as best he could, though she had no thought that he would try to communicate with Robert. Before her captors removed her from his sight, she quickly seized a remembrance of his look as well, for no one knew when next they would meet, if e'er.

Rollo
Argyll Chieftan

OCTOBER 25TH 1307
THE LAND IF ARGYLL

Twenty-three-year-old blonde-haired John Macdougall, Lord of Lorne, on the southwestern coast of Scotland, was cousin to the traitorous John "The Red" Comyn, he who had been slain by Robert Brus, setting off the explosive conflict at hand. Since that event the Macdougall clan had proven to be a formidable enemy to the army of King Robert. In the battle of Dail Righ the previous year, Lorne and his army of wild Argyllsmen fought fiercely with little more for protection than boots and blades, soundly routing Robert and his men. If there were ever two sworn enemies, Brus and Macdougall would certainly be best chosen.

This day, however, Lord John lay on his bed of straw in the lord's hall of a small and aged wooden castle, several miles from the vanguard of the approaching Brus army of six hundred men. The rain drizzled day was full on to noon but the room was dark, for John had ordered the windows covered with heavy curtains and blind shutters.

His left shoulder was sorely wounded. His ill temper, and too quickly drawn swords in the hands of two drunkards, made it so. He was one; the

REBEL KING SERIES – THE HAR'SHIPS

other they buried a fortnight past. He groaned to stand, he groaned to sit, he groaned to lie down. No servant's fretting or pampering allowed him relief of the fetid sore, though it was continually cleaned, applied with poultices, and prayed over.

"We had best make a plan," said Rollo of Argyll, the largest and meanest of the three chieftains of the Macdougall clan who were attending their lord in council.

With great agony the lord of the castle crawled onto the wooden floor and got to his knees. His steward saw him struggling and went to his aid, only to be repulsed.

"Away!" screamed John, "I can get about near same as ye!"

The steward quickly moved back into the shadows and soon disappeared into the kitchen. John painfully managed to convey himself to the bench seat at the table.

"See ye to the window!" he ordered a second chieftain, who got from his bench seat on the opposite side of the table to peer through the parting in the curtains.

"Ye see him?" asked Lord John.

"Aye, formin' his troops at the far hill, he is."

"Wine!" commanded the ailing lord, his mood as dark as the room.

A servant hurriedly came with a flagon of wine and poured the lord's cup to the brim. John sipped, then pushed the cup more inboard, making room on the table for the support of his wounded limb.

"We must beg a truce," offered Sir Rollo, grimly drinking from his horn cup. "They have ten galleys of men and arms on Loch Linnhe a'waitin' for orders from Brus."

John grimaced at the thought of capitulating, but he was in no shape to lead a fight, and King Robert had caught him unaware, with his kinsmen scattered over the whole of Argyll and Lorne.

"Who but a madman campaigns in winter!" he asked rhetorically, but after a brief period of moaning with his pain, he reluctantly agreed.

"Six months," he said.

"They'll be back," cautioned the third chieftain.

"Aye, but in half a year I shall be fit... and it will be spring..." said John, "...and decent weather for a victory."

Rollo nodded his head in agreement, and after he drained his cup and stood, he queried of the watcher at the window, "Where are they now?"

"Linin' the far hill," returned the fellow, "a'waitin' for us to come out for the fight."

"Ye go out and talk with Brus, Rollo, and... tell him that I am not among the ones in the castle, and beg a truce 'til spring," instructed Lord John with perspiration beads forming on his brow in spite of the cold.

Sir Rollo pulled his heavy, fur-trimmed cloak over his broad, leather clad shoulders and strode out of the hall to do as he was ordered, and the other two followed him to their rain soaked horses in the bailey.

"Lord Robert will make light wit of this," said the third chieftain quietly to the others.

"I hope not," said Rollo as he swung his booted leg over the horse's rump, "else we shall all die on yonder hill for a hollow cause." With that he kicked his horse's belly and started off in the direction of the Scots on the hill.

Twenty mounted Macdougall knights trailed after the three chieftains as they rode their horses toward the army of King Robert. As they traversed the expanse of open ground between them, their pace was deliberate and slow.

"Not much army to go against us," commented Robert as he sat his horse and waited for the Argyll entourage to come into hailing range.

"Keep watch all 'round," cautioned Thomas Randolph.

"I'm aware of his tricks," replied Robert, "Edward's posted spies on our flanks."

"Just don't trust shit that don't stink," said Thomas, frowning. He turned his horse to face the oncoming knights, still approaching slowly and with weapons at rest.

In the ranks of the Brus Scots, the plinks of near freezing rain on helmets and scarce worn armor, and an occasional snort of a horse tossing his head in anticipation of action, were the only sounds heard. The small band sent by Lord John was dressed in leather chest armor and fur with a variety of blade weapons strapped all about. They reined up within speaking distance and Rollo, laid out for the bargaining a temporary truce of six months.

King Robert grumped, "Want a truce, do ye?"

"Aye, Sire," pleaded Rollo.

"I will grant yer truce," growled the king.

"Generous, Sire," replied Rollo. "And at what terms?"

Robert looked Rollo in the eye and determinedly said, "The return of my dog."

Rollo looked at the other chieftains without knowing what to say.

"My dog!" insisted Robert. "The one Lord Pembroke sent ye, year last!"

The three chieftains spoke among themselves to a consensus, then Sir Rollo spoke up to say, "That dog died... not long back."

Robert's teeth were on edge. He wanted badly to take all of their lives that very minute but he restrained himself.

"Will any other dog in the bailey do ye?" asked another chieftain frowning but trying to accommodate the instructions from Lord John of making a truce.

The Macdougall entourage was getting nervous and Robert noticed several of the knights were fingering the hilts of their weapons.

"No other dog," said Robert roughly.

"I believe it to be yer dog's hide tacked to the side of the stable," quietly suggested Rollo. "Ye be a'wantin' that?"

Robert audibly fumed. He drew his dagger and approached Rollo. The warriors on both sides drew their weapons and stood to the ready, their destriers pawing the ground. He put the dagger to the man's throat. "Ye!" said the king through clenched teeth.

"Aye," said Rollo, eyes blazing and nostrils flared, but holding his sword in its scabbard. "What be yer say!?"

"Send a man to fetch that empty skin!" he ordered.

Rollo did as he was bade all the while remembering the thrashings that he and the Macdougalls had given The Brus at Dail Righ the previous summer and other places since. Rollo figured to bide his time and his victory hour would come again.

The men on the hill made no additional aggressive move or spoke a word, waiting to see what King Robert would do once his demand of the return of the hide was met.

The knight sent on errand soon came galloping back. The rain soaked hide was thrown to the ground between Robert and Sir Rollo.

Thomas Randolph, who had taken the dog to Argyll on orders from the Earl of Pembroke, recognized the pelt as probably that of Robert's hound.

Robert looked down on what was left of his once proud and faithful dog.

"That yer cur?" asked Rollo not looking down.

"Pick it up!" demanded Robert pushing his horse next to Rollo's and getting close to his face.

Rollo paused, calculating his odds of winning against losing. He glanced up the hill and saw nothing but King Robert's troops until they disappeared over the top edge. He wondered how many men-at-arms were beyond where he could not see. He looked down at the pelt laying in the mud at his horse's hooves and decided to remain alive for another day. He swung his leg off the back of the horse and jumped to the ground. He paused again, staring at Robert.

"Pick it up!" repeated Robert increasing his determination.

Rollo stooped and picked it up. He stood and held the wet mass up toward Robert.

"Kiss it!" demanded Robert.

Standing on the ground, the chieftain paused, frowning. Hatred flashed in the eyes of both men. Rollo paused again, then slowly brought the skin toward his lips.

Robert did not flinch.

Rollo hesitated more, then quickly kissed the wet stinking skin and passed it again up toward Robert.

"Remember that when next we meet," glared Robert, coldly, "Ye have six months, then I will be back!"

"And I will be waitin'," replied Sir Rollo grinding his teeth. "Next time, 'twill be on my terms," he vowed.

Robert smiled, thinking how good it would be to kill the lot of them, and tucked the skin of his dog under his arm.

King Robert was secretly relieved, for his winter's agenda was full and his resources limited, making a half-year delay most convenient. Besides, taking this one motte and bailey wooden castle was far from subduing the whole of Argyll, and that could take an entire winter in itself.

Robert kicked his horse and pulled its head north, toward the Great Glen.

Sir Rollo wondered why their proffered truce had been so readily accepted, bought for the price of the skin of a dog, but he and the rest returned to their warm castle fires, angry but well satisfied, nevertheless.

Lord John didn't care why. He had six more months before facing The Brus. He would be ready for him then. Later, when his wound had healed and the weather warmed, he would plan for the spring.

Ian de Cameron

NOVEMBER 21ST 1307
THE GREAT GLEN OF SCOTLAND

Acrid black smoke from the burning Comyn fortress at Inverlochy rose to blend into the low, bluish-gray, rain-laden clouds that concealed the snowy summit of Ben Nevis. That brooding mountain served as background for King Robert's six hundred man army, this day lining the narrow pathway along River Lochy for more than a mile down the glen. The stolidly trudging men were soaked by the steady rain and cold, and had they not just filled their bellies and warmed themselves a bit as they set the great blaze, their bodies would be in complete rebellion against their stubborn wits.

They were dressed in scant, hard-won armor and wrapped in all manner of rags and animal skins to keep warm. Many had simple rabbit fur shoes laced over woolen stockings, or had wrapped their feet in ribbons of heavy cloth that caused bleeding foot sores with its unevenness. Still, they walked.

Robert had relentlessly pushed his troops north through the Great Glen of the Highlands, leading the long procession up the eastern edge of Loch Linnhe to Inverlochy where he laid siege to the castle, and when it capitulated, directed its destruction.

Supplies and equipment, in as many as ten sea-going galleys belonging to the Macdonald brothers, Angus and Donald, had kept pace with the army as it trekked the length of Loch Linnhe.

Angus, rotund in body and brilliant in mind, and his older brother Donald were rogue traders, smugglers of sorts, dealing in everything from spices to weapons to slaves, and specializing in transporting mercenaries. Sworn enemies of the previous English king, who wanted not so much to eliminate their activity as to tax it heavily, the brothers carried forth their enmity into the reign of the son. Thus, their financial and personal support of King Robert and his army had never flagged.

Past the northern end of the loch, where the waters quickly drew to the river's narrow passage, walking the edge of the stream's meandering way grew hazardous at times, but for the Macdonalds' galleys, following the army was even more treacherous. Constructed very like the Viking craft of their ancestors, the single-masted galleys' seaworthiness had been proven for centuries, but they were hindered by narrow or constricted waters.

Seven of the ten vessels and their sailors had thus been sent back to Castle Dunaverty on the southern tip of Kintyre, their mission and worth played out. Robert had ordered the three remaining galleys, in command of Sir Angus, to accompany them as far as possible on their journey.

Despite the travails, the lateness of the season drove the small band of freedom fighters onward into the mighty teeth of their enemies' strongholds. Winter would be soon upon them.

Andrew Stewart, the king's squire and oft-times standard barrier, followed closely behind his greatly admired sovereign as he picked his way along the water's bank. After them came Robert's brother, Sir Edward, the Bruses' nephew Sir Thomas Randolph, brother-in-law, Sir Neil Campbell, and knights Sir Gilbert de la Haye, Sir Robert Boyd, and Sir John Wallace, the latter a brother of the famed freedom fighter, William. There were also two dozen or so other formally trained knights and fierce highland warriors, most battle-scarred from earlier clashes and wars. Very few others among Brus' army were trained soldiers or fortunate enough to be mounted, but were merely simple people who believed in freedom so much that they could not help but follow.

Cuthbert and Fergus, as earnest as any of Robert's volunteers, were herding the few remaining beeves from Galloway and knew it wouldn't be long before their duties as kine keepers would end. It was Fergus who alerted Thomas Randolph to a mounted figure on the road behind them.

Sir Thomas turned and supported his weight with his hand on the cantle of his saddle to see who it was that steadily approached, but could not make out whether he was friend or foe. With a click of his tongue and a swat on his horse's flank, he trotted forward until he drew closer to his uncles.

"A rider's a'comin'," he said loudly, pointing back the way they had come.

"Maybe a herald," offered Edward, glancing over his shoulder at the steadily closing form.

"We'll know when he gets here," said Robert, all the while keeping his eyes on the trail ahead.

The steady rhythm of the oars in the lead galley suddenly ceased. Angus viewed the stream ahead and ordered the twenty oarsmen and the captain ashore, while he remained on board. He threw the men a long heavy rope, which they pulled in cadenced unison to beach the galley on the rocky shore. The other galleys would follow, one by one.

"What the hell?" asked Edward crossly, reining in his horse and squinting harshly at the scene over his left shoulder no more than thirty paces away. His disposition this morn was black as pitch and delay was apt to make it worse.

"See to it," said Robert tersely. He looked more haggard than his brother had noticed before, but it had been a long, exhausting morning. They were all tired.

The younger man spurred his horse and broke ranks with the caravan of weary soldiers. He turned and shouted to Robert, "Whoe'er 'tis followin' us is still a'comin'," and he pointed toward the distant rider.

The king nodded his head and continued his pace north without pause.

With his men tugging hard on the rope, Angus remained aboard shouting threats of encouragement.

"Why don't he get his fat arse off'n the gunnels and grab a knot of this rope for hisself?" groused the big, red-faced man on the front of the towline.

"Likely he's not a'wantin' to get his brogues wetted," lamented another, his own shoes well submerged in the cold water.

The men strained at the rope and the galley finally slid gracefully from the water to the shore. Six or seven of them went to the sides of the hull and guided it to rest well up on the bank.

"What happens, here?" barked Edward, his destrier tossing its head and dancing from a sense of excitement with the activity.

"River's choked with brush, more of a fen, really ... can't pass it," answered Angus, busily preparing to disembark.

"Damn!" exclaimed Edward.

"Worry not young Brus," replied Angus cheerfully, "we have ways."

"What ways?" Edward frowned.

Angus answered not but dangled his feet over the side of the boat and pushed his hefty little body to follow. The men steadied the hull, but in spite of their support he lost his footing when his feet hit the mossy bank, and he fell into the forefeet of Sir Edward's horse.

The startled animal reared high, his feet pawing at the air above the downed Angus, who could do naught but close his eyes and offer an instant prayer for protection. The horse stomped down hard, planting his hooves deep in the mud exactly beside the Scotsman's ears.

Edward quickly backed the animal away.

The seamen stopped to stare in horror, and seeing their lord had escaped the danger, laughed out loud so raucously that the hull of the boat quivered and the mast swayed in the wind from lack of minding hands.

Unnerved, a wet and muddy Sir Angus jumped angrily to his feet and started spewing curses at the men. The sailors tried more or less successfully to stifle their mirth until, realizing his good fortune in escaping death, the corpulent commander stopped his tantrum and began to laugh aloud himself. His men then renewed their laughter and all was well.

The trailing rider arrived upon the scene and came to Sir Edward with his right hand raised in a sign of peace as he reined in his horse. "Ye men of The Brus?" he asked in guarded manner.

Edward eyed him suspiciously. "We hain't got no food to spare."

"Asked for naught. Just rightly want to know if ye are with King Robert," insisted the stranger more coldly.

Edward ignored the man and looked back at the seamen at their task. Some were offloading the supplies the galley held while others were placing large dowel pin handles into the sides of the hull, working amazingly fast as a matter of routine.

"What the hell are ye doin'?" Edward yelled, waving his arms at Angus.

"We are fixin' to carry it overland," replied the boat's owner.

"Carry?! Ye cannot carry this... this *ark*... all the way to Loch Lochy! That's more than seven... eight miles!" spluttered Edward, still in his surly humor.

"Oh, no, Sir Edward," Angus appeased his young friend. "We shall carry it only as far as necessary to reach open water. If we must carry it more than, say, a hundred or so yards, we will attach wheels and pull it like a great wagon to where we can safely launch again. 'Tis a bother, but not anything we have not faced ere this."

As they watched, the thirty-five foot vessel rose from the mud by the great strength of the oarsmen's arms, and the sturdy sailors began to walk it around the impasse. Angus waved to the other two galleys coming to the scene, ordering them to do likewise.

"We could use some brawny arms to help return the cargoes to our galleys up yonder, Sir Edward," smiled Angus.

"I'll send ye some lads who have good boots," said Edward, then turned back to the stranger and said sullenly, "King Robert's we are. Who would ye be?"

"Sir Ian de Cameron," said the stranger straightforwardly, "and I've come to join ye."

Edward squinted his eyes against the spitting rain. "And why would ye?" he asked. "The Camerons have not been anxious to lend us aid."

"Now, I am," replied the knight, making no apology for his kin.

"Ye can wield that blade at yer side?" asked an unsmiling Edward.

"Aye," said the Cameron resolutely. "Ye'll not be havin' to save my hide in a fair fight."

"But we don't fight fair," countered Edward. "We fight to win."

Ian smiled and said, "Then, ye'll be havin' me, will ye?"

"Aye," he replied dourly, "I'm Edward de Brus, and we'll have ye."

"The king's brother?" exclaimed Ian aloud, his eyebrows raised in mild surprise.

"Aye," claimed Edward, adding quietly, "the only one yet livin'... come, I'll take ye to him."

The two men rode toward the head of the array. Within a short while, the first of the smugglers' galleys was being returned to the water, and the second and third, hefted by other stout arms for their overland trip.

. .

The entourage reached Loch Lochy well after dark, and bitter winds had gathered to whip intermittent showers mercilessly southward through the Great Glen into the eyes of the men and animals, freezing in the hair on their faces and making every movement wretched. The men scattered to find lee areas where they could boil a handful of oats and escape the horrid freezing rain, but nowhere was there comfort.

The next morning brought little respite from the previous day's misery, and after a filling breakfast of cold mutton, hot parsnips and leeks, the soldiery fell in on the trail behind Robert and began their journey anew. The oarsmen in the galleys faced laboring in sinew tearing battles against heavy waves that crashed against the hulls and sent icy spray over the decks and the oars and the backs of the ceaselessly struggling men.

"'Tis a terrible way to wage war!" shouted a well-swaddled Angus to the captain aboard his lead galley.

"Aye," agreed the captain, biting hard on a green stick and holding the tiller with an arm lock to keep his vessel from being blown onto the rocks near the shore. He removed the stick from between his teeth for a moment, and waving it to indicate the rain and wind added, "Why do we set out to make war when we must also fight such? Only fools would wish to be out here in this gale as are we."

Angus chuckled at the truth of the statement, but tried to assuage the captain's frustrations, saying, "Aye, and the Comyns and their ilk agree with ye! And bein' good, sensible Scots are no doubt holed up in their warm houses with their womenfolk and their pleasures, thinkin' they're safe 'til the snows melt. By then, I suspect, many of them will lie not in their beds... but in their shrouds." The captain nodded agreement as Angus pulled his woolen wrap up to shield his face from the stinging spray.

"Ye think they don't know we're a'comin'?" the captain asked charily, the stick between his teeth bitten nearly in half with the strain of his wrestling the tiller.

"Can't say," replied Angus in truth. "But only fearful men would think to place spies in this drear wilderness in the midst of such."

"Aye," again agreed the tight-lipped captain with an encouraged smile, "or a madman thinkin' to put the fear of God into 'em."

Angus turned forward, his once neatly trimmed bearded face feeling the full brunt of the icy wind.

•   •

Once the storm subsided and the loch's surface grew less angry, the sailors took turns rowing and covered the remainder of Loch Lochy's nearly ten-mile length in quick manner. Some of the men seined for fish, and by so doing caught a goodly mess for the evening meal.

When the three galleys at last came to the northern narrows of Loch Lochy, Robert's army was nowhere to be seen, left behind as the galleys sprinted up the loch. Angus decided to camp there and await the king, a decision the tired sailors welcomed heartily, as they did the hot flat bannocks baked to eat with the fish.

Worn out, the sailors rested soundly that night, despite the raw wind and dropping temperatures, huddling together as best they could in crudely established shelters.

Before the morning light brightened the leaden clouds, Angus woke several of his soundly snoring minions and sent them ahead to scout the waters, by then rimed with a thin crust along the shore. He handed them each a leftover bannock as they stretched and scratched and wrapped their blankets round themselves on their way out of camp in the pre-dawn chill.

They returned from their scouting expedition around midday, just as King Robert and his warriors caught up to the temporarily beached Angus and his little fleet.

"We'll not be afloat for long goin' to Oich," reported one of the scouts, mucus from his nose frozen in his mustache and beard, nearly sealing his mouth shut.

"We walked near half the length of it, Sire, and it hain't fit for galleys a'tall," chimed in the other, who fared no better than his companion. "The banks at the south end are all frore and the farther ye go north, the more of the loch is ice."

With his left hand, Angus scratched his beard before casting a look at Robert as if asking for instructions.

Robert dismounted and walked to where the three galleys lay at anchor. He quickly took measure of the supplies they held and after but a moment's pause, turned and said to Angus, "Unload the stores." Then to Edward, "See that as many of these provisions get on the backs of our animals as possible… includin' the cattle."

"What about *yer* horse?" asked Edward, thinking he would not give his destrier to pack service if Robert did not.

"I'll walk a spell," answered the king, and Edward quietly moaned at his failed ruse.

"What's yer ken, Robbie?" asked Angus.

"We can only portage one galley," the king arched and stretched his back and shrugged his shoulders to relieve his tiredness, "and it must be the biggest of the lot." Stooping to the water's edge, he removed his glove and scooped the cold liquid in one great hand, to splash it on his face and on the back of his neck as if applying a curative.

"Why so?" asked Angus.

"It will take all of us to get the big one to Oich… and I hain't waitin' to get the other two over this hump as well."

"Aye, Sire," returned Angus, and turning on his heel, proceeded to start the off-loading.

The span of glen from Loch Lochy to Loch Oich, although less than two miles, was the most treacherous of the arduous journey. The galley had to be manhandled for most of the way and by the time they reached the southern end of Oich, every man, including the king, had a hand on the vessel's hull. Many wondered what good a single galley would be to the army anyway, but none asked the question of their seniors.

The rain alternated with snow the whole way, adding to the peril and the torment. Exhausted, the army at last bivouacked where they were able to float the vessel, much to the relief of the Macdonald and his sore feet and aching back, on the southern shore of Loch Oich.

Two more such long days and the exhausted army had traversed in excess of ten miles northward, crossed from the eastern to the western shore of Loch Oich, and moved up River Oich, arriving at the southern shore of the grand Loch Ness. The weather had cooperated somewhat, for though cold and overcast, the rain and snow all but disappeared, and wind blew more southerly. Still, there was little rest. For two more days the army followed the rugged edge of the ominous loch, the single galley easily having kept pace.

Afternoon of the third day was again drizzly and cold, and made more miserable by the return of the northerly wind. The men rested and ate meagerly of foraged game and bannocks, and strove uselessly to stay warm. Frostbite on the extremities of those most often exposed to the cold was not yet prevalent, but neither was it unheard of, and several men had lost toes, making their travel even more difficult.

The horses, so sleek and magnificent at the outset of the expedition, now foraged for scarce vegetation, their ribs showing poorly under their blankets and saddles. The king made no audible comparison between them and his sinewy troops, but he had not failed to recognize it.

Gathering his weary lieutenants in a canvas shelter rigged on the moored and ceaselessly bobbing galley, Robert had lit a fire in the peat-fueled firebox that heated the small refuge to bearable warmth. There they ate hard bread and drank diluted wine in small cups as they talked among themselves.

Last to arrive, Thomas Randolph blew his nose overboard before he entered the enclosure. His head hurt, his eyes were red and watery, and he ached in every joint of his body. It made him feel no better when Robert looked up at him and asked, "Ye've caught the misery?"

Thomas sniffed, sat beside the king and thrust his ungloved hands close to the heat. "Aye," he grunted, "as have mor'n half the men."

No one was in any mood to make light of his misery and so said nothing. Thomas was right. More than half the troops now struggled through their days with little strength and less spirit. Their wits were as dull as their gray winter surroundings.

Handing Thomas a cup and a crust of the bread, Robert began his meeting with, "Urquhart is next!" The men all knew of Castle Urquhart, midway up the western shore of Loch Ness on a point of land called Strone. From there, the length and breadth of the loch could be controlled without so great an effort.

"Pray, Sire, how are we to take such a well-fortified castle when we have neither siege engines nor the ability to starve them out!" queried Sir Gilbert de la Haye.

"Robbie will know!" sharply replied Edward, affronted that Robert's judgment be so questioned.

"Gilbert is, like St. Thomas, the cautious one," offered Sir Robert Boyd.

"Caution is now useless," replied King Robert, "they know we're comin'."

"How?" asked Neil Campbell.

"Picket... he sighted us today from upstream a ways," answered Robert almost casually.

"Then we are truly done," remarked Gilbert, dropping his helmeted head into his hands in resignation.

"They know we're here..." said Thomas quietly, "so how do we take advantage of that?"

"We still may have the element of surprise," remarked Robert.

Gilbert shook his head in dismay, but Robert held his own plan to hear the thoughts of the others.

"Let's bypass this one... and pick it up later when we're stronger," offered John Wallace, almost as large a man as was his martyred brother.

"Spoken like near kin to the Comyns," charged Neil knitting his brows.

"Ye think *me* a spy?" said John placing the palm of his hand on the handle of his dagger.

"I think," replied Neil without pause, "ye have family ye want saved in yonder castle."

John looked from face to face, and finding doubt in the eyes of some of his other companions as well, removed his hand from his dagger handle and took a deep breath. "For those who would call me spy, I say to ye... I am of Comyn kin, but the Comyns are in league with the English... and the English wrongfully executed my brother William. Now I ask... what side d'ye think I strike against?" He again looked at them before continuing. "Besides, was not the castle we just burnt full of Comyns? And yet, I said naught." None rebutted this but remained quiet and sipped at their cups, including Neil, whose gaze the Wallace found no longer doubting.

Pleased that they had settled the squabble between them without his intercession, Robert passed the wine flask again and continued his talk.

"Urquhart may well be garrisoned by English troops but falls within Lord Alexander Comyn's purview. We must leave no sanctuary for the enemy along the entirety of the waterway," said Robert. "We cannot bypass anythin'. This will be our supply line from the south to the north..."

"Or our escape route," inserted Edward.

Robert glared at his brother but said nothing.

"What be yer plan?" asked Thomas.

Gilbert raised his head with interest.

"The picket I saw won't get to the castle 'til around dark," explained Robert, "so they'll not expect our attack tonight."

"Tonight?" asked Edward incredulously, thinking his brother had lost his wits.

"Our strength is in surprise, not in numbers, so we must do the unexpected, Little Brother," said Robert.

"Urquhart is well garrisoned," interjected Thomas, who had visited the castle not long before while temporarily impressed into the service of Lord Pembroke.

"Urquhart has three sides to the loch," stated the king quietly.

"And we have a galley!" whispered Edward, amazed at himself for being the first to understand.

The others, however, saw it fraught with impossibilities and said so.

Thomas pulled a stick from among those in the burning faggot and rubbed it along the side of the iron box before he spat on the tip, which hissed, the red glow turning black. Some of the others watched as he took his charcoal pencil and quickly drew a diagram on the inside of his left hand, then turned his hand to the rest, displaying the palm.

It looked like a large and angular letter 'B' stretching from the heel to the callused pads beneath his fingers.

"This is yer castle plan," he said, and with the point of the pencil he waved it on the right side of the configuration where the two arcs were and continued, "This is east, this north, and this... south of the curtain wall... all surrounded by water. The western wall, here, is the landward side, and here," he indicated the center of the wall and continued, "is the main gate leadin' out to a steep stone moat. The only crossin' point is the drawbridge."

"What's twixt the two arches?" asked Edward.

"Trough for the watergate... a bit of land, steep angle, slick with piggery shit and such, runoff for that side of the grounds, and there's rocks along the bottom in the water," explained Thomas. "Nary a man has scaled those walls and later bragged on it."

"What's inside," asked the king.

Thomas dropped his hand and said, "Inside is not flat... there are separate baileys at either end. The parapet goes all 'round with towers at both ends and at the gate. The landward side is well guarded. Off the south bailey are the constable's and garrison's quarters, and the great hall. Naught in the north bailey save stables and a smithy shop, a gaol, the small animal pens and a trainin' area for the knights... but ye'll not get in... save by crossin' the moat."

"Then the galley is of no use?" asked Edward crestfallen.

"To my knowin' there's ne'er been a success from the water side. It's been approached from the water, but they always come ashore away from the castle and attack the main gate," said Thomas.

"The unexpected!" exclaimed Edward with renewed interest.

"Aye," replied Robert rubbing his index finger across his mouth and through his auburn beard, "'tis our only chance."

After a moment, the lieutenants began their objections.

"Knights ought not have to wallow in pig shit to fight a battle," said Sir Neil Campbell.

"'Tis true," said Robert, "ye ought not... but chances of a chivalrous outcome do not exist. We can be chivalrous or we can win the war, but ye'll not be worryin' 'bout the stench of the sluiceway, anyhow, Neil, for I want ye and Wallace to lead the ground forces," ordered Robert, "and

Angus, how close to the wall do ye think we can sneak ere they know we're about?"

"If ye're doin' what I think ye're doin'... well then... Yer guess would match mine," replied Angus.

Robert then said, "Neil, take the men who yet have horses, and choose others to ride our horses so we arrive at the castle about the same time. The rest can follow on foot... but the surprise must be before the morn light."

"This wind in our faces, it will take hours to row that league to the castle," interjected Sir Angus with an anxious frown.

"But it can be done!" said Robert as he arose to leave. All eyes turned from the king to the Macdonald, and he felt the weight of the whole castle fall squarely upon his sore shoulders. Finally, he exhaled audibly and thought but a moment before surrendering.

"Aye, My King..." replied Angus.

Robert nodded his head in agreement. Being called "My King," always seemed strange to his ear, though he knew he was king... but at that moment he seemed to have inherited a kingdom of wilderness and frore, devoid of pomp.

. .

Near dark, after all the men had eaten and rested, Robert addressed them and roused their blood to the task, then sent those with the horses up the glen led by Sir Neil and Sir John toward Castle Urquhart. The rest of the nobles and the infantry followed as quickly as they could manage on foot.

Robert and his squire, his remaining lieutenants, his knights and his highlanders, some seventeen fighters in all, went aboard the galley, and with black sails billowed in the wind, headed toward the castle.

God be with us, prayed Robert, and twenty seamen's oars splashed the water in rhythmic tones.

The misty cold rain began again.

NOVEMBER 9TH 1307
CASTLE URQUHART

From the galley on Loch Ness the king could see flickers of torchlight moving north along the western shore, keeping fair pace with his own furtive speed. Having its oarlocks tied in rags to muffle the slightest noise, the galley sliced silently through the cold water. Even so, if they failed to make it to the castle and launch their attack before daylight, the entire scheme would be discovered and all would be for naught.

It was that knowledge that kept Robert's wit on edge.

'Tis a foolhardy plan, he silently tortured himself. His well-founded fear was that the domination of the Great Glen would be won or lost on this singular stroke, but he had no better plan, nor any alternate.

"Will not the torches on shore alert the castle about our comin', My King?" asked Andrew in a soft whisper.

"They know we're comin', young Stewart," answered Robert in like manner. "The torches keep their focus on the landside and away from us."

"If I was captain of the guard, I would keep a watch all 'round the wall," replied the squire, sensibly. Robert kept a straight face at the boy's innocent suggestion.

"We hope the English have gotten used to their warm beds and will take the path of least bother," said Robert, shifting his weight to look forward into the blackness and the cold, spitting rain for a glimpse of the dark castle.

Thirty-seven men were packed tightly onto the small boat. Twenty seamen worked oars at the captain's command while sixteen hardy warriors, stripped of all armor save helms and mail coats, were the ones on whose skills the entire raid was balanced. Weapons were few, but included short swords, an occasional battleaxe, and always, daggers. A Scot felt almost naked without his dagger at his waist or shoulder.

The king estimated there were two more hours of darkness about the same time that he noticed the strung-out lights of the torches were running a bit ahead of the galley.

At least we won't have to wait for them to arrive, he thought, but within half an hour the row of tiny fireballs had entirely disappeared from sight. Straining his eyes into the blackness of the shoreline once more to make sure, he finally glimpsed the barest glow of firelight from the castle proper.

"Neil and John must have arrived with the land troops and extinguished the torches," Robert whispered to Edward, who agreed, also in muted voice. All aboard the vessel knew that voices would carry far across the water.

As Robert had said, so it was, and as surreptitiously as possible, Neil Campbell and John Wallace aligned their men before the landside wall of the castle. Though they had made the overnight forced march up the loch, the men were all the same spoiling for the expected fight. However, the time was not yet, so they obeyed their orders to take their positions and lie quiet in the cold darkness to wait.

Looking at the great pile in the dark, it was difficult to make out even the shape of it, but the Scots commanders could discern the faint outline of structures upon the steep rise to the south, if only by the watch fires in the upper bailey.

As Thomas Randolph had drawn it on the palm of his hand just a few hours earlier, the curtain wall, which faced northwest, was guarded by two 'D' towers flanking the gate, and the parallel stone-banked ditch more than twenty feet deep.

To traverse that wide channel an invader would have to control the drawbridge. Built of massive oaken beams, the drawbridge spanned a broad breach between the two ends of a long stone bridge or causeway built toward the center from the sides of the dry moat.

On the castle side of the bridge there were high stone walls from the castle gate to the drawbridge, protecting the castle defenders from attack while advancing to, retreating from, or operating the drawbridge. The other end of the causeway lay open to missiles flung from the castle's defenders.

A great winch and chains necessary for raising and lowering the all-important bridge were concealed from attack by the stout masonry walls. As anyone on the western approach could see in daylight, when prudently drawn up tight, the drawbridge left invaders facing emptiness and a killing drop to the bottom of the dry moat.

Beyond, there still awaited the heavy, ironbound oaken gate and the subsequent tunnel lined with murder holes and protected defenders, and near the end, the portcullis. All must be survived before one could enter the courtyard, and there the garrison awaited.

It was as Thomas Randolph had said.

As intended, the defenses of the massive citadel loomed impregnable, especially for an army that had neither siege engines nor the time and stores to starve out the English occupiers. Being nearly winter, the weather would also work hardship on those who would lay siege while the castle dwellers lazed by their warm fires.

Thus, the Campbell and the Wallace each peered into the same gloomy drizzle and held his private thoughts lest the other think him a coward.

Atop the crenellated battlements, men along the western wall kept close watch in anticipation of attack from the broad moor at dawn, though most were confident of their safety and prowess against such.

"Where be those torches we seen a while ago, Jack?" asked a lanky man with matted hair the color of flax when he met his older and darker counterpart on the wall walk at its southernmost point.

"Gone, it seems," replied Jack casually.

"Could be that bunch we heard about last night, tryin' to sneak up on us," cautioned the first.

"And so? If there's a thousand of 'em come to attack, what can they do?" asked the dark-haired man. "They hain't moved up a single siege engine, and these walls hain't made of butter!" Jack tapped his boot against the nearest reddish stone. "Have no fear o' them beggars. From what I hear, they be no more than scarecrow men, a... a... troop of starvelin's abroad with their pitchforks and their flails, frightenin' little children."

"But, suppose it be The Brus?" the first man nervously insisted.

"Oooooh! The Brus!" mocked the second, but to make the fair-haired fellow feel better he added, "Go on back to your post and quit worryin'. I'll report what we seen to the constable on the dawn."

"Keep a sharp eye all the same," said the fairer soldier peering into the western blackness.

Jack frowned and walked his tour in the opposite direction. He was not feeling as confident as he had, but he knew he should. Everything he had told the other guard was true. The massive walls of Urquhart inspired awe in all who approached.

He made himself think of other things, and continued on his way.

Down below, the tiny overloaded galley, still undetected, maneuvered near the cliff, its bow at last sliding effortlessly onto the sea worn stones at the water's edge. The single mast wavered as if trying to hail an inmate as King Robert took the lead in stealing silently over the bow and onto the wet, slippery stones. Behind him trailed a strong but lightweight rope that he had tied securely around his waist.

As the others watched, the Scottish monarch began clawing his way up the weathered face of the rocky mound, to the very base of the castle wall, until he at last stood on a precipice on which he knew his band could maneuver, and so progressed no farther.

It is now, he thought, *that we see whether my notion will work.*

He jerked the line smartly, and aboard the galley below, Thomas Randolph went to work. At Robert's signal he quickly cut the line and tied the end of it to the odd device they had created earlier and stowed amidships in the boat. He then followed Robert's lead over the bow and onto the stony beach.

Robert Boyd directed the off-loading of Robert's contrivance, a slender, thirty-foot-long wooden pole with a four-foot long arm securely pegged and lashed at right angle. On the end of the extended arm was an iron bar, sturdy and long, almost five feet, and tightly wrapped with rope to prevent its making noise when it slipped into place. From that fell two long ropes, attached to each other at regular intervals by ropes of about a foot and a half in length. This rope ladder was carefully bundled and tied for use at the right time.

It was this that Robert hoped would permit him and his small band of men to open the fortress to his army on the land side and thus take Castle Urquhart.

Angus Macdonald, though he greatly desired to go with them, would remain on deck with his sailors and observe the movements of the sentries on the wall to warn the Scots as they worked.

Randolph quietly signaled the rest of the soldiers to gather their weapons and carry the pole to the rock-faced cliff. There they stood it on end and leant it against the cliff so that it was directly below the point on which stood their friend and king.

Boyd and Randolph scrambled up the rock to join Robert, and the three of them, pulling on the rope the king had trailed behind him, gradually dragged the awkward pole up the cliff toward themselves. Then they waited for a sign from Angus that the wall above them was not, at that moment, manned.

The signal finally was given, and the three worked in concert to push the arm with its iron bar up and over the crenellated top of the curtain wall. The higher it went, the more unwieldy it became, and at one point they thought the device might just tumble down to the beach in spite of all they could do to prevent it.

As the great iron inched close to the top of the wall, Angus signaled a pause. A guard on the wall was patrolling the walk just above them. The king and his two knights near spent all their strength, but held the ungainly device against the side of the wall and prayed that the sentry looked not in their direction.

They could barely detect his movements as he shuffled his weary way, but all instinctively held their breaths lest he overhear them. Angus again signaled that the walk was clear, and they, straining with red-faced determination, finally hefted the bar up to the very tops of the merlons, where it rested. So did they.

"Now," whispered The Brus after a brief respite, "we must push it forward so that the bar falls behind the merlons and holds there." On command, they heaved it in unison and the pole moved forward. As desired, the iron fell beyond the merlons, but before they could stop it, the pole dropped the several feet also and the wooden arm struck the bottom of the crenellation with a sharp report.

"Did you hear that?" asked the sentry of his drowsing companion.

"Hear what," the sleepy one mumbled.

"That noise! Did you not hear it?" he asked again, looking at the direction from which he thought it came.

"I heard naught!" He wished his fellow sentry would just go away. "I warrant you'll next be seein' ghosts and faeries dancin' on the moors!"

"I heard somethin', I tell you!" the more alert fellow insisted.

"Then get you out there and search out its cause! I'll be here when you return." He leant against the wall and rested his arm on the butt end of his pike. "Naught will happen 'til sunup, and that on t'other side of the bailey."

Knowing that the dullard was not at all interested in leaving his dry resting spot to investigate the sound, the vigilant sentry determined to find its source. Walking slowly out on the parapet he thought he heard something else, a slight, intermittent rustling noise.

Out a ways, he cocked his ear and was sure something was moving against the side of the wall. He followed the sound a bit farther and espied the end of the wooden arm and the bar against the battlement.

"What the 'ell?" he said softly as he cautiously approached. His companion's statement about "ghosts and faeries" still ringing in his ears, he wanted to be sure that he would not embarrass himself if he raised an alarm.

Holding his pike at the ready, he looked over the side of the wall, first catching sight of the mast of the galley swaying. That in itself being nothing unusual, he stretched over the wall farther and peered straight down.

The Scot's dagger was swift. The guard's throat was stabbed through so that he could make no sound. His helm tumbled off, falling to the rocks and sea below. Robert's great hand seized the hapless fellow by his hair, and using the man's own body weight, had him quickly follow. He landed at the base of the wall with a dull thump.

The victor of the tussle quickly eased himself up and over the wall and lay motionless in the shadows, his crimson blade ready to strike again.

Thomas Randolph next pushed himself up and swung over the wall to join the king. "Ye near dropped that losel on my head!" he whispered. Complaining further he added, "If ye had, I would not have gone to meet ol' Scratch as he did, without so much as a yelp."

"Ye would if ye had suffered my blade stuck through yer gullet," rebutted Robert, showing Thomas his bloodied weapon.

Waiting for the others to appear at the battlement, the two silently observed movement within the castle, noting where the guards were stationed and how they patrolled their assigned domains. There seemed to be little movement on the battlements of the upper bailey, at least on the loch side, which suited them well.

The men below and on the galley had watched the hapless sentry drop off the castle wall after his helmet bounced down the cliff to land in the pebbles at the water's edge. None spoke until Andrew calmly asked, "May I climb next?"

"Aye, Lad," replied Angus, and without so much as another breath, the boy leapt off the vessel and ran light-footed to where a handful of warriors awaited their turn.

The ends of the loosened rope ladder were by then extended almost all the way to the bottom of the cliff, but fell a bit short of Andrew's reach. The boy jumped for the ladder but missed. He tried again and barely caught hold of one rope with his left hand. There he dangled. His feet would not reach the ground beneath him, but he held fast to the rope and tried to pull himself up. A burly young Scot moved to give him a boost but was held back by the touch of an older man's hand on his arm.

The younger man at first seemed resentful but the older warrior, looking him in the eye, said simply, "Aid him not. This he must do on his own." The younger man pursed his lips, but nodded and stood back.

Andrew swung himself from side to side and finally caught the rope with his dexter hand. Pushing his feet against the cliff he pulled hand-over-hand on the rope until his foot reached the ladder's bottom rung, and he climbed upward with the ease of a sprite.

The older Scot quietly smiled at his grit.

Two other warriors had rolled onto the parapet floor and quickly found places to hide when Andrew's head appeared at the open space between the merlons. At the king's signal, he deftly climbed through and rolled into the shadows with Robert and Thomas.

Edward was next to appear, and one-by-one, the other sea borne fighters would follow.

In the advance party of the men on the groundside, Cuthbert and Fergus had arrived less exhausted than most for having taken turns riding bareback to the scene on their one remaining beef cow. As men all around hunkered in the quiet, the hungry cow began to bellow.

"Keep that damned animal quiet!" ordered Sir Neil, crossly.

"Aye, Sire," said Cuthbert, and he nervously tried to find the poor creature something edible. All the while, the cow continued to bawl loudly.

"We're bein' attacked by cattle herders," joked one of the guards on the western wall. He and his two companions laughed and mocked the expected army of farmers and herders.

Since Robert threw the one lookout from the wall, and his somnolent comrade had dozed off, there remained only one sentry on duty on the lochside wall of the upper bailey, and at that moment he was wondering why he was missing out on the jests of his comrades across the way.

The king, meanwhile, was secretly amassing his fighters under the very noses of the watch. His men stood and sat and lay in every shadow and corner of the wall walk, and Robert knew it would be but moments before they were so many that they could no longer hide.

Seeing an opportunity, he quickly slipped toward the staircase leading up to the parapet, and reaching the steps, spun around. Suddenly he appeared to be coming from the stairs, and with much hacking and coughing, he easily drew the sentry's attention upon himself. Walking purposefully toward the guard with his hood over his head and the rest of his cloak draped around him, Robert became an unsuspicious man on the wall.

"What brings you to the ramparts, Sire?" inquired the guard, thinking the king was of the castle denizens.

"The sound of laughin'!" replied Robert with an English accent.

"I think they be laughin' at some bellowin' cow out yonder," said the guard as he turned and pointed to the landside.

Robert's dagger flashed and within the instant the man was dead. Edward briskly strode to his brother as Robert pulled the dead man's surcoat from the body. The helmet had rolled a couple of feet away.

"The helm, quickly!" whispered Robert, pulling the surcoat around his own shoulders.

Edward picked it up and tossed it to Robert, who exchanged it for his own; then he stood with the dead man's pike so the sentries across the bailey could see him.

"Ye get all the men up?" asked Robert while taking in the layout of the citadel.

"Boyd's seein' to it now."

Edward, soon joined by Andrew, stayed in the shadows as Robert walked the guard's route.

"You hear the cow bellerin'?" yelled the nearest of the three guards on the front wall.

Robert raised his spear and laughed.

The senior man on watch approached Robert more closely, but not close enough to discern his face in the shadows. "Wake the constable about the goin's on," he ordered brusquely.

"Aye," said Robert.

The man turned and stared at him, "You sound like a goddam Scot!"

No sooner had the word Scot escaped his lips than they were forever silenced by Robert's borrowed spear thrust into the man's lower jaw and his brain. He tumbled backward, dead.

Robert gave a low whistle and the rest of the Scots warriors slipped slyly over the wall and crawled to a staircase where the wall met the garrison quarters at the southwestern end. All sixteen were now inside, and they quickly scattered about the courtyard while awaiting a signal.

Andrew donned the dead man's surcoat and helmet and followed Robert down the hill from the upper bailey to the gate towers. Thomas and Edward followed apace. Only the king and Andrew, dressed as guards, could walk near the random torch lights in the bailey, and only by the lowering of the drawbridge could Neil Campbell and John Wallace, with their more nearly six hundred, join the small force to subdue the garrison.

Inside the soldiers' quarters the captain of the guard was awake and sitting on the edge of his pallet. He was a big man with coarse features and a neatly trimmed beard, a grooming luxury attributed to disciplinary practices he continued, even being so far from the social core. He rubbed his eyes and uselessly wished for warmer weather.

Outside, Thomas approached the dovecote in the middle of the bailey. The cote was a large, cone shaped building housing doves and other like birds for the lord's table. Edward was close beside him when Thomas suddenly turned toward a sound near the curtain wall, knocking his scabbard against the cote's wooden door with a sharp thump.

Startled, the birds within flew about the dovecote, creating much ado and cooing loudly in panic.

"Damn!" spat Thomas, as he and Edward quickly hunkered down to make themselves less visible.

But the captain, hearing the birds' commotion, sat bolt upright. *His* men knew to keep a wide berth about the dovecote, especially at night. He grabbed his sword, slinging off the sheath so that it slapped against the wall, and walked out into the bailey a mere twenty feet from the crouching Scots. The cold ground nearly froze his bare feet, but he cared not as he stared into the poorly lighted area, around where many were hiding.

Seeing naught, and with his cold feet starting to ache, he slowly returned inside, still feeling that there was trickery under way. He went immediately to the ground floor barracks room.

"Get up!" shouted the captain to a contingent of guards asleep in the great hall. He went through shaking ticks and boots as were easily within his reach. The bleary-eyed men came alive reasonably fast, having been apprised the previous evening that Scots were seen nearby.

The guard captain sent one of his men to wake the constable, ensconced in the lord's apartments on the third floor. He then returned to the huge fireplace and held his cold feet out to the little warmth still emanating from the last of the previous evening's roaring blaze.

Knowing that there was now little need for secrecy, Thomas said openly, "I fear the doors of hell are set to pour demons upon us!" The two quickly surveyed their surroundings at the dovecote to assess their predicament.

"'Twould be mighty good to get to those bastards ere they are full awake and armed," said Edward.

"Aye!" said Thomas, and standing, gave a high, sharp whistle and a swing of his sword, and the shadows brought forth Scots from seemingly every nook of the upper bailey.

The birds in the dovecote complained once again.

"Birds!" said Edward in disgust.

"We'll be havin' 'em for breakfast when we're done with this morn's work," replied Thomas gruffly as the other Brus warriors gathered about them.

"Aye," returned Edward blackly, "or they us."

The invading Scots whooped their blood-curdling war cries and rushed headlong into the building, Thomas and Edward in the lead. As they had supposed, the just awakened castle guards were far more numerous than they, but were as yet unready for such an onslaught. Some were armed, others not, but none were able to meet well the flying blades of the attackers.

Hearing shouts from overhead, Edward and several others grabbed the heavy tables in the barracks and with the help of stout benches, tightly wedged them into the opening to the stairs so that those who came charging down could not pass, at least for a short time.

King Robert was near to grabbing the gate guard from behind when the loud whoop from the bailey occurred. The guard turned suddenly, startling both men, but fortunately the king was at the ready with his dagger and instinctively slammed it into the man's gut just below his chest armor. The man doubled over with a scream of pain and fear, crumpling to the ground and bleeding profusely. Robert knew he would be dead within a moment, and left him there while going about the business of lowering the bridge.

Fortunately for the king, the defenders had made the error of not dropping the great portcullis, so he and his squire went for the heavy gate at the opposite end of the tunnel. As they lifted the large wooden beam from its braces, another man with brandished broadsword showed himself, backlit by torchlight, in the gate tunnel. Andrew audibly gulped at the image, but with eyes widening, he drew his broadsword to the ready.

"Ye men need help?" asked the man in a loud, cheerful voice.

"Ye scared the shit from me, Sire!" screamed Andrew, recognizing the voice of Sir Robert Boyd.

In the gatehouse above, two guards awakened, and realizing a raid on the castle was underway, prepared to lower the portcullis, as was their duty.

The three in the gate tunnel heard the scurrying overhead and knew that the portcullis would soon fall, trapping the Scots king and his companions outside the castle with the stone causeway to the raised drawbridge beyond the just unbarred gate. Boyd instantly leapt to the staircase and rushed to the gatehouse guardroom to try and stop the calamity.

At the same moment, the king, still with hands on the great oaken beam that had barred the gate, grabbed hold and with his considerable might, lifted and carried it to the portcullis, quickly standing it upright in the channel in which the portcullis would drop. Before he removed his hand, the ironbound grate slammed hard against the beam, but could go no farther.

"Murder holes!" yelled Robert looking up at the ominous ports, "We've got to stop them ere they rain arrows on us through those damned murder holes!" Andrew dashed up the stairs, sword in hand.

Boyd arrived too late to prevent the portcullis from being dropped, but when he burst through the door into the guard's presence, they had bows in hand with arrows nocked and at the ready. The startled and scared men turned and loosed their arrows in the direction of the intruder. One whizzed by Boyd's head and thudded into the wall behind him. The other caught his right shoulder solidly, and twisted him back. As if in a dream, the bold Scot heard the dull clang of his broadsword hitting the floor as he fell backwards.

Andrew, who had followed him up the steps saw the Scots hero fall.

The English guards pulled their swords and came swiftly toward Boyd, blades flashing.

"Let them not take me alive!" implored Robert Boyd in great pain.

Andrew, suddenly shaken at the thought of his friend being taken at all, recovered enough to jump in between Boyd and the enemy, swinging his broadsword like a madman, screaming curses at them all the while.

It was two experienced soldiers against one brave youth, and none had shield but relied on sheer sword work to attack and defend. Fortunately for Andrew, the two he fought were as scared of the blades of their own as they were of the slight squire's.

Sir Robert Boyd righted himself and staggered to his feet intent on aiding the boy, but when he bent over to retrieve his sword, he fell again to the floor. Much to his dismay, blood was pouring freely from his wounded shoulder. To staunch the flow, he knew he must first remove the arrow.

He leant against the wall with the arrowhead at an angle to the stonework. Gritting his teeth resolutely, he held the shaft and pushed it back and to the side so that the arrow broke just short of the arrowhead. He then was able to pull the shaft easily from the wound, but had not the strength remaining to go to the boy's relief, and indeed, swooned from the anguish he suffered.

Young Andrew was giving a good account of himself and had

managed to slash one of the men he was fighting. The other, however, was much the larger of the two guards, and relieved of the danger his compatriot posed, used his greater weight to his advantage. In but a moment after the other man fell, he had the lad pinned against the upper part of the arrested portcullis.

Grinning delightedly at his victory over the struggling Scottish lad, the man drew back his sword to drop the deathblow on him when he felt a cold point of steel touch the side of his neck. He froze.

"Ye wouldn't harm the lad, would ye?" asked Robert in a voice that caused the man's blood to chill.

The heavy guard moved only his head, and almost imperceptibly.

"Ye want to live?" asked the king as he easily removed the sword from the prisoner's hand.

"Kill him! Kill him, My King!" Andrew urged his mentor and hero.

"We have need of this one, Lad," answered Robert in a calm voice, "providing he truly wants to live."

"What need of him do we have... he's English!" blubbered Andrew, tears of fear and relief streaming down his cheeks and from his nose.

"Ne'ertheless he will live, by my word, if he does but one task for me … and naught more," said Robert firmly.

The Englishman rolled his eyes to see the face of the one that held the dagger point on his neck. Was he really a king, he wondered, but the blade point pushed deeply enough to produce pain, and the man turned his face to the front once more.

"Lower the drawbridge!" ordered Robert quietly, "and I will kill ye not, though all other English in this castle die."

Even in the cold, beads of perspiration dotted the man's brow.

"Hurry man!" urged Robert as he pushed the blade deeply enough into the man's neck to cause blood to trickle onto his chest armor. "'Tis now, or death!"

With no other choice, the Englishman agreed and Robert went to the door, his reluctant collaborator walking before him.

"Sir Robert," the king said to his wounded knight, "are ye able to defend yerself from him?" The king motioned toward the man Andrew had felled, now nursing a deep, painful gash above his knee.

"Aye, Sire," said Boyd, tending his own injury. He took up his sword and laid it beside him in case the Englishman tried to get to him.

"Then lock yerself within 'til we're done," ordered Robert. Nudging the guard with the point of his blade, he and Andrew cleared the door and walked cautiously behind the prisoner. As instructed, Boyd bolted the door from the inside.

Having made it safely down the steps, king and squire walked under the blocked portcullis and down through the empty gate tunnel to the unbarred, but as yet unopened, main gate, their prisoner going ahead.

Andrew and the captive each pulled one of the huge doors open and they looked out. Beyond, the wan morning light was casting a faint gray pall on the span and the fields and copses wherein the Scottish army waited.

"When we reach the winch," the king spoke softly but with assurance, "ye will release the drawbridge. After that, I will walk ye across to the other side. Ye will then continue walkin' down the loch and away from the castle. If ye do as I say, ye are free to return south to yer people. Turn back this way, and ye die with the others, who will be given no quarter if they choose to fight."

With that, the man nodded understanding.

"Lower the bridge!" ordered Robert firmly. The frightened man hesitated just long enough to feel another sharp jab in his side before he started walking. Andrew tarried behind them, keeping a sharp eye on the dark gate tunnel and the portholes in the twin towers that now rose behind them.

The Englishman, as he had agreed, proceeded to the winch and removed the brake, allowing the heavy wooden platform to pull itself downward with a loud clanking and a heavy rumbling of the massive chains that had held it aloft until, with a noise like thunder, it struck its place on the stone causeway opposite. Castle Urquhart stood open to the Scots.

"Sound the horn!" said Robert to his squire as they walked the Englishman across the bridge to the road. Already they could see men running and riding toward them out of the mist and rain.

Andrew twisted the horn around from his back and blew three loud and long blasts, one to the north, one to the south, and one to the west. He staggered a bit and Robert asked, "Ye hurt, lad?"

"Nay, My King, just dizzy from the blowin'." Regaining himself, he blew the final signal to the east.

"Thank God we're in at last!" shouted Sir Neil as he swiftly rode by them and across the drawbridge, his battleaxe grasped tightly in the one hand, a targe and the reins in the other.

"Aye, it has been a long night," replied Robert shouting to the galloping knight.

"Yer horse, My King," said Ian de Cameron, and he pulled up and dismounted, handing the reins of his own stallion to the king.

"In yer debt, Sir," replied Robert. He quickly accepted the steed, mounted, and brandishing his sword around his head in a circular motion and whooping loudly, he charged into the castle among his six hundred men.

In but a moment, the horde of screaming, fiercely determined Scots erupted out of the gate tunnel into the courtyard, and most headed up the steep incline toward the barracks, expecting the English garrison to meet them en masse. Instead, the first men to come out of the barracks entrance were Scots, retreating from the battle they had earlier engaged!

The baker's dozen who had charged into the English soldiers' quarters had managed to delay the bulk of the garrison's becoming active in the brawl with their staircase barricade. The hastily assembled obstacle began to give way to the force exerted from above, and fresh troops would anon be in their midst. They already had their hands and blades full with the English they had encountered, and were well bloodied and tired, and to a man, glad of the relief brought by the screaming horde.

All, except Thomas.

He and the shoeless captain of the English guard fought on as if none other was about. Perhaps it was a personal challenge, given and accepted, or perhaps they were just so evenly matched that one could not yet conquer the other, but as the fight engrossed the hundreds of men around them, and daggers and long blades flashed in the morning light, even they began to exhaust their reserve strength and the attacks were neither as well presented, nor parried, as they had been at the beginning.

Suddenly, the captain slashed wildly at his opponent, and charged madly in for a kill, but Thomas managed to put him off. His energy expended in the attack, the captain gave way to weariness as Thomas became the aggressive one, and the captain strove to survive. Yet neither man yielded.

The regular garrison that was barracked on the floors above, and the high constable who, in the absence of Sir Alexander Comyn, had temporarily taken over the lord's quarters on the third floor, had been simultaneously aroused to action by the ground floor commotion and the sent man pounding furiously on the door.

"Sire! Sire!" the man shouted through the door as he pounded. "The Scots are in the bailey! Wake up, Sire, The Brus! The Brus!"

The constable threw back the heavy countrepointe he slept beneath and rolled to a sitting position. Immediately he grabbed his boots and thrust his feet into them, all the while growling, urgently, "Wake up, woman!"

"What be?!" mumbled the woman, barely aroused from deep slumber before being thrown into a state of alarm. She sat up in the middle of the bed, her covers held close.

"We're under attack," barked the constable. He stood and strapped on his sword over his nightshirt before clamoring into the hallway and down the spiral staircase, the messenger trotting nervously behind.

"But who would attack in winter?" she asked loudly as he departed, but got no response. Quickly, she glanced around the room, seeking a place to secrete herself from the barbarous Scots. She jumped to her feet and crossed the room, picking up a dagger from a small table on the way. Her destination was a pleasant sitting room off the main chamber wherein the earl's lady had her sewing and clothing storage, and a secret place for just such an emergency.

The constable's fearful wife, her heart pounding, crawled through a small trapdoor beneath a hearthstone. She had deftly revealed the opening, no larger than one and a half feet square, and squirmed inside the cramped hiding hole. Once she slid the hearthstone back into place, she relaxed and tried to get comfortable. She was safe. The fearsome Scots would not know to look for her there.

"Awake! Awake!" screamed the constable upon reaching the second floor and seeing several soldiers yet tarrying in their fear. "Your comrades are a'dyin' and they need you! The Brus is within!"

All the others had rushed below to meet their destiny, face-to-face, but most were held at bay in the stairwell, even yet.

The lone shirker lying abed but heard the name 'Brus' and he shrunk further in his pallet.

The constable went to the coward and struck him with the flat of his sword blade. "You will surely die on this morn if you do not bring forth your courage and fight!"

The man was too petrified to move.

"Then, die now!" He raised his sword over the man's quivering body.

The man screamed in horror as the blade came down, slashing through his ear and spilling blood and brain matter into the straw in the riven pallet. Turning around, the constable watched as the other two, craven though they were, unsheathed their swords and rushed down the stairwell to join the melee below.

The constable followed, pushing and cursing the men in his way, and reached the bottom of the stair about the same time as the Scots heard Andrew's horn sound. Seeing that there were many more English in the fray than ever there were Scots and that the Scots were falling back toward the door, he chose to issue a challenge.

"Which among you is that bastard of a Scottish whore, Robert de Brus?!" bellowed the constable vainly. Glory was what he sought and prudence left by the window.

No answer was forthcoming and the cocksure constable waded into the fight with no fear of having to do battle with the formidable warrior-king. The Scots from the galley were all but beaten, and he could taste a great victory, which would naturally be credited to him.

As Robert and his six hundred poured through the gate tunnel and into the upper bailey their battle screams were heard throughout the castle grounds. To the English it sent shivers through their spines, to the waning Scots it was music.

Fergus and Cuthbert brought up the rear and went directly to the midst of the fray in the bailey. From the hand of a dying Englishman

Fergus twisted a morningstar mace and began to engage the enemy with wide figure eight swings. All around him the English suffered, and for him, it was sweet revenge for those he had lost in the attack visited on him and his village the previous year.

When King Robert saw that the battle was gained he turned to Andrew and said, "See to the needs of Sir Robert in the gatehouse, Lad."

"Aye, My King,' replied Andrew as he turned.

As the gray rain sky became lighter, King Robert and Sir Neil Campbell remained mounted and actively fought no more, but watched as their army subdued and then mustered most of those among the English garrison who were yet ambulatory into a tight knot beside the dovecote. Some Scots were sent to search out more survivors hiding in the nether bailey near the stables and the smithy. Within a half hour they were all standing huddled together and wishing they had paid more attention to the signs of the approaching Scots.

"There be King Robert," said Thomas, roughly pulling the constable from the knot and pointing to the king. "Screamin' foul curses in his name, were ye not?" Thomas fairly pushed the constable into the immediate presence of the still mounted king and there pushed him to his knees.

"What say ye, now, Constable?" Thomas prodded.

"I pray My Lord, that you will pardon a poor man for… attempting to inspire his troops in what was… on second thought… a shameful and… unworthy… yes, Sire… definitely unworthy…manner?" the constable stammered. It was only then that he dared raise his eyes and look upon the Scot.

Robert's grave countenance and stony silence gave the man cause to doubt that he could be merciful. Indeed, the king's mood was reflected accurately in his hardness against the man who held a Scottish castle against a Scottish army.

"Yer manner is not that of one who deserves pardon, Constable, but only contempt! We shall give ye real cause to regret having set foot in this land!" With that, the king ordered that the constable and all his surviving troops be thrown into the gaol by the north gate tower.

Robert rode across the bailey to the keep where many of the dead and dying were laid. Edward and Thomas both followed on foot. Robert dismounted and walked in just ahead of the other two. What he saw appalled him as he looked across the expanse of the great hall. Men lay everywhere so that there was hardly space to walk between them to determine the wounded from the dying and the dead.

"Give me an accounting of our dead and wounded… and the spoils, Little Brother," Robert said when he finally spoke. "And take our dead outside the wall and give them a proper burial, in that grove of trees beyond the road. Is there a priest here?"

"Aye," Edward affirmed. "What of the English?" he asked, gesturing in all directions around the hall.

"Have them bury their dead, but not with our own, and take their wounded with them to the gaol. Else, I care not."

"'Twill be made so, My King," said Thomas. Then he paused a moment and Robert knew he wanted to speak.

"What's yer wit, Thomas?" asked the king.

"Sire, whilst ye were lowerin' the drawbridge, a captain of the guard led his men against us in the barracks..." started the Randolph.

"And ye want him killed?" Robert asked.

"Nay, Rob, the opposite."

"Ye want him spared?"

"Aye."

"For what cause does he deserve to be spared?" asked Robert indifferently. He was beginning to feel the exhaustion of not having slept all night.

"For bein' a damned good fighter... one we could use with us, but still, a valiant and honorable man. I fought him until neither of us could lift our weapons and we both were on our knees," Thomas stated factually. "He ne'er called for quarter nor fought unfairly."

The king looked at his nephew a moment before agreeing to the request. "Thomas," he said, "Ye are an honorable man, yerself. And I grant ye his life to do as ye please, as long as he does not again take arms against Scotland or me."

"Thank ye, Uncle."

Thomas Randolph left and went to his tasks, leaving the king to himself. Robert sat on a bench by a table and stared almost aimlessly across the room. These brave, brave men, he thought as he shook his head almost imperceptibly.

A quickly summoned body removal party came into the hall and began their grim task under the auspices of Thomas, who barked orders with clarity and decisiveness.

He will do well as a commander, thought Robert, if we could ever get enough of an army together to give him his own troops. At that moment, he was suddenly overtaken by dizziness and leant against the wall for support.

"Ye a'right?" asked Edward, as he came to give the accounting his brother wanted.

"Aye," said Robert, "simply worn." He set an upended bench against the wall and slumped upon it.

"There's a warm bed in the lord's solar on the upper floor, Robbie," offered Edward, "blankets and pillow, too."

"Nay, I'm a'right," replied Robert, closing his eyes.

With his eyes closed it made him more aware of the stench that filled his nostrils as it permeated the hall. *I'm sick of death following me about on blood-soaked bony legs,* he thought. Edward was saying something, but the king could not quite understand what it was. Then he passed into sleep.

The rowdy Scots filled the hall. Kegs of ale were tapped and cups filled for all who wanted.

King Robert awoke not, though the noise and laughter in the great hall was prodigious.

"What say we take the king to the lord's chamber," suggested Thomas loudly as the morn wore on.

"Aye," said Edward, and he set his cup of ale on a table and tugged at one of Robert's legs.

"Reckon we'll need a bit more help," suggested Edward, impressing the first two men to wander into the length of his arm.

Up the two flights of stairs the four men struggled with the limp body of the king, the scabbard of his sword bumping every step in the progression.

At last they reached the lord's chamber and Robert was unceremoniously dumped onto the bed. Edward covered his brother with the constable's abandoned countrepointe.

Presently, Robert began to snore peacefully. Edward had set a guard outside of the chamber door.

The constable's wife, all the while hiding in her secret hole neath the sewing room hearth and having no knowledge of the battle, arose to the snores, and so reminiscent of her husband's were they, that she thought the king was he. It was under this false impression that the small woman ventured forth from her covert to see if her husband was yet well and the battle won.

With the dagger she had seized earlier, she walked cautiously across the room and spoke softly to her husband, pushing back the covers to gaze instead on the face of the king. Her eyes widened and she instinctively jumped back screaming. The sharp blade she waved about at the apex of her panicked movements, but never thought to thrust it into the sleeping Scot's chest.

The guard, having seen the king alone in the room, dashed through the door prepared to meet a foe and instead caught sight of the woman in full antics. Thinking she was there to kill the king, he quickly grabbed her dagger-laden hand with his own great paw and with his other, struck her full on the jaw with such a blow that she was immediately knocked unconscious and fell to the floor.

"What be the trouble here!" yelled Thomas as he plunged, well armed, through the door.

"Woman a'fixin' to stab the king, Sire," answered the guard tersely, still holding fast her dagger hand.

"Constable's woman, no doubt," said Randolph, looking at her sleep attire, "Take her to the gaol and give her to her man, and leave the dagger here."

The guard did as he was told and Thomas closed the door on the sleeping king, who awoke not during the whole ordeal.

David de Murray
Bishop of Moray

November 12th 1307
Castle Urquhart

Robert's aching eyes opened but slightly to admit the soft daylight glowing through a nearby thick-glassed window. He could see naught else and quickly squeezed his eyelids shut and frowned. His mouth was parched and tasted of long ago swallowed ale, and his heavy head throbbed from oversleep. His stiff, complaining body felt as if it had been a hundred years at rest.

"Where am I?" he whispered in a dry, raspy voice to whomever might be close enough to hear. None responded, so he again opened his eyes. His dream field was quickly becoming solid masonry and physical pain.

At last he swung his legs around and sat up on the edge of the creaky wooden bed. Memories of having taken the castle slowly crept back into his mind, along with echoes of the cries of men in terror and agony.

The fire on the great hearth struggled weakly, its fuel nearly all consumed. Robert shivered. Still in his armor, his weapons at his side, he reeked of the combination of dank sourness from having been put to bed in rain- and blood-soaked clothes, and sleep sweats. Even he was revolted by his odor.

Robert exerted much of his strength, but finally stood, awkwardly making his way to the door. The startled sentry visibly jumped when the door suddenly opened and the king stood full bodied between the jambs.

"Aye... Sire... uh," stammered the man as he stood erect from his previously slumped position.

"Find my brother," ordered Robert hoarsely. Though displeased that the soldier was less than alert, he said nothing.

"Aye, Sire," said the man, and he hastened down the stairs to where he thought Sir Edward would be.

Robert staggered clumsily to the fireplace, and kneeling close to the wispy smoke, stirred in the ashes until he uncovered live coals. He blew on the faintly glowing embers and threw in some splinters and chips of wood from a pile of kindling on the hearth. With a bit of coaxing the flame once again rose up in warmth, and Robert added larger sticks to its core. His periodic shivers came less often by the time he heard boot steps climbing the stairs to the bedchamber.

"Ye come alive after these two days?" questioned Edward while noisily entering the room.

"Aye, alive," growled the king, still hunkered near the infant fire. Two days! No wonder he felt so insensible.

"Ye hunger?" asked Edward, and glanced back at Thomas Randolph, who followed him into the room.

"What have ye to eat?" asked Robert, not sure what he could keep down though his stomach ached for want of food.

"Ah, we been eatin' fine, Rob," offered Thomas with a broad grin.

"We saved ye a brace of spitted doves," said brother Edward, smiling as he rarely did lately, and rubbing his middle to indicate the pleasure of the meal. "Though, I must admit, had I just that much more room in my belly..." He showed a small amount between his thumb and forefinger.

"Eggs, maybe?" asked Thomas, lounging on the edge of the bed. "We got chickens a'layin'."

Robert smiled as he stood on wobbly legs. "Ye left some a'layin'?"

"We had to kill a few," grinned Edward as Andrew came into the bedchamber and at once began to unfasten Robert's armor. Robert held his arm aloft to give his squire full access to the fastenings. The youth was momentarily repelled by the odor, but returned to his duty after filling his lungs with fresher air.

"Aye," explained Thomas, "the fletchers needed feathers!"

"And the poor birds would surely freeze in this weather if we plucked 'em afore wringin' their necks," teased Edward.

"So why not cook and eat 'em once they're already mostly dressed?" Thomas smiled.

Robert winced as the battle armor came off. His light canvas tunic was next, the redolent horsehair lining still wet.

"Ye might want a warm bath, Sire," said the squire innocently, all the while waving his hand in front of his nose.

The three men laughed aloud, and Robert readily agreed.

A large wooden tub was brought from the second story of the keep to the expropriated Lord's Chamber, and pots of water were hung over the fire on every level to hurry the process of having a full tub of warm water for the king.

Within three-quarters of an hour Robert was luxuriantly soaking in hot water. His only complaint might have been that he and the water were surrounded by the cramped, ironbound tub, never meant for a man of his size. Andrew was scrubbing the king's back while Thomas loudly napped in luxury on the bed a few feet away. Edward was sitting close and giving Robert a status report on losses and gains from the taking of the castle.

Robert's mind wandered a moment, amazed at how quickly his companions had adapted to castle life. They ate well, slept well, and had little discomfort of which to complain. He had to admit, even he was as rested as he had been since... he couldn't remember when was the last time he felt so at ease. The realization made him feel a bit anxious. Somehow, it didn't seem right. He frowned.

"Push Thomas off his back," the king ordered, adding, "Snores are gettin' more than what I can hear over."

As his liege requested, young Andrew dutifully grabbed a tight grip on the blanket upon which Thomas slept and with some effort turned him onto his side. The boy smiled at the strange noises the warrior made in his readjustment.

"Go on," said Robert to his second in command.

"Angus left for Kintyre ere he froze in for the winter," reported Edward.

"So we have no galley," reworded Robert.

"Aye. They took a few victuals from the larder, and figured on eatin' fish and game along the way," said Edward pushing his chair back on its rear legs, the toes of his boots barely touching the floor. "But where they'll find game is a mystery. What little there was, we et on the way up the lochs. Anyway, by spring, the game will be plentiful again, and we have plenty of stores to last the winter."

Robert nodded somberly.

There came a faint knock on the door.

Edward slammed his chair down on all fours and Andrew opened the door, soapy bathwater dripping from his hands.

"Food for the king," said the constable's wife, struggling to hold the heavy tray level.

Andrew opened the door wide to let her in for the first time since she was carried out in her nightclothes. She was startled to see the king in his tub, and the contents on the tray shook precariously. Andrew took it from her hands and put it safely on the table.

"Will that be all, Yer Lordship?" she asked, bowing deeply and smiling broadly, and flushed bright red all the while.

Andrew turned her and led her beyond the door, but not before she sneaked another quick peek at the bathing king. Her eyes widened with girlish delight.

After the door tightly closed, Robert frowned and asked, "Who was that?!"

Edward smiled and casually leant back his chair. "The constable's wife, she's been passin' helpful, despite her husband's captivity," he answered.

"Would ye not think she might seek revenge on us with her cookin'?" the king admonished his brother. For a moment Edward failed to gather his meaning.

"Oh, ye mean, if she had the chance would she poison ye... because ye have her man?" he asked, to which Robert nodded.

"Well, I get the feelin' that she don't miss the constable a'tall..." Edward grinned with a somewhat lustful air.

Robert remembered the constable from the roundup of prisoners two days earlier, and didn't wonder at the woman not missing such an unpleasant fellow, especially if she had another to keep her company. Still, he was surprised that Edward might have taken up with her; he usually preferred his women with more girth and fewer years. The king said nothing further, instead taking the conversation on a more relevant path.

"Where are the prisoners?" he asked as he stood up tall in the tub and soapy water splashed all around.

"Yet in the gaol," replied Edward. "Thought ye might want to mete out the death sentences yerself."

Andrew, bucket in hand, climbed upon the seat of a chair next to the tub.

"I ne'er *want* to take a man's life," said Robert and Andrew, with measured flow, poured clean rinse water over the king's head. Edward handed him a second bucketful with which the youth repeated the sousing.

"Can't just leave them in the gaol," remarked Edward, sitting again.

"Nay," agreed Robert. "See what Scots are among them," he ordered, toweling himself on a large cloth brought by the squire. "Maybe they'll prefer to fight alongside us if the question is put to them straight."

Andrew had found clothes belonging to the constable in the wardrobe, and the best he took for Robert, though they were lacking sufficient length to fit well.

Though his misgivings had not been entirely assuaged, the king soon ate his breakfast, starting with the brace of doves, then fresh baked bread and sweet honey from the castle's larder, and chicken eggs, after which he was filled. He felt only sated, without pain or nausea, and thus, relaxed. As he lounged, eyes closed in momentary satisfaction, a hunter's horn trumpeted from beyond the curtain walls of the castle, jarring him back to reality.

Robert and Edward looked at each other, and the younger man stood and strode rapidly to the door.

Robert pulled his boots on quickly and shouted to Andrew, "Wake Thomas!" He walked through the door almost on Edward's heels.

Outside on the ramparts the Brus army was preparing to defend their newly captured stronghold. The drawbridge had been raised and there were calls to action across the upper and nether baileys as men were hurriedly dispatched to their posts. At last, all was set to repel whatever threat was made against Castle Urquhart.

They had not long to wait, for in but a moment, a single warrior on horseback came out of the foggy mist that withheld from view almost everything farther than a hundred yards distant. Instinctively, Robert knew there was a much larger force lurking in the hidden wood beyond. The lone man, he judged, was simply a vanguard to test the alertness of those in the castle.

Surprising Robert, the man waved and holloed the castle.

Edward waved back.

"Ye know him?" asked Robert with a facial expression curiously skewed.

"Aye," said Edward smugly.

"On what account?"

"On account that I sent him north for spyin', nigh onto two days ago," answered Edward.

Robert nodded his head in understanding but retained his frown as the larger force he expected began to show itself. Before long a whole army appeared outside the walls, over a hundred and fifty in number, having come into the clearing in a single long line. Neil Campbell and the wounded Robert Boyd stood near the king's left as Edward excitedly paced within a short span on the right. Below, Gilbert de la Haye was in the bailey commanding the men he had placed to be ready for any eventuality arising from the suddenly appearing, well-armed force before the castle walls.

"'Tis the Saint Andrew's Cross they fly!" shouted Andrew, pointing at the blue and white banner that emerged out of the fog with its bearer. "They've got to be for us, My King!"

"To my reckonin', Andrew, spies don't generally bring invadin' armies to the doors of their liege lords," remarked Robert, putting his arm around the shoulders of his squire, the son of his good friend Lord James Stewart.

Andrew thought quickly and reached into his tunic to bring forth the king's own flag. The yellow field charged with the red lion rampant was unfolded with excited and nervous fingers, and when it was completely free, the squire draped it over the battlement and held it so that it lay quietly rippling against the wall.

Recognizing the king's standard, the men on the moor sent up a great cheer, knowing then that King Robert was still within.

"Lower the bridge," ordered Edward to a man standing in the bailey just below him.

Robert looked quizzically at his brother. This newly displayed manner of assuming a command position was uncharacteristic of Edward, but not unwelcome.

The royal brother's spy and the five lords accompanying him were the first to cross the bridge and enter the fortress, followed by twenty-seven knights and the balance in soldiers of foot. The mud was thick from the constant rain and the horses' hooves slid regularly as the new arrivals penetrated the defenses of the bailey without opposition.

Watching them troop into the fortress Robert thought to himself that, though Castle Urquhart stood massive in its defenses and strength, he and his army had taken it with a little skullduggery and daring. His enemies could also be clever and bold. Were these men what they were purported to be?

"Trust they're *for* us," remarked Robert practically under his breath as he watched the procession amassing in the upper bailey.

"If for us not, then who'd they be for?" questioned Andrew hearing the mutterings while pulling the royal standard from the ramparts. He slung it across his shoulder and reached outward with his fingers, feeling for the corners of the fly end to refold the sacred banner.

"If this comes to blows, Lad, make sure my pouch of parchments ye carry is not captured," ordered Robert ignoring the lad's question.

"With my life, I swear," said Andrew who now kept a more wary eye on the entering army as he finished folding the flag and tucked it back into his tunic.

"KING ROBERT!" shouted the man in the lead of the pack. No man on the ground could reckon which man was king, for Robert had on the clothing of the constable with no insignia whatsoever, and stood comfortably along the ramparts in line with his men.

Edward quickly glanced at Robert who turned his back to the bailey, leaned one arm against the parapet wall and looked out across the wide field before him where a broad swath of fresh tilth showed where were buried the Scots who had fallen two days thence. Though it might produce more graves, this was Edward's show and Robert seemed determined to let him play it out on his own.

For one long, awkward moment, Edward panicked and could not act.

"Are we not in the company of King Robert's men?" loudly questioned the leader.

There came no answer.

Those just arrived quickly drew their weapons, and the king's knights in turn drew theirs. All around the perimeter of the upper and nether bailey, men took to their blade handles.

"Hold!" shouted Edward at last. "We *are* men of King Robert's army!"

The leader looked up at Edward as he stood on the wall walk beside Robert and Andrew. "Ye scared the Devil from me, Man!" he bellowed, and let go a sigh of relief.

"I doubt the Devil e'er was in the likes of ye!" shouted Robert, and he turned and stepped forward, having recognized the man's voice.

"Lord Brus, My King!" said the man, dismounting. "Ye have had yer jest with us this day!"

Robert replied, "'Twas a test of yer army's courage when caught by surprise," though in truth he had used the building danger to adjudge his brother's leadership.

As weapons were sheathed or held downward, Robert descended the stone steps from the parapet to greet the obvious leader of what appeared to be a well-trained, if small, army. The fellow was not large, but well shaped for a middle-aged warrior. His clean-shaven, pale complexion showed even lighter against his dark hood. As Robert reached the ground, the man bent his knee and knelt before his king.

He wore the relatively light armor of a highland knight, with a well battered shield, a coif and hauberk of mail overlaid with upper body armor, topped by an open faced helmet. A mace hung at his left side, traditional type of weapon for a bishop. It was more, of course, than Robert and his men were accustomed to wearing in these days and their fugitive state.

"Have ye given up the cross for a mace?" asked Robert when he approached the man.

"Given up naught, have I," he answered forthrightly, as if the mere suggestion of such was unreasonable.

"Ne'er before have I seen a bishop fitted out with such warrior's weeds," teased Robert. "And, yer shield would be known by no Scot I ken."

"Battle won, it was, Sire," said the leader, standing, "'Twas I who beat it to this condition, while takin' it from its previous owner. And were it not for want of paint, 'twould be white with a red cross, the colors of Jesus Christ, our Lord and Savior, for true."

Edward and Andrew, and Thomas, still wiping sleep from his eyes, had followed Robert to the courtyard and stood behind him as he stepped forward and embraced the man heartily.

"The king knows this man?" quietly inquired Andrew of Sir Edward.

"Aye," said Edward, "'tis Sir David de Murray, bishop of Moray."

"Not like no bishop I've e'er seen to now," said Andrew shaking his head in disbelief.

"'Tis the Bishop, a'right," agreed Thomas, "At the king's crownin', he was... but 'tis true he was then wrapped in more priestly robes."

Andrew glanced up at Edward with a blank expression.

"He *looked* like a bishop," explained Edward, which Andrew understood.

The king and his bishop turned and walked into the great hall of the keep where the king ordered food and drink for all the soldiers of the bishop's army. He was wholeheartedly glad to see his old comrade, now the only bishop in the entirety of Scotland standing openly in support of his cause. They sat at a large table in the great hall.

Bishop David de Murray was but recently returned from holing up in the Orkney Isles for the previous winter, after two of his good friends and papal peers, the bishops of Saint Andrews and of Glasgow, were sent to London's dreaded Tower. It was during this retreat that he decided to abandon his mortal fears, and with God's help, build an army for Scotland and King Robert.

He was indeed on the side of King Robert, preaching in every kirk and hovel he came upon for the people to rise up and join the king in a fight for Scotland's freedom from the cruel and despised English. He even preached that the faithful would go straight to heaven should they die in the service of King Robert, so fervent were his beliefs that Robert's cause was in the right. Though some were yet too fearful, others were inspired and became the hundred and fifty man army he had in tow. Of those, save the nobles and the knights, all were ordinary folk of the high lands, fierce and experienced fighters to a man.

In the company of the cleric was Sir William Wiseman, a man who held lands in Elgin and near the Comyns in Buchan. He was weary of the fight from a physical perspective, but his cheerful spirit never wandered from his wit.

Tired now, he dropped onto a bench across the table from the king and the bishop as other knights, including Edward and Thomas, and Neil Campbell, Robert Boyd and Gilbert de la Haye, joined them.

Soon, wine flowed into nearly every cup and goblet, and there was much merriment in the air. Thomas preferred the strong grain ale from the castle's larder and kept his cup filled with the dark, foamy brew. Unlike wine, ale kept poorly, and Thomas felt it his duty to "save" as much of it as he could.

Next to Sir William sat a somber man, imposing in body and with brooding dark eyes. His name was Sir David de Barclay, a cousin to the David de Barclay slain at Methven. His long, straight, dark brown hair was accumulated and tied on the back of his neck. A knight with whom no man would choose to trifle, he also was a holder of large tracts in the northern reaches.

"Where be the Frasers?" asked the bishop, craning his neck to search among his companions for the faces he did not see there.

"Mixed in with the young knights at yonder table," said Sir William, gesturing with his cup toward a rowdy bunch near the fire.

At about the same instant, a young fellow at a nearby table suddenly tumbled backward to the floor, spilling his drink all over himself. He jumped up angrily and pulled a dagger from the sheath at his belt as a second man from the same party stood and placed his hand on the hilt of his dagger. An officer quickly positioned himself between the two and spoke to them in tones inaudible at Robert's table, after which the pair glanced toward the dais and grudgingly sat down, contemplating each other blackly.

Bishop Murray picked up with his prior thought, and looking at Sir William said, "The Frasers, Sir William."

"Aye?" responded Sir William, his concentration shattered by the disturbance.

"Fetch 'em?" urged the bishop with a broad smile.

"Aye, Excellency," replied the good natured Wiseman, and he at once labored to push his tired body to its feet, and made his way across the hall.

"Why'd ye bring that ol' fellow along?" queried Robert in whispered tones.

"Influence, My Dear Robert," quietly explained David Murray, his deep voice more like a rumble than a whisper. "He is accompanied by at least a dozen experienced knights, and God knows we're desperate for trained men."

"True," nodded Robert, "but he'll be more hindrance than help when the battle starts."

"Do not underestimate his abilities, Sire. He fair comes alive at the sound of clashin' blades... and was, under English rule and 'til recent times, Sheriff of Elgin," replied the bishop as a large platter of hard fried eggs and ample slices of bacon was placed before him. The bishop closed his eyes and drew his breath deep through flaring nostrils and smiled a truly angelic smile.

"Thank ye, Heavenly Father, for providin' all this bounty unto yer 'umble servants." As his powerful voice rolled out across the hall, his rough companions quickly bowed their heads and most in the hall made the sign of the cross upon themselves, though many had full mouths and hands. "We thank Ye, Lord, for the victuals Ye had the English gather up here for our use, and also that Ye made sure it is such as men most often lust to eat. Bless us as we go out to face our enemies, and cast them into confusion and fear. We can take care of the rest. So we pray in the name of our Savior. Amen," concluded the bishop. The word was repeated by many voices and the momentarily devout went on with their meal.

After blessing himself he silently repeated words that only he understood, again made the sign of the cross, this time in the direction of his companions. He then opened his eyes and began to eat eagerly, as would any man who had been in the wood subsisting only on locally foraged camp food for as long as he. And he thoroughly relished each morsel.

Having so recently eaten, Robert sat with the others, but ate very little. He listened to their conversations and watched the men around the hall as they ate and drank their fill. It had been a long time since they last enjoyed such comforts, for the newcomers as well as for his own contingent of warriors. His men were completely different, now, in this place, than they had been before, when by sheer will they were driving themselves to do whatever was necessary to take Castle Urquhart.

"John Comyn's organizin' against us, My King," offered Murray between mouthfuls, breaking into Robert's reverie.

"Aye, I know," said the king. "How does he align his followers, so far?"

"'Ppears like David de Strathbogie, John's son, will be against us. And Sir David de Brechin. Lord Mowbray is back, trailin' a company of English knights that he will surely send against us…"

"John de Strathbogie's son will move against me?" interrupted the king, finding it hard to accept. David's father had been one of Robert's most trusted allies and gave his life while attempting to help the queen and other distaff members of the royal family escape to the Orkneys.

The bishop nodded. "And, of course, John Comyn, himself. I have no ken of any …"

"That's why we need to move with haste, David. Quicker we hit them, the less likely they'll be opposin' us with great force," Robert said, sipping at his wine.

"Aye," said Murray, "'tis true, but, as the nub of cold weather is upon us… 'tis also true that it's good ye have this stout, warm castle to winter in."

Robert answered not but changed the subject, "'Twould be good… for the men… if ye held a proper mass on the late afternoon."

The bishop stopped eating and paused before he looked at Robert solemnly and whispered, "Ye know, Rob, that any who follow yer cause are already excommunicated?"

"I knew Longshanks had persuaded Rome to excommunicate me after I killed Red Comyn."

The bishop nodded. "And so it spreads to yer army... even to bishops," said David Murray with a sly smile.

"And how do ye ken that?" asked the king.

The bishop again smiled. "'Tis surely a good day for a mass."

"Then surely ye shall have it," said Robert returning the smile.

Sir William Wiseman, trailed by two others, wound his way between table and chair back to his place.

"These be two who claim be yer kin, Sire," said Sir William, taking his seat.

Robert looked at the two men. "How so, am I yer kinsman?" he asked.

"My Lord, may I introduce us?" asked the larger of the two men as he bowed.

Robert looked at him expectantly.

"I am Sir Alexander Fraser and this is my brother Sir Simon," said the hefty man.

"There was a Simon Fraser from Oliver Castle with us at Methven," remembered Robert. "He was a distant cousin to me, and to my wit, a great patriot of Scotland."

"Aye," agreed Alexander, "and cousins we were to him, as well, Sire."

"Captured and executed in London town, he was," interjected Thomas Randolph, sadly, though realizing the others already knew.

"And ye, Sire, would be...?" asked Sir Simon of Thomas.

"Sir Thomas Randolph," said the king, "my nephew."

"Randolph. Thomas Randolph." Sir Simon repeated, and then asked, "Were ye not captured in that same battle?" Simon suspiciously narrowed his eyes and added, "Some folk say ye were, but then, how can that be? If ye were captured, how is it that ye sit among the likes of us?"

Thomas liked not the man's insinuation, but for the love he had for Robert, chose to remain silent, taking a long gulp of ale from his cup and turning away from the Frasers.

"Some say ye tucked tail and hied as a whipped dog to the English whores to save yer stinkin' arse while Christopher Seton, the king's dear sister's husband, was hanged!" said young Simon, a deep frown exposing the depth of his temper.

That was all! No longer could Thomas Randolph hold his umbrage at the insult, and leaping to his feet, drew his sword from its scabbard as he moved toward the Fraser, whose blade also swiftly came forth.

Robert rose to his feet, holding his hands outstretched between the two angry knights. "Let us not waste good Scottish blood 'twixt cousins!" asserted Robert vigorously.

"He holds me in contempt, Sire! I demand atonement!" insisted Thomas heatedly, pushing forward against the king's outstretched hand.

Simon brandished his weapon and glowered toward Thomas. "I

would that ye allow him come receive his 'atonement' on my foible, My Lord!" he shouted.

The Bishop of Moray continued eating, but kept his wary eyes rolled upward and on both men who, it appeared, could begin to fight over his head at any second.

Alexander Fraser pushed his impetuous brother back, holding his arms. The other men in the hall turned their attentions to the altercation between the two knights, and as the two hurled epithets and threatened to slay each other, the area around the dais table became tightly crowded and filled with shouts urging them to commence.

The king tried in vain to allay the anger between his kinsmen, but with the crowd calling for blood, he realized the futility of his efforts.

"Enough!" shouted Robert to the eager faces around the dais.

The crowd calmed at the king's voice so that he could be heard.

"Ye spoilin' to fight?" asked Robert of the Fraser and the Randolph in a loud, angry voice. "Then put yer blades on the table and fight!"

The crowd of warriors again raised its mob voice and the king again raised his arms for silence.

"Let no man interfere, or fight with another! I order it so!" demanded Robert heatedly. "These two alone are yer entertainment!"

Thomas and Simon glared at each other in cold hatred as they unloaded their weapons onto the table.

"See that neither man receives help from another," ordered Robert to Edward as he pushed his way through the excited crowd and headed to the other side of the room.

"Aye," said Edward, and he moved to the inner circle of shouting men where the tables and benches were being cleared for the impending action.

Andrew saw the way of the king and followed.

The two antagonists stripped bare to the waist. When ready, they moved toward each other, and around in a circle they went, figuring each other's possible strengths and weaknesses. They were broadly of the same size and weight and both were young and full to the pith of mutual malice.

Thomas received the first blow to the left side of his face, wildly struck by Simon.

The fight was on. The spectators chose sides and even laid bets, and the room was filled with their shouts and goading.

Robert and Andrew stood stoically in front of the fireplace, barely able to hear anything above the din of those observing the fight across the room. Both watched the action as best they could from where they stood, but their thoughts were entirely different. Whereas the boy's face showed his excitement and even delight, Robert's held sadness and a growing sullenness. Finally, the king spoke.

"Draw together my kit, Andrew," he said in a determined voice, "and yers."

"Aye, My King," submitted the squire, turning to keep his eye on the action. The ovations and groans were growing more intense, as was the fight.

"Now!" insisted Robert.

Andrew peered at his lord with knitted eyebrows, "Now, My King?"

"Hie out now!... then saddle my horse," insisted Robert, and he turned toward the fire. Andrew kept moving, albeit hesitantly, toward the stairs, but his mind and his eyes were still on the combatants, when he could catch a glimpse of them amidst the swarming onlookers.

The boy glanced back toward the fireplace just in time to see a fiery, six-foot log fall to the floor and roll against the legs of a wooden bench and a table, where half-eaten plates of food yet laid. He shouted, "Fire!" but none heard him above the noise of the crowd.

Running back to see to the king, Andrew found him at the hearth, pulling other burning logs from the andirons and splaying flaming embers in all directions. Already one tapestry smoldered and would soon burn.

The king's surely lost his wit, thought Andrew as he stood agape, momentarily transfixed at the sight of the flames being spread by the king himself.

Robert glanced up to see Andrew staring at his handiwork, and with a frown and a wave ordered him to carry on as he was bade.

Andrew left immediately for the topmost floor.

Picking up a nearby chair, the king raised it above his head and brought it down hard against the table, breaking both to pieces, which he picked up and threw on the burning logs. He fed the flames with anything he thought would burn, including grease and meat from the platters and wine from cups and jugs.

Thomas and Simon were inflicting hefty blows on one another when not wrestling each other to the ground. There was more than a little choking and kicking and gouging, much encouraged by the onlookers. It was a fairly well balanced bout as both men were suffering near equally to what they were meting out.

One of the voyeurs, nearer to the mischief the king was making, felt unusually warm, far warmer than he had. Ascribing it to the fact that he was so actively attempting to control the fight with his yelling and acting out, it was not until the acrid, stinging in his throat that he screamed, "SMOKE! I SMELL SMOKE!" He grabbed the man nearest him and yelled, "Something's afire!" They both turned toward the fireplace and there stood the king, nearly surrounded by fires, his great sword drawn and ready.

The men saw the infant flames spreading with the alcohol and grease over the ancient timbers of the floor and began to scream in panic, alerting others among them. Soon, the crowd was ignoring the fight and staring instead at Robert and his set fires.

Even the two exhausted fighters stopped, and for a moment, watched open-mouthed as did the others. The king had indeed gone mad!

At the first movement of the mob, the king raised his hand and stepped in between the burning logs and the men rushing to quench the fire, stopping their advance. No one understood the king's actions, but none wished to face his wrath or his sword.

"Ye men want a fight?" started Robert, his eyes shining angrily in the light of the growing flames. "A fight for Scotland I have ready-made for ye! Yet ye choose to fight among yerselves for no good reason!" He looked at the men in his army with a searing truthfulness. "Ye have a short while in plenty and comfort, and ye cease to be an army, becomin' instead a pack of snarlin' animals wantin' blood to be spilt for sport! Ye have become like the old Romans... who put Christians to death for entertainment!" Robert paced in front of the mounting blaze laying his broadsword across his shoulder.

The men murmured among themselves in an attempt to understand the king's wit. Robert clarified, "Get all ye want from this keep. Larder... weapons... what e'er ye'll need... for soon, all will be but smoke and ashes!"

"I will personally cut the head off any who tries to extinguish the fire," swore the king, and he held his great sword with both hands and pulled it up to position, ready to strike.

None dared to cross the invisible line Robert had drawn with his posture.

Suddenly the men scattered like sparks from a smithy's hammer. Thomas and Simon fingered the bloody wounds on their faces and winced. Revenge, thought Thomas, sometimes is painful no matter the injuries dealt to the other party.

The two battered fighters picked up their weapons from the table and glared, perhaps less loathsomely, at each other. After all, they were kinsmen, in a roundabout way.

Only his brother and the bishop remained in the great hall with Robert as the two fighters left to gather their remaining things.

"I was lookin' forward to a night in from under the stars," lamented David Murray, looking up at the thick blackness that roiled up from the fire, filling the whole ceiling. Soon, the entire room would be consumed, and then the rest of the keep.

"They forgot who our enemies are," replied Robert. "We can't win without the discipline of living off the land!"

"Aye," replied the bishop, "nor without God."

"Same," answered Robert, his face stern and resolute.

"Ye've not given up on God, have ye, Robert?" asked the bishop as a friend.

"Nay," replied the king, "but the Holy See has surely abandoned the likes of us."

Edward had not the mind of a philosopher nor of a cleric, and so thought of more practical matters as he noticed the flames licking upward on the tapestries lining the walls. The smoke grew thicker in the lower part of the Great Hall.

"The larder, Brother," said Edward, to no response from Robert. "The larder?" he emphasized.

"Take men 'nough and get the stores out as best ye can ere the smoke kills ye," ordered the king.

The bishop rose and casually walked into the courtyard. Robert followed and stood beside him. "Ready for that mass now?" asked Robert.

"In the lower bailey," replied Sir David.

"Then we'll execute the prisoners by the piggery where their already dead comrades are stacked about," planned Robert almost nonchalantly.

The bishop hesitated a moment in his gait, then walked on, speaking to men that he passed, telling them of the sacred mass he would perform in the nether bailey.

Stores of victuals and lamp oil were being drawn from the basement larder as Edward came to his brother once again. "What about the wounded?"

"Most are in the stable now," Robert said, "Get the horses and gear out... load up as much grain as we can carry on the backs of the beasts, and go!"

Andrew came quickly through the keep door loaded with the pouches of the king's and one of his own.

"My horse saddled?" asked Robert not looking at his squire.

"Right away, Sire!" Andrew threw the pouches on the muddy ground and ran quickly toward the stables to fetch the king's stallion.

Sir Neil Campbell came to the king and asked of what service he could be to the forced evacuation, the heavy smoke now wafting across the entire upper bailey, stinging eyes and throats, and panicking all the creatures in pens, cotes, and dwellings.

"Get reinforcements and bring the prisoners to the piggery," ordered the king.

"What of the kitchen workers of the keep?" asked Sir Edward.

"Do with such what ye will..." replied Robert, " My interest is only with them that have the will to fight against us!"

The rains began anew. Robert shook his head in disgust. "Have we no cleft in this dreary weather?"

Andrew brought Robert's mount to his side and handed the king his surcoat against the rain and cold.

Robert threw the coat over his shoulders and pulled the hood over his head. "If this keeps up, 'tis damned sure... we'll all die of the misery," he bemoaned.

He looked back at the keep. Standing in the rain, he momentarily longed for the warmth of the hearth and a dry place to rest, but as he watched, tiny flames lapped the exterior of the narrow, open windows. His men still were retrieving booty from various parts of the keep and stacking it pell-mell in the bailey mud, away from the rising inferno.

Robert shook his head inside his hood; no one noticed. His horse whinnied and snorted. Robert turned and absent-mindedly patted the beast on its nose. "Ye railing against my decisions, too?"

Neil Campbell, along with six other knights, marched the quaking prisoners out to the piggery. There they gathered in the freezing rain beside their fallen comrades, stacked cordwood fashion. Disheveled and shivering more from the fear of this moment being their last on earth than from the cold, they knew what was to come next. They had seen it happen before when they were the victors.

So had the women who stood wherever they could find shelter from the rain and began to wail for their doomed men. Others shed tears for the men they had lost two days earlier when the castle was overrun by King Robert's army.

Andrew returned to the king's side. He looked sadly at the poor women hiding tears away in their kerchiefs. The constable's wife was among them, and despite Edward's assumption of her lack of feeling, was as tearful as the rest. The boy was glad that the rain streaked his face, or some might think him as lachrymal as they.

"Scots women cry, too," said Robert when he saw the expression on the lad's face.

"Aye, My King," replied the squire softly, "and some of these are Scots as well."

Robert patted the lad on the back and sighed wistfully.

The whole of the courtyard was clamoring with activity. While men readied livestock and stores and weaponry for the trip, the lone faithful bishop was saying an abbreviated mass for his hapless flock.

"Where be my mason?" asked Robert of his squire, hoping to spare him the sight of such slaughter.

"I will find him, My King," replied Andrew, and he ran off toward the stables.

Robert again made note of the fire's progress. Flames were roaring out of the second story windows, extending their tongues well up past the next floor, and the whole of it wrapped in hellish, choking smoke. *Another Scottish castle dying by my hand,* he thought with a twinge of regret.

He returned his attention to the sorrowing in the bailey. *No need to hold these prisoners in dread any longer,* he thought. Breathing in a deep, heaving breath, as if it were his own execution he faced, he walked to the piggery to address the condemned warriors.

Between the pigs' filth and the rain-sopped dead men, it was a vile and putrid matter.

Robert approached the loathsome place and pushed his boots deep into the mud to assure that he would not lose his footing, and slowly drew forth his great sword, resting it across his right shoulder.

"I will stand here for but a short time," began the Scots king. "If Scots can fight for English interests... then Englishmen can fight on the side of Scottish interests."

The doomed men, some blubbering so hard that they barely heard what he said, were all puzzled at the king's words, as were the Scots who held them prisoner.

Robert stood solidly and continued, "Any man who wishes to swear oath of fealty to me had best do it ere my feet leave this spot, else ye will lose yer head where ye now stand."

Many of the Scots quickly pushed to the front of the crowd and got on their hands and knees in the mud, begging their king's forgiveness, and there immediately swearing allegiance to him forever. Some Scots and all the English feared to trust this offer from the self-crowned king, and hesitated to come forth.

Robert turned his head as if to move away, and the English constable rushed forward and knelt before the Scot, also swearing fealty.

Robert saw the pale man quaking in the mud and the rain, and for the sake of his wife, who had been kind to his company, he ordered him to take her and go home to England, ne'er to cross the boundary of Scotland again, adding, "'Twill be yer death if I see ye again on the soil of my kingdom!"

The overwhelmed man thanked the monarch profusely, for his life and his freedom, until his wife rushed out to help him up. The two of them then left that place before the Scot could withdraw his generosity, disappearing into the thick smoke that lay about the bailey, and Robert never caught sight of them again.

The English soldiery were the very last holdouts, but none could perceive life beyond that moment, and so they also sank to the mud and made oath of their fealty to the Scottish king. The king reminded that if they should ever break their word, they would find justice swift in coming and long in suffering ere they died. They all swore and each held his oath in earnest.

Robert walked the few paces to his horse and climbed aboard. He was riding away from the site when Andrew arrived with the mason. The older man was strong and stout and had worked on many castles in the employ of both English and Scots in his time. He knew the structure of curtain walls and of keeps.

"I need for ye to take this bastion apart, Mason," said the king from the back of his horse.

"Aye, Milord," replied the gallant builder.

"And yer needs to accomplish this task?" asked the king.

"Six strong men and a draught horse," returned the mason.

"'Tis yers," ordained the king, "save one provision..."

"As ye order, My King," said the man. "What be yer provision?"

"That ye eat not the horse 'til the work is done," smiled the king, winking at Andrew.

The man returned Robert's smile and bowed.

King Robert nudged his horse forward, walking him through the gatehouse and across the drawbridge. The men who had kit or stores to tote picked up and followed. A few had newly won horses, which were put to use hauling foodstuffs.

As the lengthy procession disappeared into the fog-laden landscape, the fire in the keep burst through the roof with a thunderous roar as the air was sucked violently through the double doorway of the great hall, creating a giant chimney of the stone walls of the keep. Fly ash danced like freed spirits over the whole of the surrounding grounds.

Simon Fraser

November 16th 1307
Sanctuary of Saint Duthac in Easter Ross

The king purposefully led his growing army, increased to slightly more than eight hundred, to the small sanctuary where his queen, his daughter, and his sister Mary, along with his good friend and sworn protector of the Brus women, Sir John de Strathbogie, Earl of Atholl, had been captured more than a year before by Lord William of Ross.

The abbey was surrounded by trees that were constantly bent by the northwest wind, thus forming them into gnarled and grotesque shapes. Their lack of leaves in the barren season lent even greater severity to their strained appearance.

King Robert reined his mount twenty paces from the entrance; Edward pulled up on his right side, and Thomas on his left. Behind them trailed the army.

The weather had turned colder and the nearly constant rain began to fall as snow. The ground was not yet covered completely and the wind whipped the snow around in the air gingerly before allowing it to rest. Woolen surcoats with hoods cinched tight around their bearded faces served well their owners against the cruel climate this day.

"This Saint Duthac's?" asked Robert.

"'Tis. Some changed from summer season," said Thomas, who showed healing bruises on his face, "but 'tis the same."

Robert dismounted and walked to the entrance of the old building named for the local and revered saint who had died in Tain some hundred and fifty years earlier.

"Why has yer brother brought us here?" asked Sir Gilbert, his breath wafting away in vaporous puffs on the air as he spoke.

"Be damned if I know," said Edward as he tightened his grip on his surcoat. His own breaths were steady and full, and were dispersed just as rapidly by the wind.

Robert ran his gloved hand along the stonework leading up to the doorway. Elizabeth passed through this portal, he thought wistfully before he opened the double doors and entered.

"Daylight wanes," said Thomas, "Reckon to pitch camp on this ground?"

"Bobbie ne'er said not," answered Edward.

"I'll make it so," replied Gilbert turning his horse back toward the troops.

Robert removed his helm and went to the chapel within the chapel where he knelt to pray. Within moments a clutch of timid but curious monks entered and quietly waited until the king was finished.

At last he stood and saw the men awaiting his departure from the altar. He removed his gloves and came to them with empty hands, showing he meant no harm to them.

There was one among them by the name of Joseph, who stood forth as spokesman for the company of clerics. He quietly spoke, asking, "Sire, be ye here to burn us down?"

"Why ask ye that of me?" returned Robert, a bit surprised at the blunt question.

"We are threatened constantly with destruction, Sir Knight, for we sheltered the Queen of Scotland within these walls not long ago," answered Joseph.

"So has it been relayed to me," spoke Robert sadly, "for I am yer king and she, my queen."

The other monks bowed courteously and left Joseph and the king alone to talk.

"What happened on the day the queen was taken?" asked Robert seeking a first hand accounting.

At the monk's subtle motion, the two men walked together while Joseph told the king about how the women and the earl were so near accomplishing their escape by sea when the Earl of Ross forcefully entered the sanctuary. He had personally thrashed some of the monks for their refusal to break their vow of silence by answering his urgently posed questions.

Joseph opened a door to a relatively small chamber. "This is where yer women stayed durin' the short time they were with us, Sire."

Robert ran his bare fingers along the edge of the writing table in the room as he looked about him. The window overlooking the sea taunted him, as it must have taunted Elizabeth, for the sea, and her freedom, had lain so close to this room. He saw the meager beds, no more than sacks of straw laid about on the stone floor, so inadequate for his lovely queen. Yet he realized that this was all the monks had to offer, and of the same ilk as those on which they themselves lie every night.

He thought deeply of Elizabeth, Marjory, and Mary... she so recently married to Sir Neil Campbell that they had no time to themselves before they were torn apart by the pursuit of the enemy.

Where are they now? Wondered Robert lowering his head in grief.

"Revenge will be mine against Ross for his part in this deed," swore Robert aloud as he gritted his teeth and gripped the pommel of his broadsword until his ruddy knuckles grew waxen.

"My King, lay aside this lust for revenge else it blacken yer heart and blind yer soul," counseled the holy man earnestly.

"My soul has been condemned by Pope Clement already, and those of my kin and all who give me aid. Perhaps ye had best look to yer own spirit, kind monk, lest Rome cast it into hell with mine," the king warned the cleric.

For a moment the two men stood quiet, neither knowing what to say, Robert finally breaking the silence. "I shall leave. It is not well that I should endanger yer lives... and souls... by remaining here."

"Nay, Sire. Stay as ye will. If Rome sees us as rebels... so be it!"

The king broke into roaring laughter at the thought of the gentle monks being considered 'rebels' by anyone. Yet, he knew that affording him shelter was a clearly rebellious act, and his eyes brimmed with tears, either from the first hearty laugh he had enjoyed in months, or from recognizing the kindness and courage of the small man.

Joseph offered the help of the monks to the king and withdrew to allow him to be alone with his thoughts.

Within a quarter of an hour, Robert had examined everything about the small room and absorbed how his Elizabeth and little Marjory and the others must have felt when the Earl of Ross and his men crashed in through the door, weapons drawn.

He shall pay a heavy price when next I meet with Ross, he swore to himself.

Sadly making his way to the sanctuary's front entry, he stepped out into the snowy air. For a moment he stood outside the doorway and looked about, taking in the grayness of the wintry scene. The cold and the colorless aspect of the surrounding countryside matched his dark mood as the sun dropped lower in the sky.

At last he bade his lieutenants enter, and he was first joined by his Campbell brother-in-law.

"This the place?" asked Sir Neil.

"Aye," answered Robert as he held the door open for him and the others to enter.

"We're just inside the tree line, yonder," said Edward as he came to Robert. "The men are findin' shelter as they can."

"I would that we could all sleep within this holy place," returned Robert, "but the good brothers have not enough room for all our lads."

Bishop Sir David Murray entered the place of sanctuary to speak with Robert, and was engaged in conversation with him when Brother Joseph returned. For a moment, the quiet little man failed to recognize the bishop in his battle garb, and when it came to him that the warrior speaking with King Robert was the Bishop of Moray, the awed monk fell to the floor on his knees. It had been many years since a bishop last set foot in Saint Duthac's.

The bishop turned and put his gloved hands on the man's head and blessed him.

Later, in the evening, King Robert sat for a long while staring into the flickering blazes of the fireplace and absently eating.

He was greatly stressed between pining for his captured family and his desire to wreak havoc on the Earldom of Ross. As he pushed a bite of saltless meat deep into his jaws and chewed with slow deliberate bites, his eyes narrowed and glared, then widened and danced, acting out the images playing dreamlike across his tortured mind.

The thoughts of revenge were sweet. Separation from his loved ones was bitter.

The men with him in the monks' kitchen watched him carefully. After the incident at Castle Urquhart, whenever the king mused dejectedly on a fire, his men feared a recurring episode. They wanted to be ready to grab their kits and run.

Sir Neil Campbell grieved as well, but only stabbed the oak table repeatedly with his dagger. It was not difficult to understand his thoughts, either.

Edward was outside with the remainder of the men, who camped in the trees in quick-made debris shelters or in one of the army's few tents. Edward was somehow becoming more attached to the lesser knights, as some referred to them: the archers, pikemen, and various other soldiers of foot who actually comprised the bulk of the Scots army. They, in turn, liked his rowdy, unpredictable nature and easy camaraderie.

•   •

By morn it was briskly clear and sunny, the wind had quelled to but a breeze, and the snow clung to the twisted tree branches in delicate, graceful lacework against the bright blue sky. Exquisitely beautiful in its frigidness, it was a new day, and King Robert, a new man, set for new action against an old enemy, William of Ross.

A traveler staying at the abbey less than three days thence, had revealed in passing that he had begged lodging for a time in the castle of Skelbo. The Earl of Ross had also been a visitor there, said he, and was observed meeting with, the traveler surmised by their words and actions, some of the more prominent barons of Sutherland.

"Let us go now and take Skelbo," offered Neil. "We'll have the cock and a few scrawny chickens cooped for the takin'!" He grasped at the air with one hand to emphasize his statement.

Sir Neil's suggestion began a discussion among them as to the possibilities.

Castle Skelbo was to the north of the sanctuary but a day's ride for one, if he were fortunate enough to find a boatman to ferry him across the narrows of Dornoch Firth, but what of an army?

"'Twill take us four days at least to go meanderin' the army around the tip of the firth," opined Bishop Murray.

David de Barclay and William Wiseman, most familiar with the area, agreed that it would take at least that and perhaps more. Then there was the possibility that they would have to lay siege, and an educated supposition of the loss of no less than a hundred lives.

"We could be at Skelbo for most of the winter," offered Wiseman.

Robert breathed deep in frustration. He felt that he was near to delivering a long awaited deathblow upon his enemies, and yet... there was an army much stronger than his own to the east under the command of John Comyn, Earl of Buchan... and if Lord John were given time to muster the combined troops of Mowbray, Brechin, and David Strathbogie against him as well...

On the other hand, he could not allow Ross to join his forces with Buchan's.

"What to do?" questioned the king.

Elizabeth de Burgh

NOVEMBER 17TH 1307
ROYAL MANOR HOUSE AT BURSTWICK-IN-HOLDERNESS

Elizabeth de Burgh stood at the mullioned window and tried to see through the oppressive grayness. The whole of the outside world was covered in a blanket of thick fog, preventing her from seeing anything more than a few yards away.

The house fronted on the road that paralleled the river and its dramatic cliffs all the way to the coast, but the window by which she paused was on the back of the house, from where the land fell gently away to the peat bogs and rose to the blue rolling hills beyond. How she longed to see the sparkling bog, so beautiful in spring when purplish pink flowers covered the area in such wild profusion that they created a sinuous carpet throughout the lowland.

Now, in late fall, all was bleakly painted in shades of browns and grays and nothing bloomed to break the monotony. The days grew shorter and the nights closed darker about her than ever before in her memory, and Elizabeth felt the cold and the dark to her very core. Without Robert at her side, the world was a far different place than it had been.

She turned herself back toward the room in which she spent her days and nights, with no more to occupy her mind than the most mundane of tasks. She and her two "ladies in waiting," one of whom was nobly born but addled in her years, had little in common on which they might converse, leaving many days when Elizabeth barely spoke, and then usually only to the man who cooked for the household.

The Scottish queen settled herself on a low stool in the fireplace and soaked in the warmth emanating from the small fire laid within. As she looked across the hearth toward her companion, Elizabeth saw the old woman, head thrown back against the stonework, mouth agape, hands laying palms up in her lap.

This was the captive queen's world, and it promised to be so for many long, dreary years.

As the morning wore on, the fog burned off the moor and the clouds lifted to waft slowly around the crests of the distant hills, leaving wisps of trailing vapors drifting up from the bogs like the occasional curl at the nape of a woman's neck. Elizabeth hadn't seen the broad landscape as it came unwrapped from the fog in the occasional shower of snow and rain. This day was just another in the long line of gray days she had spent under house arrest.

Just as she grew again despairing of the sameness of every day upon another, there came a soft rapping at the room's entrance door. "Come," she called, waking the old woman.

The door opened briskly and a soldier in the garb of King Edward's guard strode across the room to the rough-hewn table, whereon he placed a small parcel wrapped in cloth and tied with a string. He spoke not, but bowed curtly and departed the room straightaway.

Elizabeth, unused as she was to receiving anything other than necessities sent by the hand of the king, found the strange package an irresistible unknown. She rose from the small seat by the fire and stared at the bundle, curious as to its origin and excited at the possibility that it might be from Robert. For the longest moment she stood gazing at it without moving.

The old woman, perhaps aged two score and ten, quietly observed the spell her mistress was under until she could no longer keep still. "Well," she croaked, "ain't ye goin' to open it?"

In another moment the young queen slipped to the table and placed her hand on the soft, mysterious offering. This day was suddenly less gray, and certainly unlike the recent others as she savored the promise of the package, the first unexpected contact from outside since her imprisonment in this place, except for one hasty visit from her father months before. She was not to be hurried in her consideration of the gift.

Finally, she slowly pulled the end of the string and set it aside to lay back the cloth covering. Beneath lay a good Scots plaid of heavy wool and a shawl of natural wool color.

Elizabeth unfolded the plaid to discover it was more than just cloth; it was a fully sewn dress, which she shook out to reveal its cut and shape. Holding it against herself, she knew right away that it would need some tailoring to fit at all properly, but she was overjoyed to have it, and the very fine shawl. Both would make for a warmer winter in Burstwick.

"Lady Elizabeth, did ye not see this?" interrupted the old crone, who was exploring the package's wrapping.

"What say ye, Mag?" asked the queen.

"There be some things here," she pointed at the wrapper.

Elizabeth looked in the folds of the cloth and found a wonderful second gift, a flat box of wood in which there lay a dozen pieces of paper, two writing pens, sealing wax, and a small flask of ink. The box bore the emblem of Richard de Burgh, her esteemed father.

"Oh, Da," she whispered neath her breath.

She took the top piece of paper and laid it with near reverence on the top of the box and sat herself at the table. With uplifted heart she opened the container of ink and took one of the pens in hand. Carefully, she drew the letters with deft strokes and soon had filled half a page with a note of thanks to her father for the warm clothing and the writing materials. The words fairly flew from her hand, so thrilled was she with the gifts. She signed it, "Yer loving daughter, Elizabeth de Burgh."

Folding the paper, she wrote her father's name and "France" on its face before dripping some candle tallow on the closure and putting a seal within it from her small ring. She then set it aside, and less confidently, took another piece of the precious writing paper from the box.

"Dearest Robert," she wrote.

"I wake each morn and ache to hear yer voice and feel the gentle touch of yer hand. To sleep soft in the warmth of yer bed and hold ye again in my arms is my prayer each night as I lie down. But, ye must not come to me but in our dreams, My Lord. I shall meet there with ye each night 'til we are again free to meet in the sun, I so warrant ye on my immortal soul. Ye remain the center of my heart, Dearest Rob. And though I know not where ye rest, 'tis there I shall be when ye need me. Ye have always my undying love. Elizabeth."

By the time she finished writing her name, her eyes were full of tears and several large spots of the salty fluid had splashed upon her writing, blurring it. She gently folded the missive and wrote his name on the face, then sealed it as she had the one to her father. She started to place it with the one she wrote first, but stopped.

Suddenly she beheld a vision of Robert receiving her paper and demanding to know from whence it came. He would then, she knew, try to reach her, though she be near York and not in Scotland. Thus she took up her pen again, drawing beneath his name the words, "In the hollow of God's hand."

She rose slowly from her place at the table and took the slim note, pressing it to her heart as she crossed the room to the fireplace. There she knelt and leaned into the cavernous opening to lay the letter upon the glowing coals. As tears rolled down her face, she silently watched the paper burn and curl in the heat until there was nothing left.

John Comyn
Earl of Buchan

NOVEMBER 17TH 1307
CASTLE MORTTLACH OF BUCAN IN SCOTLAND

In Buchan, some five leagues from the northern shore of Scotland, lay Castle Mortlach, occupied by Sir John Comyn, earl of that land and cousin to John 'The Red' Comyn. The whole of the realm had been fissured by 'The Red' Comyn's death, and the national wound ran bloodier with each passing day and deeper than anyone could have imagined.

Leading a long train of knights and baggage, Lord Sir John Mowbray and Sir David de Strathbogie, Earl of Atholl, rode side by side through an intermittent, light and silent snowfall. They were well armed and armored for Scottish highland nobles, and both rode handsome black Friesian mounts as they approached Mortlach from the south.

Lord Mowbray had been appointed guardian of the murdered Comyn's lands by the late English monarch, and certainly had a vested interest in this civil war against King Robert. Many of the knights he had in tow were English and under the baron's command.

Beyond his fortieth year, Mowbray's head was mostly bald and the hair remaining on the back and sides was trimmed short as was the closely trimmed gray- and red-peppered beard that encircled his thin-lipped mouth. Indeed, his round reddish face was bland of other features. He was of average height at five foot eight, and stronger in will than in body.

Sir David de Strathbogie had been permitted to inherit the title Earl of Atholl in spite of his father's execution for treason. The earldom had fallen to him in his early twenties, before he was ready for such responsibility, and he blamed King Robert for seducing his father to the rebellion, and thus, to his death.

David was a larger man than Mowbray, in weight and in height, with a large shock of yellow-blonde hair cropped close, and a somewhat darker beard and mustache. He was married to the daughter of 'The Red' Comyn, and she had personally sworn revenge upon The Brus for her father's bloody death. No doubt her rage rankled her husband's already burdensome hatred for the Scottish king.

The fresh snow seemed boundless across the landscape of rolling hills before them as the trailing army of nine hundred warriors left a wide swath of displaced and trampled mud and snow while advancing toward the castle.

There were lesser nobles, knights, and squires on horseback, and of course, hundreds of foot soldiers, including a large contingent of bowmen.

A trumpeter from the entourage announced their coming to the still distant castle, and with full flags fluttering in the light breeze, they were a mighty sight to behold, their colorful parade contrasting garishly with the stark whiteness of the land.

Lord John Comyn and his younger brother, Alexander, stood among their garrison as the castle guard amassed on the curtain wall of Castle Mortlach. "We'll show them damned rebels who controls the north of Scotland now, My Brother," said the larger man quietly. He was clearly exultant that this mostly English army had arrived to put an end to The Brus, once and for all settling the score for his cousin's vile murder.

For the most part, Mortlach Castle was of a three-story block design, surrounded on three sides by a curtain mimicked by a deep, wide, dry moat. Along the inner courtyard were quarters wherein the trades were practiced and livestock sheltered. In the center of the courtyard was a deep well, ample for needs of the denizens. It was a comfortable, though not extraordinary, fortress and refuge in this time of threatening calamity.

Alexander was grinning broadly. Buoyed by his brother's mood, his spirits were merry and his eyes danced with simple-minded excitement as he watched the approaching array. He suddenly exclaimed, "Make them pay for the takin' of my Urquhart, we will!"

Laughing, Lord John wrapped his hefty arm around his thinner framed brother and shook him near off his feet in comradely enthusiasm.

"Ye happy?" asked Alexander with another child-like grin.

"Aye," replied John, "Worry not Alex ... I'll be takin' care of ye, just as always I have."

Alexander nodded with a contented smile and stepped forward to the ramparts where he pushed the snow from the top of the wall and watched it drop the more than twenty-five feet to the ground. The wind caught some of the loosed crystals and blew them back across his face, causing him to squint and blink, which he did not like.

He climbed into one of the crenellations in the wall and folded his skinny legs so that his back leant against one merlon and his feet the other. Leaning his arm on one knee, and watching the panoply before the wall, he became temporarily preoccupied with how his vapored breath, drifting in front of his eyes, paled the images of the oncoming army. *They look so wee from here,* he thought, *and now grow dim as well.*

"Alexander," his brother interrupted the simpleton's reflections. "Stay back from the edge lest ye fall."

"Aye, Milord," he said, though he never took his eyes from his daydreams. John shook his head and walked away. He seldom knew what his poor brother understood and what he didn't.

John left Alexander and sought the more stable ear of Sir Reginald Cheyne, a Scot serving as the English Warden of Moray. He was an older man and a close ally to the Comyn family for many years. His face was cragged and weathered, with an almost bush of a beard that seemed to grow unabated in every direction.

"Well, Old Friend, we at last have means to run that gang of traitors from our lands," Lord John greeted the knight.

"Aye," agreed Sir Reginald, "Brus has been reported with no more than a thousand in number... and in poor circumstance at that."

The lord indicated disagreement with a gentle shaking of his head. "Macdougall sent a herald only yesterday sayin' it was many more than that," he replied, "Many... many more than that."

Sir Reginald laughed aloud, "He's but tryin' his excuses on us! God knows, he hain't goin' to fancy havin' to face up to Little Edward. He'll have to tell him why he ne'er stopped them renegades when they came right through his demesne."

Both men laughed derisively, as Sir John cast his eyes again on the approaching army. He was smugly satisfied he had chosen well *his* course of action, and The Brus and his piteous rabble could soon bewail their own.

The arriving troops were more than a half hour filing across the bridge spanning the snow covered dry moat and entering through the gatehouse into the open bailey. There stables lined the curtain wall, along with the smithy and the sheepfold and pigpens, and houses, too, for cotters who worked at those tasks, and for the foragers.

The camp followers quickly claimed adequate space in which to set up their hearths and cooking spits, and any man who knew what was good for his belly left those spaces to the claimants.

The earl and the baron dismounted, leaving the care of their horses to their squires, and strode pridefully on foot, through the dark gate tunnel into the inner courtyard. The knights followed in like order, and there Lord John graciously greeted all with an abundance of pomp, including the blare of trumpets at every interval and colorful banners, and many boastful words, which were then returned by the new arrivals.

John wanted nothing more than to extend his best hospitality for his friends, who were for the most part, equally as anxious to rid the land of Robert de Brus as was the whole of the Comyn family.

However, as the exchange of stately words of praise and of braggadocios deeds droned on for more than three-quarters of an hour, those tired, lesser-armed travelers of lower class who had walked to Mortlach, stood. Intended by the barons to be merely background for their more important selves, they eventually grew distracted and bored.

One of these nether soldiers fell asleep and dropped his buckler on the toe of the man next to him, who in turn jumped around and pitched his halberd onto the helm of the fellow behind him. There was certainly discordant clanking and cursing for a moment, but those involved quickly came to full attention once again, when their immediate superiors frowned and swore in harsh and muffled tones that they who stood not the time would partake not of the food.

The day's feast was being prepared for the guests of more import, and the delicious smells from the kitchen and bake house wafted forth across the small area, filling their nostrils so that their bellies began to growl. The foot soldiers gritted their teeth and continued to bear the rhetoric.

John Comyn droned on for another quarter hour with naught more of substance to add to his ranting. Finally, he brought the proceedings to an abrupt halt with, "Them that feel the need for prayers ere the victuals, the chapel is yonder," and he pointed to the arched doorway only twenty feet away.

The hungry congregation at last cheered him greatly, much to his delight.

Lord Mowbray and Lord David, the only ones offered seats at the onset of the speeches, arose and greeted their host with the most delicate of chivalrous dignities.

"Stirred the very blood of them, ye did, Milord," patronized the baron appropriately.

"Aye," agreed the earl as the two men came to Lord John's side.

"We'll quash this rebellion for the sake of our alliance with ol' Edward's son," added Sir John leading the group toward the doorway to the second floor great hall.

"We'll pike Robert de Brus' head and parade it the width and breadth of Scotland," boasted Lord David, thinking that such an outcome would no doubt appease his wife.

"We all are fixed for the meanest revenge... The Red Comyn deserves at least that," grimaced the baron, the only one of the three who had no blood ties to Red Comyn.

A squire on the inside of the twin doors to the great hall peered intently through the slight space between the two, and seeing the three men approach, turned and whispered toward the six trumpeters, "They're comin'!"

Banners swished gaily as the brightly polished horns came into position and blared the twelve loud notes to announce the coming of the lord and his guests. Two young squires struggled at the task, but they swung wide the heavy doors to the great hall.

Upon entering, the visitors were surprised at the spaciousness of the room. As the earl quietly commented, "It is far greater on the inside than appears possible from the outside!" It was true that the apparent narrowness of the structure surrounding the courtyard belied its actual dimensions. Further, the heavily beamed ceiling rose to a height of more than forty feet.

Along the southern wall were nine tall arched windows with frosted glass panes that allowed the pallid light of the day to filter in, and upon the opposite wall fell large, magnificent tapestries brought from the Holy Land. The whole effect was splendidly beautiful, though not overly lavish.

With a lift and turn of his head to see behind him and a brief wagging motion of his index finger, Lord John instructed the waiting players to begin.

The sweet sounds of the harp and the lute started gently as the strings were nimbly plucked by the musicians. There were also pipers, who would play later.

Lord John Comyn, his brother, Alexander, Lord David, and Lord Mowbray assumed their seats on the dais. Their upholstered chairs stood in a row behind the rectangular, heavy oak high table. Once the four men were seated, there remained two empty chairs, one at each end of the table.

Also on the dais were two trestle tables, situated perpendicular to, and at either end of the central high table, and considered a part of the 'most honored guest' configuration. As a number of barons took their places there, other landed gentry and renowned knights filtered into the room and sat below the dais at tables flanking the great room on both sides. Each man had a specific social and political position at table, and within the hall.

On the wall behind the center table, and between two sets of three high-arched windows of colorful stained glass, was the huge English banner referred to as "the three leopards," charged with the images of three lions posed in side view, one above the other, each with an extended forepaw. It was displayed as a symbol of the Comyns' fealty to England's King Edward. Draped centrally across the front of the high table was a banner showing the coat of arms of the Earl of Buchan, an azure field and three gold sheaves of harvested grain.

Lord John wanted the appearance that he, the most high of his noble guests, and the English crown were totally in control of the castle, and of the war against The Brus.

"Shows as the likes of London, it does," remarked the baron taking in the sight.

Lord John was visibly pleased, and he smiled and nodded his head just slightly so to appear to agree with his guest, without looking like a vaunter.

The few women attending were seated at the sideboard along the windowed wall, with the exception of the earl's wife, who was seated at the table to the right of the high table. Everyone placed in the middle of the hall faced the dais.

As the servitors began their work, several of the squires attending the guests helped organize the large serving trays of pottage on the surveying board. A convenience for the serving of food, the surveying board stood along the wall near the passageway to the kitchen, from where busy menials, young men and boys, lugged the heavy, hot victuals.

Overseeing his banquet being served, the earl was already congratulating himself, as most of the nobility seemed impressed with his hospitality. Though it was costing him a small fortune, at least by his standards, he needed this show of largesse and ability to accomplish his aim of ridding the countryside of the rebellious Brus riff-raff.

War talk was as abundant as the wine and ale throughout the hall. The guests began to drink and talk loudly as the servitors brought around the pottage of vegetables and venison.

"Have ye a plan?" asked Mowbray, pushing deep into his upholstered high-backed chair and sipping rather timidly from the purplish liquid in his goblet. He thought best to subdue his thirst for fear the wine would bring forth an unwanted loose tongue.

"Aye," replied John, "...well, perhaps,... somewhat of a plan."

"A plan, Milord, or not a plan. Which is it?" asked the young Lord David impudently. "'Twould seem that it is, or it isn't, for surely it cannot be both." He sat unbending before the trencher of steaming hot pottage placed on the table in front of him as he spoke.

In normal times that tone of voice might have drawn daggers, but the new Lord Atholl was not yet seasoned in the way of colloquy, which was taken into account by his host. The Comyn was not so foolish as to let a wee, probably unintended, insult sully his alliance, and so, he sidestepped the say.

"My spies tell me that The Brus has gone toward Ross," said John Comyn touching a spoonful of the thick soup to his lips to test its temperature. It was too hot. "Far as I can reckon, he's there yet." Before he could continue, the young earl again interjected himself.

"Is yer plan to go after him, there? For if it is, I would not accompany such a scheme."

Comyn gritted his teeth to restrain his tongue, blew on the spoon to cool its contents, and then sipped it down before saying, "If My Lord Atholl would exercise a bit of patience, I will explain my intentions to his satisfaction!"

"Do, please, continue, Milord. I do not wish to delay the capture of Brus and his band," Atholl said, simpering.

John Comyn rolled his eyes heavenward in a vain hope of divine guidance that he knew would not be forthcoming. *We'll ne'er get this gang put together*, he thought, shaking his head.

Before he could again speak, the musicians sounded a trumpet call and the many servitors arrived at the high table with roasted eagles, geese, ducks, doves, and sparrows. The carvers, kneeling before the diners, ceremoniously disjointed the birds and served them in the order of largest to smallest, placing the pieces on fresh-cut bread trenchers and lavishly dressing them with sauces. Those who were invited into the hall were given the upper crusts, traditionally deemed more desirable, while the less highly regarded lower crusts would be distributed to the bailey campers, who accepted them readily.

While all this was taking place, and without warning, two fully armored knights on great steeds flung wide the double doors to the great hall and noisily entered.

There was just as sudden a silence among the rest as knights and barons alike turned completely around toward the doors, to see the cause of the commotion, and partly unsheathed their blades to be ready if danger was the reason.

Trumpets blared behind the two knights as their horses' hooves clattered across the polished wooden floor.

"Praise be," announced Lord Comyn, greatly relieved, "it's Brechin!"

Sir David de Brechin next entered the room, smiling broadly, waving his hands in the air and bowing low several times from his ornate saddle.

"One of the unsat chairs," muttered Strathbogie, glancing to the empty seat on his right side.

Brechin was in his early thirties, a clean-shaven, impetuous man who, as evidenced by this act alone, had a certain flair for the presentation.

The crones and young women alike craned their necks to get a better view. As he glanced across the women's tables along the outside wall, the interloper smiled broadly and brought coy smiles to their faces in return. A girlish giggle or two was also heard within the jovial sounds of the gathered male guests.

"He *is* bonny," softly remarked one of the young women to none in particular.

"Aye," agreed another, "but I'll not say such to my husband."

"Good wit," returned the first, her eyes still following the newly arrived knight.

"Greetings Milords, one and all," he announced loudly in a pleasant baritone timbre upon doffing his heavy cloak. "I bring my magnificent self, twenty-three knights, and a near like number of esquires, some experienced in chivalrous combat and some not, and three hundred forty-seven sons of the land of Angus… to fight for the demise, or the exile, of the pretended king of our beloved Scotland, *amen*."

Some of the rowdy knights around the hall repeated the 'amen' in practical unison and pounded their pewter ale cups on the tables, while the others but peered in amazement at the young man's brash ingression.

John Comyn liked the sound of the muster list, though not the comment about "exile," and he stood to greet Brechin as a lanky squire led the latecomer toward the high table.

Brechin, as was his habit, greeted all who approached him while he made his way toward the high table and his appointed seat.

"Kindly popular, aye?" taunted Mowbray as he and the Comyn watched the younger knight make his way to the dais.

"We need for him to have his day, else we may miss ours," retorted Lord John, and the baron changed his manner.

"He and his adds us up to more than two thousand for the fight," he said.

Pleased, Comyn smiled, "Aye… and together, we can win!"

"If together, we can remain," blatantly cautioned Lord David, overhearing the two men. He seemed at that moment callow and envious of the handsome new arrival's welcome.

"Aye, young Strathbogie. 'Tis always so. And what say ye if ye get naught yer way? Do we stay together for the sake of the cause?" asked Lord John, slowly turning, with one eyebrow cocked high to look at the younger man.

Lord David huffed a long sigh. He realized that through his hubris he had misplayed his hand and lost some of the political advantage he had held upon his arrival.

"I hate The Brus worse than any of the lot of ye," he snarled, putting forth an angry demeanor. "My father followed him, to his own doom!"

"And did not yer father's death proffer ye the earldom all the quicker, aye?" goaded John Comyn.

David Strathbogie knew when to answer naught.

Brechin at last arrived upon the dais and gracefully bowed with due respect. His host received him to the high table. "Sir David, welcome to Mortlach," said Lord John.

"Thank ye, Milord," replied Brechin, "I am humbly honored." Another bow, but merely symbolically, this time.

"Please, yer place," offered Lord John pointing to the waiting chair on the other side of Lord David, and motioned for a servitor to attend the knight.

David Brechin glanced at the young Earl of Atholl as he passed behind him, ready to offer his hand, but the peevish fellow was sourly twisting tiny dabs of meat from a perfectly roasted spit of sparrow breasts and laying the morsels upon his tongue, studiously ignoring the knight. The shunning might have gone unnoticed had it not been for the keen eye of Sir Reginald Cheyne, himself just arriving at the table.

"Yer chair awaits as well," said Lord John to Cheyne as he pointed to the seat on the other side of his brother, Alexander. The latter was paying little attention to the conversation but was merrily enjoying the tasty morsels of fowl flesh as the carvers parted limb from body and meat from bone for his plate. He had great difficulty keeping his outer fingers reserved and out of the sauce, and thus had to recurrently dabble them in the bowl of water presented often by his patient squire.

Sir Reginald took his assigned seat, pushed his pottage aside and began to nibble on a couple of the small sparrow breasts that had been prepared for him by one of the carvers.

Lord John sat, at last content that the key players in his proposed cabal were elbow to elbow at his table. It was not long, however, before the small talk was used up and all grew silent at the high table. Again, Cheyne noticed first.

"What about those fine speeches I heard just a bit ago in the courtyard," Sir Reginald asked, referring to the tension at table. "Were they for naught?!"

"Naught?" frowned John Comyn thinking to be discredited once again at his own table and by his own advisor, since he made most of the bluster.

"Words are fore'er naught... deeds tell the tale," replied Mowbray almost mindlessly.

John quickly rose to his feet. His chair slammed to the floor resoundingly.

"Ease, Milord," suggested Cheyne. He was standing and holding his hand over Alexander's head toward his friend. "Did ye not say ye would cut the heart from Brus and burn it to a cinder 'pon yer fire? That ye would feed his body to yer hounds and send his head to be piked and rotted on London Bridge beside the traitor William Wallace's?"

"Aye," agreed John Comyn. He had said all.

"And is that not a deed worthy of the lord baron's say?"

"Aye," again agreed John Comyn.

"NAY!" screamed David Strathbogie.

John turned slowly in the direction of the say. There sat Strathbogie, glaring eyes and flared nostrils. His fists balled tightly, he began pounding the top of the linen clothed table. The dishes of victuals and goblets of ale and wine round about went bouncing with every blow.

At least it got him sayin' somethin', angrily thought Lord John.

"Ye have great love for Wallace, have ye?" asked Brechin, a look of surprise on his bonny masculine face.

"We *all* supported Wallace when Wallace was about and in his heyday!" he responded testily to Brechin, though he had been too young to remember the Wallace's heyday firsthand. "But that is another matter! That which galls me still is yer lack of decent respect to one of ye...!" he screamed, adding, "Have ye forgot that *my father's* head is piked on London Bridge!"

"But piked much higher than that of the Wallace," reminded Mowbray after a brief pause, trying to interject a modicum of levity into the tense situation.

The whole table laughed at the macabre jest, with the exception of Strathbogie.

"Fix to defend yerself ye ol' man!... or any of the rest of ye bunched against me and mine, besmirchin' the name of Strathbogie!" screamed Lord David as he stood and drew his broadsword, cutting the air above his head to show his skill.

Brechin ducked low to the table as he spooned more of the venison pottage into his maw, but was otherwise unaffected by the display.

Still, the music stopped.

The hall again fell quiet as all eyes were upon the unfolding drama of the high table.

Lord John fingered the hilt of his broadsword and glared at the young whelp who defied and embarrassed him in front of his guests.

David Strathbogie stood to the ready.

John Mowbray rose to get out from between the two and backed himself to the wall.

Cheney, too, got to his feet, leaving poor Alexander at the table, too fearful to budge a muscle.

Lord John breathed deep as he contemplated the potential for his next act, knowing full well the future of Scotland balanced on the scale. His fear and subsequent hatred for Robert de Brus overwhelmed him more than the satisfaction of bloodying his blade on this "ill-mannered brat," as he would later describe Strathbogie.

He took his hand from his weapon.

Strathbogie was curious but remained on high alert, both hands tightly gripping the hilt of his own sword.

Lord John stooped down to right his chair from the floor.

I could easily bring a deathblow to that neck, thought the Strathbogie, looking down at John. And in no more time than it took for a dropped coin to hit the floor, he moved to make the strike, but John's eyes staring into his own prevented the follow-through.

For a long moment the two stood only a small space apart, Strathbogie still brandishing his broadsword, and John standing and facing him with only his chair between them.

"I fear, Milord, 'twas my poor witted comments that set this to action," began Sir Reginald as he came cautiously atwixt the two men, "Ye know we are all comrades here," he continued gently with his sincere but most awkward apology; "It was but jest... for... yer friendship."

The two men still retained their pride and their fix of mind.

"I relish not yer frivolity," said Strathbogie angrily after a long moment of thought.

John then pushed his chair to the table and approached young David, well within range of the still poised broadsword. "We are earls," spoke John to David's ear alone, "Even Mowbray, here, is but an actin' earl..." Lord Comyn poised himself so that the taller man could see into the great hall without shifting his eyes far from himself. "And we survive on the support of our underlin's... thus, 'tis poor politics to cut off too many of yer friend's heads... who as well have underlin's. 'Tis the death of The Brus we commonly seek, not one another's. "

David Strathbogie considered John's pleas and soon calmed, though he looked at John to discern if he was yet being jested. At last assured of his host's sincerity, he sheathed his broadsword. "Aye, 'tis The Brus we would see dead," he agreed.

At that point, no one was fool enough to restart the laughter on any account.

John patted his fellow earl on the back to reassure him of the earnestness of his peers in attendance.

The musicians played again.

The hubbub of the hall gradually resumed.

The members of the high table quietly returned to their places. Alexander Comyn almost fainted with relief. Only Brechin gave a bit of a smile as he pushed the empty pottage bowl to the forward of the table and drew to himself a trencher of eagle meat well sauced and smelling delicious.

At Lord John's behest, a squire retrieved the chair of Lord David and righted it.

David sat.

John Comyn reseated himself, and to show his intention to hold Strathbogie as an important figure said, "Let us hear yer wisdom for the catchin' of The Brus, Sir David."

Lord David stuffed a large portion of meat into his mouth, and mixing in a generous swallow of wine as well, and used it as a means of delaying the telling of that which he had not yet thought.

"Eh?" coaxed Lord John.

Strathbogie grunted and continued to chew while nodding his head to signify he was ready to answer as soon as he was able to speak over the food in his mouth.

John understood the meaning and dipped his fingers into the bowl of scented wash water, wiped the dampness onto the tablecloth, and plucked a juicy morsel from one of the eight plates of fowl meat in front of him. Pulling it into a more manageable portion, he put it into his mouth, while waiting for Lord David's forthcoming pronouncement.

"I imagine..." spoke Strathbogie, "that this Brus... is *not* a man, a'tall!" All at the table paused and looked at him.

"Ye daft? That hain't a plan!" uttered Brechin.

"Rest yerself, Brechin," offered Mowbray.

Brechin looked at Mowbray with a disbelieving air before he sighed and returned to his trencher.

"A-a-ch, he's been hearin' the ravin's of that Dungal Macdouall down in Galloway," dismissed Sir Reginald, shaking his head in reproach.

"What's Sir Dungal's truck with our doin's, here'bouts in the north?" asked Mowbray.

Sir Reginald gathered that Lord David and David de Brechin too wanted an answer, so he continued with what he had heard:

"Sir Dungal's wit has left him from the doin's of The Brus," related Cheyne. "As the story goes, one moon-filled night, the Macdouall caught up to The Brus. Standin' alone he was... on the far side of a creek, and... no doubt thinkin' he had the bastard in his grasp, Macdouall sent his best champion boltin' across the water to challenge him. Well, 'ccordin' to the master of Castle Buittle, The Brus skewered his man with a single flash of his sword!" Aware that all eyes were upon him, he acted out the deed with one of the shafts used to roast the small birds they had just savored. The room was quiet as death.

"Well," he continued, enjoying the telling, "Sir Dungal sent more of his men, one after another, across the burn to lay low The Brus... and The Brus slaughtered ev'ry one." He had his audience in his spell, and he thus lowered his voice to keep them straining to hear. "The king's eyes glowed red and his armor shone silvery, and he fought like an unholy demon... 'ccordin' to Macdouall. And this is told to ye as I heard it from a herald sent here'bouts by ol' Dungal himself." He took a large swig from his wine cup.

"Then what?" asked Mowbray, entranced with the story, his eyes wide and throat dry.

The Warden of Moray told the end of the tale, at least as far as he knew. "Dungal vanished..." he paused to draw his listeners one last time into the tale before adding, "...behind the walls of Castle Buittle, fearful and demon filled. Thus, he did little to stop the slaughter when Brus came through Galloway at the end of summer last, harryin' the folk so that they packed kit, kin *and* stock and fled for the forests of England! Them that were caught and resisted were felled on the ground where they stood!"

The high table was solemn and stared at Sir Reginald as if he had delivered the deathblow to the group's efforts.

Then Strathbogie spoke up, "That's what *I* meant!... The Brus is not a man but a myth... we are fightin' a bunch of ol' women's camp tales, as well as Lord Dungal's fears, and... as well as the man himself..."

Sir Reginald took deliberate advantage of the pause and looked across to his table members, then said, "My God, Gentlemen, take possession of yer wits!"

The men began cautiously to talk among themselves in worried tones.

"My Friends!... My Friends!" Lord John exclaimed as he stood and held his hands up to signal his guests for a breath of silence. When they were hushed he continued, "This kind of talk does our cause no good. Keep yer beliefs regardin' this matter privy... ye must... else, I fear, we are lost!"

"Our beliefs about this tale is but one point," spoke up Sir Reginald. "Second point is, we must swear allegiance to one another, and third, we need a battle plan with some serious wit about it, in order to kill The Brus!"

Alexander Comyn, sitting quietly and unnoticed beside his brother, spoke up in his elementary way, "Why not get the Earl of Ross on our side?"

John frowned at his brother for interfering in matters he generally knew nothing about, but David de Brechin, who had no ideas of his own, declared the simpleton's mutterings 'a brilliant idea'.

"I think ye are all gone mad," declared Reginald, "to allow these stories fixin' Robert Brus as a wispy spirit that cannot be destroyed like any other mortal!" he paused to measure the expression of each at the table, and continued, "Ye give strength where it is not due... and I warn ye... pay heed that we are not beaten by our imaginations!"

"But it was yer story," protested Mowbray, confused by Cheyne's conflicting statements.

"'Twas simply my tellin' of fairy tales to entertain... to make children mindful... naught more than that," replied the Warden.

"Pray, sir, what action would ye propose?" asked Mowbray, pushing Cheyne.

The tale having been told and the spell broken, de Brechin returned his attention to his trencher when a breast of peacock was pushed to him by the servile disjointer kneeling at the opposite side of the table.

"If all hold to the cause, we can and will beat this rebel."

"And, Sir Reginald," started Mowbray, "*what about* Lord William of Ross?"

"Many of his people would rather join with The Brus and die," replied Cheyne.

"But, of course, owe fealty to Ross," spoke Lord John.

"Aye," nodded Cheyne, "they are bound to Ross."

"Let them!" interjected Lord David de Strathbogie.

"Sir?" questioned Lord John.

"Let those who wish to... die with Brus!" asserted de Brechin.

"And what of their oath to their lord? Should they betray him?"

"He would, and has, betrayed others."

"Back to yer father, are we, Sir David?" said Lord John, tired of the drama.

"Ye'd see diff'rent had he turned over *yer father* for hangin'!" spat David crossly.

"My father ne'er ran with The Brus," gainsaid John. The younger earl could think of nothing to reply, and so sat red-faced and glaring at his tormentor.

"I advise ye not to push Sir David too far," whispered Cheyne in the ear of Lord John.

"If he hain't up for keepin' handle on his earldom, then I'm willin' to!" returned the earl in an almost quiet voice.

Cheyne withdrew from John's ear and said, "Where be the spirits for our cups? How is it that more than two Scots can get together without a good whisky?"

Lord John ordered the drink to be brought to the table then turned to Cheyne and in a quiet voice said, "Ye've not far to drink poor David to his slumber and silence, but I can drink much... and still be lively."

"As I would have it Milord," replied Cheyne.

John studied the face of Cheyne for a long moment then commanded, "On the morrow next, go to Ross and turn him to us."

"Aye, Milord."

David de Barclay

November 17th 1307
Outskirts of London in England

Freezing rain relentlessly stung the faces of all in the train of Sir Ingram de Umfraville and Lord Dungal Macdouall as the two Scots and their servants made their way toward the city of London. There lived forty-five or fifty thousand people, perhaps more, making it the largest town in all England. It was also the winter residence of the king, whom the Scots had traversed the length of England to see.

Neither man had been to London before, but riding horseback along the deeply rutted roadway south, they both knew the great center was not far beyond the rolling hills. They had earlier noticed an increasing number of wains full of produce, animals in flocks, herds, gaggles, and pens, and both horses and people carrying great burdens of wool, fuel, foods, and drinks to feed and clothe and warm the great hordes that sojourned there.

If the increased traffic were not enough to alert them to the town's proximity, its foul smell soon did so. With the town's large population, there was a generally repulsive odor that wafted well into the countryside downwind of the metropolis. When first they smelt it, de Umfraville gagged and threatened to spew forth his morning meal, but as they rode on, the malevolent air grew less obtrusive, or their noses more tolerant, or perhaps the breeze merely changed direction.

It was not as if the smell were unknown to them. Each village and tiny hamlet produced the same or similar combinations of odors from human and animal habitations and wastes. Nay, it was more the power of the stench that overwhelmed their sensibilities and left them revulsed to the point that they pulled parts of their clothing across their noses and mouths.

On they traveled until they reached well into the town and found themselves looking to the left and the right, staring at the bizarre people, the many two- and occasional three-storied houses and shops, some with overhanging upper stories the horsemen had to take care to avoid. Else, they could find themselves suddenly unhorsed and lying in the filthy, narrow street, wherein all the offal, excrement, and refuse of the town was dumped to be washed away by the rain, or ground into the mud by the hundreds of feet tramping through each day.

The citizens of the place were as curious and impolite as the horsemen, gawking and laughing at the oddly dressed strangers come into their neighborhood. Some recognized them as Scots and made faces and insulting gestures, shouting insults or turning their backs on the two nobles and their entourage.

Reaching the river, the caravanners could barely make out the great white tower of their destination, off to the east. They grew exceedingly quiet as they approached the well-guarded keep, mostly because of its bloody past that chilled the bones of Scots and English alike. It had well earned its lurid reputation in its two hundred year existence as the place where many nobles as well as commoners were imprisoned until their deaths were horribly meted out on Tower Hill. Umfraville and Macdouall both knew men who had died there.

The mere thought of such was enough to raise the hairs on the backs of the necks of the uneasy Scots. "Ye likin' this more'n me?" growled Lord Dungal uneasily.

"Nay," frowned Umfraville, "but our choices have come down to this."

Within a few minutes the men and boys arrived at the Lion Gate of the Tower. Beyond, over the barbican, flew the "three leopards" flag. That, too, was of little comfort to the Scots.

Since they were expected, they were allowed instant passage across the drawbridge. The horses' hooves resounded hollowly across the wooden span and the Scots felt suddenly alone in the thick fog and the cold rain. When they entered the barbican tunnel, which curved around to the left, every noise they made echoed off the cobbles and the stone walls in the near pitch-black passageway.

Before they could see the other end of the tunnel, a horrifying roar suddenly echoed all around them, causing the already stressed horses to rear and jump about, tossing two of the knights from their saddles, one to land hard on the rounded cobblestones, the other, smashed against the tunnel wall.

"What in the name of Holy Christ was that?!" asked a wide-eyed Umfraville loudly as he fought to regain control of his mount.

"Damned if I ever heard anythin' like that afore!" answered a shaken Macdouall, crossing himself quickly. "I'm damned if I e'er want to again, and that's sure!" He stretched out to catch the reins of one of the loosed horses, only to hear another roar, though not as loud as the first. The horses were once again unnerved, rearing and whinnying and prancing about, and the two without riders retreated at a gallop the way they had come.

Those who could were preparing their weapons and shields for an attack, from what, they knew not. Another roar, loud as the first, sent shivers up their spines.

"Let's get the hell out of this tunnel and into the light where we can at least *see* the devils, and have a *chance* to save oursel's!" shouted Macdouall, and struck his spurs deep into the flanks of his horse. The animal fairly bolted through the rest of the passageway and into the light beyond.

"Wait!" shouted Umfraville. "Wait!" was all he could say as he whipped his horse with his reins and dashed after Macdouall. The others in the troupe hastened to follow, leaving the two downed knights in the blackness.

"What from hell's gate was that?" exclaimed Sir Dungal, his dagger belatedly flashing from its sheath as soon as he had a hand free to pull it.

"Came from inside the tunnel, it did," warned Sir Ingram, his eyes bulging and darting back and forth, seeking the source of the supposed danger.

"Look yonder, man!" said Macdouall pointing his dagger toward an opening within the barbican wall. Barely four feet into the open archway was a smaller arch, heavily barred with iron. They and the two remaining knights dismounted their skittish horses and approached the entrance on foot, weapons at the ready.

Peering into the small opening, the men saw a great, tawny, black-spotted cat at rest, looking at them with greenish eyes and lazily waving its lengthy tail. They stood agape, unable to move away, unable to speak. Finally, the creature broke the gaze in which it held the Scots and began calmly to groom itself, its long, facile tongue licking its paw and foreleg. Standing well away from the deep-set window, the humans watched, fascinated, as the cat was approached by a second, which laid next to it and nuzzled its shoulder.

"What be them things?" the Macdouall asked no one in particular.

"They look like the three lions on the royal flag," whispered Sir Ingram.

"Lions, then?"

"I know naught, but they look…" Suddenly an even more horrific roar from just behind them swallowed them up entirely and shook them to their very bones, causing the youngest knight to lose his water, which trickled down his leg and into his boot.

All four spun around instantly, Sir Dungal and Sir Ingram facing the beast behind them with only a relative modicum of trepidation, their weapons held forward to fend off the attack, but what they faced was another caged cat, even larger than the others. Alone, it paced uneasily back and forth within its own iron-barred cubicle without any apparent interest in the men. This one had no spots, but was tawny, and had a great wreath of brownish hair about its massive head, and a swatch of similar hair on the tip of its tail. Its demeanor was one of agitation, and its enormous paws padded silently in almost constant movement.

He complained loudly in protest of his captivity.

"What be that?" asked Dungal, his eyes wide with amazement at its size and obvious power.

"Lion, from Africa," replied Ingram. "I am for certain that one is a lion. I have heard they have such a mane."

"It don't look the same as them two," protested Dungal, but his companion had no response.

The men remained nervously alert, but were able to retrieve the two stunned, but otherwise only bruised, knights they had abandoned in the tunnel. The six of them were not unhappy to leave the dark tunnel and return to their horses.

Middle Tower thrust upward from the bed of the moat. The twin tower structure had double portcullis gates and more English guards.

"Once in," said Macdouall thoughtfully, "maybe ye ne'er come out again."

"Ye want me to go alone?" asked Umfraville, hoping the answer was 'no.'

Dungal breathed deep with an audible shake as the guards approached to check their identities. "I'll stay," submitted Dungal as he sheathed his dagger and prepared to intimidate the entrance sentry.

"Sir Dungal Macdouall, Lord of Galloway," he announced in his most commanding voice, "and my companion, Sir Ingram de Umfraville."

"And your business here?" asked the tower guard flatly.

"The king's business, man!" said Dungal, determined to impress the underling. "We have an audience with him on the morrow."

"Wait here, Milord" ordered the sentinel in the same dull voice, and he walked away from them.

"Harrumph!" commented Lord Macdouall, disappointed.

The rain, though it had lessened, still rent the air in frozen darts and randomly pinged on the armor exposed to it.

Sir Ingram looked to the top of Middle Tower, where uniformed sentries peered down on them, crossbows cocked and ready to loose their deadly bolts if circumstance so demanded.

"Take kindly to strangers, they don't," said Umfraville pointing upward.

Macdouall's eyes followed the gray dappled stonework to the top of the tower. There, three heads, contrasted by the gray sky to their backs, peered back. Their stance was anything but friendly and Sir Dungal swallowed hard and shivered, perhaps from the cold, or perhaps from the fear.

The four knights in the train twisted uncomfortably in their saddles and kept a close hand to their weapons. The squires and pages were dullards by want of experience in these matters and as such were just excited to be on such an adventure.

The tower guard returned. "Your folk will need bed in the stables with your animals," he ordered, indicating the squires and servant boys. "The rest of you follow me."

The two portcullis gates creaked and slowly ascended into the gatehouse above. The array proceeded through the tower gate and into the outer ward where the pigsty and stables were.

"Reckon they want no thievin' here'bouts," teased Dungal nervously.

Umfraville was not amused by the comment and chose to ignore it. Macdouall breathed another deep sigh as if fate's culmination of all things evil were about to pour directly upon his head.

In command, the guard grabbed the reins of both nobles' horses and held them fast. "Dismount," he ordered.

Macdouall and Umfraville did as they were bade and directed their companions to do likewise.

Only the nobles and their knights were allowed to proceed on foot through the second curtain wall at the gate in Bloody Tower. Looming before them in the inner ward was the great and terrible White Tower of death.

How many stories of horror have escaped these walls, wondered Ingram rhetorically to himself, when the subjects of them never lived to tell, truth or lie. None will ever know.

'Twas then he noticed Lord Macdouall, who again swallowed hard, his head spinning and his breath coming in short, panicked gasps.

"He a'right?" asked one of the knights as Umfraville came to the earl's side and held him from the ground.

"Take hold of yerself, Milord!" hissed Umfraville emphatically, but in a low tone to keep the words from other ears.

Lord Macdouall agreed, and with the shake of his head, he raised himself to his full height, thrusting his shoulders back.

The knights were squired to quarters inside the tower proper, and the two nobles were escorted into the palace where the lush trappings and opulent bedrooms were far beyond any either of the two men had encountered before.

Below their window was a courtyard, on the far side of which lay the great hall, which abutted the southern curtain wall. In the soft mist beyond the two walls and towers was the River Thames, where small vessels traversing the waterway seemed, for want of clear light and definition due to the day's weather, to float on air.

"Well, here we be," said Umfraville throwing his helmet into a nearby chair. He stripped his completely soaked surcoat and rain wetted armor from his body, and dumped all carelessly in a heap on the luxuriant Persian rug.

"Aye," said Macdouall, rubbing the silk bed covering and feeling the softness of the down comforter folded neatly at the foot. "Don't seem such a poorly death," he sighed.

"Will ye get that from yer wit, Milord?" groused Umfraville, aggravated with his traveling companion. "Ye'll not pay for these quarters with yer life, but with yer gold," he added.

Macdouall sighed deeply once again and within moments his resigned mood changed back to one of dread. "Ooohhh," he moaned and sat on the side of the bed. "I see devils from the bowels of hell aloosed once again 'pon my poor lost soul," he whined, rocking back and forth, his eyes fixated on the emptiness of the space between him and the elegantly plastered wall.

"God in Heaven... a single bed and Dungal Macdouall! Will this be a sleepless night!" rhetorically sighed Umfraville. He was becoming more concerned by the minute for the sanity of Lord Dungal, and apprehensive of his superior's behavior at their appointment with the king on the morrow.

• •

Umfraville was an unfit human being on the early morn for, as he had expected, he was tossed by Dungal's nightmares for much of his sleep. Lord Dungal, on the other hand, awoke exceptionally cheerful after having self-purged his devils within those same terrifying dreams.

"Where be the eats?" asked Dungal in a loud and jovial voice as he paced from the north window to the west one in his wooly under leggings, fists tightly interlocked at his buttocks.

"Ye be as those caged beasts at the barbican," suggested Sir Ingram He sat up in the bed and rubbed his red and tired eyes that wanted only to re-close.

"Glorious morn!" shouted Dungal waving his arms toward the

clouded sky through the window.

"God save us from this day's likely disgraces," mumbled Umfraville as he stumbled from the tangle of bed-covers and began a search for the chamber pot.

"Do how?" said Dungal not understanding his companion's mutterings.

Umfraville said naught but continued his business without a word. He soon came to Macdouall's side. "Yonder..." he said pointing out the window to the long building across the restricted courtyard, "be the hall."

"Make haste for it, I say," smiled Dungal, "Hope they're servin' up one of them African cats. What say ye?"

"I think not today," replied Ingram sarcastically.

Within a quarter of an hour the two men were making their way toward the great hall, though Umfraville was still adjusting his clothing. As they strode briskly through the drizzling rain, they passed men and women standing under the overhanging thatch and against the side of the building, trying to keep out of the morning's splatters.

The soft rain bothered Dungal and Ingram not at all after the soaking they had taken the day before, and neither man paid heed to those waiting. Upon entering the hall in anticipation of a grand breakfast, both displayed amiable countenances.

The great door closed behind them. There was silence.

"We... we get to the wrong place?" asked Lord Dungal.

Umfraville looked around and saw a mere two figures in the center of the vast hall and none more.

"What be this a'happenin'?" spoke Dungal in a hushed and fearful voice.

Umfraville shook his head slowly, watching as one of the figures raised a loaded crossbow and loosed a quarrel on a hay-filled suit of clothing suspended at the far end of the building. The bolt found well its mark, completely passing through the straw figure and slamming hard into the upended table behind it.

"Good shot, My Lord Gaveston! Without doubt the rascal is dead!" congratulated the second man in loud tones that echoed in the spacious hall.

"My God, Dungal," whispered Umfraville, "that be the king!"

"King?!" asked Lord Dungal forgetting their hushed tones.

"Keep yer voice d..."

"Who runs freely in my hall?" said the second silhouette in a loud commanding voice. The man pointed a loaded crossbow in the direction of the two shaking Scots.

"'Tis Lord Dungal Macdouall and Sir Ingram de Umfraville, Sire!" said Umfraville, after which he and Lord Dungal bowed deeply.

Fortunately for the Scots they remained bowed ingratiatingly, for the bolt in the cocked crossbow was loosed by the king to whiz over their bowed backs and thud into the large wooden door they had entered only a moment earlier.

The king and his companion giggled and laughed loudly to see the mixed expressions of surprise and fear on the two visitor's faces. As their amusement at the Scots discomfiture receded, the king asked, "For what purpose are you interrupting my leisure, Lord Macdouall?"

"Food!" cried out Dungal in petrified agony, "food was what we came for... My King!

"Come forth," commanded the king, adding in a mocking tone, "and you shall have food."

Lord Piers Gaveston again sniggered and returned to his activity. The marksman paid little attention to the trifling words and actions of the Scots as he pointed his unbent crossbow to the floor and pushed his foot into the stirrup on the front of the contraption. With a claw hook dangling from his belt, and a great deal of strength, he grabbed the bowstring and pulled it back toward his chest, releasing it carefully onto the cocked triggering device.

"We have business with ye... Yer... Majesty," groveled Umfraville with another bow.

Dungal's bright outlook had surely been dashed. He now twisted the tail of his finest tunic with intense anguish as welling tears blurred his sight.

He at last summoned the courage to speak, "I... was the one... one... what sent King Edward... yer sire...uh, Sire...them two de Brus brothers for his pleasure."

The young king looked at Lord Dungal intently, "Galloway?"

"Aye, My Lord King," bowed Dungal again.

The king eyed them thoughtfully before he suddenly turned and in a loud voice said, "Bring a king's breakfast for two Scots who aren't afraid of Robert de Brus... pretended 'king' of Scotland!"

There was noticeable sudden activity in the kitchen area as the banging of pots and shouts of the head cook were heard. Meanwhile the king walked around behind the Scots, looking at their scruffy clothing and odd accessories, not at all what one might wear at court. Still, the Scot had called him "Majesty." He liked that appellation. He liked that very much.

Piers suddenly laughed aloud, disturbing the king's thoughts, and pleased with his own.

"What charms you so, Milord? Pray share it with us, that we all might be amused." With that King Edward approached the other Englishman and affectionately put his arm around his waist.

"Sire, I was just thinking... I have the perfect name for the Scottish pretender... 'King Hobbie!' 'King Hobbie' is what I shall call him!" He grinned broadly at his jest.

"Do you mean... 'hobbie'... like the falcon?"

"Yes, Sire! I think it a fitting play on the name of one who thinks of himself as a fierce hawk, but is too small to hunt anything larger than larks or sparrows!"

The king chortled at his friend's witticism and grabbed him around the neck and kissed him full upon the lips, as lovers would behave in private places.

The two Scots were dumbstruck.

Piers laughed in the midst of the kiss and pushed the king backward.

The king was angry for a short moment, then laughed heartily to match his companion's mood. He then turned toward the motionless Scots.

"Sit." he commanded, wagging his index finger in the direction of a bench at a nearby table.

The two men looked at each other, but did as they were bade.

The cheerful Earl of Cornwall handed the cocked crossbow and a bolt to the king.

"I am weary of felling straw warriors, Brother," pouted the king.

Lord Dungal swallowed hard thinking he and Sir Ingram would be the next chosen marks, as Gaveston studied on the problem for a moment.

"How's lamb?" he asked, his face suddenly brighter.

"Lamb, you say?" the king queried with knotted brows.

"I fancy lamb to eat directly," smiled Piers.

The king at last caught his companion's meaning. "Excellent choice! Lamb it is!"

Dungal sighed with relief.

A boy from the kitchen was sent to the outer ward where a variety of animals awaited in pens and shelters for their turns to grace the table of their king. He soon returned with four bleating winter lambs, leading them into the hall with short ropes around their necks.

"Aha!" exclaimed the king upon their arrival, "Tie three to yonder post and hold the fourth at the fireplace.

The page, a youth of less than nine years, mutely did as his king ordered and left the fourth lamb tied to the leg of a chair in front of the roaring hot fire.

"He's bein' cooked on the hoof," joked Piers in broad manner.

The king was pleased as he laughed and handed the crossbow to Piers. "You shoot first."

Piers took careful aim, but just as he released the bolt Edward crudely grabbed a large portion of the archer's butt cheek, causing him to jolt and the quarrel to lodge itself forcefully into a roof timber.

"Dammit!" Gaveston screamed angrily at the king, "You made a mess of that!"

The king, having thought his joke great fun, now frowned and pouted a bit, for he had not been so reproved in all the months since his father's death, but it was hard for him to be cross with Piers. After all, Piers had merely overreacted to his play, he thought. Then he giggled, and approached his lover with teasing and tickling, until he, too, chuckled.

Well aware of his privileged relationship with the king, and in spite of his sudden outburst, Piers knew he was well advised to keep Edward pleasantly disposed toward him. He quickly re-bent the bow, placed another quarrel on the stock, and aimed it again at the lamb, fairly dancing from the heat of the fire.

This time, Edward behaved himself so that the earl would not be angry with him and the bolt was loosed on true course. The lamb dropped as the swift, short quarrel passed cleanly through its heart and lungs and drove deep into the masonry at the back of the fireplace.

"There's one for the dinner table," smiled Piers, turning to hand the weapon to Edward.

Servants brought thick slices of bacon and fat-fried eggs with fresh biscuits and light French wine to the hungry Scots.

"Eat!" directed the king as he waved his hand for the page to bring the next live target to the encounter.

Lord Piers bent the bow once again and laid the deadly dart along the stock. "Your quarrel," he said as he handed it to the king.

Lord Dungal and Umfraville looked on and ate hungrily. The second lamb was thrown into the fire from the force of the missile slamming into its middle. The page hastened to yank the animal from the fire by the rope at its neck as the smell of singed hair gripped his nostrils.

"You got him not through and through," bragged Piers with a smirk.

"Dead all the same!" retorted Edward, frowning.

"Next!" barked Piers, taking a second crossbow from the table. With his back to the complaining lamb and holding the crossbow at about the height of his knees, he bent down and aimed the instrument between his legs. The page was yet completing the tying of the rope holding the lamb in place when the quarrel flew effortlessly through the small creature's flesh, dropping it as quickly as the first.

Piers fairly danced as he held the bow above his head and swung about singing; "I'm the best that e'er was, for I'm the best that e'er was!"

The king was piqued and cursed his luck, but Piers was not fearful for this was but how the two played with each other.

"I'll fix you," said Edward ordering up the last sacrifice. The kitchen boy was barely in place when the king took his stand with his back to the lamb. The boy started to tie off the tether, but Edward ordered him to stand fast.

The lad stood his ground and was not fearful until he saw his king place the crossbow on his shoulder and point it in his direction. Dungal and Umfraville ceased eating and watched the rest of the drama unfold.

The king looked up at the beams in the ceiling, adjudging his position relative to the fireplace in order to align his shot. He glanced back at the stock. The goose feathers on the quarrel tickled his nose and he twitched. Piers sighed at the feigned drama and looked instead at the far wall. Edward smiled and at last loosed the bolt.

Swish... thud!

It missed both boy and beast.

Piers began to laugh, and the king in turn became so angry that he turned on the lamb with his dagger and stabbed it twenty-three times, well beyond its death. He dipped two of his fingers into the fresh blood and rubbed the crimson fluid on his lips. He then turned and walked purposefully to Piers and again kissed him on his mouth, smearing blood well across both their faces.

Piers pushed the laughing monarch to the floor and wiped his face with the sleeve of his silk tunic. "You son-of-a-bitch!" he grimaced.

The king laughed all the louder as Piers sat at a far table to sulk. "Wine!" he ordered, and he dropped himself slouchily across a pillowed chair.

"Ye think *that* king will want to talk about helpin' protect Scots from The Brus?" asked Lord Dungal in earnest.

"I think *that* king gives naught for naught," cautiously whispered Sir Ingram as he set about finishing his fine meal.

William de Ross
Earl of Ross

NOVEMBER 19TH 1307
CASTLE SKELBO IN THE EARLDOM OF ROSS

The sail wavered, flapping loosely, then billowed as the captain of the small galley turned the vessel about, catching a following cold wind from the north blowing across Loch Fleet. The rushing tide fairly thrust the galley through the narrow channel entrance to the inlet, and Bishop David de Murray stood on the deck holding fast to a mast cleat when he first saw Skelbo Castle standing atop a fairly high distant mound in front of him.

"That Skelbo yonder?" asked young Andrew coming to the bishop's side.

"Aye," the man replied. "'Tis." The two stared at their destination as their boat neared the shore.

Skelbo was originally constructed of wood and later covered in plaster to make it look like stone, a not uncommon practice. A large, gray cube of a keep surrounded by a curtain wall, with towers at the corners and the gatehouse, it was atop a slowly rising motte that would necessitate a fairly strenuous walk after they debarked.

"What do ye know about yon castle, Andrew?" asked the bishop.

"Naught, Sire," answered the youth. "Why?"

"Twenty years syne or so, our good king Alexander the third died. His only heir was his daughter's little girl, Margaret, Maid of Norway. She was to come right here, to Castle Skelbo, to be Queen of Scots."

"Then why was she the Maid of Norway? Why not the Maid of Scotland?"

"Her mother was Norway's queen, having married King Eric the Second, thus the Princess Margaret was born there. When King Alexander was killed in an accident, she became queen. That young milksop, King Edward, was pledged to marry her."

"But she didn't come?" he asked, at which the bishop shook his head sadly.

"She died at sea on her way here, poor child. She was but half yer age, Andrew."

Andrew made no comment, but felt sorry for the death of the child. Still, he thought it would be foolish to let a little girl be queen anyhow.

As the galley traversed the tidal bay, the two Scots watched the captain and his crewman as they deftly handled the craft, but Andrew's thoughts had changed directions.

"Ye think them in Skelbo will cleave off our heads?" he asked after a time.

"Not without a fight," answered the bishop. With a grin meant to reassure the squire, he pushed aside his cleric's cloak to reveal the hilt of his well-used mace and his leather and metal body armor.

Andrew smiled with the confidence of youth and pushed back his own surcoat showing that he carried a sword.

"Let's hope Lord William has more sense than to try and thrash the likes of us," said Sir David, looking again toward the castle.

"A bishop and a boy sent to capture all the earldom of Ross," said Andrew wagging his head in disbelief. He squinted his eyes into the early afternoon haze.

"Capturin' it is not King Robert's plan," said the warrior bishop quietly.

When near enough to the shore, the galley's anchor splashed through the water's surface, and the esquif on the stern of the galley was quickly lowered.

"Seems warmer here than in Tain," remarked fourteen-year-old Andrew.

"Passin'ly so," agreed the bishop, and as he directed Andrew to the small craft and the oarsman awaiting them, he added, "This be our boat to Skelbo, Lad."

"But, why does the captain not take us to the shore?" asked the squire, a bit put out.

"Because the galley could be trapped ashore until the tide comes back in. The outgoing tide will all but empty this shallow basin within a few hours. The esquif can make it to shore and back with its shallower draught."

"Ye'll be a'payin' me now?" called the gnarled old galley captain, hurrying aft. He had the wizened face and knobby hands of one who had plied the seas and inlets for most of his long life.

"Trust ye not a bishop in the service of King Robert of Scotland, man?" he cajoled as the captain reached him.

"Coin of England's king is what spends hereabouts, Milord Bishop." He held out his leathery palm to receive his due, but his passenger offered naught but a cold countenance.

"Ye wait *one* day for my return," said the no longer affable bishop, "and I will see ye get yer English coin when we're safely back in Tain."

The captain grumbled, but delayed little before he waved them on. He feared the bishop's papal magic more than he feared losing his passage money. *Besides...* he thought, in an attempt to console himself... *that's twice the coin if I take them back!*

He sat on a barrel lashed to the mast and hefted a jug of whisky onto his lap. He watched as the esquif with the two men and the boy made its way toward the shore.

"Poor thick bastards," he said aloud, and he drew a great swig of the fiery liquid, swallowed it in one gulp, and felt it burn all the way down his throat. "But then, who's the fool after all. They hain't ne'er comin' out of there alive..."

He sighed and wistfully fingered the lip of the jug.

"...And I hain't ne'er gettin' my two coppers for all my trouble." He drank again.

When his man returned with the esquif, he decided they would set sail for... someplace he could pick up another passenger, or a cargo. *No need to wait on the two o' them,* he thought.

But, by the time the oars were shipped and his sailor back aboard, the captain had changed his mind. He would stay and see who won, having made a bet with the devils in his own mind.

· ·

Across the broad brae and up the hill and brazenly across the drawbridge went the Bishop of Moray and Squire Andrew, both on foot. Entrance was easy once they identified themselves. The Earl of Ross, then senior in the castle, allowed the double gates and the portcullis to be opened to them.

"Watch for chicanery," cautioned the earl to Lord James Sutherland as they observed the two Brus Scots below them, entering the gatehouse tunnel.

"Aye, Milord," replied Sutherland.

The earl shivered, pulled his surcoat tighter, and started down the tower's spiral staircase toward the great hall in the keep.

The baron followed.

Once inside, the earl sent the baron ahead to greet their guests while he remained behind curtains to view their deportment before he exposed his person to them.

"Welcome to Skelbo, My Lord Bishop," greeted Sir James with a modicum of genuine warmth in his voice as he walked toward the pair.

The Bishop of Moray turned toward the greeting, as did Andrew.

"We are pleased to be among gentlemen, and thank ye for yer hospitality," returned the bishop. He pushed back the hood of his heavy robe, loosed the frog at the neck and shed it into the waiting arms of Andrew, who loosely balled it and threw it onto a nearby bench seat before removing his own.

Sir James took curious note of the battle-weary mace exposed by the bishop in the doffing of his robe, thus making it the first blow struck in the delicate art of diplomatic negotiation.

The Earl of Ross peered evermore intently, understanding the meaning of a Scottish weapon strapped to the waist of a man of God, and gaining no comfort from it.

He watched when, after a moment more of pleasantries, James Sutherland disappeared from the great hall and went to the kitchen to order food for their guests. The earl continued his concealed vigil, thinking to find secret meanings to the pair's unexpected arrival.

To his pure vexation, the two merely sat stoically at the table and said not a word between them. Instead, they waited, silently and patiently for Lord Sutherland to return.

The earl grimaced; he frowned.

Sweat beaded on his forehead and droplets began to run down his back between the shoulder blades. He recognized his own fear, which spawned anger deep within his anxious heart, and he abandoned his peep-hole to scream and curse in private, but everyone in the keep was easily within earshot of that tirade.

The bishop smiled, whispering to Andrew, "We've won the first skirmish to our mission."

Andrew did not understand, but it was all right, for steaming hot food was momentarily placed before them.

"The food here is far more interesting than the inhabitants," remarked the bishop through a mouthful.

"Aye," agreed Andrew as he gnawed on a juicy leg of roasted goose.

• •

No one representing Ross presented himself for conversation, but left the two of them quite alone in the great hall well after they had finished the meal. As the afternoon light grew feeble, the bishop tired of the game. All at once, he decided they would go to vespers at the small chapel within the castle, and snatching up the boy by the arm, half dragged him across the quickly darkening courtyard.

"Where we lightin' out for?" asked Andrew, his face twisted in puzzlement.

"We need to straighten yer mortal soul to the will of God!"

"I hain't the one ye came here to fix!" cried the lad in protest.

"Perhaps not," smiled the bishop, "but 'tis how I'm playin' it out, Laddie."

The chapel door creaked on its hinges as they entered. No candles were lit within, and only the wan light of dusk penetrated the dark.

Once in, the two set about their worship, striking a pose of reverent prayer before the rail.

They had hardly begun the rosary when the door suddenly swung wide and slammed against the interior wall. There, silhouetted black against torches held in the hands of the six guards behind him, was Lord William of Ross, standing his full five-foot-five-inches and obviously livid.

Andrew started for his sword, but the bishop signaled for him to stay his hand. If he could attain what he had come for without it, he would shed no blood at Skelbo this day.

The unnerved earl, however, was fully prepared to spill blood and could no longer contain his fearful curiosity. He screeched as one who has lost control of his voice and his mind simultaneously, "Is The Brus nigh onto takin' his revenge on me?!"

The bishop quietly crossed himself before he stood and slowly turned toward the open door. Andrew's smaller frame followed suit.

The bishop purposefully rested his hand on the pommel of his mace and paused. For a long moment the two men glared at each other until the bishop broke the silence. "King Robert sends fair and peaceful greetin's to ye, Dear Earl."

Lord William frowned. "Fair and peaceful?"

"Aye."

"Ye jest at my expense, Bishop!"

"Nay, Milord. I jest not, for King Robert desires only a truce with Ross."

The earl stepped forward into the chapel, still with suspicion on his mind, and ordered his men to bring their torches to light the small room.

"A truce?!" he asked in surprise.

"'Til summer next," nodded the bishop.

"I believe it not..."

"Think ye that the Bishop of Moray and a mere lad would be sent to *take* the whole of Ross?" asked the bishop.

"I have heard much of this "king's" trickery!" spat out the earl. "And I want *not* to fall victim to his revenge... though I have expected it... for surely he knows that 'twas I captured his lady and kin!?"

"He knows," said the bishop sternly, and continued to gaze directly at the earl.

"If I should say that I want this truce, then The Brus will think I am not prepared to defend my lands," the earl quavered in his resolve, but stalwartly regained it to lie, adding "though I am!"

"My Lord, King Robert knows well how ye've gone beggin' for English troops, and received naught for yer trouble," gainsaid the bishop.

Ross' anger swelled anew but he wisely retained his countenance. On the wall above the bishop's head the earl noticed the silver crucifix. It had been there all his life, but now, in the flickering torchlight, it seemed to him that it moved. *Perhaps a sign,* he thought, *but of what? Was the movement caused by that damned Brus' emissary? Or was he really an emissary of the Pope?* Ordinary priests had powers he could not imagine, and he was negotiating with a *bishop!*

He chewed at his lower lip as he mused the conundrum. He was cautious and fearful, and it showed in his eyes.

At present he had not the men-at-arms to defend his borders, or even his castles, a fact apparently known to Brus. Were he to accept such a truce, it would forestall any action by The Brus' army until summer, and surely by then King Edward would send troops to help him stave them off!

"Are ye... anointed to sign for Lord Robert, or... whoever?" he chose his words carefully.

"I am *appointed* to sign for Robert de Brus, *King of Scots,* and none other," replied de Murray.

"Aye," mumbled Ross, "'king'."

"Ye acceptin'?"

"Aye, I'll be acceptin'... 'til Whitsun next, 'twill be."

"One more item of negotiation, Sire," said Murray.

"I agreed to yer truce, what more?" shot back Ross.

"A personal matter," returned the bishop just as quickly.

"Personal?"

"My lands ye had fouled in Moray!"

The earl sneered.

"I want them set straight again," growled the bishop, "by spring next."

"And did yer '*king*' direct ye to make this a part of his treaty?"

"Nay, but I will excommunicate ye if ye don't," said Murray with a slight smile.

"Ye are excommunicated yerself," gainsaid Ross. "Ye can't do it."

"I will and can if my lands are not put to order by spring!"

The earl wrinkled his face as if his very soul were twisting it. "I reckon I can't by spring... not enough men to..."

The bishop raised his hand and looked at him sternly. "Ye will or suffer the fires of the Devil's own flames."

The earl squirmed but his fear allowed him no way out. Then he blurted, "Accepted!"

"On both matters," prodded Murray.

"Both," sighed Ross, starting for the door. "Come, we shall draw up the paper!"

"I need no paper betwixt us," offered the bishop.

"Perhaps not, but I have need of this agreement bein' penned to paper in regard to The Brus."

The two men and the boy walked back across the courtyard to a quiet corner in the great hall to author the document of truce. On the morn, in the presence of witnesses, they signed, each principal receiving a true copy.

Afterward, Bishop David de Murray and Andrew Stewart the squire returned to the edge of the water and signaled for the captain to send the esquif for them. Needless to say, the captain was passing amazed to see them at all and sent the esquif in great haste for his paying passengers.

Once aboard, the anchor was raised and the small vessel's sail went up to catch the wind. The cleric and his charge stood at almost the same spot on deck that they had occupied when they approached the castle, and watched it as their transport drew away from it on the noonday tide.

The bishop stood quietly, well satisfied with his success, and the boy watched the sea birds wafting around the small galley for a few moments before he finally said, "Sire, I have a question."

The bishop turned to look at him but said naught.

"Why did the king have me come along?" The bishop smiled at him without speaking until the squire added, "Truly."

"Why do ye think, Andrew?"

The boy thought a moment and said, "Well, I don't fancy it was because I am such a mighty warrior!" He smiled at his tall companion, who burst into a roaring laugh that rolled across the lake and echoed back from several sides.

He grew serious again, but still with a smile said, "Andrew, yer heart is as stout as most men twice yer age, and if such need be, I would welcome yer bein' at my side in battle. Ye have proven yer courage many times. I have it on the word of King Robert."

The boy, embarrassed, looked down at the water before saying, "But, why..."

"I would suppose that our king wisely wanted ye to understand that... not all to rulin' is in the bloody fightin'. Sometimes, it takes a wee bit o' talkin' as well," reasoned the bishop.

Young Andrew sat on the barrel lashed to the main mast and ruminated a long while on what had happened in his presence.

MacKie

DECEMBER 7TH 1307
TOWN OF INVERURIE IN GARIOCH IN SCOTLAND

The King of Scots had, for the present, laid aside his well-nurtured hate for Lord William of Ross, for it played hard against him in this deadly game of chess. His bishop had won him a cessation of hostilities with Ross until Whitsun next, and Robert swore, he would have Lord William as an ally, or dead, by the end of Whitsuntide.

Until then, he was free to fight the war of his choosing.

He knew that, if he moved quickly enough, he could have the north of Scotland in his grasp before the English could reinforce their winter-stranded troops or re-supply key castle strongholds garrisoned by Comyn factions and English occupiers.

Thus, King Robert's poorly clad and meagerly supplied army, living mostly from the seasonally grudging hand of Mother Nature, left Tain straightaway and headed southwest, to skirt the western reaches of Moray Firth, then northeast again, to Elgin.

Castle Elgin was well fortified and well manned when the army of Brus fiercely assaulted it, and though the attack came as a surprise to its defenders, the castle held.

Knowing that he could eventually starve the castle, but knowing also that time was not his friend and that his army would be diminished greatly in such effort, the king thought again. Spring, and perhaps an influx of English reinforcements, was waiting at the end of the bitterly cold winter, and there were campaigns of greater import yet to fight. Thus, Robert moved on with his troops to his own lands of Garioch, abutting the lands of Buchan. From there he would direct preparations and lead attacks against the strongholds of the Comyn family.

As winter's cruelty would have it, the landscape they beheld in Garioch was also barren, save for the scant ranges of pine trees. The sky was gray and the seasonal cold, misty rain was oft in the air and freezing to their clothing and equipment. Yet there they set their camp, as there was no other place as fit for the purpose.

Robert's hand slapped the rump of the huge warhorse he stood beside, and the beast and its rider took off at a gallop, headed toward the southeast.

"That Thomas Randolph runnin' off?" asked Sir Edward after sloshing through the muddy field to stand beside his brother.

"'Twas," replied the king. He turned to meet Edward and together they walked back to the manor house in which they were temporarily holed up.

"Hain't that the direction of Aberdeen?" he asked.

"'Tis," the king again replied in his terse fashion.

Edward frowned and licked his mustache into the corner his mouth and chewed on the ends, then said, "Ye hain't much for tidin's this morn, Rob."

Robert slogged on in silence.

Edward gave up pestering the king, but continued to follow.

In the open field ahead lay bivouacked the army of Brus, now numbering over eight hundred. They were tired men and women. Some were ill, and others had sores on their feet from the walk of the last three weeks, which had taken them across half of northern Scotland. The fact that game was scarce only heaped the misery that much higher.

"Hardy souls," sighed Robert surveying the field.

Edward shrugged thoughtlessly. The army was expected to inure itself to hardship.

Suddenly Robert seemed to lose his balance, and would have fallen had not Edward jumped in surprise and caught him.

"I told ye about gettin' yer rest!" groused Edward in reproach.

"I'm a'right!" insisted Robert. He pulled himself to his full height and adjusted his broadsword, strapped to his side under his surcoat.

"Ye're wore to a nub," argued Edward. "Ye're losin' weight, too. How long have ye been not eatin'?"

"I eat as well as any," Robert indicated the population of the field with a swing of his hand, and otherwise ignored his brother's say. "Let's see to their condition...," he said, moving to the thick of the bivouacked army.

"Awh, dammit, Rob!" whined Edward as he picked a clod of mud from the ground and slung it away.

Robert smiled but Edward never knew it.

The king spoke to many as he moved through the rag-wrapped troops. Sundry ones he knew by name. Most all he left them with a chortle on their lips and determination for the cause of freedom on their minds.

The two brothers came to the outer perimeter of the field, where archers were honing their skills at a full hundred paces. Murdoch and MacKie were drilling a number of others in the art of killing with the arrow.

"Ye men set to rain death on the Comyns?" asked Robert, coming up to Murdoch.

Those in the immediate vicinity turned toward the distinctive voice and shouted their general statements that they were, indeed. Robert turned with a smile to Murdoch, who replied, "Aye, Sire, ready and itchin' to do the deed."

"Be sure, for they'll be comin' for us, right enough," said Robert. After he perused the archers he signaled them to continue their practice while he watched. As man after man drew back his bow and released its arrow, he wondered in a melancholy moment, just how many of the brave lads would be dead by season's end. He walked along the row of warriors as they continued their shooting, but stopped short beside a relatively diminutive bowman.

"What manner of recruit is this?" asked Robert.

"This one's part of the bishop's bunch," answered Murdoch.

"What is yer name, Lad?" asked the king, but the fellow answered not.

"He don't speak, Sire. And since he can't give us no name... we just call him 'Mute'."

Robert stood almost motionless in front of the lad, who appeared to be less than twenty years old.

He fully lived up to his name, speaking not a word. Nor did he acknowledge the king's presence other than to stare at his chest with scarcely an eye blink. Robert looked across the distance at the targets. Each was a wooden post about as tall as a man, with a palm-sized black mark across it at about the same height as a man's heart would be. Robert noticed the one in front of Mute held eight of ten arrows within the mark, and the other two had barely missed it.

Edward scrunched up his nose with curiosity. His only comment was, "Too small!"

"This lad any 'count when the battle starts?" asked the king, still studying Mute's stoic face.

"I hain't one for sayin' such," replied Murdoch, "but show him the enemy and he turns into a pure killin' thing with a dagger, short sword, and now, a bow. And he learns everythin' I teach him real quick."

Robert had no reason to doubt Murdoch but frowned out of confused disbelief. The young conscript seemed unaffected and continued to stare straight ahead, as if seeing distant dreams.

Robert, resigned to remaining ignorant at this point, turned his attention to the army's main body.

"Send more foragers out," ordered Robert to Edward, then added, "Run them all through the trainin' drills... again!... and again!"

"After walkin'' all this way..." asked Edward, "...ye wantin' them to train?"

"Aye," replied Robert, "Keeps their minds off their hunger and off the idea of foragin' on their own. Ye know how some just wander off and we ne'er see them again."

"Aye."

"Then keep them at their weapons! If ye don't, their weapons will fail them in battle for want of bein' familiar!"

"Rob, these men live, sleep, and eat with their weapons! Ye can't treat them like squires still wet behind the ears!"

"I had rather make them work now than bury them later because their wits were too slow! Edward, I need ye to help me get them through these terrible times, when all has been given... more will be required!"

"Rob, they *have* no more to give! If ye do not let them rest, they'll be of no value to us when the battle is afoot!"

"They can rest when 'tis dark." He looked at his second in command and knew that Edward believed he was in the right, and was trying to protect his men. All the same, he said matter-of-factly, "I shall give the order myself!" The king started to speak but his brother stopped him.

"Nay, Rob, I shall order it," he said, acquiescing against his judgment.

"Then do it now! And Edward... " he paused, looking at him coldly, "ne'er question my orders again!" Robert hated having to push his only surviving brother.

Edward nodded, then turned and started walking in the direction of Gilbert de la Haye. Only a few yards away, Sir Gilbert was the knight who seemed most to enjoy putting the men through their routines of discipline.

Suddenly, someone behind Edward shouted, "Sire!" Turning around, he saw his brother lying on the turf, unable to rise, a young soldier kneeling beside him.

Edward rushed to him followed immediately by Haye. As he knelt looking down at his fallen king, Edward's heart was pounding.

"Rob! Are ye injured?"

"I can't get up! My strength is gone from me, Edward. I cannot stand!"

"My God in Heaven! What felled ye?"

"I know not! Help me to stand, ye and Gilbert, and get me off the field afore all know that I am down!" whispered Robert through gritted teeth, "...and let it look as normal as possible!"

A scared Edward looked about him. A handful of wide-eyed onlookers all but completely encircled the trio, blocking them from the view of others, still at their tasks.

"None seem alarmed save those of us here with ye, Rob, but I have no wit about getting' ye to the house without the others seein' ye!" He could not remember ever seeing his brother so, and suddenly realized that tears were rolling down his cheeks. A gnawing fear lay leaden in his belly.

"Put my arm 'round yer shoulder, the other around Gilbert's, and laugh and jest as ye walk," said the helpless king. "I do not think I can move my legs."

"As ye say," replied Edward and he and Gilbert pulled Robert to his feet by his arms and his belt and held him fast. The witnesses to the king's feebleness accompanied them to the house to prevent close inspection of the situation as they poorly mumbled jokes and pretended to laugh all the way across the muddy field and up the alley to the manor house, standing on a small hill.

The party burst through the door and into the front room, dragging the king's feet.

Sir Robert Boyd was first to reach them. "What's this?!" he asked as they laid the king upon the floor.

"Rob just kindly flopped to the ground like a child's doll," explained Edward. His fears were growing larger by the moment.

"Is he wounded or bleeding anywhere?" asked Boyd.

"Nay, he didn't say so, and I've seen naught of it. He just went down of a sudden." His voice trailed off into a whine.

The mistress of the house came into the room, and quickly assessing the situation gave instructions. "Get him to his bed," she ordered, "I'll send for the mid-wife!"

"Midwife!?" asked Edward in complete surprise, "He hain't bornin' no babe!"

"She knows about nursin'," she said, "and hain't *nobody* else here'bouts knows as much... Ye want her brought or not!?"

Edward pinched his face in anguish. His eyes rolled toward the floor where Robert laid almost motionless. He then clapped his hands on either side of his head. He moaned and waffled to and fro with indecision. He looked to Boyd for an answer.

"Get her," he said in a rational voice, "but speak the cause to no one!"

The woman hurried to the door of the kitchen and called a servant to her. "Bring Fiona," she demanded, "and say naught to another livin' one!"

"Aye, Milady," said the young kitchen girl, and she ran straightaway out the back door and toward the village.

The king, barely conscious, saw Boyd over him and bade him to come close to his lips. Robert Boyd knelt beside his king and put his ear within hearing distance to the king's faint breath.

"What does he say?" asked Edward when the king stopped trying to speak and lapsed into peaceful slumber.

"Don't know," was the reply. "Somethin' about Kildrummy."

"He may be dyin', and has seen Nigel and them we lost at Kildrummy!" fretted Edward. He slumped to the floor beside his brother. "There's no blood... yet he's same as dead," he muttered in his sorrow and self-pity. "What will become of us?!"

"Let's get him to his bed in the upper chamber," directed Sir Robert, and he helped Edward and Gilbert manhandle the totally limp body of the poor king up the stairs to his pallet.

They stripped him of his armor, weapons, and wet clothing, and covered him with warmed woolen blankets, for he was clammy cold.

Andrew Stewart rapidly knocked on the chamber door before slipping through it without permission. King Robert was Andrew's entire life, and when he heard what had happened from the kitchen maid, he was half frightened from his wit.

"The King!?" he asked breathlessly as he reached mid-room and a few steps from the king's pallet.

Boyd stood on the far side of the bed. "He lives yet," he sighed with guarded hope.

Edward, who was slumped at the foot of the bed muttered, "Urquhart, again, only worse."

"Worse, for sure," agreed the somewhat transfixed Andrew as a tear for his protector and friend traversed his cheek.

Edward slowly got to his feet, looked upon the all but spiritless body of his brother, lying on the pallet. His heart sank all the more for he knew that, even if Robert lived, command would fall to him until the king could resume his duties. He also knew that he had not the ability to command that his brother had.

From a small stand against the wall he retrieved a crock of whisky he had secreted there the night before, and he began to drink in deep and long swigs.

Robert Boyd understood the portent of Edward's drinking and angrily stormed from the room yelling to the women below: "Where's that midwife?!"

Andrew stood at the King's head, tears still glistening in his eyes. He could not resist touching a lock of Robert's wet hair splayed about on the bed. All else was unheard and unseen by him as he worried for the life of his lord.

David de Graham
Templar Knight

December 11th 1307
Port City of Aberdeen in Northeast Scotland

The wind howled relentlessly about the scant buildings on the southern side of the town of Aberdeen.

Sir Thomas Randolph was hunkered next to the largest tree trunk he could find within the perimeter of a hundred-foot wood and there, across the way from the small chapel, he waited in the cold night shadows. He shivered with the wind and nursed a small skin of whisky now and then.

Two men, beggars by the look of them, slowly moved through the near alleyway toward the chapel, apparently in no particular hurry. At first Thomas watched them intently, as he was to meet two Scots at this place, and he grumbled that they were not the pair for whom he waited.

Damned prayin' beggars, he cursed to himself, and remained still and silent while awaiting 'his' pair. Just knowing that the two men he was slated to meet were nowhere to be seen caused him to doubt the worth of his squatting alone in the dark and the cold for another moment.

"Could be their galley sunk," he muttered half-heartedly.

Overcome by a great shiver, he stood, thinking to stamp his feet to warm them and keep the circulation to his toes. Glancing back toward the kirk he noticed that the two beggars had vanished. He wrapped his surcoat tighter about his huge body and adjusted the rag he had wrapped around his helmet.

As he brought his hands back below his shoulders, a cold steel blade was laid across his throat from his right and he smelled the breath of the one who held the blade. He froze, swallowing hard.

He felt a second blade quietly push at his wrap and a pointed pressure was applied between his chest armor and the heavy leather belt that held his broadsword. *Wish I'd gone to pray for myself,* he thought, realizing the sudden and sad state of his lot.

"Yer name?" quietly demanded the one over Thomas' right shoulder.

Being on spying mission, he knew not whether to answer in truth or with a lie. He swallowed hard again, in hesitation.

"Speak," insisted the assailant.

Thomas replied in a weak voice, "Who be ye?" He could feel the blade bite into his skin and winced, regretting asking.

The man on his left came 'round to stand before Thomas. The hood on his robe hid his face but Thomas recognized the clothes.

"*Ye beggars!*" he raged. "Bein' robbed by beggars, am I?"

"Yer name," insisted the other as he tightened the blade to Thomas' neck.

"Thomas Randolph, dammit!" he replied getting more angry by the second.

"Well Sir Thomas," said the man behind his right ear, loosening his hold, "we are here to meet with ye."

Thomas pushed the blade away and turned to face his would be killer.

"Which of ye is Sinclair?"

"I am Sir Henry Sinclair," returned the other man.

Thomas turned again. His eyes narrowed in the darkness as the solidly muscular man pushed his hood away from his full-bearded face. No more than that could Thomas identify without more light.

"Not beggars?" sighed Thomas.

"Not beggars," assured Sinclair with a slight chuckle.

Thomas took a long swig from his skin, blew a satisfying whisky breath, and shook his head in relief, then offered a drink to his newly acquired "friends."

Sinclair waved his hand in refusal of the offer and said, "Let's get inside where we can build a fire."

The three men entered the priory through a small side door. A candle lantern had been left burning by one who was expecting them. Picking it up, Sir Henry led the way through several dark passages and into the building's great hall. He immediately crossed to the fireplace and within minutes, had a warm fire ablaze.

Great hall or not, the room was small and sparse of furnishings. All was covered with dust from having been in disuse for some time.

The second man, a gaunt figure with deep, piercing dark eyes and a fairly short beard, found himself a seat and dusted it off. His manner made him seemingly ready for a fight at any turn, and evidence of his quarrelsome way was displayed across his right cheek in the form of a deeply gashed scar. When he parted his robe in the front to sit, he revealed a slash of crimson on his inner garment.

"So, he's the Templar," said Thomas almost casually.

"Sir David Graham," offered Sir Henry, still stirring and poking in the fire.

Graham bowed his head a bit but not so much as to give Thomas the idea that he was submitting to being in an inferior position.

"Thought Templars let their beards grow down 'til they covered their peckers," Thomas said dryly, and pulling a large dusty chair closer to Henry, sat on the edge of it and held his hands toward the fire.

"I suspect that would not be very long for *ye!*" retorted Graham.

Thomas stood up with fire in his eye, but Henry interrupted his intent.

"A long beard would tell all that he is a Templar, a right unhealthy state at present, so he cut it! Did not King Robert speak of Sir David to ye?" asked Henry.

"He did," returned Thomas, still staring at Graham, who sat stoically several feet away.

"Did he not tell ye to meet us here?" again asked Henry, attempting to give tempers time to cool.

"He said such," replied Thomas, fishing his whisky skin once again from beneath his surcoat and taking a sip.

"Did he speak of the persecution of the Templars by King Philip of France?"

"He said they needed a place to hole up and I was to see if the idea was good for our bailiwick," explained Thomas.

"On October the thirteenth, a black, black Friday, the Templars were set upon by Philip's minions. There were thousands, over the whole of France... swooped up in a single day and night and locked away in many diverse places... declared as heretics by Rome and their properties confiscated by Philip."

"King Robert and his followers are on the wrong side of the Pope, our lands and wealth have been stolen by Edward, and our people are put to death!" argued Thomas, somewhat unsympathetic with the plight of the Templars.

"Aye," agreed Henry, "that is true enough."

"I scarce escaped with my life," interjected David.

"Ye should have taken due warnin' from what Philip did to the Jews only year last," replied Randolph, still not looking at Graham.

"But, they were *Jews!*" said David, daring Thomas to compare Templars to Jews.

"Roastin' on the same spit, ne'ertheless," gainsaid Thomas as he turned to see the light from the fire on David's angry face, its deep scar seeming to twitch with the fire's flicker.

Then Thomas asked, "Is this the same Sir David Graham, Scottish knight, who was with the English against the Wallace at Falkirk?" All the while, Thomas stared fearlessly into Graham's eyes.

"I go where I am sent by my liege lord!" scowled David.

"And, I figure, ye were sent to come spy on the likes of us by yer liege dog, Edward!" returned Thomas.

Graham threw open his beggar garb to expose the full red cross with splayed ends embroidered on his surcoat. "Hear tell, Randolph, that ye were ol' Pembroke's lapdog, yerself!"

Thomas muttered defensively, knowing it was true.

Graham reached for his broadsword tucked within his cloak.

Thomas moved not from the edge of his seat but continued to stare at Graham as Henry Sinclair jumped between the two, shouting, "I vouch for Sir David's fealty... He *shall* swear it himself, to King Robert!"

The three men stood frozen in silence for a full quarter-minute.

Then Thomas took a deep breath and said at last, "What is it ye want of King Robert that ye are willin' to swear such?"

Henry scooted two more of the heavy chairs over the flagstone floor and set them close to the fire. He sat in one and beckoned David to the other. Graham, with a look of resignation, sat in the chair across from Randolph.

Sinclair cleared his throat as if preparing to speak. He said naught but drew forth a pouch that had dangled from his belt, opened it, pinched up a bit of dried meat and offered it to Thomas.

Thomas took the pungent French made meat without a word. He was hungry.

Henry, in turn, offered Sir David meat but he had meat of his own and so refused, instead retrieving his cache.

"Now, perhaps, hot blood will be cooled by full bellies," said Henry in a calm voice.

Thomas ate, as did the other two.

"I know many Scots that would be pleasured to be eatin' this, tonight," said Thomas after finishing his portion.

Henry passed the pouch to Randolph who helped himself to more.

"Aye… many a Scot right here in Aberdeen would be so pleasured."

"We have two barrels of this dried meat on the galley," said David.

Thomas remained quiet, feigning disinterest.

"There are seven Templars who will fight for King Robert's army, if ye will but protect them from the French," offered Sir Henry.

"Seven!?" asked Thomas in a surprised voice.

"That's the full lot from our galley," said David. "We ken not how many others escaped, but I think there must have been many."

"And gold?" asked Thomas.

"No gold," returned David, shaking his head.

"Where's all the gold and treasure ye Templars are supposed to have?" asked Thomas insolently.

"We're offerin' seven… seven worthy knights to fight by yer side, Sir, naught more," said Sinclair, ignoring Thomas' question.

"Yer seven," said Thomas pointing to Graham, "and ye're one," he said pointing to Sinclair, "makes eight… and then there is me!"

Thomas sat back in his chair as if *his* point were fully made.

"A'right," said Graham. "There be nine… I understand ye not!"

"'Tis easily understood, Sir … we need to get that castle, yonder, shed of the English."

"Aberdeen?… Aberdeen Castle? And the nine of us to do the takin'?!" sarcastically asked Graham.

"Robert sent me to take it," said Thomas smiling, "…but I reckon nine can take it all the faster!"

"I told ye this was a thick witted idea, Henry!" shouted Sir David, jumping to his feet. He grasped at the air with his long fingers in pure frustration, "We can't have *nine* goin' against a fully garrisoned English castle!"

"Ye can easily say no," taunted Thomas quietly, "but then… that would leave me to take the castle, alone, when ye refuse."

Sinclair sat back into his chair and looked at David. "He has a scheme afoot."

"But, he is speakin' in riddles and witless prattle!" complained Graham.

"Let's hear how he has wit to play it out," suggested Henry.

Graham returned to his seat and propped his elbows on the arms of the chair, lacing his fingers together across his middle. He *would* listen to Thomas' plan… but was prepared to be unimpressed by it.

THE MANOR HOUSE IN INVERURIE IN GARIOCH

For six long, fret-filled days Andrew remained at the foot of Robert's bed, his arms folded across the disheveled heap of covers splayed at the king's feet. His head would nod from time to time and sink to his arms from lack of sleep and the boredom of the vigil. Robert was rarely to himself, and when he was, they tried to ply him with broth and medicines concocted by the midwife, who regularly came and went during the day.

Scant light leaked through the roughly woven curtains covering the window nearest the bed. At the other end of the long room the curtains on the window were pulled back into a knot. Two chairs stood askew between the sleeping squire and Robert Boyd, the latter pacing almost constantly in front of the window through which he could see various parts of the rebel army milling about below, in the town, in search for victuals, or honing their killing skills in training. Armorers were diligently at work in the only smithy around. Fletchers carefully feathered the shafts of newly made arrows. And there was an almost constant ringing of metal on metal.

The most part of the eight hundred man army had been unaware of their king's illness, and may not have worried even if they had known, for many in the company had witnessed the several days when Robert failed to be among them at Castle Urquhart... but those who were aware of the king's plight this time, knew it was different.

Robert's grand chain of successes seemed to have abruptly ended.

"Christina," exclaimed Robert Boyd aloud.

Andrew jumped at the sudden noise and tried to focus on the brighter end of the room where Boyd stood silhouetted against the small rectangle of light.

"Say ye, Sire?" asked Andrew, still sleep muddled.

"Christina of Carrick!" answered Boyd with a determined grin on his face.

Andrew realized not the significance of the revelation and returned his head back upon his folded arms.

"Laddie!" commanded Boyd in a louder voice.

Andrew's head again jerked up, eye's blinking. "Aye, Sire."

"Fetch one of those highlanders that Christina brought the king, spring last!"

Andrew jumped up, wrapped himself in a cloak, and did as he was bade. Boyd watched through the window as the lad traversed the muddy byways between the houses and trade shops, headed for the main encampment of makeshift tents laid out on a fallow field at the south end of the town.

Robert Boyd made his way down the stairs to the lower part of the house. There, near the fireplace, lay poor drunken Edward. Someone, compassionately, had thrown a blanket over him. Two dogs belonging to the owner of the manor house laid about near his lifeless hulk.

Boyd, jaw set, shook his head in pity for the poor man. In the next room he heard Gilbert de la Haye and Neil Campbell at playing a crude game of chess. When Boyd entered they ceased their game and looked to him expectantly.

"How is the king?" asked the Campbell.

"As if dead," said Boyd in a tired voice.

Gilbert and Neil both winced at the news.

"Will he die?" asked Neil, not really wanting to know.

"Dear God in heaven!" expressed Gilbert *certainly* not wanting to know.

"I am sending three of Christina's highlanders to fetch her here," said Robert.

"Over the Mounth to Carrick in winter?" asked Gilbert with raised brows.

"The king's not himself enough to know her company," remarked Sir Neil.

"She is a woman of many interests," explained Boyd. The others nodded. "One of these is knowledge of medicines. We must keep the king alive with our poorly ways for ten days... 'til she gets here."

"Back over the Mounth in winter," again remarked Sir Gilbert, thinking that it could perhaps be done once, but not twice.

"Not so," said Boyd, "she resides with kith about forty leagues south at the coast... near Dundee."

"The English have domain over those parts," worried Gilbert.

"That's why we are sendin' *three* highlanders," returned Boyd, holding up three fingers. He then added, "I want ye two to put all the whisky ye can find here'bouts in the stable."

"Horses takin' to havin' a wee dram?" asked Neil, teasingly.

"'Tis Edward," he replied.

"Edward?"

"Aye," nodded Boyd, "Edward. We must sober him up and keep him sober. He is our commander at present, and the spies that we have lurkin' about Mortlach tell us they see the Comyns sendin' spies to search us out. 'Twon't be long ere they find us lingerin' here."

"Ye have a plan?" asked Neil.

"Aye," returned Boyd, "If the Comyns find us here so disarrayed we will surely be killed, each and all... I ken to leave on the morrow's first light."

"Where'bouts ye headed?" again asked Neil.

"*We* are headed... toward Slioch."

"There hain't naught at Slioch save wilderness!"

"Aye," replied Robert as he turned to leave the room, "pack the animals with all the victuals they can heft. Eight hundred and forty people, e'en Scots, eat more than we have."

. .

On the dawn Sir Robert Boyd's plan was begun. The less than twenty knights on horseback led the procession, followed by John Wallace, who, being the nearest to Robert's height and build, was dressed in the king's armor, helm, and tabard, and rode his great destrier. Only the knights surrounding him were aware that King Robert was borne on a wain behind the procession with a canopy rigged to cover the seemingly lifeless monarch.

Andrew, riding before John Wallace, cleverly thought to attach the flag of the red lion rampant to a staff and fly it as he would were Wallace actually the king, all the while not knowing if he would be privileged to carry the royal banner into battle afore King Robert ever again.

Sir Edward was swinging his broadsword, swaggering in the saddle, and yelling as many curses as he could muster to color his drunken vision of killing Lord John by flaying one strip of skin at a time from his "bare arse" and feeding it to a murder of crows.

His fellow knights were giving him a wide berth.

Next followed riders who were not knights, then the seven hundred, more or less, warriors of foot, carrying their weapons and kits and bundled with as much as they dared to wrap on or hang from their bodies. The king's wain came after, and the remainder of the company; the camp followers led the pack animals, loaded to capacity with victuals, tents, blankets, and sundry necessities.

Slioch in Drumblade was sixteen miles to the northwest across Foudland Hills and a first hint of the light rain's turning to snow whipped in the wind.

"Where ye reckon they're repairin' to?" asked one villager to another as the king's caravan walked by.

"North's the way they're headed," answered the other.

"If the king dies, they'll scatter to their hovels, quick of foot and tails tucked, I ken," opined a third.

"What say ye?" said the first, "There sits the king, fit for the ridin', out in front of them all!"

"'Ppears so... but I heard from a friend whose woman knows the midwife, that 'tain't so," said the third villager. "Hear told, the king be near dead!"

"Still," said the second, "he looks plumb lively to me!"

No one noticed a young villager by the name of Eustace, who rode a palfrey from the village toward the southeast, intending to swing wide around the entourage and hie for Lord John's Castle Mortlach, with blood gold on his mind.

Reginald Cheyne

DECEMBER 17TH 1307
CASTLE MORTLACH

More than a month syne, the six ringleaders of the resistance against The Brus in the north had come together to protect their interests. Sir Reginald Cheyne had been chosen from among the six to go to the Earl of Ross and persuade him to join their efforts, but as yet he had not returned.

In the meantime, half of the nobles' amassed army, under the command of Sir David de Brechin, roamed the countryside looking for King Robert. Reports, true and false, came forth from spies scattered across the whole of their demesnes, but the Brus army seemed to have melted into the frozen landscape.

Lord John Comyn's initial passion for revenge upon The Brus was quickly being supplanted by pure fear.

Now, in Castle Mortlach's great hall, Lord John and David de Strathbogie sat in the gathering darkness and sipped potent liquor while awaiting news of longed-for progress in the hunt for their elusive enemy. All about them candle lanterns were being lit, and lighted candles were quietly placed on the table before them.

Also upon the table lay Lord John's sword, stained recently with the blood of the latest spy who failed to bring him news of the whereabouts of The Brus and his army. He vowed to do the same to any of his spies who came to him without having news of his quarry.

Across the table from Lord Comyn, Strathbogie matched the earl, drink for drink, but also ate, sopping the bread in the bottom of his trencher with the remaining gravy. At the sudden appearance of the candle flame, placed close before him by the serving boy, his yellow head jerked back, breaking him from the trance state into which he had drifted.

John looked at him with sullen eyes.

"Ye think I'm drunk, do ye?" asked David, who in fact, was somewhat dulled by drink, but not yet drunk. The earl said nothing.

David let the earl brood, knowing he would soon again speak. He was right.

"Brus is winnin'... and we've not had the first skirmish!" admitted Lord John, grinding his teeth in remorse and resentment. "Now... we but lay about, drinkin' up our very wit and strength... and the supplies dwindle as well."

"Brechin is out searchin' with half our army," protested David, thinking that was an accomplishment enough, at present.

"And when does he catch up to them?" asked Lord John, but Strathbogie had no ready reply. "And what happens if he should?"

John turned his head away. Most of the room was dark as ink, with just enough of a glimmer of light from the fading day remaining to give form to the windows above the dais. John could not believe the wasted days and wasted supplies, and with no conflict.

The steward of the castle softly entered the great hall.

"Milord," he said as he came to John's ear.

"Say," demanded the irritable earl.

"Sir Reginald returns from Ross."

The earl jumped to his feet and said with great bombast, "Why does he wander elsewhere in the castle when we are awaitin' his news?"

"Sire, he came through the postern gate but moments ago, with a body strapped across the saddle of a palfrey," replied the cowed steward.

"I understand not! *Whose* body?" cried John, becoming more agitated with every breath.

The steward glanced at the bloodied sword on the table and knew not whether to speak or remain silent.

His dilemma was soon resolved by Cheyne, who burst through the doors of the great hall, the body across his shoulders, and tossing snow in every direction. "Of course ye understand not!" He shouted as one accustomed to the out of doors.

John and David both had their eyes wide open with amazement as Cheyne dropped his load before them onto the stone floor and walked the few paces away to warm himself at the fire.

"Who be this ye've kilt and set at my feet like a cat bringing in a dead bird?" asked John.

"Ach, warm him a wee bit and he'll tell ye from his own blue lips," returned Cheyne, chuckling.

"Tell me what?... from a dead man," said John tiring quickly of the not so obvious game.

"Why, he knows the whereabouts of Brus!" broadly grinned Sir Reginald.

The earl looked confusedly at the lifeless body on the floor for a full quarter minute before he suddenly realized the potential of the news. "Arouse this man!" he demanded of his steward.

"Aye, Milord," replied the much relieved servant. He pulled the villein to the fire and laid him next to where Cheyne stood on the hearth.

"Ye think of this entrance speech all the way from Ross?" asked Strathbogie without even a glance at the lifeless man.

"Nay," returned Cheyne, "I found him wanderin' yonder on the trail about noon. He said he was from Inverurie and that he knew where Robert Brus was next headed!"

"And did he tell ye?" anxiously queried Lord John.

Cheyne just said, "He wanted gold for his news, and I said he could have it... but he passed out, from the cold, I reckon, 'bout an hour ago."

"But did he say *where*?" insisted John, moving toward the fireplace.

"Slioch!" laughed Cheyne.

Both John and David's minds went reeling.

"Slioch is a wilderness... what castle have they there to capture," asked David rhetorically.

"He's but lied to ye, Sir Reginald... for the gold," offered John, but his curiosity still pounded heavily in his brain.

"Nay, he has *more* to tell for the gold," responded Cheyne.

A slight moan from the young man brought Strathbogie to the threesome around the fire.

"He lives?" asked David.

"Sounds so," said Reginald as he gave the slowly rousing fellow a firm shaking with his foot.

The lad's eyes opened enough that he realized his surroundings.

He blinked several times before swooning.

"What's yer name?" asked John hurriedly, but the poor fellow had lapsed again into a stupor.

"His name is Eustace and he hails from Inverurie," said Cheyne.

Lord John frowned at the knight and asked, "Ye keepin' information from us?"

"Keepin' naught," said Cheyne with a smile to soften John's harsh edge. "Ye asked me not about his name!"

David bent over the groaning man, carefully looked at his frosty body, poked him with his dagger, then suddenly slapped him hard across the face. Eustace's head rolled back as blood began to trickle from his mouth.

"Why'd ye do that?" asked the surprised Cheyne.

"I'll do as I see to do," returned Lord David.

"'Bout knocked him witless, ye did," said Cheyne as he stooped to see if the man was still living.

"I was just makin' him lively," explained David.

"Or newly dead, perhaps," replied Cheyne, gruffly.

John had no feeling for this peasant, but if the man actually happened to know something, he thought it best if he were alive for the telling. John turned and demanded of the steward, "Victuals!" The steward, eyeing the bloodied broadsword yet again, gladly did as he was bade.

"What's the news with Ross," asked John changing the subject and giving the would-be informer a chance to find his wit.

Cheyne, not wanting to say news before the groggy Eustace, nodded in the direction of the table. The three men sat at one end of the board, and the bare candlelight cast ominous shadows across their faces. While the melting ice on his clothing dripped water with his every move, Cheyne poured himself a hefty whisky and sipped, deliberately delaying the telling, watching how the pair squirmed in their seats awaiting his fixing in his mind the perfect statement. Then he said simply, "Lord William hain't sidin' with us."

Shocked silence.

Strathbogie exploded. "I knew he was a damned snivelin' coward!" he screamed as he pounded the table with his fist. The half filled glasses and Lord John's sword bounced noisily with every blow.

"What's his reasonin'?" asked the more rational Comyn. His voice was gruff and tinged with disappointment.

"He signed a treaty with Brus... e'en showed it to me... claimed he had not enough troops to keep Brus and his ten ... maybe fifteen... thousand men from takin' the whole of Ross!"

John and David took the news with almost simultaneous moans.

"Ten... fifteen... thousand...?!" asked John, again moaning loudly before belting down his whisky. "Perhaps we should sign a treaty as well!"

"Forget not the story of Dungal Macdouall, Milord," offered Cheyne in caution.

John's eyes blinked as he replayed the story in his mind for the significance. "Aye," he said at last, "but wherein is the lie?"

"Ask our churl when he comes to full life directly," winked the smiling Cheyne.

A serving wench slipped quietly through the large oak doors of the great hall with two trenchers of food that she placed on the table before the three men. Sir Reginald took one of the trays and motioned for the other to be given to Eustace, shivering and moaning in the puddle created by the melting snow and ice on his frozen jerkin and trews.

Cheyne turned toward Eustace as he was handed the food and said cheerfully, "Top crust for ye this day, Laddie!"

Eustace slightly nodded and hungrily began to eat with his dirty and about frozen fingers. After nearly four days without food, he cared not whether it was top or bottom crust. Either way, it was perhaps the tastiest crust he had ever had.

.   .

Within an hour the well fed Eustace was but a frightened prisoner, sitting on a bench seat pushed back from the table about three feet. His hands were bound together and he absent-mindedly licked at the remaining gravy still in his youthful beard. His head ached, as did his entire body. Candles in clusters lighted either side of him and more were on the floor at his feet. Two guards, in the near shadows to the rear of him, flanked him on both sides.

Lord John Mowbray had been summoned to join the three to complete a panel of inquisition. Mowbray was someone to whom King Edward lent an ear, and might be of value on the panel, the Comyn had realized. Thus, the four-judge panel sat on the other side of the trestle board from the prisoner. Stubs of candles were stuck in a mass of drippings directly to the top of the table.

Eustace, presently regretting ever having the thought that he could profit by his wits, was surely on trial for his life.

The four mumbled among themselves for a short while, no doubt agreeing to the punishment ahead of the judgment. Cheyne encouraged the other three to hear the prisoner's say before killing him for a liar and a rogue.

Lord John started with his prime question, 'Ye have somethin' to say about The Brus?"

The prisoner nodded.

"Well?!" barked the Comyn. "Speak!"

"I know where he was headed near a week ago."

"Slioch." said John stealing Eustace's answer.

"Aye," replied Eustace, now not sure he had anything with which to barter for his life, much less gold.

"How many ride with him?" Lord John spoke again.

"Six or seven," said Eustace.

"Thousand?" asked Strathbogie, his eyes fairly glistening in the wan candlelight. Eustace began to think of the four as devils come to carry his soul to hell.

"I can't count a thousand… I thought ye meant hundred," answered Eustace. "I asked the priest at the chapel in Inverurie how many, and he said six or seven hundred!"

Lord John turned to Cheyne. "This is not to Ross' count," he said in a whisper.

"Remember Dungal," whispered Cheyne.

"Milord," interrupted Eustace, "can I have gold for this tellin'?"

One of the guards slapped Eustace on the side of the head with his gauntlet for the question. Eustace flinched and moaned all the more, holding his bleeding ear with his tied hands.

The earl ignored the plea and the moans, saying, "Ye are tellin' this lie just to get my gold, be ye not? The Brus travels with thousands, not hundreds… Aye?"

"Nay, Milord, I warrant ye, I spake as the priest spoke it to me," pleaded Eustace in a faint and disarming voice only frightened, beaten men use.

"No gold for the likes of that!" said Lord John emphatically.

"I know of more… for gold," said Eustace weakly, determined to carry gold back home.

A single English pence was placed on the far side of the table by Strathbogie. "I'll pay to hear his tale," he said.

"Not gold, but silver for yer next lie," said Lord John tauntingly.

With hands tied together, the villein stood a bit and reached for the precious coin. Strathbogie's impulsive dagger plunged deep into the tabletop just ahead of where the coin laid. Eustace's hands jerked back quickly.

"Yer say first, vermin," said Lord John.

"Aye," replied Eustace meekly. "'Twas the day I left home… I heard gossip about their king."

"About the king of thieves?" rhetorically slandered Strathbogie.

"Aye? What was this gossip?" said John preparing to be unimpressed.

"The King Brus be near dead, if not full dead by now."

There was stunned silence all around.

"Can I have the pence, now?" asked Eustace, meek but still greedy for the coin.

"Guards!" shouted Lord John.

The two guards came forward into the light. "To the dungeon with this lyin' baseborn bastard! Hang him, we will… 'twixt the morrow and Christmas!" Lord John ordered.

As he was being dragged squirming, his need to speak in haste was more desperate by the second and he blurted in the most voice that he could muster, "Milord! Milord!… does this mean the pence is not mine to keep?"

David de Strathbogie laughed, retrieved his pence from the tabletop and tossed it at the man hitting him in the mouth. The coin fell to the floor. "Ye'll not need a pence in hell," he mocked.

Lord John and John Mowbray joined in the laughter. Reginald Cheyne observed in silence.

Eustace played his last card with more voice than he thought he had, "If king hain't dead... I know how to make him so!"

The laughter stopped.

"For yer damned worthless life, Lad, ye had best not lie now," warned Lord John.

"I have not lied. I will not lie to ye... but I want gold for the doin' of this deed."

"How much gold?" taunted Mowbray.

"As much as ye are willin' to part with," answered Eustace, thankful that he was no longer being dragged to his doom.

"Agreed," said Lord John offhandedly, thinking he would make a bargain in the air with anyone who was as big a fool as this one.

At the signal from Lord John, the guards allowed him to return to his bench seat so that he could tell the earls how he would certainly benefit their cause.

"Say ye?" spoke John Comyn, offering the man a last chance to speak.

"I have..." he started then paused, choosing his words carefully, "I m– made friends with a few of the Brus followers as they laid about in Inverurie," he again paused, knowing his precarious life was surely at a pivotal point. "Th– They– they wanted me to join... their army."

The imaginations of the members of the inquisition being pricked, they listened.

William Wiseman

DECEMBER 18TH 1307
IN THE REGION OF SLIOCH IN SCOTLAND

For five arduous days the more than eight hundred men and women of the army of Brus worked their way toward Slioch, a mere three leagues northwest of Inverurie. To feed the multitude and have stores for a greater trip to no one knew where, the men foraged constantly for winter game around the Foudland Hills. Everything that they had brought with them, from food, to shelters, to weapons, was packed upon the back of horse, pony, or villein, but at last the meandering entourage reached Slioch, on the north side of which lay a large bog.

The king rarely was conscious of being in this world, and was oft in the nether world of his own dreams. The medicines, prepared by the midwife who saw to the king's needs at the manor house, were being administered in due course but seemed to have little, if any, beneficial effect. King Robert Brus, the heart and soul of the fight for Scotland's independence, was sinking deeper into his dark malady and no one to help.

Sir John Wallace disguised in the king's garb still led the procession. Edward Brus certainly longed for at least one more cup of whisky, or of anything that smacked of strong spirits, but Robert Boyd carefully monitored his begged-for libations. He knew well that the king might not soon revive, if he revived at all, and that Sir Edward thus had a most demanding role to play if the army were to winter out another two months.

Sir William Wiseman and Sir David Barclay hailed Boyd with shouts and waves of their gloved hands, and as they rode to Boyd's side, their mounts kick up clouds of powdery snow. Boyd wheeled to meet the pair.

"What ye want?" he called.

The two nobles drew rein before him. Edward, not wanting to be subject to Sir Robert's "incessant harping about not caring for anything" except himself, spurred his horse to the knot as well.

"We ken this area," said Wiseman, "and have a place of safety in mind."

"'Tis not far, offered the heavy Barclay, squirming continuously for a more comfortable position astride his warhorse.

Sir Robert paused and looked at the draft horse coming toward him, blowing goodly puffs of vapors in the cold air and dragging the precious cargo of King Robert on a wain.

"This place… 'tis fit for our king to rest a spell?" he asked.

Sir William nodded with serious countenance and pointed west, toward the bog.

"Ye thinkin' a soggy, dank bog fit for my near-dead brother!?" loudly ranted Edward, trying to be forceful in his demeanor.

Sir Robert Boyd raised his open hand to quiet Sir Edward. "I would hear them out."

Edward again sneered and grumbled, abruptly wheeled his horse and kicked it hard to catch up to Wallace.

"Within the bog is a hillock… fifty or more acres of mostly pine woods jutting into the bog and surrounded on three sides by the black ooze," said Wiseman.

"'Ppears as a …sort of… wooded fortress with the bog as moat," offered Sir David.

"Castle to protect us… or bottle to trap us," philosophized Boyd, adding, "We'll have a look."

"Castle or trap, almost don't matter," lamented Barclay, and he turned sadly toward the horse pulling the king's transport and laboring its way up the low hill through the drifts. "Done for, we all might be."

"Hain't a'kennin' that!" refuted Boyd, jerking his horse's reins to turn west. He refused even to think of the king dying. "Let's see this bog 'fortress' of yers!" he kicked his horse and the others followed suit.

Within half an hour, they arrived where the hillock peninsula attached to the higher, dryer land. A level space close to the bog held small shrubs and winter grass covered over by the accumulating snow.

Further out on the spit was the fifty-acre wood that rose upon the hill, the bog stretching broadly on both sides to form a natural barrier, with the outer shores having stands of pines of their own.

"An unsuspected place to hole up for a while," suggested Wiseman.

Boyd sat his horse with the others until the wain reached them.

"King awake?" asked Boyd.

Andrew, who rarely left the side of the king, sadly shook his head.

"Wait here 'til I ride the land," ordered Sir Robert.

"I'll join ye," offered Edward grudgingly.

Boyd nodded and turned his horse to walk across the narrow strip of land to the wood, noticing as they passed that there were orderly rows and piles of peat lining the open areas. It appeared that the locals had been harvesting and drying the dark slabs from the vast peat field on the edge of the bog proper. Locals might present a problem for the king's army.

After surveying the peninsula, Boyd concluded that the hillock was just what it seemed to be, with no locals or others around. Thus the army, as it arrived, filed across the spit of land and disappeared into the deep wood, the soldiers and others so exhausted by the trip that they cared not where they laid their heads, as long as they could build a warm fire and bed down in the snow in relative safety.

The masons among them, usually in charge of razing castles beyond any practical use, were now charged with building a peat hut for sheltering the king at the top of the low hill. It was to be large enough to have room for the king to sleep, and two more if needed. They made a found-stone fireplace in one corner to warm the interior, and constructed a vent hole in the stick, linen, and pine bough roof. An old, well-worn, but heavy cloak covered the small doorway.

Inside it was dark, dank, and it smelled of the earth, but it was mostly windproof, and once the fire was laid, considerably warmer than the outdoors. Those who knew of the king's plight slipped him into the hovel and placed him on a pine bough pallet covered with deer hides. He remained unaware.

Andrew stacked several peat blocks to sit upon and keep vigil on his king. After piling every available covering upon his lord, he leant against the damp wall and dozed wrapped tightly in his cloak. The burning peat filled the room with the rank smell of its smoke, and the cold and shivering Andrew would sneeze and cough from time to time, but still would not give up his vigil.

· ·

Gelis was but one of several women whose husbands were killed in the ill-fated battle for Castle Elgin, several weeks before she arrived with the army at Slioch. Had she a home to return to, she would have done, but alas, she had naught such, nor chick nor child. Thus, she stayed with the army to survive as best she could, washing and mending, and cooking for a handful of men who had neither mother nor wife, nor other to do for them.

This day her menfolk had been lucky, turning up several hares for sharing amongst themselves and Gelis, and she was at the task of preparing them out in the open.

Cuthbert was hungry. His belly ached and he had a bad case of fainting misery that dogged his every move. Smelling the meat roasting was more than he could bear, and his empty stomach growled piteously. He walked toward the aroma's source until he found Gelis.

"Ye fixed a bit of oatmeal and rabbit extra... for me?" asked Cuthbert to the woman.

"And me," chimed in his friend Fergus, who was just as starved.

The woman, squatting by her fireplace, deftly turned skewered rabbit parts to and fro over the fire. She looked at the two men hunkered a mere six feet away, "Ye're neither of ye my husband," she declared. "Why should I fix ye supper? I've me men here to fix for... and they give me the hares, not ye."

"'Cause we're hungry, woman," said Fergus, and his eyes full of tears so that she felt sorry for him. "We hain't got nobody," he added, needlessly.

"Then yer to fix for yersel'es," she replied, but softer, as one speaking to a child.

"Can't fix what ye don't have." Cuthbert looked at the brown meat on the sticks in the fireplace.

"Why hain't ye huntin' then, the pair of ye?" she scolded, and kept a sharp eye on the skewered meat at the fire.

"We been a'huntin' all mornin'," said Fergus, truthfully.

"Be none of my doin's that ye can't hunt. Now, be off and don't bother me more!"

Fergus started to speak but Cuthbert cut him short, saying, "Don't 'bother' her, none. She hain't got a heart for a hungry man. Prob'ly why she hain't got a man o' her own!"

It was her turn to look at them with teary eyes. "I hain't got a man o' my own," she almost shouted, "'cause he died back yonder at Elgin! And he was more a man than ye two put together, he was, and that's the truth!"

The pair of beggars were silenced as they groped unsuccessfully for a recovering say. Finally, they stood and started to leave, but Cuthbert sagged to his knees.

Gelis rushed to help Fergus steady his friend, and settle him against the trunk of a large tree. Cuthbert was pale and weak, and he could hardly hold himself upright. She felt of his head and watched his breathing, finally asking, "When did ye last eat somethin'?"

Fergus answered, "We hain't et but once since we left Inverurie, and that just some pottage... without any meat!" he hastened to add.

Gelis looked at the two of them. Assessing the condition of their depleted bodies and disheveled clothes, she decided the poor bastards would never make it on their own, but what was she to do? She had not enough for herself and the men she served... how could she share the little and feed the whole bunch if she took these two into the fold?

It was at this point that she remembered leaving the meat on the fire and dashed to it, finding most of it done, some of it blackened. Quickly she took the burnt portion, and before she changed her mind, prepared it for the two starvelings, leaving the rest for the men who had provided the hares. She had some grain boiling in water, and added the burnt meat to the weak soup and let it boil a while longer. The resulting soup she then divided amongst herself and the two hapless Scots.

It was not much, but with a couple of oat bannocks she had made, it was enough to lend strength to the failing Cuthbert, who then slept while Gelis and Fergus talked quietly.

He found that she was mean on the English, more even than he was, for it was they who burned her home and drove her and her husband out to flee for their very lives. Grateful she was to King Robert for providing a way for her to heap a measure of revenge where it was due, though it did cost her husband his life. To her mind, he died as revenge dictated.

Across the crowded hillock lay the misery of Robert's army. The peat and wood fires burned and crackled sporadically through the wood. A haze of lingering smoke filled the area and the smell seemed to give a comfort of a home to the freezing men and women as they went about their chores of hut and tent building, be it of peat, cloth, canvas, snow, or boughs from the pine trees. Much of the army, broken into groups or parties, relied on one another to accomplish these tasks of survival. The knights worked alongside their squires, as none who could labor stood idly by to let another take on his share of the work. A protective shed was set up as a stable so the horses could be fed and watered with melted snow.

Some of the men lay deathly sick from flux, and overexposure to the wet and cold. Most knew that nothing could be done for them that had not already been done by their fellow warriors. Medicines were in short supply and the ones they had only occasionally worked well enough to return a fellow to his health. They also knew that their weapons and clothing would be stripped from their bodies when they died, to put a sword or an axe into another's hand and to wrap warmth upon another's body. Nothing was wasted that could be salvaged. That was as it was.

The masons built a shelter of peat for the fletchers who set immediately to producing more arrows. Arrows were always in short supply. They had taken advantage of the smithy at Inverurie to make a great number of metal arrowheads and many as narrow as the diameter of the shaft so they could penetrate chain mail as well as leather armor.

Amidst all such activity, Cuthbert finally awoke, only to find himself hungry still, and to hear Fergus saying to the woman with an innocent smile, "Bein's yer man's... dead...Cuthbert and me... we could be yer man!"

The thirty-year-old woman laughed and as she did, showed spaces left where two missing teeth had once helped to make a beautiful smile. Her hair was falling in tresses around her elfin face, under a rabbit fur hood made the same as her cloak. Fergus' face went cheerless at the sound of her sarcastic laugh.

"Reckon no warm victuals this night," whined Fergus. He looked at Cuthbert and shrugged, knowing they would now have to seek succor elsewhere.

"Wait," said the woman. Cuthbert and Fergus slowly turned to look at Gelis, fully expecting another round of laughter. "Ye two get us some of that peat at the front of the wood and I'll fix some oat bannocks. 'Tis all I have left."

"For us?" asked the surprised Fergus, wary that she was teasing him.

"If ye get back ere night fall!" she said, raising one eyebrow.

"Can ye help?" Fergus asked his friend.

"P'rhaps I can," responded Cuthbert. "I'm feelin' some stronger." Slowly he pushed himself to his feet with the handle of his battleaxe, and stood steadily on his own.

"Ye can, I warrant ye. As me auld mother used to say, 'nothin' beats a try but a failure'!" With that, the two started off down the hill toward the neck of the peninsula, grinning at each other and almost tasting the fresh oat bannocks the woman promised to make them.

As they neared the front of the wood, Cuthbert and Fergus practically ran for the neatly stacked peat. Along the way they had picked up a couple of short staffs to use in bringing back the heavy blocks, and when they reached the first stack, they laid the sturdy poles parallel on the ground. Cuthbert took the snowy top block from the pile and threw it to the ground, then picked up two of the frozen inner blocks that had only a scattering of snow on the edges. Fergus did likewise.

Fergus suddenly screamed in dismay and dropped the squares.

Cuthbert came to his side. Fergus was staring between two stacks of peat blocks with a look of strange terror on his face.

"What's ye got?!"

Fergus pointed downward. There on the ground was a bizarre, almost human head, dark brown as the peat and very distorted, with deep wrinkles.

In the waning daylight, Cuthbert looked, moving closer and closer to the oddity.

"What ye reckon it be?" asked Fergus in a panic, with one hand on his forehead and the other making circular motions in the air, appearing to summons an answer to the mystery from the gods. "A bad sign, it is... Goin' t' die, we are!"

"W-Well...," stuttered Cuthbert, not all that sure of the situation, "Maybe we hain't a'goin'a die ere we get our bannocks."

"What say ye?"

After short cogitation Cuthbert suggested, "I heered my da talk about such of a thing when I were a child. I reckon it might be one of them 'bog folk'."

"Bog folk?" queried Fergus, wrinkling up his nose in revulsion.

"'Boggy men', he called 'em," explained Cuthbert. "They was thrown or fell in the bogs many a year ago and ne'er come out." He poked at the head with one finger. "Some say they have magical powers!"

Fergus absorbed his friend's say, before asking, "*Ye* ken its magic?"

"I ken it's a head from a dead man... or maybe... a woman," replied Cuthbert. "Still, why do they remain whole in the bogs after all those years syne? Why do they not return to the dust they came from?"

"Scary, 'tis. Scary as the thoughts of hell's fire," said Fergus, shivering from the fright as much as the cold. After a bit the two men picked up their blocks of peat, placed them carefully on the two poles, and left the boggy man's head where it laid. As soon as they were out of sight of the peat stacks, their thoughts changed from bog folk to that woman up the hill and the bannock supper she was to fix for them, and their stomachs tightened all the more.

• •

About noon the next day, the wind blew light flurries through the pine trees, singing a low dirge as they swayed back and forth.

"Riders!" warned a picket at the edge of the peninsula fortress.

Sir Neil Campbell came to the side of the picket and stared at the gray-white landscape. "I see naught," he said straining his eyes.

"I don't see 'em, neither, Milord," replied the picket from within his heavily wrapped shoulders, "but a whinny I heard, a'comin' from near the tree line, yonder." He pointed into the gray.

Both men stared in the direction from whence the sound came, and shortly appeared horsed figures emerging out of the snowy mist.

"Warn the others?" asked the picket.

"Nay," replied Neil, "'tis the three we sent to fetch the Lady Christina."

The riders drew closer, and Neil removed his sash and waved it to and fro and shouted to get their attention. Seeing him, the riders nudged their mounts to a faster gait and reached the two quickly.

"Had a hell of a time tryin' to find ye, Sire," said the first rider to reach Campbell.

"Let's hope the Comyns don't have yer luck," replied Neil.

"Where be the king?" demanded a woman's voice from the knot of horses and riders.

"Lady Christina!" greeted Neil, walking toward her.

Christina of Carrick dropped lightly from the saddle of her horse. Her booted feet sank into about eight inches of snow. Heedless, she pulled a bedroll from the neck of the horse as she repeated her request. "Where be the king, Neil?"

"This way, Milady," said Sir Neil, walking out onto the spit of land toward the wooded hillock. Christina followed, letting her less than pleased observations be known as she went. As they strode through the snowdrifts, she looked around at the many people hovering over cooking fires, or shivering in their poor shelters, trying to keep warm with glowing peat and branch fires.

Finally, she asked, "Yer king is deathly sick and ye've fixed yer mind to hole up in this Godforsaken place?"

Sir Neil answered her not, considering the question rhetorical.

Reaching the peat shelter wherein the king laid, Sir Neil graciously pulled back the cloak that covered the opening, allowing her to pass to the inside.

"Good Lord, what a stink!" exclaimed Christina, having made only one step into the hovel. After her eyes adjusted to the darkness, she discerned Robert, lying as if dead on the pallet across the tiny room from her. Andrew struggled to arise from the foot of the bed on which he had been sleeping, but made a poor try of it before falling backward across the feet of his king.

Christina went straight to the boy, removed her fur-lined gloves and put her hand on his forehead. "Ach, fevered," she said. She tried to awaken Andrew to ask about the king, but he wouldn't come to himself. Instead, she turned and put her hand on the king's brow.

"No fever... hain't got the same symptoms, anyhow," she mused. Her entire being was immediately locked onto her medical mission. Her eyes darted around the small room. There, beside the smoldering peat fire set a tiny bottle containing a greenish oil. She picked it up, uncorked it and whiffed the bitter contents.

"Wormwood!" she uttered, wrinkling her nose, "Ye been givin' him wormwood?"

"What say, Milady?" asked Campbell, who had remained at the door.

"Damned wormwood!" she would have screamed had Robert not been so ill.

Neil, retreating helplessly from her verbal assault objected, "'Twas what the midwife said *give* to him!"

"Near killed him, ye have!" she cried. She returned to Robert's bed and put her hand again on his forehead. He was so cool that she took back his covers and laid her ear upon his breast. Almost immediately she showed an expression of relief and stood, covering him up, again.

"He hain't dead, yet," declared Neil in defense of the medicine.

"Hain't dead… but nobody's *saved* him as yet, neither!" She took the bedroll she had brought with her and from its folds, carefully retrieved a small, wooden, hinged box.

"Can ye?"

"Bring me a clean cook pot, water, and rags a'plenty!" she commanded ignoring his question. "And feed this fire!" She pointed at the nearly depleted ashes.

Neil nodded, and stone faced, left to gather the requested items.

"My poor sick Robert, and a sick boy… freezin' men and freezin' women livin' in the open like cattle!" she said sadly of the huddled army outside. "We can ne'er win like this!" She opened her medicine chest.

• •

After fulfilling the requirements of the Lady Christina, Neil Campbell gathered the remaining ten commanding knights in the largest shelter on the peninsula.

"Why are we gathered?" asked David de Murray, wrapped tightly in his cloak.

"To speak quietly of what we may find is inevitable," started Neil.

"What may we find is inevitable?" asked Edward sourly.

"The king's dyin'," replied the Campbell. The others looked at him with various depths of frowns and fear.

"Christina's arrived," said William Wiseman, hopefully. "Air she not helpin'?"

"The Lady Christina will do all in her power to heal the king… but, if she cannot…" he heaved a sigh," …what do we do?" returned Neil, nearly choking on the words.

"I like this naught," said Sir Simon Fraser, his head hunched down in his wolf fur cowl.

"Since he is our friend, as well as our king, we like it naught… and since none of us here has the least notion of goin' on with this war without him… we like it naught…" Neil looked at his companions in the candlelight of the room. "But, if Robert, for whatever reason, is unable to complete the war and remain on the throne, we shall all be hunted down and executed by the English. Without him, Scotland be England's! None of us can claim the throne of Scotland, except possibly ye, Edward!"

"Good God, No!" panicked Edward.

"Then our only other choice is to flee to the Continent. If we can make it to France or Flanders, we might live out our lives comfortably. John de Balliol seems to have done well in his exile, and might offer succor to us as fellow Scots... on the other hand, he might have black enough heart against The Brus to wish us ill." He sighed wistfully and added, "And what will happen to my sweet Mary... and Robert's Elizabeth... and the other women imprisoned for our sakes..."

There was a long silence before the next one spoke.

"Been lost to my flock, I have... I have neglected yer souls for too long. We shall pray to Almighty God that yer 'inevitable' does not happen!" said the determined Bishop Murray. "We're celebratin' mass this afternoon, and ye all must be there!"

"'Tis Sunday?" asked Sir David Barclay raising an eyebrow.

"'Tis Sunday... I declare it... Sunday! As if it had to be Sunday for a man to pray," said Murray with a scowl.

"Still need a plan," insisted Neil, sadly.

"My brother cannot die!" screamed Edward as if his words made it so.

"Yer brother can, and will, same as the rest of us!" interjected Robert Boyd calmly. "But we shall pray that he lives many years more, and in good health!"

"Amen," several of the knights whispered and crossed themselves.

Edward sank to his knees knowing it was true, then muttered, "Ye a dram of spirits in all this Goddamned camp?"

"Not for ye, Sir Edward," said Robert.

Edward put his gloved hands over his face, and as his hood dropped over his head he appeared more like a heap of rags than a man. He was in pure anguish, knowing he needed a drink to face all this, and knowing just as well that Sir Robert was well right to withhold it.

"We shall muse on this," said Gilbert de la Haye, his spirit at low ebb.

The rest mumbled in general agreement. None wanted to realize the potential truth.

John Wallace took the king's tabard off, carefully folded it and laid it on a doss within the shelter. "I can pretend to be our king, but naught more," he wearily said.

"We're havin' mass for the well bein' of the monarch... and for the rest of us... within the hour," said Murray. "In that wee clearin' by the stable shed."

"Aye, so shall it be, Bishop," replied Boyd.

The men filed out of the hut. As Boyd started to leave, he turned to see Edward still seated on the floor, his head buried deep into his clothing.

"Ye can hide for the moment, Edward Brus, but if Robert dies," Boyd paused, "ye will be the *only* man in Scotland who can hold this rebellion together one more day." He stood silent for a full minute staring down at the motionless heap in which he placed such hopeful expectations.

Edward moved not a muscle.

Boyd sadly left the shelter, wanting to scream loudly at the gods of war for leading them into this predicament, and on the other hand, wishing he could plead with the gods of mercy on behalf of the eight hundred.

. .

As evening came on the same day, the army of mostly villeins was still talking about the words of David de Murray, Bishop of Moray, who, with tattered robes over his chain mail jerkin, made his best attempt to solicit the benevolent help of Almighty God. Further, he had asked each Scot listening to search his or her heart, and pray to become a greater warrior for God's work of freeing Scotland from her many enemies, and for the full recovery of their good King Robert.

David de Brechin

DECEMBER 19TH 1307
CASTLE MORTLACH

"What are ye doin' back here?" asked John Comyn as Sir David de Brechin entered through the door to the great hall of Mortlach Castle, snow still covering his heavy surcoat and his boots purely soaked through.

"Have ye not a flagon of ale to present to me ere ye start the inquisition?" said Sir David with a black look.

"Ale!" demanded Lord John to the squire standing near. "Now, I say again... What're ye doin' back here!?"

"'Tis cold, and I need more provisions," replied David doffing his coat and he threw it to the top of a nearby table.

"After all this time, ye have not killed The Brus?" asked John putting his face near to Brechin's.

Brechin backed away from the old earl's hot and fetid breath. "Sire, ye simplify the task! Brus is not to be found. I ken he's gone south 'til spring."

"He's gone for sure, but to Slioch!" retorted Lord John.

"Slioch?" asked Brechin, incredulously. "What's in Slioch? No castle... no town of any size... just farmlands and wilderness!"

"Spies," replied the earl, "spies who tell me The Brus is in Slioch!"

"Yer spies, Milord, have lost their wit from the cold!" said Brechin. He sat backwards on the bench seat, his elbows propped on the table behind, to await his ale.

The earl remained standing over the baron, staring menacingly at him as a sign of domination. The baron turned on the bench and away from the earl, expecting the ale momentarily.

Lord John walked around the end of the table, sat across from him and stared again at Brechin.

"What exactly did yer spy say?" asked Brechin at last realizing he was not going to escape this intimidation.

Lord John reared back on his seat slamming the palms of his hands on the top of the table. "Now that I have yer ears perked…!"

The earl told Sir David about Eustace the turncoat, and how he knew of the Brus army being in Slioch. He told him that the king was deathly ill, and that Eustace had agreed to slit the throat of the king as he lay abed … and that, if the time were ever right for a strike, it would be now.

"And, where is this lad, now?" asked Brechin.

Lord John squinted one eye and with a half smile, pointed downward, indicating the gaol at the bottom of the donjon.

Brechin nodded indicating that he understood, then asked, "Ye turnin' him loose to do this killin'?"

"Fearful of it," said John.

"Fearful?"

"Aye," Lord John continued, "He would know how to kill The Brus, if he were allowed to do as much, said he."

"And this could harm us?" asked Brechin as his ale was set before him.

"He has seen how we are here arrayed," replied the earl. "I know not what he will say or do once he is in the Brus camp. He stands up to torture not at all."

Brechin took a deep draught of his ale, and stared into the cup before saying, "Feed him well and allow him to leave with me in two days time."

"And what will ye do with him?"

"Send him into their camp ere they ken the rest of us are close," returned Brechin with a laugh. "If Brus lies about Slioch near dead… then let this spy's blade find the murderer's throat. Once the head is cut off… the snake will die."

The earl raised one eyebrow in skeptical agreement, then adds, "I would have him dead after he has done our biddin'," he ordered.

"Kill him?"

Lord John did not say yes, but he didn't say no. "I want him not wanderin' about the land, whinin' that I owe him gold... or *nothin'* of that ilk," was all he did say. The baron, being an astute young man, understood.

"The Brus camp at Slioch will be eliminated, Milord... to the last man."

The earl nodded agreement, and for the first time in a long time, felt eased about The Brus.

Brechin again drank deep from his cup. "Have ye any supper for yer champion?" he asked.

Piers Gaveston

December 20th 1307
The Tower

"What you reckon young Edward wants with the two of us this day?" asked Henry de Lacy, Earl of Lincoln.

Aymer de Valence, Earl of Pembroke, who shared the uncomfortable hallway bench with his peer, only grunted. He was thinking of another time not too far past when he waited for this whelp's father at Lanercost Sanctuary, worried that his days were numbered by the fingers on a single hand. "How in hell should I know," he at last answered with a frustrated sigh.

"When he was under my tutelage, I tried to mold him aright," Sir Henry prattled on. "He will need a Keeper of the Realm in his absence… perhaps it will be one of us," he speculated.

Pembroke turned his huge and muscular body, and leaned on the armrest of the bench to show de Lacy his back.

Henry got the message and so cleared his throat, frowned and kept his mouth shut. At last Sir Henry could stand the situation no longer and wanting to draw Pembroke into a conversation to quell his own nervousness, suddenly and awkwardly asked, "Heard you were sirin' a son… with one of your… uh… war wenches."

Aymer grunted and mumbled.

"What say, Sire?" said Lincoln cupping his hand to his ear as his eyebrows raised.

"Said… Girl!" grumbled Pembroke harshly.

"Not a son?"

"Girl… two girls… twins!," reluctantly explained the hefty earl, frowning and fingering the pommel of his dagger.

Lincoln's tongue wagged naught more and remained so for some time.

Between sighs and sniffs and snorts, little else was heard in the corridor, save occasional high notes from Edward on the other side of the hefty oak door separating the two waiting nobles from what sounded like a frolic of madmen.

"What you reckon…" again started de Lacy but was cut short by Pembroke's darting glare.

De Lacy rolled his eyes after his dour companion returned his stare to the door opposite them. He then stood and began to pace apprehensively, waving his hands in a rehearsal of answers to questions that he imagined would be asked.

The door suddenly swung open and the elaborately uniformed servant bowed low. "The King will see you now, Milords."

Sir Henry was anxious for… whatever the king wished to disclose… while Sir Aymer didn't seem to care. He was there only because he had to be; that was obvious.

The two were ushered into a large ornate room with a fairly good-sized stained glass window at one end that allowed the day's light clouds and occasional sunshine to illuminate the whole of the chamber. Three anterooms, a small private dining room, a garderobe, and sleeping quarters opened off the main area.

Standing at center stage was the king, his back to the entering men. They could see only a glorious purple robe, trimmed with gold and ermine, splayed across the floor and swooping up gracefully to the narrow shoulders of the king. He was standing and admiring himself in a looking glass held by two lackeys. The attending tailor fussed over the garment's smallest details, thus pleasing the king and increasing his purse simultaneously.

"Come," said the king as he waved the men deeper into the room, never taking his eyes off his own splendiferous image. Both Pembroke and Lincoln felt awkward coming into the situation, but he was king, and they were his earls, bound to him by troth. They came forward and bowed to the king.

"Greetings, Sire," they said in near unison.

He smiled as he glanced up at their reflections, then looked again at himself in the glass.

"I have made my decision," he announced as he took a quarter turn to the mirror to admire his presence from that angle. "Do you like it?" he asked.

"Your decision... Milord King?" said de Lacy, somewhat puzzled.

"The robe, of course... for my wedding, foolish earl," he replied, tilting his head upward, as the two men were both taller that he.

"I'm sure the French'uns will bow low to the likes of that raiment," spoke Aymer, successfully covering the not so subtle sound of sarcasm in his voice.

"Ah, yes," agreed de Lacy, taking his cue from de Valence and smiling and waving his hands, feigning delight.

"What's your *other* decision, Sire?" asked Aymer, wanting to get down to business and get out. The tower always made him anxious, as he imagined himself being held against his will at the whim of the monarch. He didn't like things that were beyond his control, and he certainly didn't like the new king's appointment of the Earl of Richmond in his former place as Warden of Scotland. *Hell,* he thought, *Richmond has done naught for the submission of Scotland all winter, except lock himself in Bothwell and enjoy my well-stocked larder and my women.*

"Brother Piers!" the king sang out.

The door to the sleeping quarters swung open and in came Sir Piers Gaveston, a smile on his face and that perpetual haughty look about him. His attire was immaculate and would have appeared that he had been dressing from the king's own wardrobe, were it not for the fact that Piers was larger and far more broad shouldered than his lord.

The king kissed the air in Piers' direction. Piers entered as the cock of the hen yard.

"Lord Piers is married to my sister's daughter," Edward said by way of prelude to his telling of the decision.

"So we have heard," replied de Lacy trying to maintain a pleasant smile.

"He is my brother... now," he continued.

Aymer frowned and looked at Piers for any clues to the worth of the king's last statement. None was forthcoming.

Edward went to Piers dragging the heavy train behind, the poor tailor following. The king stood on tiptoes and kissed Piers full upon the lips. Piers remained stoic and regal.

Both earls were a bit embarrassed at the scene. Aymer thought *Fate played a cruel trick in making Edward king, when Piers so suits the part.*

"Tell them now," insisted Piers.

"Yes, yes... I shall," Edward said, shifting moods.

"My Dear Earls," he began with an official sounding voice, "I am off to France for a bride of my own, as you know..." he smiled at Piers, "and it will be your honor to tell the other magnates of this court that Sir Piers Gaveston is hereby appointed Keeper of the Realm in my absence."

Aymer groaned under his breath. Henry was shocked at the news.

Edward giggled unabashedly at the looks on the faces of the two earls. Piers held his arms out to them to accept him. Sir Henry bowed politely and Aymer reluctantly followed.

"On your knees, My Earls," commanded Piers.

Henry and Aymer looked at each other as if a poor joke were being played on them.

"On your knees," childishly coaxed the king, having returned to his mirror.

Sir Henry de Lacy, Earl of Lincoln, fearful of the circumstances, obeyed his king.

Aymer looked down at de Lacy and back at Piers and Edward who had smirks on their faces. His anger smoldered. "We will inform the court, My King," he said through gritted teeth. "Come, Sir Henry... 'tis time to take our leave."

Henry was confused. He started to stand, but looked up at Edward who was certainly looking down at him, and went back to his knee with bowed head.

"All my young life I looked up at you, Lord Lincoln. Now it is your turn to look up at me," cruelly spoke the king.

Henry was dumbstruck. Aymer grabbed him under the arm and lifted him to his feet, and led him solemnly from the apartment. The earls heard gales of laughter as they left.

Unruly brats, Aymer thought as he helped Sir Henry limp wobble-legged down the corridor.

"I hate this tower!" Aymer mumbled under his breath to Henry.

"And I hate that goddamned king and his so-called brother!" said de Lacy angrily as he pulled his arm away from Aymer. He straightened his shoulders and walked more erect than he had for quite a while.

Pembroke smiled and picked up his gait. He had to in order to catch up with the man who had just recovered his dignity.

December 24th 1307
The Brus Camp on the Wooded Hillock in Slioch

"Ye reckon we might get another bannock, this afternoon?" asked Fergus of Cuthbert while the two men gathered pine branches to fortify their existing shelter.

"'Twon't harm nobody to ask," Cuthbert answered.

"'Twon't for sure," grinned Fergus. He gathered the stout branches in a bundle and dragged them off toward the two men's shelter.

Suddenly, another pair of hands seemed to come from nowhere to grab the boughs, nearly pulling Fergus over backward.

Fergus turned, ready to strike, his far hand reaching for the handle of his dagger... until he recognized his laughing annoyer.

"Eustace... from Inverurie!" he exclaimed excitedly. "Look 'Bert, it's Eustace from Inverurie!"

"I see who 'tis," groused Cuthbert, who had lost no love for the man.

"Good of ye to come fight with us," said Fergus, genuinely happy that his one-time companion had followed them into the wilderness. "Ye have a mind for a bannock?" he added.

"God help us," muttered Cuthbert. He thought to himself, *We don't yet have a bannock in hand and Fergus is already sharing it away.* "God help us," he repeated.

• •

Christina had asked for and miraculously gotten two narrow beds placed in the tiny space, real beds, with wooden frames and ropes to hold the mattresses, and thus, Robert and Andrew off the dank earthen floor.

Her primary accomplice in arranging for such things was fourteen-year-old Baldred Airth, a blonde-haired squire belonging to no particular knight since his benefactor, the knight he served, had been killed. Thus, he was free to help any who requested his services. He was hoping to be recognized by a single knight soon, perhaps from the house of Brus, for he was known to be their far distant kin.

With Baldred's assistance, Christina had most nearly brought Andrew's fever down to normal using snow-packed rags, and she had begun giving Robert a new regimen of medicine of her own concoction. She got her first glimmer of hope when Robert, whom she had bathed with clean, warm water and "brought to life" enough to swallow honey and cider vinegar laden medicines, groaned as if having a terrible nightmare.

Christina smiled and softly kissed his hand. "Dear Robert, die not now, for ye have much yet to accomplish!"

Robert, his head on a makeshift pillow, turned toward her as if he had heard her quiet whisper. She hoped it would fall on God's good ear, as well.

. .

As the afternoon waned and the temperature dropped again below freezing, the snow that had melted on top refroze, putting a shiny, treacherous coating of ice across the broad hills and narrow footpaths. Fergus, Cuthbert, and now, Eustace finished gathering their daily portion of the quickly dwindling inventory of harvested peat. Blocks that once were cast off because snow was piled on them, now were retrieved and gladly used.

The three men, laden with peat, traipsed through the wood, their hopes for food depending heavily on Cuthbert's clever negotiating skills.

That morning, scouts Murdoch and MacKie had brought word to the camp that the Comyn-English army was nigh. Thus, as the three worked their way toward Gelis and her cook fire, they passed about a hundred workers building a bulwark in the trees nearest the narrow isthmus to their camp. The hundred were jamming poles solidly into the hastily constructed peat and earthen barricade, the sharpened ends facing out toward the enemy at proper heights to impale approaching horses and riders. The earthwork bristled, a deadly trap.

Farther back from the entrance, and less than a man's waist in height, were immovable fortifications of wattle and daub, lashed sturdily to and among the trees. Because of these, the peat gatherers had to snake through the area, causing them more time and effort on the icy hill.

As the three men finally arrived and stood before Gelis, Cuthbert opened his negotiations. "Ye tradin' bannocks for peat, today?" he asked with a charming smile.

"'Ppears ye've added another mouth to feed," she replied as she casually glanced upward from her seat in front of her cook fire.

"Aye. 'Ppears so," grumbled Cuthbert.

"He be our friend Eustace, from Inverurie," chimed in Fergus.

Cuthbert rolled his eyes upward. The intruder was no friend of his.

"I recollect," said Gelis. Her eyes remained on the bubbling pot. "Set yer peat down yonder," she pointed her wooden spoon toward the base of a nearby tree.

The three men did as they were bade and returned to hunker by the fire, as much for the smell of the pot's contents as to warm themselves. The four chatted intermittently, about matters of no import, until at last Cuthbert said to Gelis, "We got our place fixed."

The woman nodded.

"We fixed it up better so ye'd let us be yer man," blurted Fergus.

Cuthbert grimaced.

Gelis nodded again, with a slight upturn at the corners of her mouth.

"When we be yer man, will ye cook more than a bannock for our supper?" asked the smitten Fergus with a silly grin on his face, his eyes glassy.

"I ne'er said ye could be my man," objected Gelis.

"Nodded, aye... did ye not?" asked the confused Fergus.

"Just to tell ye I understood! That's all!" she quietly demurred. Fergus' expression fell, but she continued as if she had given it no thought before. "O' course, it would make sense in a lot of ways for us to band together." The men said nothing. "'Twould be safer than bein' alone," she said, and the men's faces brightened a bit. "And to keep warm at night, two's better than one... and three's better than two... and four's..."

"Eustace here, don't count," interrupted Cuthbert, frowning.

"Why not?" asked Fergus.

"'Cause he ain't invited to our bailiwick... that's why!" bullied Cuthbert.

"Can he hunt?" interrupted the woman.

"Aye, I can," spoke up Eustace.

"That would be a boon," she made her point. "Three huntin' can feed all better than two."

"True, that is!" Fergus nodded agreement.

"And 'twould be warmer," again suggested Gelis.

Cuthbert fumed, but knew he would be out bargained, with Eustace having hunting skills. He had to come up with something to make it look as if he were the better negotiator. Finally he proposed, "Ye fix us *each* a bannock of our own?"

She shook her head. "Could have, but not knowin' about yer friend, I asked only enough extra rations for ye'uns... On the other hand, I'll portion a bit of this rabbit stew and a wee leg-part or so, to split betwixt the three of ye," she bargained.

Fergus' salivating tongue ran across the hairs of his moustache in anticipation of the meal, while Eustace, having been relatively well fed recently, looked less appreciatively upon the boiling pot of weak, herbless stew.

Gelis said, "Come back directly, when it's done." She stopped and looked at them sternly. "And..." she emphasized.

The three men met her gaze.

"...keepin' warm is one thing...but, there will be no dallyin' under the covers!"

"Aye," they agreed in unison.

"We'll fix a better door to our wee 'keep' and be back to fetch our supper..." replied Cuthbert with another of his charming smiles.

Well past sundown, when the three men strode up, three oatmeal bannocks were set by the fire garnering an added toasting from the flames.

Cuthbert's hungry eyes fairly glowed when he saw them.

The three Scots again hunkered across the fire from Gelis. She looked up to meet only the stare of Eustace. The other two definitely had their eyes on what was most important to them... the food.

"Ye found enough oatmeal, I see," commented Cuthbert, but Gelis again shook her head.

"Two are for ye, the third is for others," she explained.

Cuthbert disappointedly nodded.

"Who?" asked Fergus without thinking.

"None of yer concern," scolded Gelis, "None whatsoe'er!"

Cuthbert took both of the warm round breads and split them into three fairly equal parts as Gelis, true to her promise, portioned out rabbit stew into three cups for the men.

The stew was hot and the men blew across it to cool it off.

"Sink some snow in it, 'Bert," suggested Fergus, settling a lump into his own cup.

Cuthbert nodded, considered the idea, then scooped up a bit of snow and plopped it into his cup.

Eustace, having eaten well with the English before being sent on his murderous mission, thought the stew was swill and practically filled his cup to the brim with snow to dilute its taste.

When they finished, Cuthbert and Fergus hungrily eyed that third bannock. "Nobody's yet come for it..." Cuthbert pointed out.

"They'll be along directly," insisted Gelis.

"Can we ha'e a pinch of it?" asked Fergus.

"Maybe two pinches?" pushed Cuthbert.

"NAY!... no a crumb for the likes of ye!" barked Gelis sharply.

Cuthbert sighed deeply, but he, like Fergus, sat back on his haunches. Eustace was already leaning against the tree where the peat was stacked. The bannock was somewhat agreeable to his taste, but after the snow in his cup melted, his stew was even less savory. Still, it might be all he would have until he returned to the English, so he drank it down, hardly noticing the scraps of meat as they crossed his tongue.

Cuthbert had an idea, and taking a found silver trinket from around his neck and handing it to Gelis, he bartered, "Give ye this for the bannock."

She examined the necklace before holding it around her own neck.

Thinking he had struck a bargain with the cook, Cuthbert reached for the bread, only to have his hand smacked.

"Not for the bannock, do I take this!" the woman said, holding the bauble toward him.

Cuthbert paused. Words failed him. Finally he asked, "If not in trade for the silver, then what? Who air ye savin' it for? "

Fergus excitedly leaned forward to hear.

She leaned in, almost touching the faces of the two men, and whispered, "Puttin' it out for the wee folk, I am."

"Ye mean like, elves … and fairies and such?" asked Fergus, again glassy eyed.

"Aye," said Gelis, "For them what's goin' to save our king and win us this war!"

Eustace perked his ears at any news of the king.

"Elves?" said Cuthbert, disbelieving. "Elves are gettin' our bannock?"

"Aye," said Gelis showing her nearly beautiful smile.

"Ye've a good heart," sighed Fergus in true admiration.

Cuthbert again rolled his eyes and pushed his head deeper into his hat.

Eustace, like the others, still hungry, continued the thought, "Fergus be right, Gelis…Ye've a wonderful good heart… but…"

"But?" asked Gelis, frowning.

"But… the wee folk I learned about at me ma's knee, so wee tiny air they, that this bannock would be too much for the whole of their kind!"

"Aye?" said the woman, suspicious. Eustace nodded. "So ye want me to share it with the lot of ye, instead?" asked Gelis.

"Ah, a few pinches of yer delicious bread hain't a'goin'a change whether them wee folk help us or not!" cajoled Eustace.

Fed up with the whole idea, Cuthbert interjected with sarcasm, "I think it would be a perfect amount for the little folk… maybe, if anything, ye should add a big cup of yer stew to it, and a flagon of wine, too!"

Gelis frowned and replied crossly, "We hain't got any wine! Ye men get to sleep… I'll be along directly… after I do me good deed." With that, she broke off the negotiations and trudged off into the dark with her precious bannock.

It was not long after Gelis returned and went to sleep that Cuthbert's eyes opened. His head was full of his wife, and home, and he had dreamed that they were having supper with his children about. Gathering his wits, he was quick to realize that his arm was clearly around the sleeping Gelis. Though she felt good in his arms, he gently slipped his arm away, and silently left the shelter to take his relief.

Perhaps his exit awoke Eustace, and he lay thinking about how to complete his intended task of murdering the sleeping king. He had earlier spotted the shelter that he was certain held the ailing king, but he would have to approach carefully since people were often moving in and out. *Perhaps not so at this hour*, he thought, and checking to make sure he had his knife, he pushed back the covers and slipped out into the night.

Returning toward the hut, Cuthbert glimpsed the tall figure leaving it. Nothing but a shadow, the departing specter crept quickly away, making no sound as he softly moved among the barren trees. After checking to see if all was well in the hut, Cuthbert followed the path taken by Eustace, a dark presence moving against the trampled snow.

Unaware that he was being followed, Eustace, his head filled with thoughts of gold, made his way toward the hut where King Robert lay. Within ten yards of the hut, he slid his blade from its sheath, an act witnessed by Cuthbert.

When Eustace drew closer to the king's sanctuary, Cuthbert became convinced that his distrust of the newcomer was well placed, and moved quickly to head him off.

"Out for a piss?" he asked in an unrestrained voice.

Eustace spun around, holding his blade hand alongside his leg. "Just... uh, aye, I am!"

Cuthbert nodded and grabbed Eustace's wooly collar, pulling the suspected assassin to his face. "A ways from yer pissin' ground, are ye not?" asked Cuthbert.

"Got turned 'round in the wood..." explained Eustace. He thought of bringing his knife up and laying the Scot's throat open with a quick slash, but if he failed to kill him quickly, there would be no escape; his plan would be foiled, and he would be summarily killed.

"Which way back to our 'keep'?" he smiled, using Cuthbert's word for their shelter to put the other man at his ease. Cuthbert merely pointed, and waited for Eustace to head back to their shelter, then followed.

After Eustace retired to sleep, Cuthbert remained awake to watch. He had no proof of what he thought the man was about to do. Even Eustace's knife was somehow back in its sheath, but he trusted him not at all.

As the night passed slowly, Cuthbert nodded off and picked up a snippet of his previous dream: the eating. In the midst of his somnian feasting he made himself awaken. His belly was aching from hunger. Shaking his head to clear it, he got to his feet and went searching, hither and thither in the direction Gelis had gone, until he found her offering to the little people. Having been left by the rill upon a small altar Gelis had made of stones, it was frozen.

He quickly pocketed the bread and climbed the icy hill toward the watch fires. He laid the bannock atop a warm stone at the edge of a fire until the bread was almost warm again. Then he picked it up, and pushing the oat bannock into his mouth in ravenous bites, chuckled to himself, *I bet Eustace figured to beat me to this feast!*

Thinking he had outwitted Eustace twice somehow made the stolen bread even tastier. In no time he had chewed and swallowed every last crumb, and had not felt more sated since leaving Inverurie.

Early next morning, Gelis was certain all was aright with the world. It was obvious to her that the wee ones had had the time of their lives eating her food; they had left not the tiniest ort in spite of what Eustace had said. It was going to be a fine day!

Her euphoria was suddenly shattered when the whole of the hillock seemed to erupt in screams of fear, in shouts and blowing horns, and warriors hastily pulling their kits and weapons together to meet the enemy down the hill. Most quickly mustered at the "entrance" to the wooded area, as that was the likely approach for any attack.

Archers crouched behind the earthworks and other fortifications, the horseless knights and foot soldiers behind them serving as a second line of defense. Others rushed to their preassigned posts at the edges of the peninsula where it met the large bog.

But all grew quiet, again. A light cold breeze rustled softly through the thick evergreen trees. Being a winter day, the cold clear sky lent but faint grayish light. The army of Brus held every weapon at the ready, every muscle taut, knowing the enemy was just beyond the wood line, ready to strike.

Suddenly a scream arose from one of the front ranks. Then ten agonizing screams, then twenty, and more.

Neil Campbell, forward with the archers, could be heard shouting.

Robert Boyd stood with the second line forces a mere forty yards back and was hearing nothing but screams of pain and Neil's encouragements to his troops coming from the front line.

"My God!" said Boyd, his heart suddenly pumping faster. "The bastards are overrunnin' the barricade!" Then, his sword and shield held in expectation of imminent attack, he shouted loudly, "Stand ready, lads! Keep a sharp eye!"

Neil, lying against the foremost of the earthworks, heard Boyd's charge to his troops. "Damn it to the gates of hell," he swore. He turned and grabbed the arm of the man next to him, pointing and saying quietly, "Make yer way to Sir Robert Boyd, up yonder, and tell him what's happenin' here!"

"Aye," replied the soldier, and he scampered from tree to tree up the hill, once sliding down the ice and having to re-climb the same incline. Several times he barely missed being hit by enemy arrows, but his dash to report to Boyd was successful.

"Sire, I'm to tell ye that the yellin' is to make them bastards think we're bein' struck mor'n we be!" he said. "Their shafts are mostly landin' in the trees, but they don't know it. It's a trick that Murdoch thought up to keep 'em aimin' too high!"

"Damn good trick it is, too!" said Boyd, relieved. "Ye had me convinced!" He breathed a deep breath and said, "Get back to yer feignin', Lad."

"Aye, Sire," the messenger grinned and bounded back the way he had come.

Lord John Mowbray, meanwhile, having watched as his archers sent flight after flight of missiles in the direction of the hill, was grown certain that the hundreds of arrows had softened up The Brus' vanguard defenses. Mounting his own fine warhorse, he ordered his horsed knights, both Scots and English, to storm the bastion in the wood.

"Ye sure ye've got them pummeled?" cautioned Sir David de Brechin.

"Just listen, ye fool!" expressed Mowbray, pointing at his ear. "Listen to them moanin'...can't yer years tell ye that the time is ripe?" He gathered the reins and took up his shield.

"Hain't seen no blood, no bodies," gainsaid Brechin.

Mowbray snarled and drew his sword. "Stand ye aside, Coward! This rebellion will be routed within the hour!" With that, he kicked his horse's flanks and started toward the hill.

Brechin's eyes narrowed and his nostrils flared at the slander, but he backed his mount to allow the other knights to pass by him. As they trotted away, he thought, *My revenge will soon be dealt ye, John Mowbray, by them that follow The Brus.*

"Here they come!" shouted Sir Neil. His archers sat up, stopped their screaming and nocked arrows into their bowstrings. All were ready as they listened to the thunderous roar of mounted knights charging full speed across the frozen ground at them, John Mowbray in the lead. The Comyn-English knights could ride only three or four abreast along the entrance road, but were multiple rows deep behind the leaders. After them ran unmounted knights and foot soldiers by the score.

Even while the enemy approached at the gallop, several squires moved swiftly across the ground behind the Campbell and his archers, collecting English arrows for returning to them that sent them.

"Hold, lads!" commanded Neil to the archers. He wanted the sharpened poles at the front of the barricades to first take their toll.

Still running full tilt, Mowbray's knights traversed the narrow isthmus and crashed through the edge of the wood, spreading out to dominate the wider and higher areas as they entered the pines. Mowbray reined in his mount and allowed the lesser knights to pass into the tree line ahead of him.

Hearing their onslaught, Neil smiled, knowing that his ruse was working.

There suddenly was a terrible cacophony of men screaming and of flesh and armor colliding with the vicious bristling "hedgehogs" as horses and knights reached a mere twenty yards into the wood. Those behind the first wave had no knowledge of what had occurred. They knew only shouting, cheering, and screaming of animals and men. Trained to charge regardless of what happened to the ranks before them, they did so, and many of them and their horses also ran into the cruel spears. Some hung there, helplessly impaled.

Those who could, limped or crawled away, but few made it past the outer perimeter of the tree line. Seeing the devastation wrought by the trap, some in subsequent waves were able to avoid the remaining deadly points, while others wheeled their mounts in retreat, charging back through the oncoming unmounted troops.

Seeing that the poles were no longer effective, Neil ordered his archers to loose their arrows into the fleeing troops. The first flight was most efficient, striking many men and horses, but the gap for arrow range grew greater by the second, and succeeding flights were less deadly.

"After them, Lads!" shouted Neil rushing from behind the barricade, his sword pointing the way to his troops. Out came their swords and daggers, and they went screaming through the trees in pursuit of the fleeing enemy. English and Comyn wounded, many having made it to the edge of the wood with their lives, quickly lost them to the swift blades of the Brus Scots.

When Sir Neil and his crew took after Mowbray's, Robert Boyd and Gilbert de la Haye moved their forces downhill to the row of stationary mantlets.

The Campbell stopped with his men at the border of the protective trees and looked at Sir John Mowbray astride his destrier, shaking fist in the air and slinging curses into the deadly woods of the hillock. Then he saw the English archers with their Welsh long bows line up across the way.

He immediately ordered a retreat. Running helter-skelter through the protective pines, the Brus Scots heard a volley of arrows crackling through the branches. At least five of Campbell's men were felled before they were able to get to the safety of the barricades, but two made it back in spite of their wounds.

Lord John arrived in his own camp livid at his grand and failed first blow to rid Scotland of its most evil scourge, Robert de Brus.

David Brechin, still stinging from the slur upon his name, noticed Mowbray's horse favoring his hindquarters and rode to the side of the baron.

"The Brus bloodied yer stallion?" he asked.

"What say?" growled Mowbray. "This hain't a time for jest!"

"Yer horse is limpin,' Sire. 'Tis no jest."

Brechin reached to the rump of Lord John's destrier and with a swift jerk, pulled an arrow from the animal's hip. The mount reared and writhed in pain, nearly casting its rider to the ground. Brechin examined the arrow and handed it to the still fuming baron. "'Ppears to be one of ours," he said, delighting in his subtle retaliation. That the arrow was one of their own, retrieved and shot back at Mowbray as he was retreating, was not lost by either noble.

Mowbray jerked the reins, and forcing his wounded horse to the fore of his troops, again screamed curses into the wood, finishing his diatribe with, "The hour may be yers... but this day hain't yet done!"

The Brus Scots laid out a barrage of jeers that could be heard loudly into the Comyn camp.

Haye and Boyd, watching the whole event play out from their position up the hill, knew that Mowbray's army would pay heavily if he tried directly attacking their "citadel" again.

"Reckon we ought to go out after them?" asked Sir Gilbert, always one to want to settle matters sooner, rather than later.

"Let 'em bubble in their own juice," answered Sir Robert. "Let's see how badly they want to get us off this land."

"Our victuals are near gone; they'll just starve us off," said Gilbert.

"Not so long as we can eat horses, they'll not," said Boyd, pointing to the dead and dying mounts of the English knights.

He called several men to him and said, "Get their dead laid out and stripped of their worth, and tie them to the tree trunks at the front. Give 'em new targets for their longbows," instructed Boyd. "And take as many of our stout lads as ye need to get those dead horses to the cooks... Good eatin' we'll have tonight!" he added with a smile of pure satisfaction.

"Aye," said the knight closest to him, "we'll need the archers to give us cover, Sire."

"And take yer shields. Have one carry and protect another," suggested Boyd.

The men did as they were bade, scavenging armor, weapons, and everything else of value on the dead English, which left the bodies more or less bare. They were then strung up in full view of their living comrades, striking anger and fear into each of the Comyn and English soldiers who saw or heard of the barbaric act. Boyd knew that it would. He was hoping that, as a result, the Mowbray led forces would be prone to making more mistakes, acting from anger rather than training, fear rather than logic.

Indeed, there were many among them who surmised that if the Brus rabble could do that to such experienced mounted knights... then their magic must be truly extraordinary.

Mowbray retired to his tent to sulk.

. .

Murdoch and MacKie, wrapped from head to toe in white, long-haired goat skins to blend in with the snowy landscape, took leave of their companions, and with packed quivers, set out for the edge of the wood to stand duty as pickets. There, unlike the other sentries, they could hide in all but plain sight and observe the goings and comings of the enemy.

After watching the opposite contingent for nearly half the remaining daylight hours, the brothers were finding it difficult to keep aware. The younger of the two began to drift in his purpose, and quietly asked Murdoch a hypothetical question.

"Reckon we could pick off a couple of them longbowmen from here?"

"Maybe... but we'd have to shoot at the same time," answered his brother, and so they determined to try out their theory.

Upon Murdoch's signal, the two expert marksmen emerged from behind two trees, and between them, put eight arrows into the air before the first ones hit their targets. All the victims fell within seconds of each other, sending the rest of the men at the front of the Comyn camp scrambling well back into their own tree line. Downed first were the nearest two Welsh archers, followed by three wounded with two more killed.

"Only one chance to do that," said Murdoch. "They'll be more careful after this." They were well pleased with the havoc they had caused with but eight well-placed arrows, and mused on the possibilities.

"If we had a couple of them longbows like them fellows use... we could throw arrows anyplace in their camp," MacKie said admiringly.

"Aye," agreed Murdoch. After a thoughtful moment he added, "By tomorrow's cock crow, Milad... we'll have ones of our own!"

MacKie raised his eyebrows and smiled.

Much of the early afternoon was spent repairing defenses at the entrance of the Brus camp, while the opposing bowmen lobbed shots as opportunity dictated.

In the Comyn-English camp, Mowbray continued his sulk sitting in his tent, eating and drinking away the short daylight hours in irate disgust.

Brechin, in the meantime, organized Mowbray's army to the best defense of their position, and placed pickets and formed up the longbowmen to fasten Robert's army to the peninsula, knowing they had no way out except into his waiting hands. Under his command, there would be no seven hundred angry Scots charging across that narrow land-bridge, while his far *more* than seven hundred lay about taking a leisurely stew for a last meal.

The peninsula "fortress" was clearly under siege.

. .

Robert's eyes blinked.

Christina sat on the edge of his bed, staring at his handsome face and wondering what would be the next course of action to rid her kinsman and one time lover of this affliction that had taken him so near death.

"Elizabeth?" he hoarsely whispered, "Elizabeth?" his voice trailed off as he desperately tried to focus his bleary eyes.

"Aye, Dear Rob," she said, having no need to correct his mistake at that moment.

"Standin' tall in the heather, ye are…" he mumbled almost inaudibly, his unseeing eyes gleaming with his love for her.

"Aye, My Sweet, waitin' for ye, I am," she replied softly. He sank back into the deep sleep that held him captive, and tears welled in her eyes. "Oh, Robbie, that I were yer good Elizabeth," she whispered, "Aye, that I were."

"Say ye?" mumbled another soft voice nearby.

"Naught save prayers, Andrew," she said quietly to the boy as he raised himself from his bed on one elbow.

"Need prayers, we do." he replied, weakly.

"Glad ye're feelin' a mite better."

"'Tis but a wee mite, Milady," returned Andrew, laying back.

"Ye hungry?" she asked.

"Could eat a horse!" said Andrew with a wan smile.

"And that's what ye'll have this day… so I've heard," she said. She went to his side and straightened the lad's ragged covers to better serve his needs. Her own son, Robert's son, was only five years Andrew's junior, and she thought the two were not unalike in many ways. She remembered seeing Andrew in the hills of Carrick with Robert earlier in the year. He had such a cheerful way about him, and his now pallid cheeks were then rose colored from the sun and wind.

It occurred to her that the lad had aged a great deal in the months since. *Both of ye have paid heavily for this war,* she thought, glancing back at her king.

"Ready to break yer fast, Milady?" asked Baldred with a smile as he pushed the cloak to the side of the doorway and entered.

"Aye, and there's a young man here'bouts, says he can eat a horse!" replied Christina.

"Then, horse it will be, Milady," said Baldred with a wink.

Christina smiled at the lad and waved her hand for him to go and fetch the food, saying, "Same for me, as well."

. .

Though MacKie had reservations about doing so, Murdoch invited

Mute to accompany them on their raid into the English camp. The youth was about the only marksman in his ken that Murdoch admired more than any other, save his brother, and being so young, the lad could one day even surpass himself... perhaps.

Presented with the offer to acquire his own longbow, Mute agreed with a single nod.

As planned, they would make their way into the enemy's wood and wait for an opportune moment, with Murdoch being the first to deliberately chance being sighted. If he were seen, he would run and lead the pursuers away from the other two, who were to use the uproar to escape to the Brus camp. If the enemy failed to see him, he would return to the darkness with his plunder and Mute would try next, with the same stipulation. MacKie would go last.

They managed to find another goatskin cloak to cover the additional member of their party, and after dark, the three slithered the length of the ice covered isthmus on their bellies, slowly, so as not to catch the eye of any pickets from the English camp.

Reaching the tree line beyond which the Comyn troops were bivouacked, they silently made their way through the snowy forest toward the area where the mostly Welsh archers were settled with their longbows. Their fires lit well the inner camp and left the outer perimeter relatively dark, while the frozen snow allowed the reivers plenty of reflected light, even in places the fires' glow failed to reach.

Slowly they crept, each choosing his own route, none making a sound, silent as shadows until they were so close that they could hear the soldiers breathing in the cold night air. There they stayed, awaiting an opportunity to make their move, until the men drifted off to sleep and the fires burned low. It was then, while the bowmen's snoring helped muffle their movement, that the three sneak thieves acted on their plan.

Murdoch first moved into the light, slipping around a tree and up to a bow and full quiver laid beside a giant of a man, sound asleep neath a low shelter he had constructed facing the fire.

MacKie, watching his brother simply walk up and take the weapons and melt back into the trees, cursed to himself. *If I had known 'twould be so easy, I would have become a thief at an earlier age!*

Just as agreed, Mute next appeared, at another campfire close by, where were several bowmen huddled together in the open, sharing covers and body heat. Bent low and moving soundlessly, the second reiver slowly and carefully picked up three bows longer than he was tall, and returned to his hiding place.

Murdoch had stood and placed an arrow in his newly acquired bow, just in case there was trouble, but Mute proved to be a deft nimmer. As he and the bows disappeared into the wood, Murdoch realized he had held his breath almost the whole time Mute had been in the open.

Then it was MacKie's time to act.

Mute placed an arrow from his quiver onto the string of one of the stolen bows and pulled back, but found the full strength of his arm barely budged it. Surprised, he set the longbow with the others and pulled his own bow round from where he had carried it on his back. He, too, was ready if MacKie were seen.

MacKie, dagger in hand, stepped carefully into the clearing and quickly scanned the site for easily purloined longbows, but found unhappily that the sleepers closest to him were guarding their weapons very closely, their fingers wrapped tightly around the long, yew wood curves. Treading carefully among the sleeping archers, MacKie kept low and wary. Spying a tree with numerous unstrung bows leaning against its trunk, he started toward it, not realizing that he was being watched from that very quarter.

As he stepped up to the tree, his eyes glancing from bow to bow, he reached to take the finest of the lot when he felt a great tug at his leg. Glancing down he saw a grinning visage looking up at him, its huge hand clamped firmly around his ankle!

Without even thinking, MacKie struck at the fellow's throat with his dagger as he would have a wolf's, causing the grin to be replaced by a look of shock and panic. The hand fell from MacKie's ankle and went immediately to the man's throat, there to try and stop the blood gushing forth from the wound.

MacKie lost not a flicker of movement before he had swept up an armful of the light weapons and started across the open area in the direction of the Brus camp, leaving the dying, bloody Welshman struggling to get up. That hapless lump made it only to his knees before his heart failed and his body pitched forward, but it was enough. His falling woke others nearby from their slumber, and the sight of crimson oozing through the snow on which he lay brought them to their feet and their tongues to action. Shouts went up from all corners of the field, and MacKie was seen dashing into the trees.

Weapons came to hand quickly and a dozen men went after him, followed by a half-dozen more. They had caught only another glimpse of him when the foremost pursuer crumpled onto the snow, an arrow through his heart. Another two fell in short order, one after the other, and the pace of the Comyn jackals slowed markedly while the Brus hare crashed on through the wood and out the other side, sprinting by the English sentries in his white goat-skin, hollering loudly to hail his fellows across the barricade.

Startled at his coming from behind, the pickets could not make out whether he was a man or an apparition, and thus acted against him not at all. Having been alerted, however, they were ready when their own men came tumbling noisily out of the wood, almost to be impaled on the sentries' pikes.

By then, MacKie was safely catching his breath among the trees on the hillock and out of reach, but Murdoch and Mute were still within the domain of the Comyns and their English henchmen. In the dark snowy wood, in their pale garb, they had thus far escaped detection. Each knew the other was yet in peril, for each knew he had killed only one of the last two felled chasing MacKie.

The older man stood stock-still and listened to the chaos around him. It seemed there were soldiers running everywhere in the wood, looking for other possible interlopers, and it would only be moments before they spied him, or Mute.

Damn! he thought. *Mute! Just a boy, and no doubt afeard out of his wits! Poor dumb child won't stand a chance!*

Murdoch tried to judge where the searchers were from the sound of the ice being broken beneath their feet. His instincts told him they were too near to remain where he was, and so he started forth, only to find himself facing the huge man whose bow he now held. Murdoch started to raise the bow, but the man crossed the space between them in a single step, smacking the arrow away before it could be loosed. His great hands then went up to Murdoch's throat and started squeezing until the air in Murdoch's lungs burned to get out and the world started falling gently away.

Suddenly, the hands stopped choking him and Murdoch fell to all fours. When his eyes would again focus, he realized he was splattered in large quantities of sticky red blood. *My God!* he thought. *I must be all but dead!*

Gasping for air, he waited to die, only to have something hit him on the shoulder. Beside him stood the feet of Mute. Lifting his head, he saw the body of the huge Welshman prone behind his rescuer. The man's throat was a scarlet gash all the way across; his was the blood on Murdoch.

Mute struck him on the shoulder again, and motioned for him to stand and follow. His wits not quite functioning, Murdoch did as the young archer urged, and both started wending their way out of the Comyn wood. As his faculties returned, Murdoch used the power of the hard-won spoils he carried to place a few arrows well within the camp they just left and dropped three men, causing others to dampen their campfires and scramble for cover.

He and Mute then drew near to the bog and began to pick off the sentries that stood between them and their own camp. Within minutes, there were no guards visible, and the two Scots had nearly unopposed exit from the wood, though they had no reason to feel secure. An arrow flew between them before they reached their haven across the isthmus.

• •

Sometime during the night it again started to snow heavily, making it almost impossible to see from one camp to the other, and it showed no sign of stopping as the sun brought its pale illumination to the scene.

For the Brus followers, there was again plenty of horsemeat to eat. No matter how the welcome addition to the hungry army's menu was prepared, or even eaten raw, the heavy meat had been a godsend. Generally, there was next to no food available on the land occupied by the Brus Scots, and the only other food they had was what they had foraged on the way. Thus the slaughtered destriers were like manna, given by providence, albeit via a bloody battle. Even though rationed, the meat would not last long, but, if worse came to worse, they could slaughter and eat their own mounts.

For the moment, the three remaining dogs in camp went about their business, unaware of their good fortune.

The sun had not been up for more than an hour before Robert Boyd heard of the brazen midnight raid on the enemy by his best archers. He immediately summoned the three longbow thieves to his hut for an interrogation concerning their night's work. Though he secretly admired their courage and their good fortune, he was not pleased.

When they arrived, he motioned for them to sit or hunker down since the ceiling of his shelter was so low. Even so, there was hardly enough room for the four of them to be inside the structure.

Boyd looked at the three stalwarts before he cleared his throat and asked Murdoch, "Ye runnin' this army, now?"

"Beg pardon, Sire?" replied Murdoch with brows raised in surprise.

"Ye went o'er yonder last night, to pick yer own fight, did ye not?" pushed Boyd, frowning.

Murdoch scratched his beard before answering. He knew that Boyd was angry at them, but not why. "We worried 'em some," he finally answered. "Hain't that what we be here to do?"

"Ye do not go off on yer own and do *anythin'* without bein' told to! Ken!?"

"Hain't we here to kill them bastards afore they kill us, Sir Robert?" asked Murdoch. He was earnestly not aware that he had done anything wrong.

"Ye hain't to leave our camp or start a fight, 'less I, or another of the knights here'bouts, says to," commanded Sir Robert. "Do ye understand what I'm tellin' ye?"

"As ye say," answered Murdoch, though he still did not understand the problem.

Boyd was satisfied that he would obey, nevertheless, and decided not to belabor the situation. "This one of the longbows ye captured?"

he asked Murdoch and pointed to the bow slung across the man's back. MacKie sat almost vapidly; he hated being chastised. Mute watched, uncharacteristically, and was interested in everything that was said.

"Aye, 'tis," replied Murdoch, handing the bow to Sir Robert. Robert hefted the bow and was amazed at the slight weight and the balance of the weapon. He grasped it in his extended left hand, and with his right, pulled the string back to his cheek as if he were preparing to shoot. He then relaxed it without letting it loose, and repeated the action. "Seems more than twice as strong as our shorter bows," he surmised.

"'Bout right," agreed Murdoch, smiling. "Arrow'll go right through good armor!"

Boyd handed the bow back to his foremost archer. "Ye kill some last night?"

"Aye, a heap," said Murdoch.

"Ye fixed for another go at it?" asked Boyd.

"Back across the peat, ye mean?" he answered with a question for the sake of clarity.

"Aye," said Boyd, "Make a wide berth...Get behind them in the wood, stir 'em to keep 'em unsettled. Take some twenty or so of yer archers."

Murdoch and MacKie smiled. Mute, as usual, showed no emotion.

"They might be lookin' out for the likes of us comin' again, tonight," said MacKie.

"Or, they might reckon ye're not fools enough to go at 'em again," replied Sir Robert.

Murdoch raised his brows, not knowing the answer.

"I'll lead a bunch of foot to jump them from this side, so don't shoot none of us," forewarned Boyd.

"Their trees are same as ours, Sire," said Murdoch, "Can't shoot too much for hittin' one... lots to hide behind."

"I want them to be kept uneasy... 'Tis all," he returned. "We can..." his say was suddenly broken by a scream of pain relatively close by.

Three of the four pulled their blades and went outside. The air was thick with snow.

"O'er here!" cried a voice out of the paleness.

Boyd got there first and dropped to one knee beside the man who laid dying, bleeding and bubbling through the wound from an arrow fully through his chest. Others came to the knot of warriors, only to be rebuffed by Sir Robert.

"Stay back!" he shouted. "Ganged together we be easy kills!" As if to punctuate his statement, an arrow plowed into the ground near the wounded man. Murdoch spun quickly around and placed three arrows in the direction from which the spent arrow came, to be rewarded by a cry of pain.

The men spread out instantly, both to avoid becoming targets and to search for other bowmen.

"What is afoot!?" shouted Sir Gilbert from his common hut with the other lieutenant knights.

"Hidin' in the snow... English longbows!" replied Boyd. He held the hand of his wounded soldier until he died, then laid it reverently across the man's chest before standing. Throwing back his hood, he cocked his head and held his hand aloft to signal silence to the others.

Another scream came to his ear from the left and a muffled cry for help from the right, but more distant. Like veils or sheer curtains hung all around, the snow made him all but blind and nearly deaf. How could he defend against what he could neither see nor hear?

He lithely stepped behind a tree as he heard a sudden commotion grow nearer in the wood. After crossing himself, he stood with his sword at the ready as the sound came closer, and jumped out from behind the tree when he thought the time was right. He recognized the man and yelled to the others, "He's ours!"

"They're ev'rywhere, Sire," said the man through great gasps of air.

"They get to our horses?" asked Boyd.

"I ken not..." was all that came from the man's mouth. Boyd heard the distinctive swish and impact of an arrow, and the man he was talking to suddenly arched his back and attempted to reach for the barb that pierced him, but it was too late. He fell dead, and Boyd saw that there was a second arrow lower down in the fellow's back. He had carried it with him as he made his way to warn the others in the camp.

"We'll get the bastards if we have to go after them, tree by tree!" he promised the brave messenger. He remembered Murdoch's comment that a longbow could put an arrow through "good armor," and here he stood in no armor at all. "Use yer shields!" he hollered to his command.

Sir Gilbert and the young knights hastily suited themselves in mail and chest armor, those that had it, and grabbed their weapons and shields before storming out of their shelter.

"Reckon we ga'e them the notion?" asked MacKie as he and his brother set out into the whiteness.

"I reckon," agreed Murdoch.

Suddenly, all turned to face a terrifying war whoop from within the camp, and were greatly relieved that it came from Sir Simon Fraser. He wanted all to know that he came to fight, and his brother Alexander so close to him that he risked being hit by Simon's bearded battleaxe. Boyd ordered them to move out through the trees, which they did, though greatly cumbered by snow.

Approaching Gilbert de la Haye, Sir Robert commanded urgently, "Ye and ten protect the King!"

"Aye," agreed Sir Gilbert, and set off at a run to rally ten or so stout warriors and surround the hut wherein laid Robert, some two hundred feet away.

Bishop Murray strode fearlessly into the clearing and knelt to give the last rites to the fallen men, ignoring the snipers' arrows that still thudded into tree or ground occasionally.

Seeing John Wallace setting out with his arms, Boyd told him to go back to his hut and put on the king's tabard and arms, and return to him. Wallace trotted off to obey, passing William Wiseman and David Barclay. Boyd sent them off to check the perimeter at the bog's edge.

Boyd was doing all he knew to protect the encampment from the infiltrators, but wished Robert were able to do so in his stead.

Shortly Wallace returned in the king's garb and asked Boyd what were his instructions.

Sir Robert shook his snow-covered head. "Snow's too thick to see much of anythin', but we've got to find out how badly we're damaged," said Boyd. "Where's Edward?"

"Dossing down," replied Wallace.

"Damn that useless brat! *He* should be here in his brother's place, not me! *He* should be!" Boyd looked at Wallace and angrily repeated again, "*He* should be!"

Wallace said nothing.

The brash young Cameron joined them, but before he could say anything, Boyd sent him off, saying, "Round up a bunch that might have shields and put a guard at the horse shed... stay to the inside walls so they can't see ye!"

Sir Ian nodded and ran to carry out his orders.

Out among the trees an English bowman saw a large man with the arms of the great Robert the Brus and a commanding knight giving orders to a young one. Swift and quiet, he nocked an arrow and drew it back carefully, for he was sure he would not have another such chance to kill the Scottish king.

As the string touched his cheek something struck him hard in the side, causing him to turn as he released the arrow, and suddenly he could not maintain his stance. His legs no longer able to hold him up, he fell, and lying in the cold snow he looked up into the face of Murdoch, an archer like himself.

Two young squires brought the shields of the king and Sir Robert Boyd. The two Scottish nobles placed their helms securely on their heads, and swords and shields in hand, started off at twice a sword's length apart, moving into the unknown wood to bring order to the chaos about them.

As they walked, they passed a number of dead and wounded Scots, but there were living men among them, too. Afraid and unable to see through the curtain of snow, they awaited someone who could tell them what to do, but they did not expect to see the king.

When they recognized the king's arms, and saw the king and one solitary knight moving bravely forward into the unknown, their courage returned. By ones and twos, Scots rose up out of the snow, and taking up their pikes and their axes, their swords and their flails, fell into line beside their king. Soon, there were dozens of them spread out across the small area of land, and steadily walking in harm's way.

Wallace played the part of the king as he thought the king himself would play it, and when an arrow glanced off his helm, he flinched, but caught sight of the archer who shot it. With a war whoop that he hoped would rival the king's very own, Wallace charged directly at the bowman, who leapt up and fled before the Scottish king.

More rallied to the king, and the sweep for the enemy grew constantly wider.

Killing arrows seemed to pour indiscriminately from the whiteness, and the Scots kept their shields high. As they came upon an enemy, someone would quickly dispatch him with a thrown battleaxe, a dagger... or a stone, if that's what was handy. It was not long before there were few invaders willing to wait until the army of Brus found them. Most had run away, and could be heard fleeing across the frozen bog.

"So that's how they got past our pickets," said Boyd, looking out across the snow covered marsh. "'Tis frozen solid enough to cross it. We'll have to put pickets all 'round the hill to keep this from happenin' again."

"'Twill take about e'ery man, woman, and boy to do that proper," said Wallace as he removed his helm and wiped the sweat from his brow.

One English archer, having fled across the ice, looked back at the place he had just left and saw two pale figures standing in the snow. The tall one took off his helm and raised his arm to his head, and as he did so, the bowman pulled an arrow from his quiver and placed it against the string on his longbow. In but a second the fellow drew back the string and released it to propel the arrow through the cold air. The taller man abruptly reeled and cried out, grabbing his left shoulder with his right hand.

The Englishman smiled in satisfaction and continued on his way.

• •

Christina and a much-improved Andrew were talking quietly. He was telling her how the king would have taken back the camp, if he were well enough and in his wit. It was not that he disagreed with how Sir Robert Boyd commanded it done, but he had a definite vision of how King Robert would have seized the day and swept the foreigners from Slioch.

Hearing their quiet voices, King Robert was again aroused from his sleep.

"Christina?" he asked, slurring his words, "That ye?"

"Aye, Dear Rob, 'tis."

"Elizabeth… I thought I saw her… ?" he said groggily.

"No, Rob. She ne'er was here," said Christina trying to get him to come to reality, though it broke her heart to tell him so.

Robert turned his head, shakily raised his weakened arms and put the palms of his hands over his face.

"My King," started Christina, "We are in the most dangerous of circumstances."

Robert blinkèd and looked around the hut. He recognized young Andrew and smiled faintly as the boy waved to him, then closed his eyes.

"Cold," he said, trying pitifully to pull up the covers.

"'Tis," agreed Christina, and she brought the blankets up to his chin. She ran her long fingers through his hair and studied his face as he drifted in and out of consciousness.

Watching his king's battle to live brought tears tumbling down Andrew's cheeks. For the first time, he realized his lord's tenuous condition. As long as the king was peacefully asleep, the boy was childishly hopeful that The Brus would arise at any moment and resume his life in full fitness. Now it hit him that, at best, Robert would have a difficult and dangerous journey back from the brink of death.

The king remained semi-conscious for about half an hour, just long enough for Christina to get more medicine into him and feed him a clear broth that she had prepared daily, waiting for the opportunity. Then he fell back into his deep slumber.

"He goin' to live?" asked Andrew, who had finally gotten the maturity to see that his liege lord and good friend might be mortal after all.

"Aye," returned Christina, soberly. "He must!" She washed his face with a warm cloth, and adjusted his coverings to make his deep sleep more comfortable.

"Poke up the fire, Lad," she said, preparing for another all night vigil.

Andrew's chin quivered a bit as he stood over the king, but he turned and did as he was bade.

• •

"We left dead on the hillock," reported the Comyn archer who was himself a Scot.

"How many?" asked Mowbray.

"Milord," he swallowed hard, "five… maybe ten for the each of us," he stammered.

Mowbray's lip curled, and he turned to Sir David, "They'll be comin' for us this night."

"We'll post extra pickets," replied Brechin.

"Nobody sleeps!" snapped Mowbray forcefully.

Brechin bowed a bit, giving an appearance of acceptance, but holding back any sense of approval for the command.

"Hain't all, Sire," interjected the archer.

"What say ye?!" returned Mowbray harshly.

"Saw their king... I'm fair sure," he answered.

Brechin and Mowbray both were stunned, but tried not to show it.

"Why should ye not? He is their... 'king'," bluffed Mowbray.

"Sire, 'tis the word among the men that their king was, well, dead," came back the bowman. Before he could continue his thought Mowbray interrupted.

"Reckon there'll be a new word among the men now," snarled the baron.

"Aye..." started the man again when Brechin interrupted.

"We need not bring dead... and *dangerous* dogs, back to life," he offered.

Sir John paused in contemplation then said, "Sir David is right. Speak of the appearance of that so-called 'king' to no one... nor must any else who saw him, either... ye ken!?"

The archer bowed in agreement, anxious to tell the rest of his news and be gone. "But, Milord, I think I kilt him as we came across the ice!"

Henry Sinclair

DECEMBER 27TH 1307
ABERDEEN

The storm that covered Slioch stretched to the eastern coast and the town of Aberdeen, where the warmth of the water held the temperature slightly higher than inland, and the snow that had accumulated was quickly disappearing due, in part, to the occasional spitting rain.

Despite the weather, the sounds of the Christmas holiday were still ringing happily in the streets, and each and all had the remnants of their feast goose yet to eat. In many houses Yule logs still burned on the hearth, and some had rooms heavily dressed for the season in the old Druid traditions of holly, ivy, and branches from the oak tree.

"We ha'e no more daughters!" screamed the innkeeper's wife upon realizing that one of the men standing before her was none other than the despised Sir Thomas Randolph. He and Sir David Graham had abandoned their warrior raiment, and trying to mingle with the town's citizenry without being conspicuous, were dressed instead as ordinary travelers.

Thomas frowned, not liking her inference that he was there to steal her daughters.

"I am only here to purchase a flagon of ale!" He tried to reassure her, but she would have none of it, throwing up her hands and running to get her husband, who was baking bread in the kitchen in the back of the Red Lion tavern.

Sir David, with a wry smile, asked, "Been here before, have ye?" It was all he could do to contain his merriment at Thomas' discomfort.

"Nearly two year ago," Thomas answered. He really didn't want to get into a discussion of his having served under the command of the earl of Pembroke while the earl searched Scotland for King Robert.

"Give them their ale... and get their coin, Wife," scolded the innkeeper.

"How can ye say such when he and that wicked English earl... took away our two beautiful children!" she sobbed into her apron.

The innkeeper removed his paddle of bread from the oven and laid it down then took his distraught wife into his arms to comfort her.

"What will we do?" she asked, continuing to sob.

"What is there to do?" he replied, tears rolling out of his own eyes. He, too, suffered greatly from the mistreatment and theft of his daughters by Aymer de Valance, and from overwhelming guilt because he was powerless to prevent it.

"Perhaps he knows their whereabouts?" she said, sadly blowing her nose into her apron.

"Serve them their ale, for now," suggested the man as he led his wife back to the entrance to the barroom. When he drew the separating curtain back to let his wife through, he glared at Thomas with hatred, but knew to say nothing to his face. "Thanes!" he said under his breath like a curse.

At her husband's insistence, the woman did as she was bade and delivered the ale to the table where Thomas and David were uncomfortably settled in each other's company. When she again looked upon the face of Sir Thomas, the tears flowed anew and she could not help but wail.

"Stop yer caterwaulin' woman!" griped Thomas, laying a couple of pence on the table, "I ne'er took yer lasses." He hung his head over his ale, ashamed of his part in the girls' abduction. "'Twas Pembroke," he added quietly.

The woman wept all the more, retreating from the table.

"A charmin' soul, ye are, Thomas," soberly chided David, taking up his foaming cup.

"'Tweren't my doin'!" insisted Thomas, as sullenly as he felt. He, too, lifted his cup and drew in a goodly quantity of the dark brew.

The innkeeper came out of the back to retrieve his wife and comfort her for their loss.

"Ye're stirrin' the waters where we need to cast our seine," complained Graham.

Thomas ignored the comment.

About that time Henry Sinclair entered the tavern to meet with them. As Thomas moved to summon for another ale to be brought, Graham said, "Let him do his own orderin'! Ye'll set her off afresh."

Thomas rolled his eyes, but let Henry fetch his own drink.

Sinclair leaned on the heavy wooden board and ordered whisky, laying down a coin for it. The woman cried great tears and whimpered all the while she poured the drink into the cup. Henry saw a tear or two fall into his liquor, but took it anyway and ambled toward the table to join his friends.

"Old woman cried in my whisky," he complained, stirring it with his index finger. "I'm just glad she didn't have a runny nose," he grinned and licked his finger, then sipped from the cup.

"Seems as though Thomas ran off with their daughters time last he was here," explained David, as much to rankle Thomas as enlighten Henry.

It worked in both instances. Thomas grumbled and Henry looked upon him in surprise.

"And these are the ones ye were expectin' to help us capture yon castle?" asked Henry with a certain note of reproach in his voice.

Thomas nodded, blacker than ever. His lips tightened. Then he pulled his dagger and laid it before him on the table.

Sir David laughed openly, letting Thomas know he was unafraid.

"Ye two mind yer deportment," said Sinclair.

Thomas drank.

David drank.

Thomas postured in the doing, but re-sheathed his dagger.

"We will speak to them after the others have gone home... or to bed," he said.

"We'll be drunk ere then," advised David.

"Then ye won't have a mite to say about it, will ye," said Thomas, curling up one side of his mouth.

Later, as he had said, Sir David laid across the table asleep, and while Thomas was bleary-eyed, he still sat talking in hushed tones with Henry, going over details of the plan to capture Aberdeen, town and castle, for King Robert.

They noticed that all others had left the tavern and summoned the innkeeper to the table where the three sat. The keeper and his wife were in dread of Thomas Randolph, but determined they would not wilt before him. They wanted to know anything that he knew about their young daughters, and as soon as he was at the table, the man asked.

"Where are my daughters? Do they yet live?" In spite of himself, he sobbed.

"Aye. Last I heard they were well."

The woman overheard and began to cry, joining her sniffling husband at the table.

Thomas sighed. This was not in the plan.

The man gained control of himself, but the woman continued to weep.

"She cry *all* the time?" asked Sinclair.

His tone of voice vexed her and she cried all the more, using her apron to hide her contorted features from view.

Thomas gently took her wrist and put her hand into her lap before telling her, "Ye're goin' to be a grandmother."

The wife's eyes grew as wide as saucers and spilled over again.

"Don't cry the more, woman!" said Thomas, trying to stem the flow.

"Which one?" she asked softly, "Lula or Lela?"

Thomas shrugged for he never knew, or at least, didn't remember their names, but said, "The younger one."

The woman smiled through her tears. Her husband was pleased to have word of the girls, but he knew that was not the reason for a man like Randolph to have come all the way to Aberdeen, especially in winter.

"Why came ye back here?" he asked.

"To kill English," bluntly replied Thomas.

Sinclair nodded his head in agreement.

The innkeeper looked quizzically at Randolph and said, "Figured *ye* were English!"

"Nay."

"Ye lolled around here with that earl. That Pembroke!"

"I was payin' a debt I owed him."

"Some debt, it must ha'e been!"

"'Twas."

"'Tis now winter," interrupted Sir Henry, wanting to get back to the real subject they came to discuss. "The castle partially depends on the town to provide victuals, save what's sent from London and stored within?"

"I sell naught to the English," replied the innkeeper. "They come and drink… sometimes." He still had his eyes on the hated Thomas.

"But ye know those that do supply them," returned Sinclair.

"They will murder us all if we don't step around to their orders," said the innkeeper. "What do ye want from us?" he asked, his hands showing signs of nervousness.

"We want some men who will help us."

"Help ye do what?"

"Keep the English pinned behind their walls," interjected Thomas.

"Ye don't know what ye ask!" exclaimed the innkeeper. He looked around as if he were afraid of being overheard.

"Are my bairns still with yer lord?" asked the wife, still weepy.

Thomas smiled, "Aye. I've been asked to be Godfather of his child."

"But he's English!" protested the man.

"He surely is English," remarked Thomas, "but he is also the father of yer grandchild. Ye can hate him for bein' English, ye can hate him for takin' yer daughters… Hell! Ye can hate him for any number of thin's! But like the rest of us, he is not all bad!" he said, remembering Loudoun Hill, for which Pembroke paid a great cost, Thomas was convinced.

The woman could not staunch her tears, and her husband had nothing more to say.

"My woman is tired, Sirs. We are closin' now." He stood and started guiding his wife to her bed.

"Will ye help us, or nay?" asked Henry.

"We're closed, now," was the only response. As they climbed to an upper room, the woman began to wail again.

"What's she keenin' for, now?" moaned Thomas, wiping his hand down his bearded face.

"Hain't goin' to be easy," remarked Henry thinking about the innkeeper's fears and hatreds. He stood as he turned to Thomas and said, "Let's wake Sir David and get us back to the chapel."

"That hain't goin' to be easy either," Thomas observed, looking at the large man sprawled asleep on the tabletop.

The next morning, David Graham groused and whined, his temperament standing on the shoulders of his overindulgence the evening last. Henry still slept, but Thomas was up early, filled with a wit full of ideas.

"What ye reckon if we turn this great hall into a school for warriors?"

"Who cares," said David still holding his pounding head, and occasionally vomiting on the flagstones behind him.

Randolph ignored the unsuitable answer and began to imagine the whole of the chapel, small as it was, somehow turned into a secret training area, away from spies.

Anxious to have an agreeing soul to play out his idea, he awoke Henry from his bed of hay in the corner near the fire.

Henry awoke shivering and wrapped the meager blanket tighter around his body as he came to his senses.

"Any dried meat left?" he asked.

Thomas pitched him a pouch and began to describe his plan to breathe new life into the all but abandoned building.

"The English will kill us," sighed Henry.

"The English will *try* to kill us, no matter! They think we are less than men… unwillin' to defend oursel's, and unable to run them back to Londontown… with their tails tucked tight betwixt their bony legs," grinned Thomas.

Eustice

DECEMBER 29TH 1307
SLIOCH

Robert Boyd was suffering severely with a toothache, and lying on his pallet with a poultice on his jaw when Murdoch and MacKie came to his hut. The commanding knight guessed their mission by the telling of their faces.

"So, ye want to raise havoc, do ye?" he started after they paid their respects.

"Aye, Milord," offered Murdoch with understated passion. "Sore fixed to revenge, we are."

"Ye archers are mighty important to this campaign," replied Boyd coming to a sitting position, frowning with the pain.

"We will do as we are told," returned Murdoch, "but we're the ones that can strike from…" His say was suddenly broken by the distant sound of trumpets.

"See Sir Neil… and report back to me the matter of the trumpets!" groaned Boyd as he attempted to get to his feet.

"Aye, Milord," said Murdoch, and he and MacKie made haste out the doorway and through the wood to the barricade at front of the peninsula, arriving winded and with their sides hurting.

Sir Neil stood where he could see down the road, and Eustace was serving his assigned picket duty nearby.

"Sir Robert… wants to know the why… of the commotion," Murdoch panted out.

Campbell said nothing but pointed down the snow-covered dirt road running between them and the Comyns and their English hirelings.

There came a parade of knights in armor, on fresh destriers, and with colorful pennants and flags flying, followed by foot soldiers trailing as far around the bend in the road as they could see.

"Who be that one in front?," asked MacKie squinting his eyes against the brilliant white snow for a sharper look.

"'Tis the *grand Earl of Buchan!*" exclaimed Eustace as he stood erect, in complete awe.

"He right, Sire?" asked Murdoch, surprised that the tailor from Inverurie would have known such a thing or acted in such a manner.

Sir Neil nodded then added, "Be comin' for us within a day, no doubt."

"Why not now?" asked MacKie.

His brother elbowed his side for asking such a blunt question of a noble. MacKie grunted in temporary pain.

"'Tis a'right men," said Sir Neil before answering, "They'll need to drink a spell and set a plan."

"'Ppears to have plenty of soldiers to make a plan with, Milord," observed Murdoch.

"Most likely, three to every two of ours," surmised Neil with the utmost seriousness. "Go report to Sir Robert what we have seen and said here."

"Aye, Sir," he replied.

The brothers did as they were ordered and when they had told Sir Robert the story, they again asked permission to take a few bowmen across the peat field to harangue the enemy. Their request was refused; Sir Robert knew it would be a desperate attempt, and that no significant advantage could be gained compared to the risk being taken.

They, however, were disgruntled. "I ne'er would have asked him if I had thought he could refuse us!" griped Murdoch.

• •

Around noon, King Robert was again stirred from his dreadful sleep.

"Welcome to Scotland," greeted Christina in as cheerful voice as she could muster, though she was aware of the perilous situation they faced.

Robert blinked and rubbed his eyes with his weakened hands. "Christina… what is afoot?" he asked weakly with a raw, gravelly voice.

"Have a wee bit of this broth, and I'll tell ye," she said as she sloshed her special blend of herbs around in hot, weak soup. She hoped he would gain some strength from having meat juices in the medicinal tea.

She knelt at his side as he forced himself to rise on one elbow and sip the elixir. He then pushed the cup away and fell back to his bed. "Yer promise... ," he prompted.

She turned and called Andrew, who was again practicing his skills of war with Baldred outside the hut. The odd thought of the two boys never being able to apply those hard learned skills crossed her mind as he poked his head around the curtain.

"Aye, Milady?" he said with a smile.

"Run tell Sir Robert Boyd that the king is awake," she relayed.

"Aye, Milady," he replied, then, still smiling, waved to Robert before dashing away, Baldred in tow.

Robert returned his smile, albeit weakly.

"What has happened to my brother?" he asked immediately, anxiety filling his voice, realizing it was not Sir Edward Christina had summoned. He then quickly followed with, "How long have I been all but dead?"

"Shh!" she tried to soothe him. "Yer brother is a'right and ye have been ailin' for more than three weeks," she explained.

Cold air from the doorway blew in again as someone pushed the curtain aside.

"That the squire?" asked Robert. He could not make out the standing figure, silhouetted by the brilliant light reflecting off the snow outside.

Christina turned. Her eyes adjusted to the new light. "'Tis but a young man from the camp," she said, recognizing Eustace and thinking he was sent to guard the hut.

"Aye, 'tis," he said as he stepped into the room and pushed his cloak to one side, revealing a dagger hanging from his belt. Somehow his attitude alarmed Christina.

"Ye have no truck within! Go outside to stand the guard!" she ordered angrily.

"Ye are my promised gold!" He said to Robert, and he shoved Christina out of his way, throwing her down to the dirt floor.

Robert tried to arise in Christina's defense, but could not. He fell back helplessly.

With nothing on his mind but the promised gold, the tailor from Inverurie drew his blade and moved the short distance closer, and none to intervene. He loomed over Robert and raised his dagger for the deathblow, hearing the king whispering prayers, preparing to die.

Christina scrambled to stand and reach into the folds of her skirt for the slit she had constructed there. In a blink of an eye she brought forth the dagger she carried strapped to the thigh of her right leg, and reaching around Eustace, plunged the blade into his belly.

The assassin only felt Christina reach around and hit him hard in the stomach. He turned and laughed at her, neither feeling nor seeing the scarlet spreading across the middle of his jerkin. She hit him again, with all her might, and this time he felt the blade rip across his belly. With a piteous cry he dropped the dagger and stumbled backward from her, holding the painful burning in his gut as his legs lost their will to stand.

"Kill my Robert, ye will not!" she said vehemently as she stared down at him with contempt.

Eustace could not believe that his pathetic life was about to end and tried again to stand. Christina quickly grabbed Robert's large broadsword, and with the point against the wounded man's chest, pushed him back to the dirt floor and didn't stop until the blade stained the ground below with his blood.

Eustace' anguished scream was short, and then there was silence but for Christina's breath, which came in great heaving bursts.

She was shaken, not for what had happened, but for what had almost happened.

"Ye'll make a good knight," said Robert, trying to laugh.

She dragged the broadsword to his bedside before dropping it and sat heavily in her chair. After a moment, she threw her body across Robert's and cried bitterly.

Robert ran his fingers through her hair, remembering long ago when they had been lovers, and the children they had together. He still loved her, perhaps even more now, for he missed his dear Elizabeth, whom he had not seen since sending her to Kildrummy after the battle of Dail Righ.

Robert Boyd stepped through the door, nearly stumbling over the dead Eustace.

"What happened here?" he asked.

"Lady Christina has most courageously saved the worthless life in this bed," answered the nearly exhausted king.

"Sire! Lady Christina, are ye unharmed? Was he alone?" Boyd placed one hand on the hilt of his sword.

"He was alone," said Christina, standing. "And we are unharmed," she looked at her hand, covered halfway up her forearm in the blood of the dead Eustace. Blood was spattered across her apron and on the bed covers of the king, prompting her to add, "In spite of what ye see." She wiped tears from her face with her unbloodied hand, and bowing to the king, said, "Sire, I shall have the body removed from us. Sir Robert, please allow no one in until 'tis done."

"Certainly, Milady."

She covered herself with her long heavy cloak and went to find Andrew and Baldred to tend the corpse.

"My God, Rob! What happened ere I came?" asked Boyd.

"An assassin, intent upon my death for promised gold, sent by... one or more of my enemies. In his entrails ye will find a blade, placed there by Christina with as much courage as any man I know." He closed his eyes a moment, and after a deep breath said, "Now ye ken what went on in here, what's happenin' out there?"

Sir Robert assumed Christina's chair, and the two warriors talked for a long time. Boyd was relieved, as that was the first the king had been alert long enough to make any sense of anything.

The first decision they made was to attack the Comyn army at dawn, before the newly arrived Buchan had opportunity to array his and Mowbray's troops for an attack. A second force would be led by Sir Gilbert, leading a large contingent on the enemy's flank by crossing the frozen bog in the hours before daylight.

Andrew and Baldred had come quickly. The young boys retrieved Christina's dagger from the body and laid it inside the hut. Andrew took Eustace's dagger from the floor and its sheath from his belt, and gave it to Baldred, then the two youths dragged the attempted murderer's remains down the hill.

"What happened to Eustace from Inverurie?" asked Fergus, seeing the body thrown to the ground like so much rubbish.

"What happened?" echoed Cuthbert.

Andrew told his understanding of the story in unvarnished fashion.

"I knew he weren't a'right!" said Cuthbert as he kicked the body. "I ne'er liked him!"

Fergus removed the dead man's hat and said, "I always liked his hat!"

"Hae it, then," snarled Cuthbert. Fergus placed it on his own head with a smile. Looking again at the body, he asked, "How about his cloak? Ye want it?"

"It's bloody! And it has a slit in the back!"

"It'll wash... and I can mend it," responded Fergus.

"Hae that as well," Cuthbert shook his head. Within moments others came to see the man who would have been the end of King Robert and hear the story of his killing. It wasn't long before the body had been picked clean of everything.

Cuthbert set him upright against a tree. He wasn't fit for being laid out with the others.

Atop the hill, Christina returned to the hovel.

She found Boyd sitting beside the sleeping king.

"Were ye able to talk to him, Sir Robert?" she asked quietly.

"Aye, Milady," he almost whispered.

"What said he?"

"We attack on the morn."

"Just like him... yet he is not at all like himself!" Tears again welled in her eyes.

"He is our king… we will obey."

"The army will follow ye if ye lead in his name," she said.

Boyd nodded, knowing it was true, but added, "Edward, they would follow faster."

"Edward is no better off than his brother!" she replied.

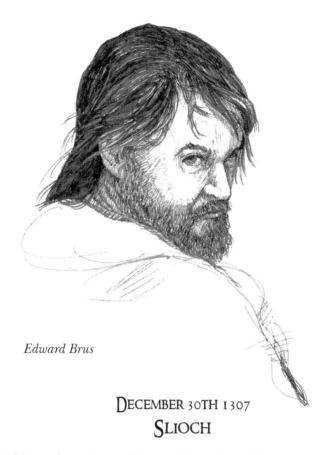

Edward Brus

December 30th 1307
Slioch

In his weakened state, his own life at low ebb, King Robert was not told of the struggle of Sir John Wallace to recover from the shoulder wound he suffered in the king's stead.

Lady Christina had nothing in her box of medicines and herbs for the warrior's loss of blood and the ensuing infection that would not abate. He writhed with pain in his lucid moments, and no doubt, would have blessed his insensible ones. Thus it was that, in the darkest hour, before the light had even tinged the black with the grayness of the day, God wrested the valiant soul from the agonized body of good Sir John Wallace.

Sir John's "fought for" weapons were given to others who needed them to continue the battle. His body was ceremoniously carried from his bed and laid beside the bodies of other brave Scots who had learned, all too well, the full price paid for the regaining of lost freedom. Eventually, by natural progressions, they would become a part of the land they held so dear.

Two hours before the death of Wallace, Sir Gilbert de la Haye silently had gathered his men and set out across the bog to conduct a surprise attack on the Comyns' flank. Crossing the treacherous, frozen bog in total silence, they took their positions and waited until light, when the main body would attack straight on the enemy camp.

. .

Indeed, across the way in the earl of Buchan's command tent, Lord John was preparing his raid on the Brus camp, with the intention of launching it as soon as the sky was full light and the sun had warmed the air, at least enough to take the worst chill away.

As he envisioned, all were to be on foot, except himself and a few others, with knights in the vanguard, just behind the foot soldiers. They, bearing shields, would take the arrows' first flights. The combined army would then start at one end of the peninsula and simply work its way to the other. Though far from classic warfare, it seemed to be a plausible solution to the "rebel infestation" of the Comyn stronghold of Buchan, and to Robert de Brus as well.

"I am leavin' this freezin', God-forsaken neck of Slioch by this day's end! And as I depart, before me will be displayed the head of The Brus... on a high pike... and surely lookin' dour of mouth and weepin' sanguine tears from his dead, evil eyes," claimed Lord John Comyn, imitating with great passion his vision of The Brus' sad face upon the pike, after which he broke into a raucous and wine-influenced burst of laughter.

"Aye!" agreed his obsequious minions. "Aye!... Aye!..." they shouted rousingly at the appropriate places in his performance.

"Near sunup 'tis... We eat!" ordered Lord John to his companions. Lord David, Lord Mowbray, Sir David Brechin, and other top field lieutenants assembled for a pre-dawn breakfast of broiled eel and fresh honey bread, washed down by free-flowing wine. "A man should never make war... or love... on an empty stomach," he threw out to elicit another round of cheers and merriment.

. .

On the peninsula, gathered around the fire in their hut, the generals in the weakening army of Brus met to plan the final details of the array to carry forth the attack on the Comyn forces. While they agreed on some specifics and disagreed on others, all knew that their only chance to survive after Slioch was to escape from this corked bottle in which they had placed themselves.

While they argued back and forth about who was to charge first and who would follow whom, Edward Brus laid in his bed and listened. His name was never mentioned in their discussions, meaning they had no faith in him even though he was a knight of considerable prowess and renowned courage. He grew resentful of their slight.

As the planning session wound down, and the Scots leaders prepared to depart and take command of their respective forces for the grand... and many felt, final... charge, Edward unexpectedly arose from his doss and with glaring eyes looked about at the subdued knights.

"I will lead the army," he said calmly, but malevolently.

"Ye?" asked the surprised Bishop.

"Am I not the King's brother and a knight of Scotland?"

"Sire," said Sir Robert, "We thought ye were... afflicted!"

"Nay, ye didn't," Edward said. "Ye thought I could be dismissed... as a whore after yer pleasure! But I am no whore, sirs! I have been with King Robert from the beginnin', before ye had turned yer faces from England and raised yer heads as Scots! And I will take command of this army!"

None of the men answered Edward, but looked at each other in bewilderment.

"Squire!" he commanded loudly, "Bring my armor!"

Standing just outside the hut, his squire scrambled to obey his lord.

"Ye sure ye're feelin' fit to this, Edward?" asked Boyd.

Edward curled his lip giving a cold, determined demeanor. "Ye think me not up to the task, Sir Robert?" The two stood unmoving, a few feet apart, as Boyd considered whether to challenge the man he had so recently cursed for not taking this very step.

"As ye say," replied Boyd, withdrawing his question though not his misgivings.

"Then prepare to follow me! Have the horses readied immediately," he ordered. "I go see my brother ere we gather." With that he ousted them, dumbstruck, from his presence.

• •

The squires would normally put the knights' chain mail into small barrels of sand and roll them along the ground to remove accumulated rust and dirt. To clean the metal parts of some armor and weapons, they would scour them with sand and other polishing agents. Nothing was 'as usual' at Slioch. They had no barrels. No suitable sand. Nothing.

Thus, all of the metal on the Scots' armor and weapons was tinged reddish brown with rust and the stain of blood.

Edward Brus was soon dressed in his metal studded, boiled leather armor and his chain mail. With his squire trotting beside him with a torch, he set off in the lightless, frigid morning to see King Robert.

Entering the king's hovel unannounced, he was no more than a darkened figure in a darkened room, the fire light flickering off his helm gave the only hint as to his size and presence.

Christina awoke and gasped. "Who are ye?!" she demanded.

"I have come to talk to my brother," he said, telling who he was and what he wanted in a single breath.

"Edward!" she stood and moved to poke the fire for a bit more heat and light. "Ye are well enough to join today's battle?"

"Someone must dare to stand in the king's boots, or yer next visitor might be yer last!" He looked around at the cramped room, at Christina, and for a long moment, at his sleeping brother. "If it should be that we fail to..."

"I will kill him... and then myself," she interrupted his thought. "They will not have him alive, Milord." Edward nodded. The woman had allayed his concern that his older brother might be publicly butchered as all his younger brothers had been.

"Is Robbie awake?" he asked abruptly.

"Ye can shake him, but gently."

Edward went closer to Robert's side and looked down at him. His first thought was of how much thinner and older the man in the bed seemed than when he had been brought to this place. He hesitated just before his gauntleted hand would have touched the king's shoulder.

Instead, he turned, commanding Christina, "Send his squire to me when the king comes to himself."

"Aye, Milord," answered Christina. As he left, she wondered at his managing to assume the warrior role with such daring strength in his manner, and yet was afeard to awaken the king, his own flesh and blood.

• •

Lord John's morning meal was suddenly interrupted by the knight commanding the pickets, who presented himself saying, "There be somethin' ye must see... I pray, Milord."

The fellow had such a queer look on his face that Lord Buchan decided to respond. Thus, he and his mostly besotted entourage traipsed through the hodgepodge of English, Welsh, and Comyn Scots warriors, then in the midst of readying themselves for battle.

At the edge of the wood where began the broad flat area once of interest only to the local peat harvesters, the knight, ahead of them with a torch, suddenly stopped and pointed.

In the wan early light, across the land area approaching the peninsula, the pale image was far from clear but there was no doubt about its being there. It sat at the head of the strip of land that connected the "mainland" to the peninsula fortress.

Taking the torch from the knight, the earl brazenly walked halfway toward the curiosity and strained his eyes all the more.

"What is it, Milord?!" shouted Lord Mowbray, too fearful of mischief to sally forth.

Strathbogie grunted, downed his filled goblet, and repaired to the earl's tent for a refill.

"'Tis a man, obviously naked," exclaimed the earl, "sitting in the midst of the trail!"

The earl gathered up his drink-enhanced courage and moved a bit closer. David Brechin lurched in his wake.

"What ye seein' now?" again asked the baron.

The earl shook his head and turned his face to Brechin. "Ye'd figure a man with so damn much curiosity would be ahead of *me* a'lookin'," he whispered.

"Could be a trap, Milord," expressed Brechin eying their dismal surroundings.

"Oh, could be," replied the earl creeping forward, his eyes straining for clarity against the poor light.

The earl grunted as he stood erect, took several draws of his broadsword to clear its sheath, and propped the blade across his shoulder so that he was prepared for trouble. Still, he wanted not to appear frightened to his watching men.

Sir David anxiously fingered the hilt of his sword.

The archers along the Comyn tree line set arrows in their bows, ready for action if need be. Mowbray's English knights, some only half dressed for battle, quickly mounted their destriers, their squires handing weapons up to them in haste.

Lord John suddenly brought his sword to the ready. "God damn...!" he cried as his eyes widened. "God-damned passin' strange!"

Brechin straightened. "'Tis that hell-bound sorry spy we sent to kill The Brus!"

"Aye," agreed Lord John, "but why does he sit as if frozen... and... with something other than what God placed there betwixt his legs?"

Brechin passed by the earl to get a closer look.

"He *is* frozen, Milord," reported Sir David.

The earl sighed with relief that his senses had not completely failed him.

Brechin drew close to the corpse. Seeing neither pocket nor purse about the man, he thought, *Reckon my silver coin be gone.* He picked up the odd thing between the dead man's legs and walked toward the earl, casually tossing it to him.

The earl fumbled the thing in his unencumbered gloved hand, then caught it firmly. It was dark brown and hairy, and he turned it for a better angle. He needed but one glance. Beholding an ugly face with squinted eyes and a drawn mouth that appeared to him to be an evil spirit straining hard to conjure the worst spell ever placed on any man, he dropped the red-brown head as if it had regained full life in his hands.

"What is it?!" he asked, looking down at it on the ground.

"Head of a boggy man," explained Brechin, unruffled.

Bad, bad luck, thought John. He took the point of his broadsword and poked at the eyes of the raisin-like orb.

Brechin picked up the mummified head. Knowing that it was considered by many to be a portent of evil, he held it by its hair and slung it back to the Brus Scots on the other side of the land bridge, shouting, "*Ye* are the ones with the bad luck!"

Cuthbert and Fergus, watching from beyond the tree line, grinned at each other in the near dark. Their tomfoolery had roused fear in the great earl and interrupted preparations for the coming battle, which was more than either of them had dared hope for when they hatched their adolescent plot.

Eustace from Inverurie had, at last, aided the army of Brus.

. .

King Robert groaned in his sleep. Christina came to him with her broth of herbs, hoping he could be awakened to take more. She knew he was returning to life because of the brew, but wondered if there would be time enough to get him well.

The two squires, Andrew and Baldred, sat just outside the doorway as the sky grew light enough to paint the countryside with a faded gray pallor, made paler by the snow. Andrew, not yet over his illness but determined to ignore it, sniffed and coughed continually. As he sat, he withdrew the king's flag from within his jerkin where he always carried it. Speckles and splatters of blood from the many battles it had witnessed dotted its yellow field and red lion. That gave it special meaning to the lad. He was, at least temporarily, the standard bearer to the king, and as long as the king yet lived he was bound to this blessed duty and honor.

Within the folds of the flag was the ring of gold with which King Robert was crowned. The king had worn it in every battle, save Methven, when he was set upon so quickly he never thought to put it, or his helm, upon his head.

Baldred ran his fingers across the sacred flag. Andrew smiled because he had acted the same when first the banner was presented to him at Loudoun Hill, some seven months earlier.

Andrew put the crown on his lap, crumpled the flag on top of it and picked up one of the somewhat straight branches he had cut that morning and whittled to look as much like a regular flagstaff as he could, working under dire circumstances.

"Who carries the Saint Andrew's flag?" asked Baldred.

"Ye can," said Andrew.

"Me?"

"Aye," confirmed Andrew. "It's yonder," he continued, pulling back the door covering and pointing to the foot of the king's pallet. "That's what the second staff is for. Go fetch it, and take this to Lady Christina," said Andrew, straightening the obviously bent circle of gold and handing it to Baldred. He was totally awed. "Well, take it!" Andrew insisted.

"Should I carry it… like that? I mean, shouldn't it be on a pillow… or… somethin'?" said Baldred, his eyes wide.

"Hain't got the likes of such," returned Andrew.

Wiping his grubby hands on his just as dirty trews, Baldred took the crown and backed into the hut, turning around to say, with some trepidation, "The crown, Milady."

Christina had been dressing her dear Robert in his tabard. The crown was the last of the preparations for the king to meet the enemy, even though, if the enemy reached that far, she knew he would be dead, as would she.

Baldred returned to the outside holding the Saint Andrew's flag and straightaway began attaching it to the second staff.

"Reckon we'll live to tell of this?" he asked the other squire.

Andrew looked off in the distance a moment, answered simply, "Can't say," and continued to rig the flag to the pole.

• •

Neil Campbell had their dozen or so nearly starved destriers saddled and dressed in the coverings available to him. He knew that poor, killed Thomas Brus would have had the horses much better fed and adorned. Thomas was the finest hostler in the Campbell's ken, and always knew how to keep their mounts in top shape, even when times were bad.

Well, Thomas, he thought to himself, *'tain't as ye would have done, but I did as best I could, and I hope ye will not be ashamed of us.* He left the horses and went to see if the preparations for the battle were completed, only to hear angry shouts as he drew near.

"What do ye mean, no attack?!" asked Robert Boyd, standing in the middle of the hut and facing the challenger to his decision.

"Am I not the king's own brother, I ask again?!" shouted Sir Edward. Proceeding with his intentions, he grabbed the fox fur robe from his pallet, where it had kept him somewhat warm through his uncaring time. Now, it would serve as his royal cloak.

"The *king* said to attack!" returned Boyd, angry at the sudden change in plan.

"The king said for me, *me...* to work *my* plan," lied Edward.

The other knights were bewildered, but only Boyd stood directly against him, for it was he to whom the king had given the order to mount a surprise attack, and the king was, unfortunately, no longer available for further consultation.

"Ach, if ye wish not to follow my orders, shall we await King Robert's arisin' that he may tell ye himself?" asked Edward, knowing the answer would be nay.

"We came to this spit of land with o'er eight hundred souls," said Sir Robert, "now we are little more than seven and well outnumbered. If we await their comin' for us, we *will* kill many of them, but they will kill... *all* of us!"

Sir Neil entered the hut. With his arms folded across his chest, he stood behind Boyd. "What?" he asked.

"Edward says the king wants us *not* to attack!" replied the bishop, shaking his head.

Edward swung the cape around dramatically and held his head back to look at the rest through half-closed eyes, his mouth puckered as a pouting boy. Deftly, he flipped the cloak over his armor and fastened it around his neck to trail behind him.

"Are we fixin' to follow a madman?" whispered Wiseman to Barclay.

Barclay frowned. "Madman or no, we'll not live through this!" he whispered in return.

Edward began to speak in grand terms as he paced to and fro, as much as his confined space would allow, his fox cloak dragging in his steps. He laid forth his plan to get them all out of the wood and escape unscathed.

No one present believed it would work, perhaps not even himself.

The bishop left to walk among the men and women who were gladly making preparations to leave the wilderness of Slioch. He blessed them in his passing and secretly prayed for them all to be guided by God's hands through whatever they had to confront in the coming hours.

• •

It took the backs of four strong soldiers of foot to get Buchan in his saddle atop his huge destrier. One of his squires handed the four-foot-long broadsword to the hefty superior liege lord, and another handed up his azure shield emblazoned with three golden sheaves of grain. Finally, he sat mounted, breathing heavily and sweating from the effort.

Next in command, the Earl of Atholl put his foot to stirrup and swung into his saddle easily, and held a bit of silly drunken pride in thinking that he was completely in contrast to the old man.

Lord Mowbray mounted up with his English knights after positioning his archers at the head of the army, along the line of trees facing the Brus camp. They would be used to make the first strike, but Sir John had no illusions as to their effectiveness after their various marginally successful attempts at raids.

Sir David Brechin was forth in command, and no doubt, the most reluctant of the four to do anything not clearly his own idea, and this operation had none of his approval.

The Scottish knights, unmounted, fell in behind the two earls and Brechin. The hundreds of foot soldiers seemed to mingle with and surround them all.

Almost at the moment they were set to proceed, Strathbogie saw something moving between the trees. "Hold a moment," he called and repositioned himself to observe it closer.

Mowbray moved in as well.

The English archers readied their longbows.

The Brus archers nocked arrows as well. Both camps remained behind their tree line defenses.

The Comyn trumpeters blew their signals, putting all at the ready and causing a collective shiver to run the spines of the men and women on both sides of the open area.

"Shall we attack, Milord?" asked Mowbray.

"Stand at the ready… we shall see how they be arrayed before we commit!" replied the earl.

Sir Edward de Brus quietly appeared, riding at a walk out of the wood, the fox fur cloak draped down his back and partially across the rump of his destrier. His torn tabard, worn over his rusty chest armor and mail, showed the colors of the King of Scots and was a sign of his sheer determination. He was a haunting reminder of the king, and certainly displayed the king's brashness and self-assuredness, if he lacked his brother's follow-through or understanding.

Next to appear was the flag of the king carried by Andrew, and behind him on the same destrier was Baldred, who clung tight to Andrew's waist with one arm whilst he carried the blue and white saltire flag of Saint Andrew. Solemnly, they followed Edward de Brus into the very teeth of the lion.

"Ye reckon they'll kill us right off?" whispered Baldred, his mouth dry with fear.

Andrew shook his head but slightly. "Not ye… *I'm* the one with the *king's* flag," he whispered over his shoulder.

They rode silently toward the flat peat field. Baldred sighed deeply, having observed the wood across the way. "There are Comyns everywhere!"

"Hain't so bad, I've seen worse" lied Andrew.

"Still feel like runnin'," confessed Baldred.

Andrew gave a nervous snicker.

The eleven Brus knights on their own destriers emerged full-blown from the tree line. They were dressed in various kinds and conditions of armor, all of which was showing rusty spots if one looked closely. All had some chain mail, and some had boiled leather cuirasses and other pieces of armor. A few proudly carried family banners, others had lost theirs somewhere during the long year of warring.

Edward ambled his beast ever forward, holding its head back and high in a proud fashion, and making its steps more animated.

Lord John nudged his horse toward the front of his army to be ready to give the order to attack as soon as he saw fit.

"This rout will be easier than I thought," he said, sneering broadly. He was content with seeing the Scots coming out of their den in such wretched condition.

"Take care, Milord," advised Sir David. "Edward de Brus is treacherous and unpredictable."

The earl sneered again, outwardly ignoring Brechin's say. "But, where is their king?" he wondered aloud, truly thinking Robert was dead.

It was only a moment before the next section of the Brus army emerged from the defensive trees. "I should think he is there, Milord Earl," said Brechin, indicating a phalanx of men walking in unison.

The earl raised his hand to signal to attack.

"Ye might stay yer hand, Milord," suggested Brechin.

The earl turned to Brechin, "Why so?"

"The farther *out* of the wood they be, the less we have to chase them *in* the wood," he replied with a smile.

The earl slowly lowered his hand.

King Robert's pallet came forward, six men on either side holding the king high over their heads. He was, as usual, lying on his back and asleep to the world. Christina had placed a small cloth over his eyes to protect them from opening to daylight after having been so long in all but total darkness.

He was dressed in chain mail from head to foot. His litter was heavy with fur robes, and at his head was a yellow flag with a significant portion of the red lion draped over the edge. On her palfrey, closely following the king's pallet, Christina rode with a dagger strapped to her waist, ready to be drawn at any breath to kill the king.

As she rode in the cold, still morning, it seemed to her that the procession was oddly more an ancient funeral rite than a grand prelude to escape.

Lord John, seeing Christina riding close to the king and perhaps remembering that his own young wife had run to The Brus with six of his finest warhorses, observed, "The Brus always has a woman with him!"

"And it matters not whose woman she is, eh, Milord?" joked Brechin, still feeling his wine, but he was quickly sobered.

John Comyn was definitely not amused, and would have dealt with Brechin then and there, had he not noticed a phenomenon that he had not been prepared to see. The Comyn Scots were breaking ranks and crowding the edge of the wood to see the Brus army on the march.

The earl directed his subordinates to order the men back to their own lines, but several took to their heels instead, and fell in with the Bruses' column.

Among the Welsh, and even some English, the desertion of the handful of Scots elicited poorly squelched laughter.

The unmounted Brus knights arose from the wood dressed in their rusty chain-mail. They came walking four abreast, their gauntlets holding swords up and in front of them, along with their targes and bucklers. There were but sixty-three still ambulatory, but walk with King Robert's army, they did.

The weather that morn had been anything but spectacular, when suddenly the clouds opened, showing long shadows of a glorious morning sun.

"God smiles on us!" exclaimed the old earl as the golden rays came across his face. "This signifies we shall win!"

Could mean The Brus will win, mused Brechin silently, still disquieted that his foolish comment had hit home with the earl and put his standing in jeopardy.

Edward maintained his demeanor as his huge horse trampled the frozen body of Eustace. The foot soldiers then emerged from the wood, four abreast and proud, ready for the fight, every one holding what weapons he had with dirty, cracked and bloody hands. Many were limping with heavily wrapped feet, but none fell to the ground. They were following their king, half dead or not. They were the army of Brus.

When Edward came to the end of the neck of land he smartly turned his horse to his right and proudly led his well-tested warriors.

The old earl jerked the reins of his mount, reacting to Edward's brazenness.

Brechin snickered in his mind.

"Might reckon to attack now," suggested Brechin.

Lord John again raised his hand to give the signal.

The two standard bearers turned in kind to follow Sir Edward.

Some of the Comyn Scots' pride began to show, and they walked out of the trees toward the road and openly shouted and cheered their opposites who walked so gamely into the beards of their enemies. The Scots knew great courage when they witnessed it, and the army of Brus was flaunting it with dash.

Soon the Comyn Scots were all along the road cheering to see their countrymen buck the English and their paid-for Scottish lords, twisted to King Edward's will.

The Welsh stood back and quietly admired the spirit they were witnessing as the rag-tag warriors of The Brus walked upright from their supposed slaughtering pen.

Lord Mowbray readied his English knights for attack.

The earl was again ready to give the signal, but realized his delay had allowed the perfect moment of attack to pass. He looked at Brechin.

Brechin looked at the many who were cheering and shook his head.

Mowbray was furious and commanded his English knights to attack at once! However, Lord John sent his Scottish knights into the roadway, effectively blocking the English.

The cheering became all the louder, even from some among the Welsh and the English.

One of the Brus warriors recognized a kinsman among the Comyn ranks and shouted, "Rany! Rany, ye mutton-head! What be ye on the side o' the road with the dog-tailed English for? Can't ye see the real Scots a'leavin' Slioch with The Brus?"

"*With* The Brus? Seems to me ye be *carryin'* 'im!" The Comyn Scots nearby laughed.

"Aye, and we'd carry 'im to the devil's door and back! Come to think of it, maybe we did!" All around him his mates laughed. "And," he added, deriding John Comyn's girth, "... at least we *can* carry 'im! The lot of ye would be hard pressed to carry yer earl!"

After the laughter died down, Rany hollered back, "The earl eats pretty good... and so do his lads!" He patted his belly for emphasis, knowing the Brus Scots had run short of provisions.

"And so did we... off o' the earl's horses!" They were almost out of earshot but he yelled, "Come with us, Rany! Ye know ye'd rather die cold and hungry for Scotland than live warm and stuffed for England!"

Rany raised his arm and brought it down as if saying, 'go on, leave,' but as he walked back toward the others, he looked over his shoulder at the parade of proud, raggedy Scots, and knew that what his kinsman said was true.

Finally, the camp followers, including the last three dogs, brought up the rear. The Comyn Scots cheered them as well, just because it seemed the order of the day. All filed past in one long procession, not unlike a grand parade.

"Goddammit, ye've let them go!" screamed Mowbray, having ridden in a rage through his troops to John Comyn after the earl's knights made the roadway impassable.

The earl looked at the baron with disgust. "Ye would have me try to go against them with my own men a'cheerin' them?"

"They weren't cheerin' when first they came out of the wood!" replied Mowbray. "They were expectin' a fight! And what will yer fine Scots do when next we are met up with The Brus?"

Lord David laughed out loud at the calamity and wheeled his destrier to retire to the tent where he knew good wine was waiting.

The old earl looked down the road after the Brus army and mumbled, "'Tis a bad day to die for Edward of England. Aye." At that, he followed David Strathbogie to the wine.

The men with Sir Gilbert, who never knew anything except they were to attack the flank when the fighting started, were able down the road to join in behind the procession and march away.

The Comyn's foot-army returned to their cook fires to speak in good humor of the morning's events, not sorry at all that no blood was spilt.

"Back to Mortlach... after we rest awhile," ordered Lord John as he was helped from his mount.

Brechin smiled. *Damnedest war I e'er saw,* he mused, looking out toward the wood from which the army of King Robert de Brus had so recently emerged. There he saw only the sunlit, trampled, bloody remains of the spy from Inverurie, a tailor by trade, an assassin for greed, and a corpse by the hand of a lady.

Alexander Comyn

January 3rd 1308
South Aberdeen

Staring intently out of the high window of the once thriving priory belonging to the Knights Templar, Sir David Graham could easily see the English garrisoned Castle Aberdeen towering over the rooftops of the houses and businesses of the town. Over a mile away, it loomed near the natural harbor at the mouth of the River Cree, where commerce entered Scotland from many parts of the world, and where provisions arrived from the south to bolster the inmates of the castle.

The child-like simpleton, Sir Alexander Comyn, titular overlord of the four-story stone citadel, had recently arrived from Buchan, ostensibly to see to the fortifications, but in reality was sent there by his brother to keep him safe from The Brus.

Graham carefully observed the muddy, snow edged street, paying particular attention to those who traveled there, and how many times they passed by the priory. Below him, echoing in the deserted church building, he heard the repeated clanging of blade against blade as the six other Templars and Thomas Randolph honed their skills and taught several Aberdonian volunteers.

Thomas casually swung his sword at an obviously smaller man, one of the volunteers, whose eyes reactively blinked, causing him to lose his balance and fall backward.

"On yer feet, man!" encouraged the veteran, obviously enjoying himself.

"Ye'll just knock me to the floor again!" replied the raggedly clothed man.

"Reckon I will... 'til ye learn how not to let me," gainsaid Sir Thomas, who demonstrated. "Ye put her blade here, to protect yer head. Then ye step yer leg back, like so, since the blade is comin' at ye from here, and move back this way and return the blow. Try it!"

The man arose once again to face the blade of Thomas. He sighed deeply, but gamely held his weapon to the ready.

Thomas grinned and immediately slammed his sword toward the man's head. The man as quickly threw his sword up to defend as Thomas had shown him. The blades clashed sharply, and the smaller man jumped back without falling, but he missed making the swing at Thomas.

Thomas withdrew and relaxed his sword arm. "Now ye're gettin' it," he remarked.

The man grinned with a certain pride, but he realized that he had failed the last move.

"Thomas! Headin' this way... might be English!" called David from the balcony.

"We'll cease for now," said Thomas sheathing his large sword and signalling the Templars to stop their practice.

The volunteer, called Colin, nodded and handed his weapon to Thomas. "I'll be gettin' one of my own, somehow... if ye'll teach me good?" he said, raising his voice to question.

"Bring some of yer big friends who feel like we do about the English, and I'll give ye a dagger as well," bribed Thomas.

The man smiled broadly. He could already feel the dagger in his hand, cutting a hated English soldier. He swooshed his fisted arm to match what his mind was saying.

Thomas was right pleased with his volunteer.

• •

Later that evening, it began to snow once again, as if nature couldn't make up its mind whether to snow or rain.

Thomas wrapped the wide length of plaid wool around him and headed for the door, passing behind where his two companions were eating before the fireplace.

David Graham looked up and asked, "Leavin', Thomas?"

"Aye."

"Where ye headed?"

After a pause, Thomas answered, "I'm goin' to see a man about a gylte he has to sell."

"A gylte?" David wondered what they would do with a young sow.

"Aye, are we not goin' hungry?" Thomas glared at David and jerked his head toward the door.

The Graham got his meaning and quickly asked, "Aye, we are! Maybe he has two gyltes at a reasonable price, ye think?"

"Maybe."

Like some company?"

"If ye've a mind." So Thomas waited for Graham to dress for the cold and snow.

Throughout their discussion, Sir Henry Sinclair's eyes were busy looking from one to the other as they spoke.

"Ye wearin' that damn Templar surcoat this time?" asked Thomas feigning a grimace.

"Why not?"

"'Cause people talk!"

"Aye," David removed his surcoat, instead throwing his heavy leather cloak over his shoulders, and the two men left Henry sitting in a chair by the fire, paring a winter apple as a completion to his supper. After they closed the door, he chuckled.

. .

"Didn't know ye Templars were allowed with wenches," said Thomas as the two men trudged in the slushy snow through the quiet village.

"We weren't... but now that the Templars are no longer... I do as I damn well please!" replied the knight.

A hundred yards more, and dripping wet snow all about, they entered the Ram's Horn tavern. It was not unlike the Red Lion on the north side of the castle, but Thomas preferred to avoid the innkeeper's wailing wife and so discovered this place.

Doffing their wet cloaks, the two went straight to an empty table and sat to wait for a serving wench to come take their order. In the meantime, they looked around and took in the feel of the place. It was of ample size and warmer than many, but could have used more candles, for the room was dark as the inside of a boot. Still, one got the idea that the patrons there preferred it so.

When the man came to their table they ordered the strongest of distilled spirits for Thomas, ale for David, and when served, they paid with the coin of England, as was the custom.

After a few sips from their respective cups, Thomas suddenly spoke up, saying in a not very quiet voice, "'Ppears the English have all the wenches spoke for!" David was caught off-guard and didn't quite know what he should do. Fighting is not what he had come for, though perhaps Thomas had, it seemed.

The tavern keeper knew trouble when it bit him, and in an attempt to avoid cleaning blood off the floor, sent large horns of ale to the two knights, thinking that they might grow less hostile. Thomas frowned, but accepted the two drinks and handed one to David.

As time passed and the levels of the drinks went down, Thomas' mood went darker while David listened to the piper and was far less concerned. To keep Thomas placid, the tavern keeper sent a hefty lass with a friendly manner and juicy red lips to Thomas. She knew how to get and keep a man's attention, and within moments was nuzzling her barely covered breasts against his jerkin as she playfully sipped ale from his cup.

Thomas' attention soon turned to tugging at the ties on her bodice, which she had purposely loosened on her way to the table. As she had supposed, his eyes were arrested between the two ample mounds of sensual flesh. He turned more toward her and slipped his hand into her dress to touch her nipple. She teased and jerked away, walking several paces before turning with a coy smile aimed at Thomas.

A drunken English soldier at another table roughly grabbed at her, but she sidestepped his advance, clenched her not-so-small hand into a fist, and slammed it smartly against his nose. The soused man dropped to the floor as if dead.

My kind of woman, thought Thomas, smiling at her, and quickly drank the full measure from both his cup and the ale horn. The tavern-keep was all too willing to aid in relieving Thomas' pouch of some of its weight in exchange for a moment of time with the woman, and Thomas was searching the depths of that pouch when two coins were laid in the keeper's hand. Thomas turned, his fingers finding the hilt of his dagger as he thought that some other was buying his woman from under him.

"My treat," smiled Graham.

Thomas' eyebrows quickly rose in surprise, and his eyes darted from David to the wench.

"Somebody awaits ye," said David still smiling.

Thomas crossed the room to the woman. She quickly looked to the tavern keeper for the signal that he had been paid, and the two disappeared through the melee of patrons and entered a small back room. A young man met them at the open doorway with another horn of ale for Thomas. He took the ale but frowned at the youth, who quickly left them. She gently grabbed him by his crotch and after had no trouble coaxing him into the room.

Thomas drank deeply of the proffered ale once again, then settled the drinking horn and slipped out of his jerkin as she fully loosened her bodice strings, releasing a grand display of buxomness in the candlelit room. She reclined onto the straw mattress and drew up her skirts to exhibit the rest of her wares. Thomas was fully pleased and allowed his trews to fall about the tops of his boots, and himself headlong onto her awaiting pulchritude. His bearded lips found her ripe, red ones in a release of carnal passion.

The whole affair lasted not long after that. She laughed and caressed him in places that felt good to him, and teasingly said, "Most don't wear their swords to me bed!"

Still in her enchantment, he was then suddenly aware of his trews hobbling his feet and his sword in its scabbard, still belted around his waist, the tip having traced a pattern of his actions in the straw on the dirt floor.

Thomas' sheepish grin was changed when she kissed him once again with her full wet lips. Then she curtly said, "Up, me dandy. Ha'e more money to make this night, I do."

He grunted in disappointment but obliged the woman.

Back in the tavern room, Thomas espied David sitting at a small table and sipping a whisky, still listening to the piper. His own mood having shifted to one of peaceful amiability, he rejoined the knight with whom he arrived.

"Did ye see a lass ye like, yet?" asked Thomas as he sat with David.

"Aye," he nodded, and pointed toward the rowdy group of English soldiers in the corner. "There's the lass I'm fixed on havin'."

Thomas turned and his eye sought the wench amongst the boisterous English, finally to see a dark-haired young woman of extraordinary comeliness. Thomas was admiring of David's taste in women, but realized that his choice was all but unobtainable with the soldiers being so enthralled by her charming ways.

"Shit!" he exclaimed. "Ye must be daft! Ye hain't got a chance in hell of gettin' *her* to bed ye!"

"Ne'ertheless, 'tis my want," said David with a confident smile.

Thomas shook his head. It was just common sense that she was out of their reach, at least for now. He gulped a swig from his cup and as he did he saw from the corner of his eye, David, passing him and heading toward the corner, and trouble. "Oh, shit!... Shit!... Shit!...," he lamented as David drew to the knot, took his chosen woman by the arm and pulled her from the man's lap.

The woman cried out angrily at first, but then she looked at David's face,, and liking what she saw, acquiesced to his accomplishment.

The man whose lap she had graced was overtaken by drunken amazement. One of his companions laughed and hooted, and teased him about his wench being taken from him by a "stinkin' Scot." The fellow soon came to the full realization of what had happened, as David, with his arm around the woman, headed toward the back chambers.

"DAVID!" shouted Thomas as the Englishman ran for his back with drawn sword.

Sir David turned instantly to see the man, sword in hand, bearing down on him. He pushed the woman into the crowd of watchers and dropped to his knees, arising with the definite sting of his dagger placed well into the man's gut. The soldier slumped at the waist and paused in disbelief, as most of his weight rested on the hilt of the knife that David still held tight, waiting to see if a twist or another thrust was needed to complete the kill.

The cheering of the dead man's comrades hushed, and the whole of the tavern grew silent when the man fell limp to the floor.

"Seize him!" screamed one. Several others pulled their blades and started for the Templar.

"God save us!" mumbled Thomas as he sipped the last from his cup.

David laughed loudly at the men approaching him with drawn weapons. He drew his sword and laughed again at them, taunting the besotted poor devils to unreasonable rage.

The woman shrunk back, as did most of the others.

One of the English swordsmen rushed the blood-spattered knight, and not knowing how, found himself impaled on the foible of David's sword. The Templar withdrew his blade and circled left as the others, stepping over the two lifeless bodies, were no longer interested in a one-on-one fight, but wanted to kill David with a collective attack.

Thomas chose one nearest him and easily dispatched him, drawing attention from the four other men, suddenly between the two large knights. The crowd, mostly Scots, cheered at the spectacle. They fought, blades flashing and clanging until the four became three, then two, and the two ran out of the door and into the snowy street.

"Ye had best leave here… they'll fetch others and be back," said the woman whose attentions were the cause of the fracas.

"Not without ye," softly said David, catching her by the wrist and pulling her toward the door. She resisted at first, but mostly for show.

Thomas backed out through the door behind David and the woman.

"What ye fixin' to do with a woman?!" asked Thomas.

"Takin' her home to da'," replied David with a big smile.

There was noise in the street toward the castle.

"They're comin'," warned Thomas.

"I hain't comin' wi' ye," objected the woman, not knowing where her captors were taking her.

"Why not?" asked David.

"In the alleyway… ye can have yer want," she said, "but not more will I go, willin'ly!"

David kissed her mouth gently and said, "As ye will."

Thomas kept an eye out for the English as the other two gave in to their carnal desires at the back wall of the stable, their feet planted firmly in the ice-cold mud.

"David! Get on with it, man!" groused Thomas.

"We're talkin'," he returned.

"Ye're talkin' us to death if we don't get out of here!"

"Ye'd be amazed at what we're talkin' about."

"No, I wouldn't," snarled Thomas.

The English soldiers came closer to the alleyway, driving Thomas deeper into the shadows as Sir David and the woman continued their tête-à-tête. *Too late to warn them,* thought Thomas as he prepared for a fight, when suddenly the woman went sashaying by him so closely that he could smell her sweating body.

She feigned tears and directly approached the nearest band of soldiers. With a tearful glance and a show of high thigh from her, the five searchers lost their wit, and their will to look further for their quarry, following her into the tavern with scarcely the span of a dagger between them.

Sir David came to Thomas. "We can be on our way," he said quietly, a smug grin across his face.

Thomas grunted and sheathed his blade, and they left the area keeping to the shadows.

The woman told of her capture just as it had happened, leaving out only the part about the silver coin David had pressed into her hand and the details of their encounter. She and her "sisters" used the event well into the night to entertain the valiant soldiers who "rescued" her.

It was a full hour later by the time the two Scots picked their way back to the priory, avoiding the many soldiers in Aberdeen looking for the two "murderers!"

"Reckon we'll not be goin' back to that place," said Thomas.

"Hain't ye goin' with me?"

"And when next are ye goin'?"

"When next I take the notion to see my Dianna," laughed David.

Thomas grumbled as he playfully pushed the knight through the rear door of the priory. "'Dianna,' eh?"

Inside, they found Henry dozing near the fire.

"We brought Sir Henry naught, neither drink nor wench," chortled David.

Henry slept on.

Thomas looked at his carousing companion in silent amazement. *The dour, mean tempered knight that always delivers his thoughts with a growl... is laughin'?* he thought.

"So, Templar, what were ye and 'Dianna' whisperin' about while I hid in the sinks betwixt the buildin's?"

David softly laughed a bit more before saying, "She's fixed to be our spy!"

Thomas' face twisted. He knew not quite how to think about what his ears heard. "She tellin' *us* what the *English* are doin'? Or tellin' the *English* what *we're* about?"

David laughed again and sat in a nearby chair, stretched his long legs out before him and reared back on the chair. "She's a'fixin' to spy for us!" he finally admitted with a broad smile of satisfaction.

Thomas' face went twisted again. "Why would she?"

David smiled and with his fingers rolled into his palm he pointed his thumb toward his own chest.

Thomas frowned in anger and went for the wineskin hanging on the wall. "If she'll sell hersel' to ye ... she'll sell ye to the English, just as quick!"

With that dire warning, he drank deep from the skin and went to his pallet. It had been an eventful evening and sleep arrested his worrisome thoughts almost immediately.

David remained spraddled out in his chair with a smile on his face for another quarter hour, ignoring his companion's warning, and certainly fully pleased with himself.

Isabella of France

FEBRUARY 25TH 1308

WESTMINSTER ABBEY

King Edward's small fleet of ships had returned across the stormy channel to land in Dover on the seventh day of February. With him arrived his new bride, Isabella of France, daughter of King Philip IV, also called Philip "The Fair." The couple were married on the twenty-second of January in Boulogne, Pas-De-Calais, France. Her brother Charles and two of her uncles, Louis d'Evreux and Charles de Valois, accompanied the bridal party to England.

Piers Gaveston had managed the affairs of state reasonably well during his tenure as regent in the king's absence, but not without his overweening manner riling many of the powerful magnates of the realm.

The English nobles and Isabella's family were highly distressed by the affections bestowed on Piers Gaveston by King Edward at the landing in Dover, when Edward abandoned his pretty young bride on the dock to run to and embrace Gaveston shouting, "Brother! Brother!"

For the occasion, Gaveston wore jewelry sufficient to overshadow the king himself.

At every interval thereafter, both private and public, their affections to each other were so unabashed that the magnates threatened civil war if Gaveston were not banished from the kingdom. The intended coronation of the king and queen had to be postponed from the eighteenth of the month due to the lords' absolute outrage, but the whole affair was temporarily saved when Edward agreed to seriously discuss the matter… at the April Parliament.

The coronation at Westminster Abbey was to be, as expected, a splendidly gaudy occasion on February twenty-fifth. The king had made the error, however, of acceding to the demand of Gaveston that he be placed in charge of the whole affair, and worse than having things go wrong, there was little that went right, even before the ceremony began.

Crowds, unlike any that had been seen since the masses that gathered for the ceremonies creating the Swan Knights, had gathered outside to catch a glimpse of their soon-to-be-crowned king and his French bride, but were greatly disappointed when the coronation dignitaries all went from the palace to the abbey via a connecting doorway, never setting foot nor hand out of doors… to avoid the crush of the crowds.

Barons who had threatened not to come to the event if Piers Gaveston were to be there, and had been assured that he would not, were appalled to see him, not just there, but in the procession, carrying the Crown of St. Edward, and dressed in royal purple sewn with pearls while all the other magnates wore cloth of gold.

Gaveston not only had failed to provide enough seats so that all of the invited nobility could sit, but the ceremony itself ran hours longer than planned. Further, the ceremonial dinner was not ready even then, and was poorly prepared and poorly served, nearly at dark.

Nevertheless, the couple were crowned, with the Archbishop of Canterbury performing the service amid much glorious pomp and pious choir singing. Edward sat upon the special chair that his father, Edward I, had constructed around 1300 to accommodate the "Stone of Destiny." He had stolen it from Scotland some years earlier in an effort to obliterate the Scottish sense of uniqueness and independence.

At the coronation banquet, Lord Pembroke, no great admirer of Edward, was placed as near as he could tolerate to the high dais when the most honored potentates took their places at the grand table. Squires and servitors should have been scurrying hither and thither to accommodate the king and the queen, the royal and noble guests, and their lords, but there was no food as yet.

Flagons of wine, brought in barrels for the occasion from the French king's own cellar by the ships carrying the nuptial entourage, were plentiful at every table. The hungry guests began drinking the wine to fill their emptiness as they talked among themselves in genteel voices, trying to conceal the undertone of outright rage brewing hot, just beneath the surface of their forced facade.

Sir Henry de Lacy, the Earl of Lincoln, assumed the chair next to Pembroke and in a rather clumsy attempt at small talk asked, "How's yer twin girls?"

Pembroke grumbled, and with one hand selected a piece of the breast meat of a songbird from the half dozen he held in his other hand, pushing it into his mouth.

Waiting for an answer, Lincoln raised his eyebrows when he saw the meat in Pembroke's hand. "Where did ye find those?" he queried.

Pembroke's eyes rolled to Lincoln's direction. "Paid dearly for 'em," he said as he continued chewing, making no hint that any other answer was forthcoming, to either question.

Lincoln grew uncomfortable and wished he had not asked.

A moment passed, Lincoln looking anywhere save in Pembroke's direction. Then Pembroke spoke in a guttural, demanding voice; "Speak of the twins ne'er more!"

Lincoln nodded and got up from his chair, feigning seeing a friend up-table. He moved right, to a vacant seat two places over, to sit beside Lord John de Botetourt. Lord John de Menteith, Earl of Lennox, sat to his immediate left.

"Lady Lincoln not in attendance, this day?" asked de Botetourt in a rough and awkward tone, being more accustomed to a rugged, unsocial life.

"Not this day," he replied almost absent-mindedly. "She's ill," he lied.

"Damned glad I ne'er took to matrimony," returned Botetourt.

"Well," started his companion, Menteith, "If ye were the king, and not just the favorite bastard of yer father, I know *ye'd* not be at the high table kissin' dear Cornwall on the lips as yer half-brother there be doin'." With his dagger he pointed toward the grand table upon the dais.

The king's attention was obviously not to his bride and new-made queen, as would be expected, but toward Sir Piers Gaveston, his proclaimed brother and Earl of Cornwall.

The king giggled, running his fingers along the inside of Gaveston's leg.

"Cease yer tease, Knave," said Piers in his usual haughty manner.

"But I want you to want me," counter teased the king, acting at pouting.

"I am the king, I want for no one," protested Piers.

"You will," returned Edward moving his hand to his companion's crotch and squeezing.

Piers jumped back. The two men giggled at their private prank done in public for their own amusement.

Sixteen-year-old Isabella sat at the king's right, her family members sitting in a row beside her. She was unaccustomed to such behavior, and it was especially harsh to her honor as it was played out before her family and the magnates of the king's own realm.

Botetourt poured more wine in his goblet from a nearby flagon and tried to avoid looking at the scene so blatantly before him.

Trumpets sounded as the first offering of delicacies was presented with flames and fanfare galore. Edward stood and cheered amid the cacophony as Isabella glared at him through brimming eyes, swearing before God that she would seek revenge upon him, in her own time, and in a manner of her own choosing.

Thomas, Earl of Lancaster and of Leicester, took the empty chair between Pembroke and Menteith.

"I could kill that god-damned baseborn Gaveston at this very minute," he whispered into Pembroke's ear.

Pembroke snorted. His chews arrested as he turned to face the large body of Lancaster, sweltering in his anger. "'Tis poor luck to kill a man on a feast day," he replied with another snort.

The incensed French royal contingent sitting at the high table, including the humiliated queen, withdrew from the banquet and left the abbey in protest of the King's continuing display of affection lavished on Gaveston at the exclusion of Isabella.

It seemed as though everyone present was exasperated with the king and his playmate, but the populace outside knew nothing of the royal brewing pot inside.

"You chased off the queen and her entourage," giggled Gaveston in a singsong manner.

"More room at the table," replied the king in the same vein, broadly smiling as if having won a victory.

. .

It was near midnight and the revelers, barely having finished eating, headed toward their various quarters. Lancaster invited Pembroke, Botetourt, Menteith, and Lincoln to his appointed apartment within the Tower of London for a stirrup cup. Lancaster poured, and each in turn took his cup in toast to the others' health as they had done for much of the afternoon and evening.

Pembroke drank his straight down and wiped his mouth with the sleeve of his cloak.

"Milords all," started Lancaster, swinging his cup to his companions. The four were expecting an additional toast, perhaps to their newly consecrated monarch. "A toast... to the death of Cornwall!"

The others were stunned, but each in his own way wanted the priggish man to be deeply tucked into his grave. And so they drank to Gaveston, not to his health, but to his death.

There was a long moment of silence as the toasters meditated on their admitted conviction. Smiles of satisfaction playing on their lips were suddenly broken by the loud snores of Pembroke, lying across Lancaster's large bed, arms outstretched, and in muddy boots and all, fast asleep. The small remainder of his toasting spirits poured from his cup onto the countrepointe on which he slept.

"Where'll ye be sleepin' this night, Milord Lancaster?" asked Lincoln.

With eyebrows raised, he replied, "Not in that bed, you are to be assured, Good Earl!"

David de Strathbogie
Earl og Atholl

MARCH 14TH 1308
CASTLE MORTLACH

"I hate that goddamned Robert Brus!" screamed Lord John, throwing his trencher of half-eaten food across the solar at the defenseless squire. The boy staunchly held his ground as the dish hit his chest, splattering chicken, bread and sauce over his person, and fell in disorder to the floor. He quickly hunkered to pick it up.

"Leave the goddamned thing where 'tis and get out!"

"Ev'rything damned by God this morning, Milord?" Sir Reginald Cheney was sitting in a large, ornately carved chair stationed in the farthest corner of the solar. He had been summoned three-quarters of an hour earlier by Lord John for the purpose of planning the next military move against The Brus.

"If ye had the goddamned piles like I have the goddamned piles ye'd be foul tempered and yelpin' yer own goddamned self!" howled Lord John.

Cheney ignored the poor attempt at gainsay and offered in its stead, "Brus and his army are back in Inverurie."

The earl almost froze in place, save for his eyebrows, which raised high upon his forehead. "Ye don't say!" he exclaimed softly.

"Accordin' to my spies," replied Cheney. "My thought is to send an expedition to the region to test the strength of his forces there."

"Is Brus still alive?!" asked the earl, suddenly remembering that Robert was in poor health when last they met. If Robert were dead, he had no interest in fighting the remaining rabble.

"He's alive," said Sir Reginald.

"Reckon Ross still hain't with us…"

"Lord William still holds to his treaty with Brus," replied Cheyne.

"What say if our regulars don't fight?" John probed.

"Ye mean, like… Slioch?"

"Aye, like Slioch," whispered the earl, propping himself up on one fubsy butt-cheek.

"We'll take Mowbray's English and mix in some of our regulars… they'll fight if one or two of their own get kilt," plotted Cheyne.

The earl sighed deeply, unsure of his own men's loyalty.

"We'll make damned sure they all fight," added Cheyne.

"Take Brechin's bunch with ye as well," ordered John.

"Put Brechin and Mowbray to the task on their own," said Cheyne. "I hain't fixin' to go!"

"Well, can ye see *me* mountin' a warhorse?" came back Buchan.

Cheyne shrugged. "I'm off to Castle Duffus in the morn to restructure the defenses there."

A streak of fear found John's backbone. "Ye leavin' Mortlach?" he asked, feeling that he was being abandoned.

"Aye," offered Cheyne, "We can't all stay bunched here… there's plenty more to protect than Buchan, Milord Earl." Then added as further explanation, "I am the Warden of Moray and have many lands under my seal."

John again heaved a great sigh, knowing Cheyne to be right.

"Ye'll have this one, as well, to protect," whined the earl.

"How so?"

"I'm an old man, and alas, too sore for the battle… Done, am I," he cried great tears as self-sorrow filled his heart and wit.

"'Tis the pain in yer arse that speaks to ye," suggested Cheyne, thinking that Buchan was trying to manipulate him to his will. "Tomorrow, yer pain will be nigh gone and ye'll be hiein' for Inverurie atop yer destrier and whoopin' as best ye e'er did, Milord."

Lord John smiled, hoping Cheyne was right. Then pains from his hemorrhoids sent a wave of excruciating agony throughout his body, and he realized how dire a hope it really was as far as *his* participation was concerned.

"Send for Lord David!" he ordered, still in torment. "He's the one that's full of hate for 'King Robert.'"

Murdoch

MARCH 23RD 1308
NORTH INVERURIE NEAR OLD MELDRUM

The countryside surrounding Inverurie consisted mostly of rock-strewn pastures, just starting to sprout anew, and freshly turned sections of tilth, spotted here and there with wooded patches. A dusting of new-fallen snow, muted by the gray sky, drained the color from early spring's palette. Murdoch and MacKie, still outfitted in their cloaks of longhaired goat skins, were once again placed at the forefront of the observation outposts, this time at Old Meldrum, a tiny hamlet of but a few hovels along the Urie River.

Two leagues in a southerly direction, the remains of old, rotting wooden walls barely showed above the mound that, seventy years earlier, was a Norman built motte and bailey castle. Within sight of the castle mound the Brus camp lay, south of the River Don and above its confluence with the Urie. From there, Aberdeen was about eight leagues to the southeast.

Still all but incapacitated, King Robert was billeted in a large manor house almost a half-mile south of where he had first been struck with illness three-and-a-half months before. In the meantime, he had been carted and carried to Slioch, to a harsh freezing time in Strathbogie, then for a short visit to Kildrummy, and now back to Inverurie, all the while under the protection of his loyal army and of his Christina of Carrick, who had tended him all through the miserably cold winter.

Most of his army now laid about in villein's huts, and many others in shelters of their own invention. It was warmer at Inverurie than it had been in the mountains when they were there, and the light snow that had fallen was as much a harbinger of spring as a reminder of winter.

Christina came into the room carrying a tray of victuals.

Robert was sitting on the edge of the bed in the middle of the room, a battleaxe in his hand. His broadsword hung on the bedpost. Hard-earned sweat dotted his forehead and trickled down into his eyebrows as he worked to bring himself back to the strength he had the year before. "What ye feedin' me this day, Woman?" he asked.

"Chicken stew," she answered, putting the tray on a sideboard near the bed.

"Chicken! Again?"

"Chicken's good for ye, Milord King." She busied herself straightening up his bed.

"Much more of it and I'll be grubbin' in the byre yard for my supper!" he replied. He continued exercising with his battleaxe, making a few deft swishes in the air with his left hand, then with his right.

"Yer strength is returnin', slow but steady," remarked Christina.

As his arm gave way to the weight of the axe, he dropped it to the wooden floor where its upper tip stuck, the handle upright. There were a number of scars on the floorboards that looked like they might have been made that way. He took up a cloth and wiped his face commenting, "Not fast 'nough for me."

"Ye been workin' too much this day," she said. She pulled a chair up to his knees, and to be close, pushed her legs between and sat.

"'Ppears a wee bit of spring's tryin' to squeeze out that terrible winter," she said shifting the tray to his lap.

And my time for warring on the Comyns without their gettin' English reinforcements may well-nigh be gone, he lamented in his thoughts.

"What say?" she questioned, making him wonder if she could read his mind.

"Any word on the Comyns?" he said, changing the subject as he gingerly brought the hot bowl near his lips and blew to cool the stew.

"None, Milord," she replied, "but I *shall* have some 'woeful-soul' bring ye the latest news from the outlands within the hour." Then she paused in thought, "There is one matter."

Robert raised his head to look at her. "Aye?"

"Yer hostage has arrived," she said, almost offhandedly.

"Hostage?" he asked, frowning in puzzlement.

"Young man from Ross," said she, "son of Lord William."

Robert nodded, understanding. "That is good news." He sipped some of the stew's broth from a wooden spoon.

"Seems the earl means to keep his truce in good stead with ye, My King," she opined.

Robert sipped again. "Can we get somethin' different for later?"

"Somethin'?… Ye mean… like a piece of meat from a buck's hindquarters?"

He grinned and nodded approval as he took a bite of hot chicken and cautiously chewed to prevent being burned.

"Ye may have to slay the beast with yer axe," she teased.

He smiled at her humor, and it occurred to him that it was good to smile again.

She offered him a cup of herb tea, her special medicinal concoction. "Drink!"

"Have my brother sent to me," he said to her, setting the bowl on the tray perched on his lap and taking the cup from her hand.

"Yer brother is… ill, again," she sadly replied.

"Send Boyd and Haye, then," he grumbled. "Edward's grievin' for my sickness."

Christina was feeling untruthful when she agreed with him.

● ●

A mere six miles north of the Brus outpost sprawled the encampment of the Comyn army, one thousand strong. They fully meant to erase the steadily dwindling "Brus rebellion" forever.

"Spy comin' in!" announced a picket, and a single rider rode pell-mell into the camp.

A guard, standing at Mowbray's tent, entered and told of the return of one of his spies. The baron waved the man in and was told of an incident along the road to Inverurie, where he and his companion ran into a fellow he now knows was of The Brus' army. Innocently striking up a conversation with the fellow to gather information, they were set upon by unseen archers, who killed his companion and would have killed him, had he not been clever enough to escape, an arrow in the pommel of the saddle on which he rode.

After the spy was dismissed, a herald was summoned.

"Take a message to the Earl of Buchan. Say that we shall be goin' for what's left of the Brus army, and that, if he wants any of the glory, he has two days to get here," said the baron.

"Aye, Milord," replied the messenger.

Without warning, Brechin excitedly threw the flap of the baron's tent back and entered, upon which the messenger was dismissed by Mowbray with a wave of his hand. "Hear they've run the Brus gang to ground," he said, eagerly wanting more news.

"North of Inverurie," was the casual answer.

"We goin' on the morn?" Brechin asked as he sat on the edge of the baron's pallet.

"We're waitin' for word from Lord John... see if he wants to 'lead' us into battle," came back Mowbray, sarcastically.

"If they know we're here," the knight protested, "they'll bolt, Sire!"

"Well, they know," grumped the baron.

Brechin groaned and shook his head in disgust.

"I doubt if the ol' earl will get off his infirm arse to sally in this direction... but if he has such a desire, let him come, I say."

"He'll just send word he hain't comin'... and it'll be too late... they'll be away!" whined Brechin.

Mowbray raised a brow. "Now or later, we'll dispense with them. Matters not to me."

Brechin left in a huff. Mowbray smiled a bit. He liked to vex the impetuous Brechin in small ways. *It's good to show who is 'cock of the walk' and who is all squawk and feathers,* he mused. Then he laid himself down on his freshly abandoned pallet and pulled his heavy covers about his neck. "Too cold for war," he remarked aloud as he closed his eyes and nodded off.

Brechin went immediately to Lord David's bivouac area to plead with the earl to make for Inverurie on the morn. The young earl quickly agreed to "go cut the ears from The Brus' head" but had a terrible time remaining upright from being too much in his cups. Showing his prowess with a large blade, he sliced the tent apart, causing Brechin to make his exit quickly. Left to himself, the earl had a long drink and soon passed out, to dream of killing The Brus.

The eager Brechin soon came to the conclusion that getting the earl involved was a dangerous idea. He went his way brooding over the facts and the baron's lack of action.

"I thought The Brus was already dead," remarked a knight standing near the earl's tent.

"I saw him bein' carried out from Slioch, and he looked dead," said his companion.

"If he hain't, it'll sure surprise a lot of folks hereabouts," the first agreed.

"Aye. He's dead... he's dead for sure," reiterated the second.

. .

The ignored and angry young Brechin decided in the night to take the ending of the Brus army into his own hands. He took his command, nearly two hundred knights and foot soldiers, and led them from their campsite before dawn. The spy came along to guide them to where he had seen Brus forces the day before. Riding all morning in a misty and cold spring rain, by midday the hunters were close to Old Meldrum.

"Yonder's his dead body," said the spy, pointing to the crumpled figure face down on the muddy road stretching before the advancing army. "The bowmen were just there," he pointed, "in the trees."

"Take those woods apart!" commanded Brechin to his horsed knights, who proceeded in an orderly fashion down the road toward the grove with weapons drawn and ready.

As they entered the tree line, the thoroughly soaked men could hear nothing but their own horses and the patter of the rain. Followed by the soldiers of foot, the horsemen moved cautiously, picking their way through the rock-strewn grove, but could find not a soul, exiting the stand of trees on the other side.

"They ran away before we got here," said the spy, wiping rain from his eyes. "They knew we would be comin' for them, and they ran away. Simple as that."

Brechin looked at him, but said nothing. He was disappointed in the extreme. This was to be his victory, when he finally brought down The Brus and his rebels after the likes of Aymer de Valence, John Comyn, Dungal Macdouall, and others had failed in the effort. He shoved his sword into its sheath, as did most of his knights, and heaved a great sigh before sending his troops back through the misty grove to return to the Comyn camp... empty handed.

"ATTACK!!" yelled Neil Campbell suddenly, and he rushed from the surrounding trees, guisarme in hand. The hook on the backside of the six-foot long weapon snatched the nearest knight to him by the neck on his armor and jerked him from his destrier. His pike went flying unattended before the knight had in mind to make the first defensive swing.

The woods were all at once alive with long shafted weapons pulling knights to the ground as other Brus warriors teamed to finish the unmounted men with swords, axes, and daggers.

Soon there was a score of riderless horses panicking and kicking amongst the trees, frightening the soldiers of foot so badly that they fled like chaff before the wind.

"On them men!" ordered Sir David Brechin, wheeling his steed toward his scattering men. As he looked to ascertain the enemy's force, they had vanished back into the wood as quickly as they had come, having killed some twenty-five of the knights, losing none of their own.

Brechin was livid. "After them, ye bastards!" he screamed at the highest pitch of his voice.

The remaining horsed knights picked their way farther into the wood where Sir Neil's men had fled. Some of the foot soldiers, having regrouped beyond the wood with blades at the ready were met only with their own knights bounding forth from the trees.

"Where are they? Where are the cowards?!" squawked Brechin as his knights began to filter back out of the woods onto the roadway.

The captain of the knights shook his head in amazement, "Weren't that many... but... it's like... tryin' to catch wee flittin' birds!"

"Get back in there and find 'em, damn yer eyes!" Brechin cursed. "And don't come from there without their heads on yer pikes!"

The men reluctantly started back in the wood, but this time with weapons poking at everything suspicious as they went. After a half hour of such, the captain returned to Brechin with nothing to report, prompting a string of expletives from his commander. Finally, he ordered the troops to withdraw and they assembled again on the road.

"Move on!" commanded the aggravated Brechin, and leading the way, he started back toward the Comyn camp.

Reaching an open field already prepared by the local farmers for spring planting, the Brechin force saw, along the far edge of the plowed ground, Neil Campbell's force taunting and jeering at them.

"Don't miss yer aim this damn time," scolded Murdoch to MacKie, whose arrow had failed to bring down the fleeing spy, now returning with Brechin's troops.

They both loosed arrows into the enemy forces with their usual accuracy.

A Brechin knight gagged as he clutched his neck and slipped uncontrollably from the saddle. Within an eye's blink, the man behind him took an arrow in his side just under the chest armor and he began to scream in pain and panic.

The two brothers and a couple of other archers continued to place arrow after arrow into the army standing along the road that bifurcated the field, while the other Brus Scots shouted insults and several dropped their trews and turned to display their backsides to the seething Brechin.

It was all more than he could bear. Pulling his sword once more from its sheath, he ordered his troops to charge across the open, muddy tillage.

The captain gave the order and his knights turned to the right toward the scant line of "rebels" some one hundred or more yards away. They lowered their lances and pikes into position and started out into the mud at a walk.

"Get ready! They're comin' after us with lances!" said Murdoch.

"Put yer brother on my horse," ordered Campbell, ignoring Murdoch's statement.

Brechin knights picked up their pace across the field.

"I'm not lettin' him out of this fight!" objected Murdoch.

"Send him to warn King Robert!" ordered Campbell.

"Aye Sir!" said Murdoch, and he sent MacKie as instructed. MacKie gave his brother his own quiver of arrows, those that were left, thinking he was never going to see him again.

"This argument hain't lastin' that long… now get," said Murdoch, and he slapped the horse on the rump. MacKie disappeared into the trees as Murdoch began pelting the oncoming cavalry with the remainder of his arrows, garnering a deadly effect.

Sir Neil and his rain-soaked men bravely stood to the ready.

Brechin led the center of the charge, his broadsword held high. Banners of many colors were waving in the wind and the continuing drizzle caused their armor to take on a shimmery glow.

"Stand fast men…" said Campbell, "hold tight to yer axes!"

Nervously gripping the long axe handles, his men awaited the last second, when they would sidestep the charging knight, and unhorsing him by hooking some part of his clothing or person, hack him to death with the axe.

The knights now urged their destriers to their fastest, seeing that they were favored in the one-sided battle against the small contingent of Scots. The huge horses' hooves were heavily caked with mud from the wet field, and in accelerating they lost traction. Some slid headlong into the waiting Campbell men, who made short work of their riders. Others, seeing their fellows go down, tried to rein in their mounts, causing them to slide and fall. Horses and riders went down in the mud.

The seventeen remaining Campbell warriors made a valiant stand, but the muddied field was a poor equalizer for the overwhelming numbers under Sir David Brechin.

Lance against flesh, knights falling to the ground being axed, blade against blade, and the screams of agony on both sides created a horrific cacophony that echoed off the hills.

Murdoch had thrown his treasured longbow over his shoulder and pulled his axe into his right hand and his short sword in his left. Most of his companions, including Sir Neil, had already fallen. Murdoch gave a loud whoop and charged the closest destrier. With his axe he caught the back of the horse's knee, bringing it down and tossing its rider within reach of Murdoch's sword blade.

The next was an unhorsed man, running at him with his sword swinging above his head. Murdoch set his feet wide into the viscous mud, ready to repel the attack, but was trampled by a running destrier. He fell face first into the muck. He groaned and tried to push up before he finally collapsed, blood running from his mouth and nose.

With the men of the Brus rebellion gone, the knights withdrew, and Sir David Brechin ambled his destrier among their crimson washed bodies. He smiled in satisfaction.

Tears filled MacKie's eyes as he watched the action from the saddle of Neil Campbell's horse. When he saw the enemy regrouping on the road, and none of his companions-in-arms standing, he spurred the horse toward Inverurie.

. .

MacKie reined in his horse in front of Gilbert de la Haye.

"The Comyns are nigh to us, Sir Gilbert!" he said sorrowfully.

"They at Meldrum?" asked the knight.

"At Meldrum... and killed 'em all," he nodded, his face streaked with tears for his poor brother, whom he had seen go down in the bloody tilth.

"Killed who... and how many are comin' for us?" Haye asked in a quick demanding voice.

"Hundred or more on horse and many more than that afoot," reported MacKie.

Gilbert de la Haye's brain was whirring as he ran the fifty yards to the fortified manor house where King Robert and the other leaders were staying. He ran through the gate and straight through the door.

"They're at Meldrum!" he announced in a loud voice that traveled throughout the house.

"How many?" asked Boyd as he came to Haye.

"Hundreds, perhaps two or three. MacKie can't count," he replied. "All we had there were killed, apparently, Sir Neil among them."

Christina, hearing the commotion below, opened the door to hear more clearly.

"What are they sayin', woman?" asked Robert.

"All the men at Meldrum are dead by the Comyns, and they are headed this way," she reported sadly.

Robert's eyes widened and filled with tears. *Just what I had hoped for... the enemy comes to us... but at what cost?* he thought.

Boyd, Haye, and Murray ran up the stone stairs to the king's solar. Robert stood, and at his behest, Christina opened the door wide to allow them in.

"My King..." started Boyd in excitement.

"I know. Who wouldn't with all that bellowin'?" replied Robert in a calm voice.

"What are our orders, My King," asked Boyd.

"Where is my brother?" asked Robert, temporarily ignoring the question.

"Below," said Murray, "Asleep."

"Shake him from his stupor... he needs to be a part of this," insisted Robert.

"I'll get him," said Murray, and he left the room.

"Will ye sit, My King?" suggested Christina coming to Robert and steadying his stance.

"This is good medicine for me, Lady Christina," said Robert, visibly forcing himself to keep on his feet. "I will lead the men into battle."

Christina gritted her teeth but said not a word. Nevertheless, Robert read her face.

"I am fit... am I not?" he asked her.

"Ye're hale and fit in yer heart, Sire, but not for sword work," she earnestly replied.

He sat heavily on the edge of the bed. "I must be with my men..."

"My King," started Christina, "with our enemy at the gate, perhaps it would be wise to gather the troops... as many as can be mustered... and send them against the enemy this very minute."

Robert blinked and looked at Robert Boyd and Gilbert de la Haye. "Make haste to move against the enemy... Edward and I will follow."

"Our five or six hundred against their two or three hundred, we should easily win," interjected Gilbert.

"That is probably not their full company," cautioned Robert.

"Then they are fools to split it in such a way," returned Gilbert.

"Fools... or tricksters," said Robert, picking up his battleaxe from the floor and laying it on the bed beside him.

He's goin' no matter what I say, thought Christina.

Murray returned with Sir Edward in tow. Edward was rumpled and limp of limb from being freshly awakened, but clearly understood the implications at hand.

Robert continued to sit on the edge of the bed. "Murray, ye and yer men from Moray... Is Barclay still alive?" he suddenly asked, seemingly confused about what had actually happened and his illness dreams.

"Aye, My King," returned Murray.

"And Barclay, then..." he continued, "and those two Frasers... and Wiseman as well... go as vanguard to those who seek us out."

"Aye, My King," agreed Bishop Murray, "but Wiseman left two weeks ago for the northwest."

Robert looked surprised at first, but continued, "The rest of us will be directly behind ye."

Murray briefly bowed and left to get his men kitted to leave immediately.

"Ready my horse, Gilbert," said Robert, "and get the remainder of the troops set to be the aft guard."

"Aft guard?" he questioned, "for the king?"

"No time for particulars, we've got a battle to win... be at it!" he commanded.

"Aye, My King," said Gilbert, and with a quick nod, disappeared out the door.

"Reckon ye've got a plan?" asked Boyd as Edward slumped to a nearby armchair and propped his weary head on his fist.

Robert sighed deep at the sight of his brother.

"Got some of it... the rest will come when we get there," he replied.

"God grant it to ye," prayed Boyd as he plucked Edward from the chair and led him out.

There was a quiet moment as Robert sat on the bed and Christina stood over him. "There's naught a word that I can say to dissuade ye from yer notion?" she asked.

"'Tis critical that I be there," he replied. "'Tis the beginnin' of our return to victory, or the end of us all. Should we not win this battle, 'twill make no difference if I am here, or there..."

"Go ye, then," she said, "I knew ye would from the first... but it chafes my heart."

From the drawer of a nearby chest she retrieved his saffron tabard with the red lion. "Yer surcoat, My King," she said, releasing its folds.

He took the brightly colored cloth and looked at it as if it were a relic from a life long since past. Christina had patched it as best she could, and washed out the blood of John Wallace, who was wearing it when he was mortally wounded.

He sighed deeply again. "Is this my folly?" he asked her.

"Nay, my dear Robert. 'Tis not yer folly... 'tis yer destiny," she said, tears welling in her eyes.

She unwrapped his stored away chain-mail... the full-length coat, the leggings, and the coif... and began to dress her king for battle. He had not only to fight the Comyns and English but his infirmity as well, while carrying scores of pounds of protective metal.

From outside they could hear the noises of people preparing for battle, as the bishop gathered his men from Moray on the orders of their king, to move against the Comyn force that had come to kill them all.

MacKie, anxious to retrieve the body of his dead brother, went with Moray's vanguard force.

"Knowing this day was nigh," said Christina, " I have had them make ye a special saddle with a high back, where ye can be girded about yer chest, to keep ye upright, My King."

Robert frowned at the idea but said no word in protest. He was reluctantly grateful she had had such a notion. She was being so formal toward him and so fatalistic at his going that he began to think she held little hope that he would survive.

He took her hand and started to say his goodbyes, but she interrupted.

"Tell me no farewells, Robert Brus, for I'll be ridin' at yer side," she announced.

Robert's eyes narrowed slightly. He wasn't sure what she had meant at first, but was quickly relieved of any confusion when she threw off her long skirt and blouse, and bound her breasts with strips of cloth and a tight fitting linen tunic, over which she put on trews and chain mail of her own.

"Ye can't do this!" exclaimed Robert.

"Can and am," she flatly said as she continued.

"What about our bairns?" he asked.

"As it happens to ye, 'twill happen to me as well," she philosophized. "Our bairns will either be earls... or orphans." She then twisted her hair to a knot atop her head and tied a helm cap over it. Slipping her Carrick tabard over her head, she cinched it with a wide leather belt over which she strapped on a broadsword and the dagger she always carried under her dress.

"Ye've thought of this for a while," he said observing the completeness of her dressing.

"My greatest fear," she replied, standing tall and looking every bit a warrior knight. "But I will do my part and yer bidding."

"Then, I bid ye stay here," he said.

"Only that, will I *not* obey," she replied, as if motivated by a solemn oath to a higher power than the king.

Robert had no more to say and Christina opened the door and called to Robert's squire to come escort his liege lord to the manor's courtyard and his awaiting destrier a new, well-trained Welsh Cobb that had an almost white coat.

"Where is *my* horse?" asked Robert.

"Killed by the enemy and et by yer men, My King," replied Andrew matter-of-factly.

The king of all the Scots nodded, and with a boost from Boyd and Andrew, he was aboard. Sir Gilbert strapped him onto the special saddle, covering the harness and the high saddle back with Robert's royal tabard. Christina mounted her dappled palfrey and took a place beside the king. Sir Gilbert rode on the other side of Robert to steady him if need be.

"On yer command, My Liege," offered Sir Gilbert.

Robert spurred his new horse through the courtyard gate. There his arrayed army stood.

"Look!" yelled one, "'Tis King Robert!"

Cheers followed as Robert waved to all his warriors and the gathered townsfolk, then drew his battleaxe from the saddle sling and pointed it toward Old Meldrum. Sir Gilbert gave the war whoop and Andrew and Baldred moved ahead of the king with the flags. Sir Robert Boyd and Sir Edward rode immediately behind their king.

The remaining part of his army, still cheering and whooping, zealously followed.

. .

Sir David Brechin halted his troops just south of Old Meldrum, thinking it too late in the afternoon to finish the Brus army by the time he reached Inverurie. Waxing ecstatic over his victory against the seventeen outpost keepers, he decided to rest and bivouac in an open field surrounded by a wooded area.

Tomorrow will be a good mornin' for killin' what remains of the rebellion and by leavin' Mowbray and Strathbogie behind, I shall get all the credit, he pleasantly mused. As his reverie continued, it occurred to him that, perhaps, there would even be an earldom in it for him from the grateful, King Edward.

The latter part of the gray afternoon finally gave way, and the sun hazily appeared in the western sky. This omen was Brechin's confirmation of his rightful choosing.

Sir David de Murray, leading the men of Moray, was at least a half hour ahead of the second army led by King Robert. Within a mile of where Brechin was camped, he saw sixteen riders coming toward him leading another seven horses by the reins.

"Comyn or ours?" asked Barclay as the men approached.

"The trappin's on the mounts are Comyn," replied Murray, who pulled his weapon partway from its sheath.

"Damned friendly for Comyns," said Barclay, seeing the approaching riders wave as if trying to hail them.

When they were close enough, Murray recognized them as being men assigned to the outpost and slammed his sword back into its scabbard.

"Thought ye were all dead," said a smiling Murray to the apparent leader.

"On the one side of the enemy line, all are dead, Sir David," explained the fellow, "but Sir Neil had us run in 'tother direction, so's we could sneak back, and pick up the destriers of the dead Comyns while the rest were a'chasin' Sir Neil's bunch."

Murray and Barclay smiled at the Campbell's cleverness.

"Goin' to miss Sir Neil," lamented Barclay, his smile quickly gone wistful.

"Ye know the whereabouts of the Comyn troops that killed him?" questioned the bishop.

"Aye, Sir. Camped, 'round that bend up yonder, they are, and some English mixed in, too," said the man pointing northward along the road.

"Fall in behind the knights," ordered Barclay, "and parcel out the remainin' mounts to them that are used to ridin' but hain't got horses."

• •

"Brus army's a'comin'!" screamed the picket as he pulled up sharply at Brechin's tent. "Half mile away!"

"My God! They're here?!" yelped Brechin.

"Aye, Sir. Here and full arrayed for a fight!" reported the picket excitedly.

Brechin grabbed his sword from his pallet and rushed onto the muddy field half dressed. He had been inside resting and savoring his earlier victory. The campfires were burning as the men were laying about preparing their evening meal.

"TO ARMS! TO ARMS!" he shouted at the top of his voice as he ran through the seasoned knights, some of whom were already preparing for a fight. Brechin had been so comfortable with his superiority over The Brus' "rabble," that he had not even observed the details of his surroundings, and hadn't a clue to a battle plan or even possible defensive strategies.

Their captain, a knowledgeable soldier, directed his knights to their positions and the men hurriedly set about defending themselves. Brechin naturally credited himself with being a brilliant leader when he saw the men marshaling in such an effective array.

Murray's army came down the road and began to filter out across the tree line on the opposite side of the field from the Brechin army.

"Remind ye of earlier today?" said the captain.

Brechin nodded his head in quiet agreement and said, "Except there are one hell of a lot more of 'em, now. Still, we have greater numbers than they have."

"Let them come chargin'," suggested the captain, "We can sit right here and cut them up with our archers before they reach us."

"Very well," agreed Brechin. "We'll await their charge."

Unknown to them was the fact that Simon Fraser, leading another contingent, had marched around by the east woods to cover their flank.

"They figure we're less than they are," remarked Barclay.

"'Tis well, for we are more than they," replied Murray. He crossed himself and offered up a prayer for his words to be true, then pulled out his mace and sat looking into the enemy camp.

Some minutes went by, but the two armies held their positions and stared across the field between them. "Why do they wait?" asked Brechin's captain. "They are arrayed for a charge, why do they pause?"

Brechin sat without reply, scanning the field for signs of other troops arriving. Colorful banners strung on his knight's lances and others held by their squires fluttered almost noiselessly in the light afternoon breeze. The sleek, well cared for Destriers snorted and pawed the ground waiting for action, their masters sitting astride, outwardly unmoved.

The captain thought he saw movement in the woods to the east when a bit of sun glinted off a buckler or a sword. "They have troops to the left of us, Sire!"

Brechin looked where he pointed, but saw nothing.

"I saw a flash off metal!" insisted the captain, fearing that Brechin considered him daft.

"A'right, we'll move forward, and set the left flank a'facin' the woods.

Across the field Barclay watched the rearrangement of the Brechin men and said, "They've caught sight of the Frasers."

"Seems so," agreed Murray, "but they hain't seen all of us as yet."

"Let's pray they don't, Milord Bishop," suggested Barclay.

"Already have," said Murray with a smile.

Brechin's forces reined in and stopped at about fifty yards from The Brus' line, which held its position.

"What ye reckon be their trick?" asked the captain to Brechin.

"Don't know," he returned. "This is like no other ..." he began but was stopped short when, without warning, Simon Fraser brought his horsed contingent to the open field and at once charged the left flank of Brechin's army.

Murray instantly gave the order to charge along the front, and Brechin, with the Brus cavalry charging at him from both sides, ordered his knights to charge as well. To the left and the front resounded a tremendous clash of men and weapons. Brechin's knights had long lances while the Murray knights had but sword and axe.

On the first encounter, Murray's men took the brunt of the charge and the lance points of the Brechin force. Scores of knights were either killed or unhorsed by the long lances, but those who survived that initial charge were thereafter on a fairly equal basis with their adversaries. Scots blood flew in every direction as the armies set to work with more personal weapons.

Fraser's troops managed to get behind Brechin's, and he suddenly realized that he was surrounded on all sides and losing badly. Before his stunned eyes his superior numbers were quickly being whittled to kindling.

"We must retreat, Sire!" shouted his captain.

Bewildered, Brechin agreed, for his bloodied men were dying all around him.

The captain broke away from the fight and screamed for his men to withdraw. As ordered, they gave way and tried to retreat, but the Murray knights and foot soldiers were upon them, dogging their withdrawal with deadly resolve.

Then suddenly, the forces under Murray found themselves facing greater numbers than there had been. The field was being overrun with men of the Comyn camp, and the superior numbers were now held in Brechin's favor.

The Murray Scots, clearly the victors and chasing the Brechin soldiers from the battlefield were, within minutes, transformed into the ones being overwhelmed and chased by additional hordes of Comyn troops.

"Trickery!" cried Murray, "Pull back and regroup!"

The Brus Scots, on horse and on foot, rushed to the far side of the field from whence they had attacked. Murray's three hundred and fifty, more or less, were abruptly facing Brechin's eight or nine hundred.

"How could we have so underestimated their numbers?" cried Barclay, gauging the enemy's force. "What had been about two hundred are now perhaps near a thousand!"

"Cease yer poppycock!" commanded Murray, not wanting to demoralize his men. "Numbers matter not! We will fight to the last man… win or lose!"

Visibly shaken, David de Brechin found himself facing the irate Lord John Mowbray. "Don't know which I hate worse, ye or that band of rabble yonder!" ranted the baron. "For all that, I don't know why I came to save yer sorry arse anyway!"

Brechin stared with fearful, rounded eyes and angrily sputtered, "I needed no savin'!"

"Ye'd be bleedin' and pukin' in the mud this second, had we not rode hot to yer rescue," countered Mowbray, disdainfully.

Brechin was furious, but knew in his heart that the baron was right. Thus, like a whipped dog, spurred his horse between the knights and withdrew to the rear, leaving the field and the glory to Mowbray.

"See anything of The Brus?" asked Mowbray of the captain, now slightly wounded and bleeding.

"Nay, Sire. Not a hair," he replied. "Most of my men are sayin' that the so-called 'king' is dead. Killed at Slioch. And I have no doubt of it. Else, where is he whilst his army is about to be slaughtered?"

Lord David of Strathbogie approached them. "We come to prate or to fight?" he challenged.

Mowbray had no choice but to yield command, though it galled him. "Ye are senior, Milord," replied the baron to the young earl, "We are at yer biddin'."

"Array to charge, then!" ordered Strathbogie. "And this time, make it last!"

Trumpets sounded and the knights took their places in the vanguard, lances high, as the others had done before.

"It's damn nigh to an hour ere sundown. We have to make this quick!" advised Mowbray.

"That will not be difficult," bragged Lord David confidently, and he rode to the center of the line to begin the charge across the muddy field, already strewn with the dead and the dying of both armies.

"We chargin' or runnin'?" asked the Fraser, his bloodied sword still in his hand.

"Chargin'!" insisted Murray, but before he began his impending war whoop, he was interrupted by the trumpet of a ram's horn being sounded behind him.

"'Tis King Robert!" shouted Barclay, his spirits soaring.

"Open the line at center!" ordered Murray. "The king must lead!"

Strathbogie and Mowbray's army started their charge, moving at a walking pace.

The King's red and yellow banner and the Saint Andrew's blue and white, both emerged at the center of the vanguard line carried by the two young squires. They trotted to the side as the trumpet continued. King Robert, still flanked by Sir Gilbert and Lady Christina, came to the fore and halted while the remainder of Robert's warriors melded with Murray's. Now, the numbers of soldiers were more balanced.

Picking up the gait to a trot, Strathbogie moved his line more quickly toward the center of the field.

King Robert, his gaze always upon Strathbogie, gathered his reins in his shield hand, and raised his battleaxe in the other, preparing to lead the charge. Gilbert and Christina drew their swords, ready to protect the king.

Those in the Comyns' line realized that the heart of the rebellion, the man they thought was long dead, was here, alive, and before them ready to do battle. What manner of necromancy had he wrought to return from the netherworld and fight more against them? Thus shaken, they neared the halfway point with less fervor.

Even if he were truly alive and not risen from the dead to fight against them, Robert's reputation as a fierce and fearless warrior was well known among the opposing northern clans, and as the charge drew closer to him, individual knights started reining their horses and soldiers on foot slowed their advance. Soon, only some few handfuls of English continued toward the awaiting Brus army and its terrible king.

Reaching the center, Strathbogie ordered the gallop, not realizing that his vanguard was melting away like spring snow neath the warm rain.

As the riders gained speed, Murray's archers slipped between the knightly horsemen and fired their deadly shafts into the approaching Comyn-English attackers, taking down a horse and its rider with one well-placed missile to a horse's broad chest. The bowmen quickly reduced the line still further.

Strathbogie fell back to let the English knights go ahead and was shocked to see only a portion of the line that started with him across the wide field. While he watched, some of even that number seemed to plunge to earth, head over heels as their mounts collapsed mid-stride, landing horse and rider close by the feet of King Robert's great white

Cobb.

Lord David, astride his horse, stood alone about thirty yards before Robert. The scene of the king, standing untouched with fallen knights at his feet was not lost on him, or on any in the Comyn army. Momentarily they became fearful at the sight and began to break ranks and run away from the battlefield altogether.

The commanders, unable to hold even a center core of fighters, also began to crumble and scatter.

"After 'em Lads!" commanded the king in a strong voice.

Charged with excitement that their king was once again animated, Robert's army at last sensed it was about to savor victory, again, and the prospect overwhelmed them. Even Sir Edward Brus kicked his mount, and shouting with the rest, took off after the fleeing rout.

Both groups went sliding and slipping in the mud all the way across the battlefield and disappeared through the wood on the other side. Only Robert, Christina, Gilbert, and the standard bearers remained.

The Comyn foot soldiers were easily overrun, countless numbers struck down by swords held by mounted knights moving through them. Brus' foot warriors swooped in to finish off many.

MacKie, his service to the king completed, and worried about his brother's body being devoured by packs of roving wolves attracted to the massive carnage, broke away and headed toward the field where the seventeen were slain, to give Murdoch a proper burial.

Robert, still holding his battleaxe at the ready, announced to Christina, "I'm worn to the bone."

"Let's get ye back to Inverurie, My King," she kindly suggested.

"Feels kind of lonely, with everybody just runnin' off thataway," bemoaned Baldred, looking about the death-strewn ground.

Andrew turned and looked at his king.

Robert knew his mind and said, "Chase after them, if ye have the mind."

Andrew smiled back and shook his head, instead remaining with the king.

At last Christina sheathed her sword.

Several of the thrown and bloodied English knights began to recover from their horrific falls and arose from where they fell to stagger about.

Sir Gilbert raised his broadsword to finish their suffering, but they threw their hands in the air in supplication. Robert caused Gilbert to hold his wrath and walked his horse toward the helpless men. He paused before them and looked sternly at each one.

"Ye men swear ne'er to raise yer weapons against me or my kingdom again?" he finally asked.

The four injured and dispirited men fell to their knees and those who could raised their empty, clasped hands above their heads indicating their surrender. Afterward, and individually, they plighted their troths that they would never assault him or Scotland again.

Robert put his axe in the sling on his saddle, and relaxed his tired arm, saying, "Ye will strip yerselves of all armor and weapons save a small blade each for protectin', and walk home to England," ordered Robert.

All agreed and began to shed their armor.

The five Scots wheeled their mounts and left the English where they stood.

"If he hain't goin' to watch what we do, I'm takin' my kit," whispered one of the knights.

"You take it and I'll kill you!" said another. "I gave oath as a knight, and I'll not let you…" with his hand on his short sword he looked at his other companions, "nor any of you… sully my honor! We'll leave this land as we said we would!"

MacKie reached the site where his brother had fallen to find that wolves had indeed been making meals of the dead warriors. Even though he saw no wolves around, his horse had gotten scent of the creatures and was affrighted, making it difficult to manage.

With tears streaming down his face, he coaxed the horse through the horror. "Ach! Poor Murdoch!" he lamented from his saddle. He was reluctant to dismount for fear the nervous animal would run off and leave him there, and from the looks of things, the wolves were not long gone.

He spotted Murdoch's goatskin cloak on the muddy ground and massed in blood. "Poor, poor Murdoch!" he again lamented, sobbing openly and wiping his nose on his sleeve. It was then that he saw it in the failing light, a yellow-eyed, snarling wolf not ten feet from his horse.

Drawing an arrow from his quiver, he nocked it and let it fly into the wolf. The predator yelped in sudden pain and fell dead beside his crimson red meal.

The horse danced all about, nearly flinging MacKie off its back, and screamed and whinnied as it saw a wolf crouching beside the ragged remains of another soldier. Thinking that the carrion was the body of his brother, MacKie loosed another barb into the second wolf, which yelped pitifully and dragged itself away.

MacKie kept an arrow nocked as the horse was made to pick its way through the offal and scattered parts of bodies. What Brechin's men hadn't hacked apart the ravenous wolves had. It was more than the heart-broken MacKie could bear.

"MURDOCH!" he screamed, and he hung his head and cried.

"MacKie?" asked a faint voice.

MacKie's eyes widened and he lifted his head. "Aye! 'Tis! Hain't ne'er spoke to no spirit afore," he said in answer.

"Get o'er here, MacKie!" commanded the urgent voice.

"Where are ye, brother spirit?" asked MacKie, shaking uncontrollably.

"In the damn wood… behind ye!" grumbled the voice.

MacKie obeyed and rode the horse to the edge of the trees. The mount refused to enter and reluctantly MacKie dismounted and proceeded on foot. "Where are ye now, brother spirit?" He heard the chilling growl of a wolf in the thicket, and eyes widened even more, he instinctively nocked the arrow again as he approached the voice in the wood.

"Where are ye now, brother spirit?" asked MacKie.

"Kill this wolf, MacKie!" commanded the voice.

MacKie stepped into a small, open area and in the waning light saw Murdoch, on the ground and leaning against the trunk of a tree, one arm around Neil Campbell and fending off a large gray wolf with a broken pike he held in his other hand.

"Shoot the damned wolf!" again commanded Murdoch, jabbing at the creature.

"Yer alive!" shouted MacKie, overjoyed. "Ye're not a spirit!"

"Not for long if- ye- don't- *kill- the- wolf*," said Murdoch in as plain a language as he could muster.

"Sir Neil alive, too?" asked MacKie, his emotions outrunning his mind.

"Kill the god-damned wolf!" shouted Murdoch.

"'Twill be good news for them at Inverurie, right enough," said MacKie, all but giggling, and presuming that Neil was still alive.

The wolf, sighting MacKie, changed its focus of attack to him, and just as he was about to leap for the throat, MacKie turned his bow and released its shaft deep into the beast's chest. Murdoch dropped his head back against the tree and exhaled loudly.

"I thought ye was a ghost, Murdoch!" said MacKie coming to his brother and touching his face.

"I thought I was goin' to be! Why did ye not just kill the damned wild dog when I asked ye?" complained the exasperated Murdoch.

"I was fixin' to, but I… I was just so happy to see ye wasn't et, Murdoch, I plumb lost the notion of the wolf!" prattled MacKie.

"I could tell!" fussed Murdoch. "Help me get Sir Neil to yer horse, if he hain't run off!"

"Any more alive back yonder?"

"Was… but hain't now," answered Murdoch pushing his lips into a frown. "Could only save one, besides myself… and did."

• •

At the manor house, just before the near full moon brought light to the curtain of darkness, about a hundred warriors arrived back where the trip to the battle had started only a few hours before. To Robert, it seemed a lifetime ago.

The villeins and cotters kept to their hovels. No whooping, no waving of flags met the returned soldiery, just the quiet spaces between the byres and houses where an occasional cow complained or a weeping for a lost loved one could be heard.

The strap holding Robert to his saddle-chair pushed deeply into his chest from the ride's jostling and even though it had kept him upright, he liked it not.

All totaled, he was well satisfied with the day's results.

With the help of Andrew, Christina walked Robert up the steps to the solar. She removed his belt and tabard, then his heavy mail armor.

He pulled his nightshirt over his head and his chest, sorely bruised from the strap that held him to his saddle. Then he collapsed onto his bed and was asleep almost before he lit.

Christina then shed the soldierly trappings she had worn, unbound her breasts and slipped into her shift. She returned to his pallet and sat on its edge. Looking at his tired face, she lightly touched his bearded lips with her own.

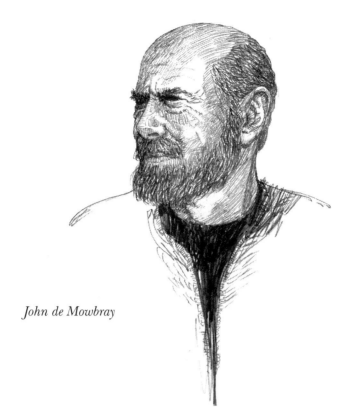

John de Mowbray

March 27th 1308
Inverurie

Two days after the battle of Old Meldrum the remainder of the army finally returned. With Sir Edward leading them, they were in gloriously high spirits and treated somewhat as heroes by the Inverurie townsfolk. The courageous men told of killing the Comyn knights and soldiers all the way to the English Royal Castle of Fyvie, some twelve leagues north, where the fleeing Comyns fortunate enough to get there alive, took refuge.

Brechin, Mowbray, and Strathbogie had all escaped the Brus blades, mostly due to the rear guard of knights they left behind them. Many of the foot soldiers simply melted into the surrounding wood and made for home after their pursuers passed. Lord John Comyn, of course, never made it to Old Meldrum, nor did he have the will or the inclination to appear there.

The Brus casualties were relatively light against the demoralized and chased Comyn legions.

Due to their success, they were able to recruit more men to their cause along their way back. Because the army had no victals or shelter for prisoners, few were taken. If not valued for ransom, they were put to death where they were captured, or were convincing in their swearing of allegiance to King Robert. Some simply didn't want to die, and having no strong ties to the Comyn chief, joined The Brus with little ado. Others wanted to be on the winning side for the cause of freedom against the English, and some admitted, for the personal weal to be gained from the spoils of war.

"Great day to be alive," exclaimed Robert as he opened the east view window to the early morning sun. From the second story, the town and the river before him seemed washed in a reddish glow.

"Ye feelin' renewed this day, My King?" asked Christina, coming to his bare back.

"Aye, that I do," he chirped, still looking outward.

Christina smiled. She raised her hand to touch him on his broad bare shoulder, but hesitated, then brought her hand down to her side.

"After ablutions and a bit of victuals, I want to address the close guard," he said turning toward her and rubbing his hands up his arms and over his chest to warm himself a bit.

She quickly redirected her attention to pouring a pan of fresh wash water for him. "I will see to yer request. Ye want yer regular lieutenants, I reckon."

"Aye," he said bending over the bowl and splashing the cold, refreshing water on his face, up to his ears, and into his hair. "None more."

"I shall see to it, Sire," she replied, avoiding his eyes.

"There be a board in the great hall large enough for the meet?" he asked, drying his face.

"Ye can have several placed side by each," she suggested with a sigh of some resignation. On the one hand she was thankful and happy that she had been successful in bringing Robert back from near death, but on the other, she was melancholy, for it would mean her return south to her kin and away from him, perhaps forever.

"Let us begin the day with a grand meal," exclaimed Robert exhibiting a broad smile.

"I shall have ye a grand meal brought up," she said, returning his smile. At last his appetite was back, and strongly so.

"Nay woman," he smirked, "today, we shall take our food in the great hall."

"Ye feel…," she started to say.

"I feel mighty and fixed for the world!" he expounded with arms high above his head.

"As ye order, My King," she said and gave a shallow bow of her head then turned to leave.

As she was pulling the door to a close, she heard a loud thud and the bedstead move slightly across the oaken floor.

"Robert!" she yelled after she quickly reentered the room to find him lying on the floor. He was struggling to rise, and she went to him and helped him to his feet and into a nearby chair.

"Reckon we'll have our grand meal, here," he said with a long sigh, rubbing his knee.

"Ye will be yerself again, Robert," she said encouragingly.

"I know... but not today," he admitted.

Christina picked his battleaxe from the floor and handed it to him, then left for the kitchen. Robert laid the weapon across his lap and secretly wondered if he would ever wield an axe, or any other weapon against an enemy again.

. .

Later that day, near the appointed hour of the meeting, Christina occupied herself and the two squires in making Robert's appearance as royally splendid as possible. She feared most the long staircase that he would have to descend from the bedroom, and so had the boys help him to an anteroom on the lower floor, next to the hall, before the summoned men assembled. She made ready the finest raiment available at her call.

He seemed tired before any others gathered but hearty to go through with his part in the assembly.

Soon, the thirty or so senior and junior lieutenants gathered in the great hall and awaited the arrival of their monarch.

The band of mostly thanes was headed by Edward Brus, who ushered in Robert's hostage, Walter de Ross. He, despite being a hostage, had readily sworn fealty to the rebellion, even though such went against his father, Lord William. Edward and Walter, nearly the same age, had become fast friends from the outset. Edward rather looked upon Walter as a younger brother, perhaps because his brothers' deaths had left a vacancy in his own existence that Walter helped seem less vast.

Robert Boyd and Gilbert de la Haye were followed by the contingent from Moray, led by the warrior bishop David Murray, and included David Barclay and the two Frasers, Simon and Alexander. The wounded Neil Campbell was carried in on a litter to be part of the proceedings.

Conspicuously absent was William Wiseman.

The balance of the group was a conglomerate of high-level knights from almost every earldom and shire within Scotland.

The men stood in groups chatting and enjoying each other's company when the door to the king's antechamber opened, heralding the coming of Robert. The excited voices quietly talking among themselves became hushed in anticipation of his entrance.

Andrew and Baldred entered carrying the standards. They ceremoniously went to either side of a large chair in front of the long table, made of several sturdy boards laid across multiple trestle legs. The room of men remained standing as Robert entered, looking every bit the King of Scots. As he walked toward them, the assembled warriors could not contain themselves to reverent behavior any longer.

The first to shout was probably the bishop, but others instantly joined in with hearty huzzahs and cheering, as if they had merely been waiting for someone to start it. Scarred and tested from their many battles, the stout Scots warriors wept, their hearts nearly bursting with pride, as they welcomed their king's return to their midst.

Robert's eyes also welled with tears at the unexpected reception from his followers. He stood bathed in their enthusiasm for a long moment, at last raising his hand for its cessation.

"Ye brave men are the pride of my life!" he expressed earnestly.

Another round of cheers went forth intermixed with shouts of, "The Brus!... The Brus!"

Robert smiled and glanced around the room at the faces of those many who fought with him and for him, and protected him when he could not fight for himself. His eyes rested on Christina who stood quietly on the side awaiting his need of her.

"A greater family has no man!" he announced in response to their continued shouts, "But we have much bloody war before us ere this realm will again be free of English occupation!"

To a man they agreed, and Robert waved his hand as signal for them to sit at the table. When they did he sat as well, in the large chair less than five paces away and facing them.

Robert breathed deep, thinking of the chosen words to tell them his mind. Another half-minute. The gathered waited silently in eager anticipation.

"We have won a great victory at Old Meldrum," he started.

The men gave a loud round of "ayes" and nods in agreement.

"Meldrum is but the first step in the fall of Buchan!" Suddenly the men grew silent, and awaited Robert's plan. "The land here is fraught with Comyn castles, and for the most part, this is their ancestral homeland. There are also a number of strongholds held by the English usurpers, some they have claimed as being 'Royal' castles." He looked at the faces of his lieutenants and said, "They may be garrisoned by the English, but they're on Scotland's soil, and they are Scotland's castles!"

Again his men lent their voices to loud agreement.

"What is yer desire, My King!" shouted Robert Boyd, causing the others to grow quiet. "I have seen the enemy and they are strong... and well arrayed... and their hatred grows toward us, almost daily."

"Good!" exclaimed the king. "We are a thorn in their side, else they would not hate us more as time goes on. When they hate us less, we no longer matter to them."

"Edward, how many men do we have now?" he asked.

"Well... the Wiseman hied with about fifty of his highlanders, and we lost around a hundred in the last campaign, at Meldrum and its trailin's... but... we've since gathered more recruits along... my guess is we're nearer to six hundred than five hundred," enumerated Edward.

Robert breathed deeply trying to maintain his strength. He listened as the congregated soldiers talked among themselves for a few minutes, giving him respite from carrying the meet. He slumped a bit, but when he looked toward Christina, she straightened her back as a signal for him to do likewise. With a great deal of personal resolve, he followed her advice.

For the next hour the talk went on among the Scots, and during that time they hammered out a plan from their own sheer determination, for they certainly did not have the upper hand. The Comyns alone were far more numerous, not to mention the English troops under the command of Lord Mowbray. Even Brechin had some English knights left that he had not squandered on poor, impetuous decisions.

It was figured that, due to Robert's convalescence, Sir Edward Brus would lead the army into Buchan and find those willing to come to the side of The Brus, and "strike to sorrow" those who were unwilling. The aim was to control the countryside, as much as possible, and force the enemy out of their castles to fight.

Such was the plan.

Only Christina could tell that Robert was worn beyond his capacity to be sensible and signed him to end the discussion and return to his chamber. He remained a quarter hour more through stubbornness, then surrendered to his body's need to recuperate by laboriously standing.

The group became silent and stood when he rose.

"Ye finish the details of the plan and let me know yer notions... I will decide the course on the morrow," he announced.

The men again applauded and cheered their encouragement. The king smiled and waved to them as Christina helped him back to the anteroom from where he had emerged an hour and a half earlier.

"Ye fixin' to give over the ghost in front of their very eyes?" scolded Christina as Robert sunk deep into the padded couch in the corner of the room.

"If that's what it takes," he whispered, closing his eyes. He easily and quickly passed into a sleep of pure weariness.

Her hands balled to fists and she shook them at him, growling in frustration as tears welled up and spilt down her cheeks. "Ye are the most cantankerous man I have e'er known!" she shouted, knowing full well that he heard none of it.

Mute

April 18th 1308
Castle Mortlach

"Why does the sun shine this very day when I've barely seen my shadow for the past five months!" whined Lord John. He was in his bed clothing still, and had wrapped a woolen blanket around himself as a temporary measure against the uncomfortably cold weather.

"I know not," sighed Sir John Mowbray, thinking the question inane. He was just aft of the older man as the two nobles crossed the bailey of Castle Mortlach and climbed the stone stairs to the parapet.

"We have fifteen hundred against him," reckoned the earl. "Why then does he still have free rein o'er... what seems to be... the whole of Buchan?"

"We *had* fifteen hundred?!" said the baron angrily. "God damn us all to hell... we _had_ o'er three *thousand!*... now we have but seven *hundred* within these walls!"

The earl was quiet as he absorbed the unbelievable numbers.

The two men reached the wall walk and peered over the curtain, looking toward the south, as did the soldiers of the guard and the Earl of Strathbogie. He stood with but two men between them and him, and when he realized their presence at the battlements, he intentionally moved farther away and looked not in their direction. Sir David blamed the other two for the terrible beating he and his men had suffered at Old Meldrum.

"That them?" asked the earl to an English knight standing next to him.

"Aye, Milord," he said pointing to an army camp of merely a handful of tents about five hundred yards away.

"Why don't we just go out and... run them off?" asked the earl. Immediately he sneezed and wrapped his blanket tighter about his shoulders and neck. He wiped his draining nose on the part of the blanket covering his forearm.

"They scatter and lurk in the wood, Sire... and when we try to seek them out they pick us off, one-by-one, like apples from the tree," said Mowbray remorsefully. "We have learned to remain lock-holed here, but they pester us with fire arrows at night and so doin' have set alight more than a few of the buildin's in the bailey."

"Then... can we not conscript more men?" asked John.

Mowbray sighed thinking how hopeless it was to explain to the earl a situation that had been brewing for the last three weeks while he had remained taken to his bed, not wanting to hear a word of it.

"Milord Earl, there will be no conscripts forthcoming from among the crofters, as many are dead fightin' for ye already, and others... turned tail and joined The Brus! Further, we see dark smoke rising from some point on the horizon every day!" he explained. "Yer lands east were pillaged of their stores and all structures burned near three weeks ago, those north, a fortnight, and west... but days thence!"

"Now, here they sit at our very gate, between us and yer southern holdin's! We must make a decision... our rations are pitifully low and we cannot even *forage* for more!"

Lord John turned abruptly and hastened to leave the cool air of the wall walk for the rosier temperatures of his fireside. The baron close on his heels, John Comyn went through double doors of the protective tower house to descend the stone staircase when he suddenly stopped as if a grand thought had struck him. "We should have killed the bastard at Slioch!" he proclaimed, eyes wide and staring up at Mowbray's, two steps above him.

The baron gritted his teeth.

I and the whole of my contingent were ready to attack at Slioch! It was ye *who feared yer men might turn on ye and so delayed ordering the assault until it was too late!* thought Mowbray. *Edward Brus had just appeared too intimidating for ye, ye cowed, fat, old, ill, earl! Ye have outlived yer nobleness, and yer day!*

He followed his liege to the great hall, and near the fire, a table laden with the last of the better meats and wine. Mowbray ate heartily,

Comyn less so.

After the meal and after the leavings were taken away, the two men sat quietly musing their entrapment, each wondering what the other had in mind.

At long length Lord John spoke, "What if we made a run for Duffus... ye reckon Cheyne would take us in?"

"I reckon he would, but ye would ne'er make a fast ride of that distance, Milord," candidly replied Mowbray.

The earl growled and stared frowning at his guest, but then softened, knowing that it was true. "Then what? What?! Where can we go?" he demanded anxiously.

"I have a plan that might work... if ye are up to chicanery," said Mowbray, leaning to the earl to gain a sense of secrecy.

The earl's head bobbed, his eyebrows heightened with interest. "Chicanery?"

• •

It was as early as the cock would crow, had there been one close at hand, and MacKie, who was again standing picket duty, shouted loudly to his sleeping companions, "The ones in the castle are makin' a run for us!"

Sir Edward, sword in hand, was out of his tent and first on the scene. "Saddle the horses!" he demanded. "Everybody wake up and kit to fight... they're comin' down on us, fast!"

MacKie nocked an arrow, but they were certainly too far away to try a shot in such poor light.

As Sir Walter of Ross came to Edward he said, "Shall we scatter into the wood as before?"

"Sure too many to go against for our size," groused Edward, still feeling the smart from his grog of the night.

Walter turned to give the order, but some of the Scots had already decided that scattering was the best course of action and had done so on their own.

Horns blared and blared on both sides so that every living thing in the neighborhood was alerted that an attack was imminent.

Meanwhile, and certainly unnoticed, four figures riding donkeys and dressed in the hooded garb of monks left by the postern gate and headed north away from the impending battle. They kept their heads bowed and well tucked beneath their hoods, revealing little more than shadow to determine their facial features. One labored his donkey so from his weight that a fifth donkey was in tow with sparse travel victuals strapped to its back.

The Brus men watching the back of the castle had their eyes open for charging knights and crafty archers. They paid little attention to the small assemblage of clerical pilgrims, who were thus left to their travels unimpeded.

"They mean to kill us this time!" shouted Edward.

"Won't if they can't find us," gainsaid Walter.

"Let's get, then," agreed Edward as he started backing up. The charging knights were almost upon them with the foot soldiers running behind.

As Sir Edward and Sir Walter withdrew, more laden with their mail armor than he, MacKie darted past, and reaching the protection of the trees, wheeled and shot an arrow at the closest pursuing knight. The hapless target, sword already poised to deny Sir Edward further use of his head, felt MacKie's arrow smash into his right shoulder. His sword was flung tumbling to the ground, and the knight reacted quickly to rein in his mount, turning the horse to the side and out of the way of the charge.

Edward ran and tried to catch the reins of his own loosed and freely wandering stallion.

"Sons-of-bitches!" cursed Sir Walter, swinging his sword at them and trying to run down his own mount as well.

MacKie was the only one who was getting any licks in at all. He would strike arrow after arrow into the charging army, in an effort to protect Edward and Walter, but there were too many of them, coming too fast.

Edward was in a panic. "For the trees… let the horses do as they will!" he yelled.

The two stranded warriors ran as fast as they could, but mounted knights were on them before they could cover the distance to the trees.

The pair stopped running and turned to fight, but it was too late. They were completely surrounded by lance, pike, and sword point. The power of their own blades wilted in their hands. They dropped their weapons and held their hands out empty.

"That one's a Brus," said one of the knights, "I saw him at Slioch."

"Aye! 'Tis! Edward Brus! I saw him, too!" said a second man.

"Lord John will know what's to be done with them," proffered another.

"Aye… to the earl with them!" shouted the second, and with his mailed foot, kicked Edward in the face.

"Where ye reckon are the rest of those bastards?" wondered another. The mix of Scottish and English troops carried that thought no further, instead cheering loudly at their small, but important, victory, and set about destroying the remains of the Brus camp, taking what little there was of value.

Edward, his face swelling and bleeding from multiple small cuts made by the chain mailed kick, and Walter glared at their captors and silently swore revenge as their hands were bound tightly in front of them with rawhide. They would be led like goats and forced to run to prevent falling and being dragged across the muddy, plowed field to the gate of Castle Mortlach.

Two enemy foot soldiers, ordered to round up the horses of Edward and Walter, proceeded to calm and catch them. However, as they turned to lead them to the castle, two well-placed arrows from MacKie's bow released the fetchers from their duties. Free again, the horses reared, whinnied, and galloped away.

Sir Gilbert de la Haye, with a hundred forty-one men, was encamped in a field beyond the small woods in which the fleeing Brus forces were scattered. He was alerted to their plight by a signal horn blowing in the trees, and came with a troop of mounted knights to investigate, but all was complete before he arrived. After talking with the men in the wood, he had the horns call all of The Brus' forces within hearing, a several-mile radius, to come join up with him.

Within Mortlach, David de Strathbogie held, with much satisfaction, both the brother and the hostage of King Robert. He was overjoyed that God had given him such a power over the formidable Brus. Still, he was also aware that his holding the two made him an irresistible target, and took steps to safeguard his fortress.

"Seems to be plenty more vermin in the wood, Milord," opined one of the knights standing guard atop the curtain wall.

"Lots of horn tootin'," added Lord David. With a smug smile on his lips, he peered into the bailey below, where Edward de Brus and Walter de Ross were hanging by rawhide thongs attached to large iron rings mounted high to the castle wall, where cattle and swine were hung to be butchered after being slaughtered.

The Brus' and the Ross' bootless toes scarce reached the foul dirt and their weapons, armor and clothing had been stripped from them. Blood from numerous tortures inflicted by the denizens seeped downward and dried, as it had from earlier beatings given by those who had taken them prisoner. Fair game they were for any casual passerby to abuse.

A couple of old crones came to the prisoners and stared at their hanging bodies, talking between themselves and pointing as if reviewing a lesson in anatomy.

A short, squatty mutt dog licked the blood from the men's feet.

"What ye reckon those two are whisperin' about?" asked Edward through bruised and swollen lips.

Walter turned his head and looked at his companion-in-chains through his one eye that wasn't yet swollen completely shut and said, "They were talkin' about yer wee pecker, Lad."

"And I thought they were pointin' at ye," gainsaid Sir Edward.

"In a pig's eye," painfully insisted Sir Walter, maintaining a bit of humor through his misery, "besides, the dog likes *my* feet best."

"So, ye got the biggest pecker *and* the best tastin' feet?" groaned Edward with a half smile.

"And ne'er forget it, My Friend," said Walter with a half smile in return.

The crones soon left when a soldier with too much to drink in his belly to be sensible, took his opportunity to clout, safely, a "high-up" member of the Brus camp. Fresh blood seeped on top of dried from Edward's nostril. Walter was dealt several body blows. They both groaned in agony as their tormentor staggered away, a hero in his own mind.

"Soon be dark," observed Walter after a while. "Goin' to get... mighty cold... ere long," he said with a shiver.

• •

The four cleric-robed escapees from the castle were well on their way north by the latter part of the day. By remaining on the roadway, actually little more than a series of meandering footpaths, they ran upon a small alehouse and hostel where they could rest.

"Why did ye set me on the most poorly ass?" whined the earl as he carefully rolled from the sad, overburdened beast's back.

"He was the hardiest of them all when we left, Milord," answered John Mowbray.

The fat, old man grunted and merely said, "Glad to find safe haven."

"This hain't no safe place, Milord!" Mowbray answered.

"Not e'en for the earl of these lands?" he exclaimed, raising an eyebrow.

"Ye are earl hereabouts no more! Now, it depends on how deep ye permit their hand to dip into yer purse, Sire," answered Mowbray.

Lord John's eyes widened. "We're monks!" he exclaimed, referring to their disguises.

"Lest ye speak softer, we'll be dead monks!" cautioned the baron.

The old man grunted.

One of the two real monks traveling in the party came to the earl and suggested that he be allowed to make the negotiations for their night's lodging, since he and his brother monk were well accustomed to such trivial transactions.

The earl pressed several coins into the old monk's hand and was relieved of the responsibility.

The four entered the tavern and easily found themselves a table in the far corner. The volunteer negotiator went to the keeper and made the arrangements. Coins were paid and the deal was done.

He returned to the small table and reported, "Supper will be a small pot of beans and one loaf amongst us, and there's a stall in the stable, next to the goat pens, for our sleep.

A tear arose in the old earl's eye, as he silently lamented what had become of him.

The ale room, modestly populated by locals, was nearly cleared out when five Scots of Brus' army entered and ordered whisky for their table.

The earl adjusted his hood to cover more of his face. He was hungry but detested beans and hard bread, and so merely picked at his food. Mowbray restrained himself less and got rather full on the meager rations. The two monks faired well, dividing the beans that the earl left in his abandoned trencher.

"What have I come to! What have I come to!" moaned the earl in low tones that were easily camouflaged within the ambient sounds of the room.

"We have done nothin' wrong," answered Mowbray. "We oursel'es have fought against England for Scotland's freedom… in the time of Wallace."

"Yet, we are put to flight?!" mumbled the earl, near tears.

"Aye," replied Mowbray, "put to flight by The Brus! Brus, who murdered our kinsmen at Greyfriars Kirk and put himself, and his kith and kin, against the Comyn family."

"Mortal enemies, we are now," moaned the earl. "I hate Robert Brus… truly and bitterly."

The five men sprawled around their table and began to brag of their exploits within the earldom, telling of how those who held faith with the earl were "slain where they stood," their crofts burned down around their dead bodies.

Struck with fear, the earl began to shake almost uncontrollably. Mowbray drummed his fingers on the tabletop as he sipped his tavern-brewed ale trying to mask the sound of the earl's shivers. The two monks rose from the table, and taking the candle, motioned for the two nobles to follow them to the byre before the earl got them all killed.

The warriors paid no attention to the exiting travelers and ordered more ale brought to them. The innkeeper gladly obliged since the invaders, for all their mayhem in the land, were the ones who now had the silver and gold, albeit stolen from his regular customers and others.

"Oh, God, if we can just make it to Banff!" earnestly prayed Lord John, feeling the accursed piles beginning to pain and burn, again.

"We'll be in Banff by noon on the morrow, Milord," mumbled Mowbray, trying to appease the poor wretch.

"Don't call me 'Milord'!" whined Lord John, "…some might hear, and ye would give me… and yerself… away!"

Mowbray nodded, blew out the candle, and leaned back on the hay, his fingers interlaced behind his head. The earl returned to his low moaning and whimpering, even as he slept. Mowbray could not believe the regression the old man had taken in such a short time. He was strong and knew how to wield power just a few short months past, but now fairly begged entrance to his grave.

"I will return with a great army and wreak hell-fires on Robert de Brus," swore Mowbray determinedly under his breath, "as soon as I can see ol' John safe to London!"

•   •

It was along about sundown when Robert arrived at the outskirts of Mortlach, where Sir Gilbert was working at a plan to save Edward and Walter, and capture the castle in one deft move.

"My Liege," he said before Robert had even dismounted, "yer brother… and our hostage from Ross… have been taken prisoner and are held in yon castle." He vacillated in the telling.

Robert laboriously dismounted and searched the surrounding campsite for a seat, finally settling on Gilbert's saddle.

"Tell me of our plight," he opened the discussion as the bishop rode up and joined them. He asked no questions until he had heard the whole story.

"How much light and hefty rope ye got?" asked Robert.

Christina knelt to Robert with a warm brew. "For yer strength, Milord Robert."

Robert took the brew and sipped. "What's for food, woman?"

"Greasy eel and swill water," she whispered in his ear.

"Sounds good…" he replied, "… cook it well done," he grinned.

She bowed slightly and withdrew to fetch him a bannock and bacon from one of the several cook fires that dotted the area.

"Ye got a grapplin' hook?" asked Robert returning his attention to Gilbert and Bishop Murray.

Gilbert explained his point of view, "Got rope and a grapplin' hook, but that hain't a'gettin' an army o'er that muddy bottomed moat and high stone curtain wall."

"Get the gear we have at our command, lay it on the ground before me," ordered Robert. "And Murray," he addressed his old friend, "get that slip of a lad, that bowman… uh, what's his name?"

"Ye mean the little fellow, Mute?"

"Aye, Mute. Send him o'er."

A thin sickle moon shown in the southwestern sky following the setting sun. The day was done. The night was to be new-made.

•   •

"We must see Lord John!" demanded Lord David.

"He left me and Harris here as guard this morn, Milord" said the large knight who stood confidently at the solar door. "He weren't to be pestered by nobody, said he!"

The impetuous earl drew his dagger, the blade glinting in the flickering light of the torch carried by the knight behind him.

Both Harris and the big man reached for their sword hilts, but did not pull their blades.

"We fixin' to see what ye're made of?" The earl's brows knitted and a smile of portended pleasure crossed his lips.

After the briefest pause, Harris stood aside.

"We'll all be in the damnedest trouble, Milord!" pleaded the second guard but, as the angry Strathbogie observed, he was not prepared to die to protect John Comyn's privacy. He, too, yielded.

"Stand aside!" ordered Strathbogie, pushing the smaller man to the wall and trying the handle. The door was bolted from within. Frustrated and cursing, he began pounding on the heavy oak door with the pommel of his dagger, making as much noise as possible.

"Ye'll be wakin' the Devil, Sire!" warned Harris, still holding his position against the wall.

The earl glared at the man. "Yer head *can* make a batterin' ram," he warned.

Three more senior knights came to the narrow hallway space. "Ye seen the earl or the baron, Lord Strathbogie?" one asked.

"Not yet," retorted Lord David at the door, "but I hear somebody a'gigglin' within!"

"That hain't the earl a'gigglin'!" offered the first guard. "That's been goin' on in there all along. Sounds like a lass, to me." He smiled and looked at the other sentry.

The angry earl pounded again, only to hear the same silly laughter rippling within.

"Open it!" ordered Lord David. Two of his large comrades carried axes and began using them to chop away and weaken the wood around the bolt. After a significant splintering of the wood had occurred, Strathbogie called a halt to their efforts and ordered the bigger guard to batter it with his shoulder. After several times at throwing his weight against the barrier, the weakened section split and the door swung open, slamming loudly against the inner wall.

All who could see inside from the doorway were aghast at the sight of two monks, one on the floor and the other lolled about on the huge bed of the lord, both as drunk as two human beings could be.

"Where's the earl?" demanded Lord David crossly.

"Where's the baron?" asked another knight.

"Off to London, sssmy notion," slurred the heavy monk, who rivaled the weight and girth of Lord John himself. He unabashedly downed the remainder of his cup's contents.

"Both... off to London-town," confirmed the second drunkard, struggling to rise from his place on the floor, but not managing to stand before he rolled over onto his back again.

"God damn it!" screamed Lord David in reckless temper, "I knew... somehow... I knew! The damned old bastard has removed himself to England and left us to defend his keep!"

"How can we?" bemoaned a close-standing man. "Lord John knows the castle and its defenses better than any other!"

"And it's a well-guarded fortress! Get hold of yer senses, and collect the knights in the great hall!" Strathbogie again screamed in fury. "To hell with John Comyn! We've got our own hides to try to protect now!" He stormed out, not knowing what to do to save his command or his own life, but determined not to let The Brus take either.

Following after him, the warriors retreated quickly, leaving the battered door ajar. The monks said nothing for a short time, but stared at the doorway through which the others had abandoned the solar.

"I'm quittin' the church," seriously confided the slighter monk to his friend, sitting alone on the solar bed.

"Why?" asked the larger one, "What would ye do, that could best this?"

The first smiled, still lying flat on the solar floor. "Le's open 'nother cask," he said after giving the matter some thought, "and drink to the cla-cla-rity of yer notion." Then he giggled, sounding just like a lass.

•   •

As Lord David and the other knights of the abandoned Castle Mortlach gathered in the great hall to discuss how to carry on a defense against the army of Brus, roguery was afoot without. The slightly moonlit early evening made a perfect cover for what King Robert had in mind.

Four figures slipped stealthily from bush to tree, making their way around toward the back of Castle Mortlach where the donjon tower stood high above the height of the curtain wall. A usually dry moat surrounded the structure, though the bottom was presently somewhat less than dry because of the spring rains.

"See the arrow slit near the top of the wall?" asked Robert pointing.

"Aye, Milord," said Gilbert de la Haye.

"Reckon ye can fling this hook to the battlements directly above the slit?" asked Robert, handing his companion a grappling hook attached to a coil of knotted lightweight rope.

Sir Gilbert, broad-shouldered, strapping Scot that he was, looked across the moat at the tower and pursed his lips in a low whistling sound, obviously having doubts. He pulled a handful of grass and tossed it into the air, only to watch it flutter down directly for lack of wind. He hefted the weight of the hook and line again, and finally said, "I can try, Sire, but I doubt I can reach it from this side of the moat."

"Give it a try!"

"Aye, I will." He proceeded to doff all manner of armor and weapons, making himself as unencumbered as he could. He then reached down and pulled some heather from the area about his feet and stuck the boughs along the back of his belt and put a small branch in his hair. Lying prone on the ground, he crawled on his belly to a spot near the edge of the fifteen-foot-deep chasm protecting Mortlach.

Not seeing anyone along the crenellated wall, he took several deep breaths and stood, swinging the hook in broader and broader circles until he thought he had enough speed, and released it… to watch it arc gracefully and fall against the side of the curtain. Quickly, he squatted low in the heather, and sure enough, there came a sentry who appeared between the merlons near where the hook had struck the wall and had a look about. Seeing nothing, he went away.

Gilbert tugged repeatedly at the line and slowly retrieved the hook, with which he immediately started the process again. Putting more force behind his circles, he let the line out to a greater distance, and let it go once more. It sailed higher than the first effort, but was too far to one side to connect with the tower, and fell into the moat, clinking several times on its way to the bottom.

Again he dropped to the heather to become invisible to the guard on the wall, but this time no one appeared. Gilbert resolved to give it one more try, and winding it up again, wider and wider, he tried also to change its angle, but it hit the ground and bounced a couple of times.

Cursing under his breath he gathered the lengthy rope and prepared to try a fourth time, when Robert joined him near the rim of the moat.

"Wait," ordered Robert, "We're goin' to go across the ditch and see if it is any easier."

Within minutes, several men, using Gilbert's camouflage trick, hastened across the heather covered field to connect with them. Already briefed on what it was they were to do, the men quickly went to work, climbing down the steeply angled walls into the moat. Robert instructed Gilbert to go with them and take his grappler and line. It was muddy in the bottom, but no more than they could maneuver through, and they soon completed their aim of getting Gilbert to the base of the castle wall.

The strongest of the lot stood with his back against the nearly vertical wall, and the next stoutest climbed up to stand on the first man's shoulders. The third did the same, and the fourth, until Gilbert was able to climb the human ladder and reach the ridge at the base of the castle. There, he stood, and with the extra depth lent by the moat, was able to spin a large enough arc that he reached the top of the tower on his first throw.

He was at first unbelieving that the grapple was lodged sufficiently to support a climbing man, even one as slight as Mute, but after lifting his own weight off the ground several times, he was convinced.

Almost before he knew it, Mute appeared at his side and took hold of the rope. Dangling from his belt was a mason's hammer.

Using the knots tied in the rope, he lifted himself high enough to stand on the lowest knot, then reached higher and pulled himself to place his feet on the second knot, and so on. Sir Gilbert held the rope out from the wall so that Mute could more easily climb, and before long he was nearing the top of the curtain wall.

All of a sudden, from the Brus archers stationed before the front of the castle, the night sky was rent with fiery streaks blazing over the curtain wall and into the outer bailey. They sailed silently in wave after wave, and the castle guard began ringing the fire bell almost immediately. The thatch on some of the buildings in the bailey readily caught fire and the castle denizens drawn to fight the sudden danger created a noisy and frantic hubbub below the castle.

Watching Mute as he continued to climb, one knot at a time, Robert was reminded of a spider climbing its slender thread, and of the spider in the cave during the dark days in the mountains after his brothers were betrayed and killed. He clenched his jaw tightly and willed the struggling youth to complete his journey and reach the arrow port.

"Ye can do it," he said in a whisper. "Climb, Lad! Don't stop!"

Higher went Mute until finally, he reached the arrow slit, his entrance to the castle. He tried to squeeze his small frame through the narrow opening but, as was expected, it was too close for even his wiry body to slip through. On the other side of the loophole, the arrow slit angled back drastically to allow an archer a wider range of fire against invaders. Thus, the edges that prohibited his entry were the least substantial parts of the whole castle wall.

He reached down and took hold of the thong holding the mason's hammer and pulled the tool up to grab its handle. Solemnly, he began to chip away at the edges of the port.

Gilbert backed away along the wall far enough to avoid being pelted by the falling pieces of stone.

"Reckon he can do the job, Sire?" asked MacKie, watching the youth whaling away at the stone with all his might.

"Reckon he's the only one who has any chance of slippin' through that slim hole," replied the king. *But, does Mute have the strength to enlarge the opening, is the real question*, thought Robert.

The hammer blows were resounding within and without. Outside mattered little, for all attention was paid to the several fires still burning in the outer bailey. Inside, in the great hall, the earl of Strathbogie was meeting with his chief lieutenants, and paid no attention to one more noise in a distant part of the fortress, but a squire minding the door at the great hall turned to listen to the odd hammering.

Mute, not realizing that his constant striking of blows had been heard, continued to flail the edges of the slit, knocking it a bit wider with each blow. He was encouraged by the early success, but the farther his blows progressed, the more solid and thick the stone would be.

The squire slowly pushed the large door open with the notion of alerting Lord David and the knights within to the echoing sound, but they seemed too engrossed in their discussion for a mere squire to bother them over such a possible triviality, and so he pulled the door to, again.

Mute was close to having a usable entrance, and continued to force his aching, exhausted arm to pound on the stone, again, and again.

Unable to contain his curiosity and anxiety any longer, the squire left his post at the great hall and mounted the spiral stairs to explore the source of the hammer strikes, becoming more pronounced with every level.

Mute stopped a moment to test the opening for possible admission. He pushed his arm holding the hammer through the slit to see if he could yet slip through sideways. A small toggle loop on his jerkin caught on a protruding edge of the fractured rock and threatened to shake him loose from his rope. Working at getting the snag released, he dropped the hammer to the floor within, certainly out of his reach.

His heart pounding as hard as had his hammer, Mute heard the creaking of an interior door and pushing his body back out of the opening, held tightly to the edges of the large stones making up the tower's outer wall.

The suspicious squire walked quietly into the room but saw no one. Still, the hammering noise had stopped just as he reached that floor, and looking into the dark he saw the hammer beneath the ragged edged arrow slit. He picked it up and found the peen was warm.

As his eyes adjusted to the wan light and he saw there was no one in the room, he crossed to the arrow port and looked out into the night. Light from the fires in the bailey cast a pale orange glow on the curtain wall merlons, and he suddenly realized there was a dark shadow approaching the opening in which he stood.

He gasped as if to speak, but it was too late.

Mute swung wide on his tethering rope and slammed into the wall at the slit where the squire was standing. Holding tight to his dagger, Mute's hand went through the widened slit and into the belly of the curious squire, who dropped the hammer and stumbled backward across the room, blood spurting from the gash in his gut. The weight of his falling body slammed the door shut on the opposite side.

The slit was still not quite wide enough for Mute to get through and the hammer was even farther out of reach.

Mute felt along the edge and figured where it needed to be opened more. With his bloodied dagger he began to chip at the stone again, with the far less effective tool.

The mortally bleeding squire within moaned and tried to get to his feet to warn the knights.

Mute worked more feverishly.

Again he tried to get through, but it still would not permit him entrance, so he backed off and whacked at the stone more. Desperate to get through the jagged opening, he pushed his head through, scraping large bloody wounds on the sides of his face and head, and then his shoulder. Gritting his teeth and overcoming the pain, he barely managed to force his body through, tearing toggles, loops and skin in the process. Then turning his attention to the wounded squire, found that he was dead and no longer a threat.

Now that he was in the tower, Mute traveled a predetermined route heading for the outer bailey. Passing the great hall, he could hear the knights still shouting and arguing amongst themselves over which courses of action needed to be taken. He sneaked outside where a page, approaching the door, saw him standing in the shadows. Mute was expeditious with his once razor-sharp dagger, and the page felt little more.

He soon found his way through the gate tower and tunnel to the outer bailey where renewed waves of fire arrows were causing a lot of trouble, but nothing to risk the taking of the castle.

"A fine rescue this is," groaned Edward as he watched the blazing shafts coming inbound. One of them struck the wall above them, scattering bits of fire all around. Several of the fiery flakes landed on them and they winced, shook and groaned as the live embers burned themselves out in their hair and on their bare skin.

"At least we're warmer," replied Walter. Both were still hanging side-by-side on the wall as if they were slabs of butchered meat.

Mute watched the patterns of the scurrying inmates for a few minutes, seeing how best to proceed according to the king's instructions.

Edward and Walter watched Mute cross the bailey, picking a blazing arrow from the ground as he went, and enter a small horse stable along the outer wall. Once inside, he threw the fiery shaft into the surrounding hay and released the horses, ducking out quickly before the fire grew.

The flames and smoke alarmed the beasts, which whinnied and snorted, and realizing they were not penned, bolted for the bailey. The fire soon breached the thatched roof and shone brighter. Several citizens of the castle saw what was happening and began to shout and scream, bringing a score of others to the well to draw up buckets of water with which to quench the all consuming fire.

Out from between a couple of the frightened horses emerged Mute, blade in hand, in front of the two helpless men. Without a pause he moved a nearby wooden chicken coop over beside them and jumped onto the top of it, but found that he still could not reach the iron rings holding the men to the wall. He slipped his feet onto Walter's shoulders so that he could get to the ties that bound them there. Walter groaned, not only at the added weight tugging downward on his wrists, but also at the chafing of his numerous wounds.

Mute cut Edward's bindings first, then Walter's, falling to the ground along with the large man. Stiff and sore, the two freed prisoners could hardly move their limbs, especially their fingers and hands, numb from being tightly bound for long hours. They all three managed to get to their feet, and mixing with the aimless horses, guided the frightened creatures toward the main gate.

There, the two men awkwardly lifted the heavy wooden beam and opened the inner gate, hoping the portcullis had been left raised. Those hopes were dashed, however, as they stared straight into the metal reinforcements on the heavy wooden latticework preventing them from reaching freedom and forbidding their comrades' entrance to Mortlach Castle. They looked about them and found that Mute was no longer there.

On the glen outside, King Robert and his archers periodically launched more fire arrows over the wall and into the lower bailey. A few even lofted high enough to land and set fire to something in the inner bailey, or so reported Murdoch when he limped painfully to Robert's side.

"Also, Sire, we'll soon be out of arrows," he added in his account of their status.

"We've got one good-sized blaze goin'… just stretch yer supplies 'til that gate comes open!"

"Aye, My King," replied Murdoch, and he hobbled away supported by his walking stick.

Inside, Mute returned with some scant clothing for the two knights, quickly filched from within an open barracks. The two grateful knights put on the clothing as best they could, and with their cold, barely functioning hands, quickly began tugging at the draw wheel in an effort to raise the portcullis into the open position. With Edward on one wheel and Walter on the other, the two groaned and grunted under the terrible strain to their awfully abused bodies. Some of their wounds broke open and began bleeding again, and every injury ached as they were bumped and scraped while at the task.

One of the castle villeins saw the two men at work and turned to alert others, but his scream for help was cut abruptly short by Mute's dagger, thrown so hard it cut clear to the fellow's backbone. Retrieving the blade, Mute hunkered motionless within the shadow of the gate tunnel, waiting to see who would next discover their attempt to open the gate.

The two old women who had stood before and discussed the naked Scots earlier, came to the tunnel seeking shelter from the various fires. Mute held the handle of his trusted dagger waiting for the moment to strike. The crones immediately recognized the two escapees, even in the near dark, and began to caterwaul to the height of their voices. Several knights turned to see the reason for the screaming, and Mute tucked the blade between his thumb and forefinger, ready to make the throw to shut them up. He even drew the dagger back, but could not release it at the elderly women.

The knights approached to see what the women, trying to disappear into the crowd, were in such an uproar about, and Mute hurried to Edward, shaking his arm. When he saw the approaching men Edward kicked the brake pin into the wheel on his side of the tunnel and warned Walter, "Soldiers a'comin'!"

Walter turned and kicked in the brake on his side. "Its most the way up anyhow," he quickly said as the two prepared for fist-to-blade combat.

Thinking quickly, Mute lay next to the dead man as the three knights passed him by on their way to apprehend the escaping prisoners.

Mute quickly jumped on the back of the closest one, and grabbing his chin, jerked it up, exposing his neck to Mute's well-bloodied knife. The young warrior quickly swooped up the man's dropped broadsword and tossed it to Walter, whose hands were recovering their feeling enough that he charged the two remaining knights. Edward's attack was with no more than his bare and bloodied hands. Forcing their aching bodies to fight on was purely a tribute to their mutual will.

Mute pulled his own short sword from its sheath and flung it to Edward, giving him a chance to survive against his armed opponent. Realizing that the youth had provided both escaped prisoners with weapons, one of the Comyn knights hit Mute hard in the face with his mail-covered elbow. He went down.

Walter and Edward fought hard, but more of the castle's garrison realized that there was a struggle going on at the gate tunnel and headed toward them.

The inner gate was open, the portcullis was up, and all that stood between the besieged pair and the outside was the outer gate. Shaking his head, Mute got to his knees, the clanging of swords compounded confusion on top of confusion in his wit.

What must I do? What must I do? he thought, trying to piece together the sights and sounds and his memories.

His head pounding, he nevertheless jumped quickly to his feet and maneuvered around the fighting knights to get to the outer gate. There he pushed upward hard, putting all his remaining heart into raising the large beam holding the two halves of the gate solidly closed. As the bar moved slightly, he pushed still harder, until the veins in his temples pulsed mightily and tears began streaming down his youthful face. His strength was near failing and he so wanted to let it drop back into place, when the massive weight was completely cleared of its iron supports, and Mute stepped back to let it fall onto the ground.

Breathing heavily, he exhaustedly swung one of the gates back into the tunnel, hoping King Robert would see the great doors wide open and come take the castle. Instead, what he was staring at was more pitch-black darkness. The drawbridge was up. Mute had completely forgotten about the bridge across the dry ditch.

In frustration, he pounded his fists hard on the impervious bridge, but the noisy clanging of battle behind him brought him to his senses. Looking back he saw more soldiers coming into the dark tunnel after them. Only Edward and Walter stood between his mission's success and their bloody deaths in a failed attempt to rescue the two valiants and capture the castle.

He slipped his slight frame back through much of the tunnel and was skirting around the four fighting men when Sir Walter dispatched one knight, the man collapsing heavily against the wall, thus blocking Mute's path. Overcome with more violent death, he momentarily shrunk back from the body, but recovered his nerve and picked up the dead man's sword. There were more of the enemy entering the blackness of the tunnel.

Mute hid in the shadows once again as the warriors went straight for Edward and Walter. With time running out for the three of them, the young man dashed up the stone stairway to the room over the tunnel. There, the mechanism to operate the bridge was housed. He tried, in the faint flicker of the bailey fires coming through the arrow ports of the gatehouse, to figure out how to release the brake on the locked wheel holding up the drawbridge.

In desperation he took the sword in his hand and began swinging it hard and wildly against the wheel. Again and again he chopped and slashed at the mechanism, until, without his knowing why or how, the chain holding the bridge upright began to rattle, and seconds later, with a great thud, the all-important gap between castle and King Robert's army was spanned.

He heard the cheers from Edward and Walter below, and saw light through the murder holes in the floor; some of the Comyn warriors had brought torches into the tunnel. Mute had no trouble distinguishing friend from foe.

Standing, he saw several bows and quivers of arrows hanging on the wall ready for use at the murder holes. He swiftly strung one of the bows and dumped a quiver of arrows to the floor. One after another, he nocked arrows and aimed through one of the holes at enemy soldiers that neared Edward or Walter, alleviating some of their distress. As each shaft found its mark Mute lost no time in finding places for more points of death for his enemy.

King Robert, having seen the thundering drawbridge fall, knew his small warrior had been brilliantly successful. With his buckler in place on his left arm, he pulled himself aboard his destrier and with a loud war cry, rode at a gallop to rescue his brother and Lord William's son, and to capture the castle.

Mortlach's defenders, seeing and hearing the approaching army, tried to seize the gate tower's upper chamber and raise the bridge, but Mute kept them at bay with a seemingly endless supply of arrows. Within minutes, groaning and dead bodies choked the stairwell, dissuading others from following in their footsteps.

Sir Edward and Sir Walter found their adversaries in the tunnel were turning tail and running into the bailey. Having been so completely occupied with staying alive, they momentarily wondered why their opponents ran, but hearing the clatter of approaching cavalry, they high-tailed for the inner gate as well, clearing the tunnel just as Robert and his knights poured through.

Lord David and his knights, previously holding council in the great hall, had been alerted of the incursion and were now in the outer bailey, fully armed and ready for the fight.

Robert rallied his troops around him by swinging his battleaxe and whooping loudly. Haye and Boyd, realizing the king was not yet returned to his former vigor, pushed in front of him to lead the mounted charge against the Comyn knights, arrayed and ready to defend the inner castle.

One of the men who rode up to protect the king was instantly struck in the shoulder blade by an arrow. Groaning, he slumped over his saddlebow, and onto his horse's neck. As Robert reached to help the man, another shaft hit him, narrowly missing Robert's hand. The twice-hit warrior grunted but once and slipped from his saddle to the sod of the bailey.

The king turned to see from where the arrow came and found that the Comyn archers on the wall walk were effectively thinning the invading Scots' ranks with a steady rain of arrows and bolts from crossbows.

Just as he wheeled his mount one of the deadly missiles glanced off his buckler.

A warrior from the wall walk saw the emblazoned red lion and realized he had almost shot Robert and began pointing and shouting loudly, "'Tis King Robbie! - King Robbie! – Kill him! - Kill the king!"

Others began searching the line of Scots, looking for the famed Brus, anxious to be the one to bring him down.

Robert growled, unwilling to be a target. Instead, he pushed his destrier through the chaos and toward the stone steps leading to the wall walk. His men of foot were close on the heels of his charger, though arrows and bolts flew thick in the air and many of their number were struck.

Still mounted as he reached the level on which the archers stood, Robert bent tight to his destrier and squeezed through the tower door leading to the walk.

The Comyn archers were aghast at seeing the King of Scots on their level, whooping his war cry from the back of his great white horse as it stamped and crowded all in its way. Several men were flung from the walk and others fled for the far tower as Robert's mount reared and dropped back forcefully on the wooden beams forming part of the walk. The whole walkway shook, as did every knight and man standing on it.

Robert nudged his horse to the battlements as his foot soldiers moved swiftly around him to engage the enemy. The Comyn archers continued to prove deadly to them as the Brus soldiers moved forward. Robert urged his steed toward the bowmen, driving them from the edge of their roost into the warring factions below.

The king swung his leg over the saddlebow and dropped to the wooden walk. He could feel the underpinnings loosen beneath his feet and knew he must take the walk quickly before it spilled the lot of them to the bailey.

Axe, sword blade, and bolts from crossbows filled the space between the rival warriors. The Comyn defenders fought courageously, but the weakness of the crossbow, the length of time it took to cock it, soon made the difference. The closer Robert and his men got to the archers, the less time they had to reload and fire. Very soon, they had no time left and threw down their useless crossbows in favor of blades, with which the Brus soldiery had trained all winter.

The walk shifted, and Robert grabbed the reins of his heavy horse, turning it back to go through the double doors of the tower to the stairs. His knights and men had almost dispatched the entire Comyn force on the walk by the time the king and his destrier got to the bailey floor. As he mounted, he realized how much energy he had expended as he felt totally depleted.

Across the bailey the flashes of swords were everywhere. In the midst of the battle stood Lord David, swinging his sword in every direction and taking life and limb as got in his way. His inexperience as a warrior showed despite his awkward success.

Brave young fool, thought Robert. *He should have taken more lessons from his father!* Robert had thought much of John de Strathbogie, both as a warrior and as a man, but his whelp had sided with England against his own blood and had yet to earn any respect or consideration from the Scots' king.

Robert Boyd was on his destrier leading his men, and the knights fighting from the ground had little advantage except their own courage. The Brus headed directly into the thick of it all.

"Retreat to the keep!" ordered David, seeing the king maneuvering toward him on his great horse.

As the earl and his contingent backed through the gate tunnel to the inner bailey and the castle, Robert followed close on as the rest of the men pushed tight to him, almost as one.

Coming at last to Lord David, Robert dismounted, and holding his axe low, circled to the right around the younger man, taking the combat to a personal level. Strathbogie was at first confident and quick, and swinging his broadsword, hit a glancing blow off the king's buckler. Robert surprised him with an instantaneous counter swing of his axe, deliberately striking the hilt of the young earl's sword.

David's self-assurance flagged, but he quickly recovered and rashly swung at the king's axe hand. Robert easily sidestepped the blow and brought his axe up and around to hit David's helm with the flat of his axe blade.

Stunned, David shook his head and prepared again to attack the older knight, his father's friend. Another wild swing gave Robert the second opportunity to damage the earl, if he so desired, but again the king chose to move aside, blocking David's balancing foot with his own, and sending him sprawling face first onto the cobblestones. Robert stood back and waited for him to rise.

Sir David stood and wiped the fresh blood from his skinned face with the back of his hand. His eyes betrayed the fear in his heart for he knew that Robert could decapitate him whenever he so desired... but he was not a coward, and so gripped his sword handle with both hands and attacked his superior opponent once again.

Robert expertly fended off blow after blow, until finally he hooked his axe blade behind the earl's knee, and with a well-timed shove, placed Strathbogie down on his back, hard, his head resoundingly hitting the pavement, his sword flying. He tried to rise but fell again, unconscious.

The battle for Castle Mortlach was ended. The men of the castle soon bunched together and dropped their weapons before them on the ground.

More torches were brought into the inner courtyard for light.

"Take the earl into the castle and tend his wounds. And set a guard to see that the surrendered Comyns and their ilk stay put," he ordered Robert Boyd.

Lord David was picked up, and with a large knight holding him up under each arm, was taken into the castle with the toes of his boots dragging uncontrolled.

"I'll see where the gaol be," said Haye.

"No gaol for these men!" said the king sharply. "Do as I say!"

"Aye, My King," replied Sir Gilbert.

It was about then that Christina of Carrick walked almost casually, as if on a leisurely stroll, through the gate tunnel, just ahead of the camp followers. Her concern was for Robert but she did not want to appear overly anxious.

The exhausted pair of former prisoners, Edward and Walter, what few skimpy garments they had been wearing now hanging in tatters from their fight, stood when she passed, not even thinking that they were all but unclad again.

"Ye men need to find yer raiment," she said, barely glancing their way. The two men looked at each other, and then at themselves, and laid down again. They were too tired even to laugh.

Having heard Robert tell Haye that the captives would not be gaoled, Barclay wiped his sword blade clear of mingled blood from uncounted fights, and slid his broadsword into its sheath before asking the king, "We killin' these prisoners, Sire?"

Robert smiled. "Somethin' special for this band, we have," he replied as he swung himself back up onto his destrier. "Get a few good men and search the whole of the castle to find any hiders."

"Aye, My King," replied Barclay.

Robert wheeled his horse and headed for the outer bailey. Seeing him whole when he came through the inner bailey tunnel, Christina secretly sighed with relief.

The prisoners were sent through the tunnel as well. Those who could walk helped those who couldn't. They were a bedraggled and disheartened lot, and sure they would soon be killed.

The bailey was littered with dead and dying and the less severely wounded. Much dear blood was spilt in every quarter by both Brus and Comyn Scots, and English, too. The courtyard was fair painted scarlet.

While Robert rode through the carnage on horseback, midst all the misery and sorrow he heard a piper's droning lament drift up from the prisoners' area. The mournful tune was apt for the occasion, and haunting for every man and woman standing within earshot, no matter on which side of the battle they had served. Some were openly sobbing.

Robert maneuvered his destrier to be directly in front of the piper and was overcome with the tune. The Scottish monarch, though the light was poor, watched the piper closely as he played, and eventually noticed that the man had stubs instead of the first three fingers on his right hand, though one could not have told it from the fellow's playing.

When the man finished, he opened his teary eyes and looked up to see Robert gazing at him sadly. He removed his hat and said nothing.

"Ye're a fine piper," Robert said. The man nodded somberly and wiped his nose on his sleeve.

"How did ye lose yer fingers?" asked Robert, thinking it remarkable that the man could play at all without them.

"My liege lord," replied the Scot meekly. "My playin' displeased him upon three occasions, Sire."

Robert nodded his head to show he understood.

The piper, holding close his pipes, sank to his knees. "I am ready," he sighed.

"Ready for what?" asked Robert, puzzled.

"Ready to… go, Milord," returned the man without looking up.

"Ye mean ye are ready to die?" asked Robert, frowning, as Christina came to his side and touched his leg. He glanced down and saw her, and turned back to the piper.

"Aye, Milord," agreed the man, tears running down his cheeks.

"Well, ye should not be so hasty to depart this life," said the king. "A piper of yer good worth is seldom found, and 'twould be a pity for ye ne'er to play again." A soft murmur went through the crowd of prisoners. "Yer friends here seem to agree with me."

The man looked up at the king with a slight smile at the flattery, but he still didn't understand what was going to happen to him. After mulling it for a moment he asked hopefully, "Do ye mean I'm to be spared?"

"Aye," said the king, "…on these conditions. First, ye must give oath that ye will remain loyal to me as yer king for as long as ye live." The piper's eyes twinkled as he awaited the rest. "Second, ye must play the pipes for me whene'er I call."

The piper nodded, expecting more, but Robert just sat quiet, looking at him. A broad smile lit his face with gratitude and wonderment. "Aye, he agreed, "*that* I will do, Sire, and gladly."

"Then ye are free to move about where ye will." The piper got to his feet and bowed to the king, but he remained among the captives. "I said ye can go free, Piper."

"Aye, Sire, but I first must ask a boon," he said boldly.

"A boon! I have handed ye yer life and a place with my household!" the king chided. "What more do ye require?" The piper's countenance reflected his fear.

"I must ask that ye also spare my good wife, Sire!" At that, he reached out and took a small woman by the hand. "We have been together since childhood, and I would not want to live without her at my side!" he declared stoutly.

Robert looked at the pair standing before him and knew that he could not refuse the man his wife. "What is yer name, Piper?"

"Oliver, Sire"

"Well, Oliver, ye may take yer wife with ye, and any other kin as well." The crowd again started to talk softly among themselves.

"If ye really mean what ye said, Sire, then I will take most of the people ye hold here, for almost all of us are kin, one way or t'other." He pointed to various ones and said, "Yonder is my brother Will, along with his wife and bairns, my wife's brother Alfred and brother Eoin, sister Fionna and her brood…"

"Alright," Robert held up his hand for Oliver to stop. "The rest of ye," addressed the king, "will live if ye but swear yer fealty to me and our fight for independence!"

"But some of us are English!" came a shout from a knight among the corralled prisoners.

"Be ye Scot or English, join me and live!" offered Robert as he paced his horse before them. "Only the dead will I not have."

"We will think on it." was another shout from among the prisoners.

"As ye will," replied the king, "'til sunup…" With that he turned away his horse, crossing the bailey at a walk, Christina at his side.

Listening to Robert as they went, Christina glanced around, still not sure Robert was safe in Mortlach. Out of the corner of her eye she saw a striking motion as torchlight reflected off a blade. She looked closer and recognized the slight frame of Mute, sitting astride a dead English knight and repeatedly stabbing the already dead man with his dagger.

"Oh, Robert!" she exclaimed, pointing.

Robert's attention turned to the matter, and it made his blood run cold. Getting down from his destrier, the king walked carefully toward Mute, who seemed to be in a trance as he continued his vicious ritual.

The king spoke to the mumbling warrior, but Mute paid him no mind. Finally, Robert knelt beside the youth and grabbed the blood soaked hand holding the knife and wrested the blade from its grip, saying, "The English is dead, Mute… the English is dead! Ye have won yer war!"

Mute, eyes staring, suddenly turned them toward the king and collapsed, sobbing uncontrollably against his shoulder. "Sire," the voice unheard 'til now spoke with great difficulty.

Robert's memory reached years back and pulled out a feeling that he knew the eyes from another frightened face, but softer and frailer… and then it flashed before him and he knew who this was that he held in his arms.

"My God! Agnes!" He was dumbfounded for a moment, and then all he could do was hold her close in his strong arms and rock back and forth. Christina, watching from where she held Robert's horse, was amazed at what she saw, for she had heard none of it. Finally, she approached the pair, only to see the close-cropped head roll back in a faint.

"She could take no more," said Robert when Christina was close.

"She?!" said Christina with astonishment.

"Aye. "Brother Nigel's betrothed. She was…" he started, still holding her close.

Christina interrupted, saying softly, "'Twas Kildrummy… the siege… ye've told me." She knelt beside the fainted warrior, and stroking her gently murmured, "Don't ye worry, Agnes, Robert and I will take care of ye. Nothing will harm ye more!"

Dianna

April 26th 1308
South Aberdeen

"Ye a'wantin' yer pleasures so early this morn?" asked Dianna, smiling as she turned to see Sir David Graham enter the Ram's Horn.

"A little bed time would not ruffle my feathers," replied David with a coy smile.

"Ye speak so quaint," she laughed, ushering her friend toward the back rooms, ostensibly sleeping quarters for the tavern's traveling guests, but more often used for guests' pleasures and entertainment.

She was quick to turn her head as another entered, roughly slamming the door. Sir David turned as well toward the abrupt noise.

"Fear not, my Dianna, 'tis but a companion in arms, Sir Ian de Cameron," he explained, and then frowned at de Cameron.

"I'll wake another of the girls for the likes of him," she said, quickly reading the situation and understanding his desire. "I'm not about to take two of ye at a time… we'd break the poor bed to the floor!"

David smiled with satisfaction as the woman disappeared into the back to fetch another tavern maid for his friend. Shortly they heard, "'Tis too early for such work!" Nevertheless, the two came back to the floor of the tavern, Dianna having a reluctant young wench in tow, her dark hair tumbled about her head like the serpents of Medusa.

She was most reluctant to follow Dianna until she looked to Sir Ian, who struck her as exceptionally handsome. Pulling her hand away from Dianna's grip, she smiled and sashayed toward the young man, who also found her fair to look upon. Ian took a step forward. She reached for his hand, and without so much as an audible word, they disappeared into the back room in which she was sleeping only moments earlier.

"Are ye fixed now?"

David smirked, and bowed sarcastically, and pointed a single finger toward the back.

"Ye startin' the morn with just a poke at me?" she asked, and as she swished by him she grabbed his outthrust finger with which she led him into the bedroom.

"I'll buy ye a hen egg and a slab of bacon, if that's what yer hintin' at," he said, watching her dress move from side to side as she walked a step ahead of him.

In the room she loosed her blouse and pulled it to her waist. "Ye want more'n this, ye'll ha'e to work for it," she teased.

"Those bonny white duckies," he exclaimed, his voice aquiver as he quickly drew her long dress up to her waist and revealed her bare, well-shaped legs and rounded hips. He put his arms around her legs and picked her up until he could press his lips to her beckoning nipples. She began to breath heavily.

"Ye'll be bustin' yer trews if ye don't drop 'em soon," she warned as she felt him pushing against her.

He followed her suggestion.

. .

Later, as the four were breaking the night's fast around a table in the corner of the tavern, they spoke in low tones since some others had collected for their morning toddy.

"Ye yet gathered more stout lads for us?" asked Sir David, nuzzling her ear.

"Ha'e two in mind for ye, but ye'll ha'e to do the talkin' to get them to go along with yer scheme," replied Dianna in a whisper.

"Where are they now?" he asked, moving closer to her.

"Been hauled off by the English to unload a ship at the docks," she said, getting even closer to his ear.

"Be comin' here when they're done?" he asked, his lips almost touching hers.

"I like bein' yer spy." She smiled.

David raised his brows searching for the answer to his question.

She suddenly sat back in her chair. "More. Six more ships to unload, there'll be this day," she returned.

David was taken aback at the sudden change of attitude.

"What's yer bur?!"

"Ye love me spy work more'n ye love me bed work," she said in a huff.

Sir David rolled his eyes toward the ceiling. He had hurt her feelings.

"This might be what Thomas is keen to learn about," interjected Cameron.

David darted an angry glare at his companion.

Ian shrunk back and said no more.

David blinked a time or two and ran his fingers through his hair as his wit overcame his temper.

"Could be, at that!" he said with a mischievous smile. He stood and lightly kissed Dianna on the lips, lingering just long enough to make her yearn for him, and then the two men left in a hurry.

The dark haired woman picked up the two silver coins of French origin, left laying on the table and handed one to Dianna. "Hope *they* come back," she said, with a hint of wistfulness.

"Ye ne'er know," said Dianna shaking her head and staring toward the oak door that was left ajar by the two warriors.

• •

Forty-two men of Aberdeen were led by Randolph, Sinclair, Cameron, Graham, and the six other Templars. Over the previous several months they had been trained, one-by-one, by the ten knights. Only Cameron was new to the group, having recently come from Inverurie at King Robert's behest to return with a report.

They moved through the streets brandishing their broadswords and daggers, and telling the people of Aberdeen that victuals are coming for them in ships arriving that day. Having struggled through a meager winter, the citizenry were excited by that, and it was not long before they were gathered in hundreds, trailing the knights and their entourage of generally inexperienced, but willing, armed men.

Thomas Randolph led them onward through the streets, stopping directly in front of the castle. There they watched conscripted Scots carrying stores from the quay, past the long row of single-story dwellings, through the barbican gate, across the drawbridge, and into the innards of Castle Aberdeen.

"What say, Friend! Don't the people of yer town need these victuals more than do the inmates of this castle?" asked Randolph to the closest of the impressed workers.

The burdened Scot was quizzical at first, but at the sight of many blades flashing in the light and the mob of hundreds of people behind his questioner, he quickly got the idea to set his burlap-and-rope-bound package on the ground and tear at its bindings. Thomas was quick to help at the task with the tip of his sharp broadsword. He then walked on toward the dock where the sailors saw them coming and began to loose mooring lines on their vessels from the cleats on the dock.

"Hurry, lads!" shouted Thomas as he started to run. The others were fast to follow and crowded the wharf with hungry Scots.

As one galley's crew were pushing their vessel away from its mooring with their oars, Ian de Cameron, screaming a war whoop that would curdle the blood, leapt from the dock to the deck of the galley. Several of the astonished sailors quickly dove overboard.

"Let Cameron and the others handle this," said Sinclair. "They'll be sendin' troops from the castle to squelch us at any second!"

"Aye," agreed Thomas, and hollering to get his trainees' attention, pushed his way through the crowd, back the way they had come. The men in his company who recognized his signal followed, but others pushed along by the swarms of people on the narrow quay.

Within the castle, the captain of the guard reported as much as he could tell of the events on the wharf below, which threw Alexander Comyn into distress.

"We have need of those English supplies!" he screamed.

"We're gettin' men arrayed as fast as we can, Sire!" the captain replied.

Alexander ran up the four flights of steps to the wall walk, and panting from being out of breath, looked out over the battlements to ascertain the situation. Below was a turbulent sea of people milling in front of the castle, pouring from the streets nearby onto the dock, and tearing at bundles of goods to which each thought they had a right. Tears began to stream down Lord Alexander's face as he could not imagine the people acting in such a rowdy manner.

Henry Cheyne, Bishop of Aberdeen and cousin to Sir Reginald, appeared on the wall walk in his vestments and shouted his loudest for the populace to desist, but his old croaking voice was swallowed up and reached no more than two floors below.

"What shall we do, Yer Grace?" questioned the simple minded Alexander, his brow twisted into lines of apprehension.

"I fear there is little we can do!" replied the bishop, his eyes fixed on the melee below. In moments, troops from the castle ran across the drawbridge and without warning began to hack to death and dismember those closest at hand. Archers aligned on the wall began to rain deadly missiles into the crowds.

"Shouldn't have gone against the king of England!" whispered the bishop, knowing his words garnered none of the ears for which they were intended, but he was truly saddened by the slaughter taking place before his eyes.

Alexander came to the old cleric, and as would a child, put his arm around the bishop's shoulder and continued to cry as both watched the food disappear into the multitude.

Thomas pushed through the crowds with as many of his army as were able to squeeze past the oncoming human tide. He saw the arrows coming from the castle's battlements and knew the English were killing the town's citizens, but the hungry throng was ignorantly relentless in its desire to attain the foodstuffs on the quay.

Finally, the Scots began giving the English some of their own medicine.

The screams of fear from the horrified townspeople mingled with the clash of weapons and the shrieks and groans of the wounded and dying, many of whom were underfoot while the fighters continued the contest over them. More of the trainees moved into the center of battle as the innocents withdrew, back into the side streets from whence they had come. The arrows from the wall kept up their relentless flights, hitting as many of the English garrison as they did the Scots fighters. Thomas drew his men deeper into the crowd to get them farther away from the archers' reach.

"Ere we lose the battle, ye must send more of the guard out!" suggested the bishop to Alexander Comyn, fascinated with watching the episode unfold below.

"I fear, Yer Grace," timidly whined Lord Alexander, "the people… the people are too much riled against us!"

"Then raise the drawbridge and await reinforcements from King Edward!" said the bishop.

"Our men are still without!" Alexander shouted, wide-eyed.

"And how," asked Bishop Henry sarcastically, "will they get inside and successfully leave the *enemy* without?" He moved his distance from the half-wit, no longer wanting to comfort him and knowing that, sadly, the leadership in Castle Aberdeen was sorely lacking, and that if this "Lord of the Castle" were not the brother of Lord John Comyn of Buchan, he would at best have made a passable sty keeper.

"Hoist the drawbridge… lower the portcullis," reluctantly ordered Alexander.

The standing captain followed through as he was ordered.

Hearing the chain of the drawbridge rattling behind them, the remaining troops turned and ran fast for the gate. A few quick-footed ones made it before the bridge raised beyond their reach. Others retreated to the barbican at the outer end of the bridge.

Thomas and David, followed closely by their men, fell upon the disarrayed warriors and dispatched them in their panic. The barbican provided no great protection from the angry citizenry for the abandoned English warriors, as the townsmen dragged them out by their feet and ears to stone them to death beyond the castle guards' arrow range.

"There be yer fate, Milord," said the bishop, pointing to one of the guards being stoned, "lest a miracle from Edward… or God, save the lot of us."

The poor Comyn wailed through streams of his tears, "My brother will save us all… ye'll live to see his grand march to our rescue!"

The bishop was, at that point, silent and took his leave of the battlements for the sanctum of his prayer room below.

• •

As the afternoon rested into darkness, few were left milling on the ravaged wharf. The entrance to the castle certainly had an oddly matched contingent of citizens and Thomas' men to keep its company penned therein, which remained cloistered for fear of the Aberdonians, armed with the booty weapons taken from the day's fight. The reduced garrison was estimated to be a poor contestant against the people in the streets. There would be no more supplies, either from England or the local vendors for their survival.

The captured ships and galleys remained tied to the pier, but the English crews that guided them to the shore of Aberdeen were no more. The waters around the vessels were choked with floating bodies, food for some of the fish and crabs close by.

The bodies of those who died on land and not yet claimed by their kindred, were stacked, awaiting a burial party to take them beyond the town.

Some of warriors led by Graham and Cameron were celebrating heartily at the Ram's Horn where, only that morning, the idea was hatched that now threatened to bring the castle to its knees.

Dianna came to David's side and pushed her arm through the crook in his.

"Yer 'spy' awaits her spoils of battle," hooted Cameron.

She gently beckoned him to follow, and he was certainly a willing servant.

Thomas and Henry Sinclair found themselves pushed through the doors of the Red Lion. Wherever they went, the pair were being hailed as heroes and consequently taken to the nearest drinking establishments, one after the other. The keeper's wife saw Thomas, and as she had done the last time, began to cry.

Thomas grumped, "Oh God, whate'er have I done now?" He started to leave, even against those many appreciative hands wanting to touch him for the heroic action he had taken.

The old woman drew a flagon of the house-made ale and held it high, gesturing an offer to Thomas, tears still falling amid a faint smile forming on her face.

Thomas was surely confused and could not get to, or away from her, for the mob of happy bodies surrounding him.

The innkeeper came from the kitchen with an armful of pewter goblets and began filling them with ale. "Get their coin, woman!" he ordered, "and stop yer snivelin'."

She put down the ale meant for Thomas and began selling the ale her husband was placing on the counter. Soon, most all had tipped a horn or cup to the two honored, and captive, guests.

The woman came to Thomas as she had the opportunity and took him by the hand. "Ye must see Lula," she said, tugging his hand insistently toward the back of the tavern.

Thomas frowned, but fearing little, especially with all the ale he had drunk, accommodated the woman out of curiosity, if naught more. The separating curtain to the back room was almost ceremoniously drawn back to reveal her two daughters sitting in chairs. Lula had a five-month-old nursing bairn in her arms and Lela had another of equal size perched wobble-headed on her lap.

Thomas blinked. *Pembroke's bastard son, or sons!* he thought, *but why are they here?*

"My daughters ha'e been returned to us!" exclaimed the woman.

"I see they have," replied Thomas peering down at the scene. "Ye here for a visit?" he asked, finding it hard to believe that Pembroke would have let them simply leave.

"They're here fore'er!" she announced, thrilled with it all. "With Lula's twin lasses!"

"Lasses, eh?" mused Thomas. An interesting smirk emerged from within his beard.

"Aye, Milord," demurely answered Lula.

He looked closely at the two bairns, "Good they take after their mother," he commented. Then he asked, "Where is Lord Pembroke?"

"Gone to England, he has," the young mother answered, "ne'er to hear of us, again."

"Ye'll be best off that way," said Thomas starting to leave.

"Won't ye ha'e that ale," urged the woman. "The earl was very generous to the lasses," she bragged.

Most unlike Aymer, thought Thomas. He returned to the ale room and joined Henry Sinclair. The woman, still shedding tears of happiness, poured two glasses of ale for the two warriors and set them on the table in front of them.

"A toast… to the day," said Sinclair holding his glass toward Thomas.

Thomas smiled, picked up his glass and tipped it toward his companion, but before he drank he said, "Yon castle hain't been taken as yet, ye know?"

"They'll be dead in their skins within two months," said Sir Henry, taking another deep sip from his glass.

"Tomorrow, I'll send the Cameron back to Inverurie with the news for the king," said Thomas.

"Ye'll have to send him on to Buchan," returned Sinclair.

"Buchan?" asked Thomas.

"Aye," replied Sinclair. "Talked a while ago to a lad fresh from there, and he said that the whole of Buchan is bein' consumed by fire."

"Did he have news of the king?"

Sinclair just worriedly shook his head. "He told me that 'twas *Edward* Brus settin' fires and killin' as many that remained loyal to their Comyn lord, as he could lay blade to."

"I'll have to see this for myself," replied Thomas.

MAY 1ST 1308
BUCHAN

Thomas Randolph leant around on the cantle of his saddle. Not knowing the fate of King Robert, he had come to see for himself the condition of the rebel army and what was happening in the earldom of Buchan.

By this time of year, such fields as would grow crops should have been showing bright green with sprouted crops and pastures should have burgeoned with verdant grasses, but instead, the fields were blackened and the trees reduced to charcoal for as far as he could see over the soft slopes of the hills. The gloomy landscape was not enhanced by the gray sky and constant drizzle.

Continuing in a northwesterly fashion for another league he came to an emerald field of new green shoots and a crofter's house that had not been razed to the dirt. There were workers milling about and taking care of ordinary daily chores as if all around this oasis were not laid waste.

"Good day to ye," greeted Thomas, calling loudly ahead.

The two startled peasants looked at Thomas, and without a word, hastened away to the byre, staying clear of the mud puddles with leaps, and striding sideways as they went. Their quick steps reminded Thomas of a dance.

Continuing on at a slow but steady pace, Thomas arrived at a spot where he was a respectful distance from the farm buildings. There he dismounted and walked toward the hovel where an old man stood in the doorway and under its protruding roof, holding a rusty old sword to his side. Thomas made sure that his countenance was open and friendly as he drew near, so as not to alarm the crofter.

"What ye a'wantin'?" the man barked suddenly, his long waggling beard accentuating the movement of his jaw as he spoke.

Thomas raised his gloved hands to show that he held no weapons. "I am but a tired, wet citizen from Aberdeen," he lied.

"Ye don't sound much like 'un from Aberdeen," replied the old man, and he gripped his sword hilt a bit tighter.

"'Cause that hain't where I grew up, Ol' Man," grumbled Thomas, becoming agitated.

"I'll take none of yer sassin' ways, ye young snippersnapper!" barked the man pointing his ruddy-brown sword toward his unwelcome visitor.

Thomas paused, again holding up his hands, this time to remove his gloves. "Looks like Beltane celebrations got out of hand, back yonder," he said, trying to start a conversation that wasn't confrontational.

"'Tweren't Beltane revelers with their torches. 'Tweren't no May queen, and truly 'tweren't no Robin Goodfeller! Nay, 'twas Brus!" scorned the man.

"Brus?" asked Thomas wrinkling up his nose in disbelief.

"Aye, 'twas that king's brother… name of Edward, went through here more'n a fortnight thence," he said, softening in his demeanor. "They fought hard with Lord John Comyn's pack, o'er hill and glen… but in the end, Brus won out… least in these parts."

Thomas looked around him. "Ye seem not to be tainted by the fires, here," he observed.

"Nay, we were not, 'cause our lord of these fields, here, gave in… and swore oath to King Robert as his liege," he sighed.

"'Ppears like it saved the likes of ye and yers, as well," said Thomas as he returned to his destrier.

"Folk here'bouts think of Lord John as our 'real' chief… not some 'come-lately'," said the man.

"And The Brus is a… 'come-lately'?" asked Thomas.

"Right lately, I'd say, forsooth," opined the crofter.

Thomas nodded as if saying he understood. "Ye got grit, Ol' Man."

The ancient one seemed pleased at the remark but chose not to respond directly. "We got water for yer animal 'round yonder," he offered, pointing to his left with his sword. "Hain't got no victuals for ye, though."

"Obliged," returned Thomas. He took the hanging reins and led the horse to a water trough by the side of the small house.

The man followed to keep an eye on him.

Thomas drank, as did his horse, after which Thomas splashed cold water on his face. "Which way did they go?" he asked as he stood, the chilling water draining generously from his beard and onto his already soaked jerkin.

The old man pointed with the sword toward the north. "Hell bound for Mortlach," he replied, still cautiously unsure of Thomas' intentions. "Best take another way… 'less ye're one of 'em!" he warned.

Thomas said nothing but mounted his destrier, and with a wave, turned and headed north. The old man watched until he was nearly out of sight. Gritting the remains of his teeth, he held his sword high over his head, shook it menacingly, and shouted as loud as he could, "I *knew* ye were one of 'em!"

· ·

The solar bed at Castle Mortlach was huge. Into its oak headboard was carved a bas relief of the shield of the Earl of Buchan, festooned with traditional oak leaves to draw favor from the Celtic gods of ancient times.

After the battle for the castle, Robert was dangerously worn, considering his recent bout with illness, and he slept for more hours than usual every night. He, and Christina, could tell that his strength was returning to him more with each day that passed.

This morning Robert sat on the edge of the great bed and busied himself flipping his battleaxe into the oaken floorboards.

"Practicin' or musin'?," asked Christina, the incessant thuds beginning to wear on her nerves.

Robert looked up at her, smiled and shrugged his broad shoulders. Then he threw the axe again.

"Ye hungry?" she asked trying to distract him from the exercise.

He plunked the axe three more times into the floor without response.

"Anxious to sit yer horse, I reckon," said Christina.

He sighed, not knowing why.

"Well, ye're fixin' to send me daft!" she said, growing irritated at his lack of answers.

Robert stood and paced off the distance to the far wall from the bed, which he calculated at some twelve paces. Taking a stance, he slung his axe for the middle of the headboard. The handle hit first and ricocheted to the floor, landing just ahead of where Christina was sitting.

Christina darted a fiery glance at Robert.

"Damned axe," he said accusingly.

"Get yer boots on," wisely said Christina, "and we'll take a turn around the bailey."

Robert sighed deeply and scratched his head and pulled at his beard in frustration. He knew her to be right; he needed some fresh air and the bailey might do well. His spies were late in reporting back to him from neighboring areas, and he was anxious to get on with the planning of his war. Here it was in late spring, and he yet had much to do.

She stood and fetched his boots from the corner where they had been for three days.

He sat on the bed as Christina helped him on with the boots. The curls from her hair dropped carelessly about her neck and he wanted so badly, at that very moment, to reach out and pull her to his bed as they had done so many times in the past.

He pushed his foot deep into the boot as she pulled upward.

"There ye be, My Lord King," she said smiling.

"My Lord King," he repeated under his breath. Robert was suddenly thrown back into the reality of the relationship.

He stood. "To the bailey," he said smiling and with renewed vigor trying to shake the thoughts of Christina as far back into his mind as possible, yet the thought of sending her away never entered.

"I have boots of my own to don," she said laughingly. "Ye'll not leave *me* in this stodgy abode."

"And shall I help ye with yer boots?" he asked smiling.

"Not proper, My King," she replied pulling them on herself.

"Independent sort," commented the king as she pulled their cloaks from where they hung on pegs and folded them over her arm.

"We be needin' our wraps?" he questioned.

"Wind's still right smart," she replied as she opened the door to allow him to go before her.

As the two passed out of the inner gate tunnel and into the outer bailey, his presence surprised almost everyone they encountered. Each would bow low and offer greetings, and wish their liege continued good fortune and cheer.

"'Ppears Edward's been mighty busy conscriptin' kine," said Robert, looking toward about forty head of cattle near a byre.

Cuthbert came to greet Robert. "Milord, 'tis good to see the likes of ye about."

Robert smiled. "Where would these fine animals be bound for?" he asked.

"Victuals for a hungry army, Sire."

Christina interjected, "Not unlike the kine that helped feed yer army on the mountainside in Strathbogie".

Robert looked at her questioningly.

"'Twas chickens that fed *ye*, My King," she said.

"Refresh my memory, Dear Lady," prompted Robert, knowing she had a point.

"In Strathbogie, Sire, when ye were at death's door, a kind and generous crofter's wife took her layin' hens, and cooked them to help start yer turnaround," she explained.

"And how fit the kine into this spinnin' yarn?" asked Robert, thoroughly confused as to the purpose of her say.

"They had cattle that fed yer folk while we were there, Robert."

He looked into her eyes, bright with the notion of a repayment of the kindness.

"How many bovine be needed by the crofters?" he asked.

"Four," she replied. "More can be sent later."

"Four, 'tis," he agreed.

"Cuthbert, ye and yer friend..." started Robert.

"Fergus?"

"Take four... three heifers if ye have 'em, and a young bull... to the crofter who helped feed us in Strathbogie," he ordered.

"Aye, Milord," said Cuthbert, and as Robert and Christina turned for another round of the bailey they heard Cuthbert's voice calling out, "Fergus! Get yer arse to me!"

She giggled. He held a stern face but she could see the corners of his mouth and knew he shared her laugh.

"Ye up for a ride?" he suddenly asked.

She paused. "Aye, are ye?" she asked in return.

Robert's smile always brought one to her lips.

The groom was called to saddle and bring out Robert's white destrier and Christina's gray palfrey. About the time the groom appeared with their mounts and Robert helped her onto her horse, there was a mighty commotion outside the curtain wall.

"Raise the portcullis! 'Tis Sir Edward!"

Edward whooped loudly as he led his one hundred and twenty-three warriors through, at the gallop and slinging mud in their wake. They all whooped loudly as befit returning heroes back from battle.

The column of returning men filed past; remarkably, all returned alive and most uninjured. "This endin' our ride?" asked Christina.

"Nay!" he said as hoisted himself into the saddle.

Edward saw his brother climb aboard and spurred his horse toward him, waving for him to wait.

"See ye're up and about, Brother," shouted Edward.

Robert smiled at Edward and raised his hand.

"Reckon a couple of beeves are goin' to be roasted this night!" prophesied Christina.

"Reckon yer right," agreed Robert, nodding and smiling. He asked Edward, "What ye been about?"

"Bringin' all of Buchan neath yer peace, My King!" bragged Sir Edward. The statement was accompanied by a grandiose flourish of his gloved hand.

"So be it," said Robert, smilingly pleased with Edward's work. "Ye can give me yer report when we return!"

"Aye, Rob," Edward said as he left to tend to his men.

Robert and Christina turned their mounts and pleasantly trotted out of the gate and across the fresh, bright green fields.

It was their first real spring day, and the pair rode faster, their unfastened cloaks waving behind them. Christina laughed as the breeze blew through her hair, loose and carefree, once again.

When they were less than a half-league from the castle, a lone rider appeared from within a close wood and charged straight for them.

Robert wheeled his destrier and drew the battleaxe strung to his saddle. Christina pulled her short sword and both stood ready for the oncoming man.

"And ye without yer mail coat," she grumbled in a half-jesting, half uneasy quip.

"Well, ye can put yer blade away," he countered.

"Nay," she argued, "ye know I can fight!"

"Aye, ye can," said he, "but ye'll not have to, for 'tis Thomas." He returned his axe to hang on his saddle.

"Randolph?"

"Aye," he replied, and he kicked his horse in Thomas' direction.

"God, it's good to see ye, Uncle!" blurted Thomas. "Heard ye were given up for dead!"

"Thought so myself a few times!"

Christina rode up to the men.

"Lady Christina!?" Thomas exclaimed, remembering her from bygone years.

She smiled at Thomas and extended her hand, which he gallantly touched to his lips.

"She's my nurse," admitted Robert.

Thomas paused and looked at her then back at Robert, openly displaying doubt.

"My... nurse, naught more," insisted the king.

Thomas nodded and changed the subject, saying, "I have brought ye news, Milord! Aberdeen will soon be in our hands! Ye'll have yer waterway to the trade lands," said Thomas coyly smiling, knowing that he had accomplished exactly what Robert had sent him to do.

"When?" asked the King, inwardly delighted, but outwardly merely pleased.

"When, what?"

"When will our victory be complete?"

Thomas' eyebrows raised in understanding. "The town is already free... and well supplied, thanks some to English ships caught at the wharf. The castle keep will fall... within a fortnight or so, I suspect. It is not very well victualed, due to the citizens of Aberdeen!" he said with pride. "Ye should have seen them, Robbie! They were grand!"

"Thomas, I am proud to call ye my nephew! Ye will take supper with us tonight in Mortlach. I want to hear more about Aberdeen," he ordered.

"I will, Uncle, with pleasure." Then Thomas shifted the subject once again, "Are ye aware of Edward's doin's hereabouts?"

"Bringin' peace to this region," smilingly replied Robert, his mount dancing with the desire for more running. "He seems well suited to the task."

"He brings hellfire and destruction to thane and villein alike," said Thomas, angrily.

Robert paused. He was unsure he heard correctly. "What say?" he questioned.

"He has set fires to burn out all who oppose ye, clear across Buchan!" groused Thomas.

"Since when did ye e'er care of such, young Thomas?" the king asked.

Thomas cast his eyes downward. He wondered himself why he should care.

"Am I not king of the whole of Scotland?" asked Robert, pushing his destrier against his nephew's mount and grabbing him sternly on the forearm.

"Aye," agreed Thomas. "But…"

"I *am* king!" The Brus stated resolutely.

"Aye," agreed Thomas, not wanting to go further against his king and uncle.

"One day, Thomas, ye will see the wisdom in what we do here," spoke Robert. "Our enemies among our Comyn kin are strong and determined. The only way we can bring them to us as allies, or at least in peace, is to reduce their strength until they have no further will to oppose us. This wealthy land of Buchan is their primary power and their asylum. Destroy Buchan, take away their asylum, and they will oppose us no more!"

Robert removed his hand from Thomas' arm and turned his horse toward Mortlach at a gallop.

Christina put spurs to her palfrey to come to his side, and Thomas followed.

May 10th 1308
Castle Buittle in Galloway

The rotted corpse of Sir Patrick Macquillen had hung, trussed body and limbs, above Castle Buittle's main entrance all the nine months since Lord Dungal strangled him for bringing the ills of the country to lay at his feet. The Brus had not been seen in Galloway since that time, and so Lord Dungal rested peacefully, satisfied that his decision to kill the turncoat knight was justified. The gods had been appeased.

Lord Dungal sat astride his destrier, leading the procession from the castle to the parade and tournament grounds in front of him. The promised and long overdue troops from King Edward, though negligible, were at last filtering into the parade area from the wood on the far side.

Following the lord was Sir Ingram de Umfraville and the goliath warrior, Gavin, who was the lord's special lieutenant and oft-times bodyguard. Behind them trailed a contingent of seventy-eight knights and many soldiers of foot, called from the countryside to fill out the body of men that Dungal thought appropriate for the occasion.

"Do I see red birds a'flyin' again' blue and white?" sneered Sir Ingram.

"Aye, 'tis Pembroke," answered Dungal turning in his saddle to face the haughty knight.

"Aye!?" replied Umfraville, seething underneath. Ingram nudged his horse closer to the lord's side. "What's Pembroke doin' here?!" he asked angrily.

"Merely to help," chortled Dungal knowing that the very presence of the Earl of Pembroke, after the Loudoun Hill battle with Brus, would send Ingram into rage. "Calm yerself, ye'll get yer share of the English troops."

"I will not again take orders from the likes of him!" ranted Umfraville.

"Then ye best be effective," coaxed Sir Dungal. He knew exactly how to play his immediate inferior, not the least of which was allowing the remains of Macquillen, now picked to a skeleton, to continue to dangle above his head.

Within moments, the two contingents met. "Hail, Milord Pembroke," greeted Dungal.

Sir Aymer raised his large hand and grunted in a semi-agreeable tone. The corner of his mouth curled in delight when he saw Ingram so agitated and knowing the reason.

"I trust yer journey was without incident, Milord," offered Lord Dungal.

Pembroke grunted again and nodded a bit. He cared not much for his current assignment and it showed in his demeanor, but it was better than mixing with those conspirators in London, he thought.

"We have pallets a'plenty for yer knights within the castle walls and tents set in the field yonder for yer men of foot," spoke Dungal, waving his hand in broad gestures.

Pembroke nodded and Dungal's portion of the contingent wheeled to return to the castle. There the hindquarters of several steers were roasting in preparation for a feast to welcome the newly arrived, and much wanted, men-at-arms.

Dungal was a plain man, and his processions and celebrations all had his approving stamp of mediocrity, as displayed in the few courses and little variety that allowed him to keep a tight rein on the purse strings. Such as it was, the food was plentiful, and he did have some overworked but comely slave women serving as courtesans, to his own house and to his guests. "A belly full and a bed full" was the saying of those in Lord Dungal's favor around Buittle.

Within the hour after their arrival, the nobles and knights began to gather in the great hall of Castle Buittle. Even with the simple trappings of Dungal's lair there was a certain protocol and pomp involved, if for nothing more than to show that he had a modicum of civil behavior.

Dungal's large chair sat empty in the center of the dais as Lord Aymer, arriving amid blares of trumpets, was shown his assigned seat on Lord Dungal's right, and Sir Ingram, to the seat on his left. Their respective lieutenants lined the head table on the side of their lord. Only Gavin stood, with arms crossed, behind the center chair awaiting the lord of the castle.

The host of knights, English and Scots, took their seats as places were available on the main floor of the great hall. The squires and kitchen maids brought flagons of tolerably good wines and ale to the guests. Tidbits of sweetmeats circulated the main table and those on the floor.

Neither Ingram nor Aymer was anxious to offer the first word to break the solid ice existing between them, turning instead to their own minions for light conversation. Umfraville was constantly reminded of Loudoun Hill and the total embarrassment he suffered and blamed on Pembroke, and Pembroke delighted in Umfraville's continued loathing.

Lord Aymer casually and deliberately withdrew a scroll of lambskin from his loose fitting robe and laid it on the table in front of him. King Edward's large seal on the document was difficult to miss, even from two seats away. Umfraville's curiosity was piqued and Pembroke knew it.

Lord Dungal watched the gathering from the peephole in his solar wall. His continual mistrust of any under his roof haunted his wit, and he had hidden spies mingling throughout the guests to report any word or act of treachery against him.

When he was satisfied that his person was relatively safe, he dressed himself in dandy fashion, and with two identically dressed guards with upheld broadswords at shoulder height following in his near wake, he was filled with pretended graciousness when he entered the great hall. The trumpets again blared, but far longer, and all the louder.

Gavin moved the centered chair back so that his lord could gracefully sit amid planned cheers that filled the hall.

Lord Dungal sat. Gavin moved him in and continued his vigil at Dungal's back.

The well-roasted meats from larger animals were placed before the feasters that the feast might begin.

Sir Ingram, who could contain himself no longer, then spoke to Lord Dungal loudly enough for Lord Aymer to hear. "Milord Dungal, perhaps ye can say why good King Edward, our protector and liege, has sent such a *powerful* earl as Pembroke, who was, but is no more, Warden of all Scotland, to us here in Galloway, with English knights and sundry troops... so obviously gleaned at *our* behest for use against The Brus?"

"Tell him, hain't none of his truck," grunted Pembroke into Dungal's opposite ear.

Dungal's eyes bulged. "If ye two want to say somethin' to each other," he said, looking first at one then the other, "leave me from the middle!"

"But, Milord! What do ye know of that scroll a'layin' afore Pembroke with King Edward's seal on it?" whined Umfraville to Lord Dungal.

The master of Buittle casually cast his eyes to the right to peruse the scroll sealed by King Edward himself.

"What manner of word do ye have from our liege?" asked Dungal pointing to the scroll.

"This scroll?" taunted Pembroke, pointing to the only scroll on the table, the one he had set there only moments before.

"Aye," said Dungal becoming curious about the scroll's content and angry because it was being withheld from him.

Sir Aymer smiled within his beard.

"Who's it for, goddammit!?" demanded Dungal. Sir Ingram hung over his shoulder, wanting to know as well.

Pembroke laboriously stood, plucked the scroll from its place on the table and said, "'Tis from the King!" Pembroke could play political games as well as anyone.

"We all *know* its from the king... who's it *for*?" bickered Umfraville.

"'Tis for ye... great knight," his words tinged with sarcasm as he handed it over Dungal's plate to Umfraville.

Umfraville's eyes were wide as he nervously broke the wax seal and unrolled the skin. Lord Dungal's eyes were also transfixed. Umfraville smiled broadly as he read. "I am made Warden of Carrick!" he said in triumph.

"Ach! Ye are jinxed," croaked Dungal.

"Jinxed!?" replied Umfraville indignantly, his smile suddenly turning to a frown.

"Aye," explained Dungal, downing his cup and signaling a servant to bring another. "Lord Percy was in Turnberry only a month or two when Brus scared the shit to his britches. Ran back to Northumberland in pure fear, he did!"

"*I* fear The Brus not," vaunted Umfraville, fingering the pommel of his dagger.

Pembroke sat and began to eat from a joint of beef.

Lord Dungal shrugged. "'Tis none of my worry, so I say."

"My Dear Sir Ingram," said Pembroke unctuously, "If ye would read the word from the king further, ye would see that we are *first* to protect Galloway. Perhaps... ye can slay The Brus here'bouts, afore ye take possession of Turnberry."

"I heard The Brus is long dead!" offered Umfraville, thinking to settle the matter.

"Then, ye know not the man," replied Valence.

"He hain't no ordinary man, for sure," whimpered Dungal, remembering his eerie encounter with Brus along the creek bank on a certain moonlit night. "He's a red-eyed hant, that one is!"

Sir Ingram cleared his throat and put his attention to the trencher before him, trying to lay the conversation about Carrick and The Brus aside.

Pembroke smiled and grunted in complete satisfaction. Umfraville's mouth, concerning their battle against Brus at Loudoun Hill, had garnered long ears in London, and Pembroke was determined to jab his dagger through Umfraville's wagging tongue.

Marguerite

MAY 15TH 1308
CASTLE MORTLACH

Knight Sir William Wiseman had been sent from Inverurie to Ross for a two-fold purpose: one, to brabble with the border citizens and the English warriors to keep them reminded that King Robert still remained a viable power in the area, and that they must therefore take seriously the short-term treaty between the king and the earl; and two, to analyze the size and disposition of Lord William's forces in case the treaty failed.

Wiseman and his highlanders caught up to the king at Mortlach, arriving as heroes amid much panoply and cups of wine held up to them as they entered the outer bailey of the castle. With them they brought many destriers and much armor they had gathered as booty.

Upon hearing of their near arrival, Robert ordered his destrier saddled and brought to the entrance of the inner bailey by his groom. With ten of his knights aligned, five on either side of him, and his brother at his right, he met the incoming contingent.

Andrew sat his horse to the side holding the king's standard high. Robert's newly acquired piper stood to the rear and played tunes to suit the warriors' ears.

After the king praised the expedition and Wiseman reciprocated with words to honor the king, the piper inflated his bag once again, and the troops were allowed to find their women and their suppers.

"Come, Sir William, tell me more over a bit of whisky," said Robert, wheeling his steed toward the inner bailey with Wiseman at his heels and Edward following next.

As the bulk of the knights were fed and tarried in the great hall enjoying their ale, King Robert and William Wiseman had a quiet repast in an anteroom near the castle's solar. Behind a curtain was the piper's wife, Marguerite, a harper, who played sweet, melancholy tunes of her own invention.

"Ye gettin' accustomed to castle life again, My King?" asked Sir William, finishing his first kitchen cooked meal he had eaten in weeks.

"Hain't sayin' I don't cotton to it... but...," replied Robert smiling slightly, his eyes drifting off as he wondered how to best chastise a loyal lieutenant for going beyond his command.

"I hear that Sir Reginald Cheyne, whom I know very well, plans to lay siege to ye, soon," said Wiseman, pushing a bit of bread through the last of the rich sauce left in his trencher and eating it.

"He had best stay lock-holed in Duffus," rhetorically advised Robert. He was aware that Cheyne and Brechin were among the last militants holding out north of the Mounth, but they were no longer a serious threat to his plan.

"Ye were unexpected," commented Robert.

"Unexpected?" replied Wiseman.

"When ye came with the bishop to Urquhart, I thought ye were old beyond yer years, and a'ready worn," said Robert, "...but ye got ambitious of late."

Wiseman knew to what the king was referring with this conversation and decided to broach the subject himself. "Ye'll not have to worry about Skelbo," he said looking the king squarely in the eye. He knew plainly that he had gone against Robert's wishes by taking the castle.

"I hear ye took it over," said Robert.

"Aye, My King," returned Wiseman, "and set fire to it, as well."

Robert nodded then added, "Ye were only to spy it out."

"'Twas o'errun with English," came back Wiseman.

"English are everywhere!"

"My King," started Wiseman, "ye may not know this about me..." he sighed gathering his thoughts. Robert frowned, thinking Sir William to be stalling and trying to excuse his actions at Skelbo.

"... but," he continued, determined to have his say, "when yer queen and the rest of yer womenfolk were hiein' for the Orkneys... nigh to two years thence... 'twas my wife that took Elizabeth and Athol in and hid them ere they reached Tain."

Not knowing where the story was going and feeling the pain of repressed memories, Robert squinted and looked hard at his table guest.

Wiseman took a deep breath and continued, "Ross caught up to her just one day afore Athol and yer womenfolk were captured."

Robert leaned forward and rested his folded arms on the table in front of him. "What are ye sayin', William?"

"My wife was sent to Roxburgh dungeon… and hain't been seen since," said Wiseman, his tear-filled eyes dropped to his trencher.

The two men sat in near silence for a long moment, each man dealing with his own loss, as well as the loss of the other. Only the harp in the background was heard. Robert pulled thoughtlessly at the hairs of his beard. William's eyes were transfixed before him.

"I didn't know," whispered Robert at last.

"I didn't think so," he replied, "but happen, it did… ne'ertheless."

"What about yer actions at Skelbo?" asked Robert shifting the subject back to his problem, though Wiseman had made it more difficult.

Sir William's lip curled in hatred, his face became sullen and brooding. "I killed them all," he replied coldly.

King Robert nodded. "Any sign of Ross? He was there, not long back."

Wiseman shrugged his shoulders. "I know not," he whispered. "Plastered logs burn right fast and hot."

"But did ye *see* Ross?" insisted the king.

"I ne'er saw him… but I imagined the damned earl to be burned clear to hell with e'ery lick of that blessed fire."

Robert sighed. He very well understood the exacting of revenge on Lord William of Ross but now was not the time. It could be disastrous… for the earl to have been killed.

At last King Robert spoke, "William, I want ye to repair to Castle Elgin and persuade them to come to the king's peace."

Wiseman's eyebrow cocked in disbelief, "Sire, we have tried twice before to take Elgin and its come to naught, what makes ye…?"

Robert cut Wiseman's say short. "The good work we have done here in Buchan, that's what!"

Wiseman mused the king's words then nodded in understanding.

"After Elgin… go to Duffus… to Cheyne, and tell him that he is nigh to the last… He stands alone. He is a reasonable man and will come to the king's peace as well. Brechin will more than likely come easily, too."

"Aye, My King," agreed Wiseman seeing the potential for failure with Elgin and Duffus quickly turning into success.

"And the royal castles of Banff and Fyvie?" further queried Wiseman.

"Banff is no immediate threat. Fyvie's supplies will be halted when Aberdeen falls," replied Robert.

"Aberdeen?"

"Aye, and do this in great haste," said Robert choosing to not further explain his words about Aberdeen. He stood, as a sign that the meeting was concluding, "We are leavin' here soon... goin' south."

"Shall I follow ye south?" asked Sir William, who rose when the king stood.

"I want ye and the highlanders of Moray to hold north of the Mounth under the command of the bishop," he said. "I have spoken to Bishop Murray a'ready."

"Aye, My King," answered Wiseman bowing slightly.

"Ye will answer only to the bishop, under me. And as yer lieutenants, take Barclay and the Frasers," he further instructed.

"Aye, My King," Wiseman answered, enthusiastically ready to do his king's bidding and especially glad to have escaped the king's wrath for overstepping his mandate for Skelbo.

• •

Bishop David Murray of Moray, Sir William Wiseman, Sir David de Barclay and Sir Simon and Sir Alexander Fraser, with a retinue of five hundred knights and lesser men, left the next morn for Castle Elgin. They were in effect King Robert's glue, holding the north in place until all else was solidified.

The king had sent a messenger to the forests of Selkirk to find the illusive Sir James Douglas, who had been conducting a surreptitious ambuscade, sneak and attack campaign of his own in the southeast of the country during the winter.

At the same time, Thomas Randolph returned to Aberdeen to finish the siege of Alexander Comyn's castle, near the quay that Robert so badly needed to be able to trade with the rest of the world.

Two days later, King Robert led his armored force of nearly seven hundred across the blackened landscape south, around the Mounth... where there was still an old score to settle in Galloway, and a short term treaty in Argyll... with which to come to potentially deadly grips. Carried along were a great number of pack animals loaded down with grains for making bannocks, and goats to provide milk. Beeves stretched for quite a way as well. For the first time, all of his knights had fought-for or conscripted weapons and destriers to ride, with many extras in tow. The men of the army of Brus felt elated and strong for their cause. Fear of going hungry had passed from their minds.

Castle Mortlach had been set ablaze and blew forth a great cloud of dark smoke. Lord John's serfs and other workers, those who chose not to travel south with King Robert but yet had sworn allegiance to him, were allowed to make for kith or kin elsewhere in the countryside.

Robert had masons stand by to dismantle the stone walls beyond practical use after the fires had cooled. They would catch up to the king, later.

Turning in his saddle to look back toward the burning castle, Robert said to Christina, "That damned oak bed of Buchan's is sure burnin' bright."

She nodded and smiled in return, for she knew that it was the fancy, carved Buchan crest festooning the headboard that galled him so.

Henry de Lacy
Earl of Lincoln

MAY 17TH 1308
THE TOWER

"'Tis *expected*, My Lord King!" whispered Hetherington at the end of a rather tedious meeting, especially considering Edward's short attention span.

"Expected?" grumbled Edward swaying to and fro in his seat, wanting release from the business of the crown.

"As your closest advisor, and one who knew and honored your dear late father, I tell you that an heir *is* expected by your subjects, Sire," reiterated Hetherington, "and right soon!"

"Perhaps her belly has not swelled to your notice," offered Edward, "It has been but four months, you know."

"My Lord, little passes unnoticed, especially as concerns the king," countered Hetherington.

"You're *spyin'* on me!?" spat Edward with fists balled as he stood over the much smaller man.

"For your sake, Sire," he answered. He trembled slightly for the might of the king he served.

"'Tis none of your affair, nevertheless!" shouted Edward, kicking the chair in which he had been sitting to the floor of the anteroom.

He stormed out, pushing through the double doors and knocking the guards on their ceremonial armor as he swished his long, dark blue robe down the corridor toward his quarters. "Damn Hetherington!... spyin' on me!" he muttered angrily as he went.

Entering his apartment he screamed at the top of his breath, "Piers!"

Gaveston appeared from an inner room where he was stripping off his soiled but elegant clothing after displaying his prowess in mock combat on the playing field.

Edward came to him. "It's expected of us... and expected now!" he screamed.

"Expected! What's expected?" asked Piers removing more perspiration drenched clothing to expose his muscular chest to the coolness of the room.

"An heir!" shrieked the king, nearly beside himself at the mere suggestion.

"So, give it to her!" responded Piers, not at all perturbed.

"A woman! ... I mean... the queen!?" asked the king.

"I have been with many women," returned Piers, amused.

"You!?" The king went pale.

"Of course!" he replied with a smirk on his lips and casually tossed to the floor his shirt of felt padding that protected his skin from the heavy, knee-length hauberk.

Edward was stunned! He had known that Piers had experienced many sexual encounters, and in fact had found the stories exciting to his own relationship with Piers. And perhaps, somewhere in the back of his mind, he had known that some of his lover's encounters had been with women, but he had avoided thinking about them as such.

He sat hard on the floor, his heavy, ample robe all around him.

Piers hung his heavy broadsword on a peg inside his armoire and asked, "We have parliament on the morrow?"

"Yes," mumbled Edward, "It's *your* head the parliament wants, you know."

Piers looked around the armoire door down on the then supine king. "You want me to stay here?"

"Of goddamned course!" he said with the contempt of a spoiled child.

"Then tell those oafish pricks that *you* are the king and *I stay*... no matter if it means war!"

"War!?" cried Edward. "War with whom!?"

"With the rest of the kingdom!" shouted Piers seemingly out of control.

"Oh, Dear God," prayed Edward, cupping his hands over his face and rolling over, twisting his robe with him. "We are finished, Brother," he sobbed.

Within a minute King Edward jumped up. "Come, Sir Piers!" he commanded boldly, finger pointing skyward as if receiving an edict from the heavenly beings, his other hand tugging at the arm of his companion.

"Where, pray, do we go?" grunted Piers frowning. He had not yet finished changing.

"To the queen's chamber, Dear Friend," shouted Edward gleefully. "The magnates want an heir! That's all! They'll leave me alone if we have an heir!"

Piers pulled back. "Hold, Sire! You need *me* not for *that*," he objected, eyebrow arched.

"Oh, Dear Brother, I do indeed need you... desperately!" he remarked as he urged his friend through the double doors and into the corridor leading to the chamber of the unsuspecting queen.

Piers was curious as to the king's mind and so allowed himself, half-naked as he was, to be pulled along like a tethered cow.

Seven ladies-in-waiting surrounded the sixteen-year-old queen in her apartment. As homesick sailors often did, they were reminiscing in their native tongue about their homeland and their easy and lively life there. The ambiance of familiar expressions and soft feminine voices and giggles quickly turned to the harsh and loud masculine voice of Edward. Several of the startled young women screamed in panic.

"I'm here to make a new heir!" he proclaimed, his prophetic finger wagging at the assembled ladies and directing them out of the suite.

"Mon Dieu!" whispered Isabella under her breath. She then made the sign of the cross upon herself.

"Faire ses adieux!" ordered the king as he waved his hand over the retinue. "Rapidement! Rapidement!" he hurried them.

Some looked protectively toward the queen, while others scattered, screaming in fear. The queen spoke in low tones to the reluctant ladies, giving them permission to abandon her. She would be safe, she assured them.

When her ladies all had scurried from the room and closed the door, she stood, and looking the king in the eyes, calmly but firmly asked, "What manner of folly brings you to my privy chamber, Mon Roi?"

She saw beyond the two men to the outside corridor where bewildered guards stood, mouths agape.

"We are here to endow you... and England... with an heir!" said Edward, authoritatively propping his fists on his hips.

"And I am here to receive you, Sire, but my bargain is for my husband, alone," said Isabella, eyes darting toward Gaveston.

Edward turned to Piers, "Close the doors!"

He turned to do Edward's bidding. "Be sure to mention *this* to Hetherington!" shouted Edward to the guards just as the doors came to.

"Give me your clothes, Dear Brother!" commanded the king.

The eyes of Piers and Isabella widened not knowing what Edward had in mind.

"Now!" prompted the king, pointing to Gaveston's trews and boots.

Piers growled in protest.

"You will like it, I promise," he softly urged.

Piers loosened his belt and dropped it to the floor.

Isabella stood fearlessly staunch, ready for whatever ploy the king had in mind.

Piers removed his boots and then his leggings. He stood in their presence fully unclothed. Edward looked upon his body then reached to the floor to pick up his lover's trews.

"Watch," he said to Piers, and he turned to Isabella. He looked at her and as he did he put the pair of trews to his face and drew in deep breaths through his nostrils.

"Shall I disrobe?" she asked coldly as she turned toward the bedchamber.

"Not necessary," he replied in an equally cold tone.

• •

"How you reckon that whoreson will skirt parliament tomorrow?" asked the Earl of Lancaster of his drinking companions, the Earl of Lincoln and the King's half brother, John de Botetourt. The conspiracy of three was sequestered in a private backroom of a popular tavern near the Tower in London.

"If he's not dealt with tomorrow, then we have no choice but to kill him!" angrily put in Lincoln.

"But, we must do it so that it seems it's a plot by The Brus," interjected Botetourt, who had good reason to hate The Brus for tricking him at Dunaverty the year before.

"Brus!?" came back Lincoln with surprise.

"Brus must be right glad to have Gaveston at court, Henry... he keeps the wind out of Edward's sails sure enough," Lancaster agreed with Botetourt.

Botetourt grunted and drank again from his cup of ale. Plans and ideas had never been his long suit.

"If Pembroke hadn't run tuck-tailed to Galloway, he might have had a notion or two," said Lincoln.

"Pembroke ne'er gave a good tinker's dam!" grumped Botetourt slamming his mostly empty cup to the table and reaching for the flagon to refresh it. "I think he seized the opportunity to get shed of the likes of us!"

"John, you're daft, for a fact," replied Lancaster.

Through the space between the curtains that cloistered the scheming nobles, Lord Henry noticed two men standing in the main tavern area. "Now, there's two that could be put to blame," said Lincoln sporting a cunning smile.

His drinking companions leaned to the opening to see about whom Lincoln spoke.

"Let's invite them in for a 'wee dram of spirits'," suggested Lincoln in a mocking Scottish brogue.

"I don't understand," admitted Botetourt.

"Then keep your wit to yourself and listen," said Lincoln as he swished back the curtain and approached the pair.

Bewildered, Botetourt looked at Lord Thomas, who with raised brows sipped more from his cup.

Within a moment, Lincoln was guiding the two men toward the private backroom with a bottle of Scottish-made spirits tucked squarely under his arm.

"Lord John of Buchan!" said Lancaster, standing when he recognized his Scottish counterpart.

The heavy man was clearly overburdened by his weight and his labored lack of energy. He moved slowly and chose the largest and best-padded seat in the small room for his own. "Milords," he introduced the other man, "my companion in arms, Lord Mowbray."

Introductions as needed went around the room, and they all sat while Lincoln began pouring the high-powered spirits.

"What brings you to Londontown?" asked the Earl of Lincoln, pouring a dram into Buchan's cup.

"The Brus, Henry," responded Lord John, frankly. He took the small whisky and drank of it.

Botetourt's angry fingers clenched tight about the rim of his cup.

"Say how? The Brus?" probed Lancaster, recognizing Lincoln's plan.

"I *am* the Earl of Buchan... do ye not see that I no longer stand in Buchan?" complained Lord John with frustrated gestures. He emptied his cup.

"Time for refillin'," suggested Lincoln, pulling the cork from the bottle. This time he merely handed it to the huge earl, who took it and filled his cup to the brim, then passed the bottle on to Mowbray.

"We have come here to get an army from the king and go back to run The Brus from our lands," said Mowbray, pouring his own cup full and passing it on to Botetourt, who set it on the table in front of him.

"Scot's warriors hain't good 'nough for you?" pushed Lord Thomas.

Lord John took certain resentment in the remark and even thought of drawing his dagger, strapped under his arm but, after a half moment of reason, that was where it remained. He satisfied himself with a grunt and a scowl.

"Now, now," said Lincoln smiling, "we have no need of harsh tones amongst friends."

"Friends, are we?" questioned Lord John.

"Do we not have common enemies within yon tower?" suggested Lincoln.

Mowbray and Buchan blinked at each other.

"Gaveston!" offered Lancaster as if it were common knowledge.

"Ye mean... the Earl of Cornwall?" queried Mowbray, his face more or less frowning on one side, his brow arched on the other.

"Yes, Cornwall!" said Lincoln, clarifying the question.

"Edward no longer cares for the people of Scotland, you know," interjected Lancaster.

The two Scots were still puzzled.

"'Tis Cornwall keeps him from helpin' you Scots, against The Brus!" lied Lincoln in as plain a language as he could muster.

Lord John frowned and slowly drank to give himself time to think of a response.

Mowbray sat awkwardly quiet. He didn't like the tone of the conversation but knew not how to gracefully withdraw.

Botetourt drank again. He was little more than an onlooker in this deception.

Lord John set his empty cup on the table and reared back deep into the padding on his chair. "So, that's why!" he exclaimed.

Lincoln looked at Lancaster and smiled behind his cup.

Henry Cheyne
Bishop of Aberdeen

JUNE 12TH 1308
ABERDEEN

"Halt!" ordered Ian de Cameron in his gruff, authoritative voice while grabbing the reins of the surprised man's gray horse.

"I ha'e a message for those in yonder," protested the messenger, pointing toward the castle. Men-at-arms were gathering round, making him very uncomfortable.

"Yer missive," said Sir Ian, holding his hand outward toward the pouch strapped to the horse's saddle.

The messenger sighed and reluctantly loosed the ties to the pouch and withdrew the neatly folded parchment and passed it to Sir Ian's waiting hand. Breaking the wax seal, Sir Ian began to read.

"Ye got provisions?" asked Cameron.

"Just for travelin'," answered the man. "They're 'most gone by now."

"Give up yer food and ye can deliver yer pouch into the castle," offered Cameron.

The man's eyes darted from one citizen to another. "Ye ha'e the castle under siege?"

"Aye," replied Cameron. "Ye can join them if ye like," he again offered.

"Will I be kilt if I stay out here?" he nervously asked, looking about him at the dour faces on the Aberdonians.

"Nay," said Cameron.

"Then ha'et," he said, handing the pouch to Sir Ian, and turning his told him the content of the castle's message. Thomas rubbed his beard for a moment then said to Cameron, "Tell these people that there will be a grand feast on the morrow for any that come here to get it!" With that, Thomas rode away.

Cameron made the announcement amid cheers and hoots.

• •

The message pouch had sailed into the open barbican just fine after the squire added a stone to give it some weight.

"Message for ye!" yelled the lad.

The starving denizens of the castle made no move to retrieve it until after dark, when the drawbridge was slowly lowered and a frightened fellow was sent forth to fetch it.

So fearful was Alexander Comyn of seeing hordes of citizens pouring across the span that he commanded it to be raised before the man had again set foot to it. "Raise it! Raise it! Raise it!" he screamed.

Turning to see the bridge closing without him, the retriever threw the pouch onto its floor and leapt near waist high to vault onto the moving structure, rolling down the other side to the cheers of his companions.

Within moments Bishop Cheyne was reading the recovered missive by candlelight in the solar of Castle Aberdeen. After he read it through, Alexander Comyn asked, "What does it say, Yer Grace? Can we expect my brother's army soon?"

"They wanted us to know that all is lost in the north, and yer brother run off to London!" snorted the bishop.

"My brother John'll come back to save us!" lamented Alexander amid sobs and continual wipes on his sleeves.

"Only God can save us now," moaned Cheyne, adding sardonically, "...and I fear he is too busy helpin' The Brus!"

Alexander sobbed all the more. "Why has God abandoned us?"

In an attempt to placate the simple minded Alexander the bishop reluctantly mumbled, "By God's good grace, the English will yet send troops to save us!"

"We have not been abandoned?" asked Alexander.

"Nay," said the cleric, "not by God... I misspoke in anger."

"But John has run off... abandoned us... left us here to die!" whined Alexander.

"Ye must be strong, Alexander, and... seize this opportunity to turn bad into good!" urged Cheyne. "God loves people who do such."

"That evil Brus!" cried Alexander, and he lay on the floor and rolled his body into a ball, much like a small child might do.

Unable to assuage the poor creature's fears, the bishop left him and returned to his more comfortable chambers.

Alexander lay quiet and pensive for a long while. He even slept fitfully from time to time during the night, but when he did, he was always suddenly awakened in a cold sweat by the thunderous hoofbeats of the destriers of the army of Robert Brus.

The morn brought yet another nightmare for Alexander. The guards on the wall were the first to observe the wheeled carts of food being moved into position, just beyond arrow range but in view of the castle. As they watched, they could smell the most enticing aromas wafting toward them, but their shrinking stomachs had not been filled for weeks as the castle's meager stores were parceled out to last as long as possible.

"What must I do!? What must I do!?" tearfully cried Alexander as he pounded his fists bloody on the oaken door of the bishop's private chamber.

Suddenly the bishop's door was flung wide and his rude voice boomed in anger, "What say ye?"

"They are eatin' below!" exclaimed Alexander.

"Good, I could eat as well," said Cheyne, thinking victuals had been somehow obtained for the castle.

"Nay… nay… ye understand not," the Comyn continued, "the street folk are eatin'… we have naught!"

The bishop rushed to his stained glass window and threw it open to be teased with the wonderful smells of meats and breads. "How dare they!" he shouted before thinking of their purpose.

Alexander fell to his knees. "What must I do, My Bishop?!"

"There is nothin' to be done," he felt his stomach twisting in hunger. "Unless ye can somehow get out there and get that food for us!" he added somewhat wishfully, not realizing that the simple mind of Alexander would take that as word from God.

The half-starved warriors within the castle were so desperate for food that, when Sir Alexander, lord of the castle, saddled his destrier to charge the citizens of Aberdeen and steal their food, all of the knights and many of the foot soldiers lined up behind him and marched from the castle.

Finding out about Alexander's expedition only after he had left, Bishop Cheyne went to the ramparts to watch the skirmish. The twenty-two archers lining the wall from side to side were his only company, and their bellies also rumbled in anticipation of being fed in short order.

The drawbridge was lowered into place and Alexander drew his sword. "Charge!" he screamed, his voice cracking, his mind set upon nothing more than relieving the continual ache in his innards.

The horde of English soldiers ran after Alexander as he galloped across the bridge, through the barbican, and down the stone entranceway to enter the street. Yelling and screaming, they stampeded down the narrow road. In the forefront, Alexander was horrified to see the food carts and the eating people transform into Thomas Randolph's citizen militia, their blades flashing in the morning light.

"Charge on! Charge on!" yelled Alexander, but he reined in his own mount to allow his soldiers to stream by him toward the waiting blades.

As one voice, Thomas' men erupted into a great roar and rushed the oncoming English garrison with vigor. Blades worked in every direction with blood following.

Arrows from the ramparts flew in support of the charging English, and though some reached their intended marks, far more found their way into the backs of their comrades.

Those leading the charging English knights were the first to fall against the pikes carried by the advancing citizen army. As they tumbled to the ground the men and women of Aberdeen came quickly to dispatch them with sword, club, hammer, and dagger.

Alexander wheeled his destrier and hied for the castle gate. "God, God... why have ye sent these heathen to my door!?" he cried, thoroughly daunted, looking over his shoulder at the unfolding disaster, his gaze turning quickly back to the open gate.

The following knights saw the will of the charge withering and threw their weapons to the ground, hoping to be spared, but they and the foot soldiers were set upon by the town's folk with sticks and stones and weapons found abandoned along the way.

Randolph and his trained men started for the melee where the citizens of Aberdeen were fighting, then halting in his tracks and holding his large arms out to his sides, he ordered, "Let them have their victory!"

"Raise the drawbridge!" ordered Alexander as he rushed across, and his guards immediately began to crank the large wheels.

Some of the fleeing English saw the bridge being raised and began to run toward it, but Aberdeen's citizens mobbed them as they tried to get away. Those who managed to twist themselves loose ran for the bridge and jumped for the edge of it as it went higher, only to fall into the dry moat.

Others purposely jumped into the lethal ditch to end their lives quickly and escape their pursuers.

Soon there was a jumble of mostly living but twisted, broken bodies lying at the bottom of the broad trench, moaning and wishing they had not followed Sir Alexander Comyn to their terrible end.

The angry citizens looked down on the despairing English with not a shred of pity.

"Rocks! Bring rocks!" shouted an enraged man in the crowd, and his fellows began to gather rocks and stones from walls and cobblestone streets, and wherever they were to be found, and brought them to the edge of the chasm and threw them onto the men in the death trap.

High above on the wall of the castle, the bishop watched the torturous deaths being meted out to the English and was compelled to stop the horror. Looking at the men standing dumbstruck beside him on the ramparts he shouted, "Now, ye shoot!"

Several of the archers obeyed and loosed their deadly arrows into the milling crowd, and none failed to kill as they struck. Other bowmen, fearing that they themselves would eventually be stoned by the crowd if they fired into the people across the ditch, lowered their weapons and ignored the bishop's command.

The bishop, suddenly overcome with the realization of what he had ordered in the heat of the awful moment, sank to the wall walk and dropped his head into his hands, "Heavenly Father! What was I thinkin'? God forgive me!... God forgive me!"

In spite of the attack by the archers, the irate populace continued to rampage. Two men carried an armored knight, dead from the battle, and tossed him into the moat on top of his dying countrymen.

Several Aberdonians tried to do the same with a freshly killed horse.

"That can be et," advised Thomas, and the idea and the carcass were abandoned.

The distraught bishop of Aberdeen had looked over the ramparts at his usually subdued flock *murdering* the men with whom he had lived in the castle for months. He had no words to utter because his mind was but a jellied jumble of horrible images.

Some of the citizens, seeing that their live targets were rapidly dwindling, began to cool in temper and their interest in revenge waned. They started to gather in groups to compare their personal exploits, excited about being free from the English and no longer fearful of the garrison in the castle.

As they filtered toward their homes or to nearby taverns, their elation only grew. Robert's plan of having Thomas Randolph form a citizen army in Aberdeen may have sparked the idea of freedom, but ultimately it was the sheer fury of the people who were determined to sunder themselves from those soldiers and minions of King Edward who kept them under heel.

Alexander Comyn was later found curled on the floor before the high alter in the sanctuary, mumbling in whispers about how his brother John was coming to save them all from evilly devised death at the hands of the heathens.

•   •

That evening, after standing outside Castle Aberdeen and working up a great thirst all day, Thomas Randolph set a guard, if for no other reason than to prevent those trapped in the fortress from getting the notion that escape was possible in the euphoria of the town's victory.

Afterwards, he headed for the tavern to do a bit of celebrating on his own.

Entering the Ram's Horn, he immediately noticed that Sir David Graham was, as usual, seated with Dianna and jealously guarding her attentions. He then saw Sir Henry Sinclair across the room and ambled over to his table, sitting on the bench opposite his. Thomas said nothing, but kept his eyes on the Graham and his woman.

"How long ye reckon the rest of the garrison will last, Thomas?" finally asked Sir Henry in an effort to converse.

"He fixin' to marry that wench?" asked Thomas nodding his head in the direction of the couple.

Sinclair looked. "Oh… Graham."

"Aye," grumbled Thomas, "Graham."

"I think he's stockin' up," advised Sir Henry. "What about the garrison?"

"Two days…" answered Thomas. "What ye mean, stockin' up… she's but a… a…"

"What's the matter, Thomas, ye plannin' on lyin' with her, too?" asked Henry, cutting right to the cause of Thomas' interest.

"I reckon to," said Thomas, uncomfortable at being so transparent in his motives. Taking a sip of Henry's ale, he added, "Be leavin' in three."

Henry sighed deeply. He was weary of conversations wherein Thomas was preoccupied with bedding Graham's woman, or someone else's. "Three what?" he said tersely.

"Days!" was the answer as he continued to watch the pair.

At last Dianna teasingly laughed and pulled away from David to go flirt with another man. David adjusted his trews, and spotting Thomas with Henry, picked up his whisky and sauntered in their direction.

"Our Sir Thomas, here, has lust for yer wench," announced Sir Henry as David came to the table.

David hesitated, smiled, and sat down beside Sinclair. Reaching into his coin pouch, he brought forth and laid a coin on the table and with one finger pushed it toward Thomas. Graham always seemed to have hard money, no matter what else was going on around him.

"Where d'ye get all yer coin?" grumped a green-eyed Thomas. "Might be said by some that ye Templars are always flush with coin."

"Ye want to have the woman or not?" challenged David, quietly.

"And if I take yer money?" asked Thomas, picking up David's cup and drinking.

"If ye take the money…" said David, "I'll get ye a drink of yer own when ye get back."

Thomas nodded his head and wrinkled his brow, "Ye don't care?"

"Have her," said David, "She's sweet and gentle." He sipped his whisky.

Thomas picked up the coin and stood to cross the room toward Dianna, David watching all the way. Randolph stopped very close to her and spoke but a few words when she held out her hand for the money, turned to look smilingly at David as Thomas put the coin in her palm, smiled brightly at Thomas, and without a pause, disappeared into the back room with him.

"When did the Randolph say he was leavin'?" asked David turning back to the table.

"Three days. He expects the garrison to last but two, then he'll be off," reported Henry, to which David nodded. Sinclair watched closely as David again sipped his drink. Then he asked bluntly, "Why are ye payin' to let Thomas be with Dianna?"

"She'll have any man that has the money," explained David.

"I thought ye were… I don't know… somethin' more than a payin' customer."

"A man could lose more than his heart to that 'un if he allowed himself," the Graham commented. "And I'd sooner give her to Thomas."

"Mighty generous of ye."

"Nay, that's just the way things are with Dianna," said David. "Besides, I'm goin' with Thomas when he leaves!"

"And ye don't want him to be suckin' a sour pickle?"

"Aye," agreed David with a wink.

• •

On the morning of the fifteenth of June, a white flag was seen fluttering over the ramparts of the castle. Thomas, David, Henry, and Ian were all on hand to watch the remaining garrison file out.

Alexander Comyn was bent over and had difficulty walking. The food for which he so quickly committed troops two days before was now his to have until sated, or until he made himself sick.

The proud Bishop Cheyne came forth to receive a portion of food. He ate little as he stood among the people, but by the time he left, he had overburdened his baggy trews and robes quite noticeably.

Having surrendered, the few men and women of the castle were allowed their fill, and were then taken to the docks two blocks away to be put into two galleys and shoved off on the receding tide. Sir Henry Sinclair was overheard as saying that, if they made it to England, good! If they didn't, better!

The bishop was the only one allowed to remain in Aberdeen, still staunchly for English rule, but agreeable to not speaking out or acting against King Robert until King Edward came to his rescue.

• •

The next day Sir Henry Sinclair stood with Thomas and David before the old Templar church on the south side of Aberdeen, where the three comrades had trained the citizen volunteers who ultimately gained a great seaport for King Robert. From that point, the king had the ability to trade with all of Europe and even England, and Henry was chosen to coordinate business activities in Aberdeen on behalf of the realm.

After the three said their farewells, Henry watched the two young warriors head toward the west, knowing they would eventually follow Robert's trail south, around the east side of the Mounth.

They were hardly beyond sight before he heard fast approaching hoofbeats from behind him, and when he turned, he saw Dianna astride her palfrey with her caboodle tied aboard. She barely acknowledged Henry as she passed, hieing to catch up to Thomas and David.

Gelis

June 23rd 1308
The Forest near Selkirk

"The Black" Douglas was moving cautiously from tree to tree. His three hundred and eighty-five men mimicked him in kind, spread across two hundred yards of woods. With each move they edged closer to the pathway winding along the western side of the River Tweed below Peebles, a small village of Scots and very few foreigners. The village was situated on the northern side of a mountainous area known as "the forest."

"Who ye reckon they be?" whispered Henry Symonds.

"Ye can see that Templar's cloak from a mile off," returned Douglas. "Must be Templars."

"Hain't they good for us?" said Symonds.

"Rich, they be, so I hear," replied Douglas, and he sneaked to the next tree. He was ready to spring his trap on the forty or so travelers.

The train drew nearly beside his warriors when James Douglas began to laugh heartily. His men knew not what to think or do.

Thomas Randolph and David Graham, leading the train, were surprised to hear the bushes suddenly coming to laughter. They turned, drawing their swords.

"All ye with me put away yer blades," shouted Douglas. "These laddies are with us!"

Douglas and his men showed themselves and Randolph lowered his sword.

"What in the devil are ye doin' James?" snarled Thomas.

"Scarin' ye to shit," laughed Douglas, "and aimin' to relieve this Templar of his hefty purse!"

Sir David Graham said, "Where is it writ that all Templars have money?"

"Not writ, just known!" answered Douglas smiling. He asked, "Where ye bound?"

"To meet up with Robbie, down in Galloway," replied Thomas, sheathing his weapon. The others in his company, picked up along the way, followed suit. Sir David kept his weapon more to the ready.

"We're fixin' to go that way, too!" exclaimed Douglas. "Rest here with us this night, and we'll all go together on the morn. Aye?"

Randolph agreed and Douglas led them to his campsite not far away, where food was cooking and the ground was softly laden with pine needles and gathered leaves.

"This where ye been keepin' yerself all the winter?" asked Thomas.

"We ne'er spend more than two days anywhere," returned Douglas.

CASTLE BUITTLE

"The Brus!" shouted Sir Ingram de Umfraville, "The Brus is upon us!" His voice reverberated throughout the great hall. There were only a few early risers and those who had been on guard during the night and taking their ease within the hall heard the alarm.

One of the English knights, who had been lying about in the hall, ran to Lord Aymer's chamber and rapped quickly on the door.

"What say?" growled the earl's voice from within.

"The Brus is upon us!" he reported in excited voice.

Pembroke got from his pallet and scratched himself in several places. "Damned bugs," he mumbled as he traversed the room. He bothered not to robe himself but spoke through the slightest opening of the door.

"Tell Umfraville!" instructed Pembroke in his rough and still sleepy voice. "*He's* the one who wants to kill The Brus."

"Yes My Lord!" said the knight, "I ken he's heard the news."

"Good," replied Lord Aymer. Then he rudely shut the door.

The knight left somewhat bewildered.

Pembroke turned back toward his bed where his companion was still asleep. He finished off the wine in his glass that remained from the night before and lay down beside her. He pushed his naked body tightly to the back of hers, reaching around for a pleasurable squeeze.

She awoke at the jostling. "Ye be a'wantin' more?" she asked in a sleepy, whiney voice.

Pembroke moved his hand down her body and she had her answer.

Within a quarter hour Umfraville had alarmed the entire garrison of Castle Buittle that The Brus was in Galloway. Lord Dungal came to the great hall hastily wrapped in a blanket to find out how imminent was the danger.

"They are up the River Cree!" explained Umfraville.

"How far?" asked Dungal relieved that they were not three hills from the castle, but aggravated that he was taken from his bed so abruptly by Umfraville's excited intonations.

"Reckon, 'bout twenty miles," answered Umfraville.

"Twenty miles is a long way off!" scorned Dungal.

"But they're killin' our folk left and right up yonder," he further explained trying to churn Lord Dungal's blood to ire.

"A'right, a'right," said Dungal. "We'll leave to catch them on the morrow."

"Why not today, Milord?" replied Sir Ingram impertinently.

"The morrow!" insisted Lord Dungal. "Fix for leavin'... today... leave tomorrow!"

"Aye, My Lord," said Umfraville with a bow, submitting his anxiety to his liege.

Dungal turned to go back to his solar, he stopped, then turned again to Umfraville, "Ye can have a few spies go yonder to report more!"

Umfraville agreed and quickly set about sending spies and making ready for his campaign against The Brus.

JUNE 25TH 1308
THE TOWN OF BRISTOL IN ENGLAND

In the Parliament held on the eighteenth of May, the earls of Lincoln and Lancaster, Lord de Botetourt, and others, with the damaging testimony of the Earl of Buchan and Lord Mowbray, exerted sufficient pressure on King Edward to cause him to agree, albeit painfully, to send Piers Gaveston away from England. Further, the estates granted him as Earl of Cornwall reverted back to the crown.

If those demands were met by the twenty-fifth day of June, and no later, the angry magnates would agree that he be allowed to retain the title of Earl of Cornwall, at least temporarily, and in his exile would serve as Lieutenant of Ireland, for which he would be handsomely paid.

Thus, the awful day arrived.

The king accompanied Gaveston across the more than one hundred miles to the west coast, to Somerset and Bristol, from where the ship would set sail carrying the earl to Ireland and exile.

The two men had chosen to walk across Bristol Bridge when going from the castle to the ship, which was docked at a pier on the River Avon. From end to end the long bridge was lined on both sides with multistory buildings housing shops and dwellings, and very little light fell on the roadway between except in the middle of the day.

By the king's order, the guards closed the bridge to other traffic so they could be alone during their parting moments.

"I loath those sneaky, connivin' bastards," lamented Piers in a low and angry voice.

"The barons and earls?" asked Edward.

"Who else in hell do you think I mean?!" shouted Piers.

"Be not so harsh and mean to me, Dear Brother," whined the king. "I did what I could... but, when I heard that there was a suspicion of a plot afoot by certain Scots and our own earls to murder you! ... well... this will give me time to find and deal with our enemies, and to mold our friends to our will... and then you can return and we can again be together! You do understand, don't you, Dearest Piers?"

"I understand that I'm to be sent to that god-awful Ireland!" his voice, in his rage, still at a high pitch.

"As Lieutenant!" Edward tried to pacify.

"Oh! Yes! There he is!" exclaimed Piers sarcastically, his arms out to his sides as he turned left, then right to an imagined crowd. "Presenting the new Lieutenant of Pigsty!"

Edward giggled.

"'Tain't funny!" shrieked Piers in his great anger. "They send me away only because I beat them in tourney... always!"

"You are not a gracious winner, My Dear Brother," admitted Edward.

Piers suddenly stopped and fell to his knees. "Please, My Good Friend, My King... *please* take this cruel punishment from me! I do not... *we* do not deserve this!"

Edward was aghast. Never before had he seen Piers place himself in such a subservient position. Tears welled in his eyes at his inability to save his dearest friend from this abhorrent fate not chosen by either of them.

It was Edward now that achieved the more sensible mind when he said, "We must give me time!" He held his hand toward his friend to help him to his feet.

Piers sighed deeply, and stood without Edward's aid.

The two continued in silence across the remainder of the bridge. There was a pause as they looked sorrowfully at each other.

"Bring me back soon!" begged Piers, his breath, in his panic, coming in sobs.

The king bravely smiled and replied, "As soon as I can, Dear Brother."

Piers turned and walked toward the ship, tied up only yards away. His heart fearful, his mind filled with sadness and anger, he sullenly thought, *I will kill them all when I return!*

Reaching the gangplank and walking to its top, he turned briefly to look at the end of the bridge where stood the king, a solitary sunlit figure against the darkness of the bridge.

Edward sadly waved.

Piers, weeping profusely, snuffled aboard as if he were about to be ferried across the River Styx.

Walter of Ross

JUNE 29TH 1308
GALLOWAY

King Robert and his army were indeed camped near the River Cree, about 30 miles west of Dumfries. He had sent spies in all directions looking for the army of English that had been reported to him as being thick in the area. Aware that there had been a large contingent of about two thousand bivouacked at Castle Buittle, he certainly did not want to take that many on in a siege or a pitched battle. Rather, he wanted to find small pockets of the enemy and grind them away faster than they could be replaced.

Circumventing the English-held castles in the area, he harried the magnates who opposed him and yet owned lands in Galloway, killing and taking what was needed to feed and clothe his army. His precious seven hundred experienced fighters had grown by two hundred, but he had also lost almost a hundred due to illness and bloody skirmishes as they went through the region.

"Robbie!" Sir James Douglas excitedly greeted the king as he swung down from his horse.

"Young Jamey!" returned the king, smiling. "How'd ye find us?"

"There's a'plenty of folks ready to point the way *ye* went," said

Douglas.

"Some come to the king's peace easier than others," Robert responded.

With the sounds of approaching horses from behind him, Douglas turned to point out Thomas Randolph. "Look who I captured for ye!"

"Sir Thomas!" the king greeted him as Randolph came within speaking range.

"Been a long time, Uncle," Thomas replied sarcastically. "What, two... three weeks?"

"Just about. Our business in Aberdeen complete?" asked Robert. Christina came out of the tent and walked to Robert's side.

"Castle Aberdeen, by force of its citizens, is yers, My King," he said smiling broadly and with pride. "Ye have yer seaport to the continent. The merchants from Flanders and Spain and Norway are at yer service... willin'ly, I might add."

Sir David de Graham, sitting on his horse beside Thomas, grunted to draw attention to himself.

Thomas readily took the hint and said, "This is Sir David Graham, one of yer newest and meanest... and worst woman chasin' knights, as is imaginable!"

Sir David was fairly taken aback by the strangest introduction he had ever had made.

Robert looked at Graham, then at Thomas. He cleared his throat and said with a completely straight face, "I would have thought ye to be describin' yerself, save for the 'newest' part."

Thomas looked at David with a frown. David could hold it no longer and burst out laughing.

Robert laughed as well, as did Thomas.

"Well come," said Robert, "'tis good to have a Templar or two in the mix."

Graham dismounted and immediately went to one knee before King Robert. Placing his palms flat together, he held his hands up to the king, who, by placing his hands on the knight's, accepted Graham into his service, at least temporarily.

Robert then invited the newly returned knights and Graham to join him for a meet to discuss the winter's activities, and future plans.

Having seen Dianna ride in with Thomas and David, Christina smiled and went to her as she dismounted. After introducing herself, Christina pointed toward Thomas and David's direction and asked, "Ye be with one of those rascals?"

"Aye," replied Dianna with a coy smile.

"Why don't we leave the lads to talk and I'll show ye around the camp," suggested Christina, and she started with the newly arrived woman toward the camp's inner area. She knew that Robert wanted to hear all the details about the last days before the fall of Castle Aberdeen, and she had no desire to listen.

"Christina!" called out the king as the two women were leaving.

"Aye, My King," she turned and replied.

"Find our new piper and have him play for us by the trees yonder." Robert wanted to cheer his troops but did not want to have his meeting drowned out.

"Aye, Sire." Christina gave a slight curtsy and turned to leave again.

"Christina!" called Robert once more. She turned and he said, "Will ye also get the piper's wife to play the harp at supper?"

"That be all, My King?" returned Christina with a sigh and wondering if she would be called back yet again.

"Aye, I have naught more," he replied smiling. The two women returned to their original intent.

Crossing the field in which the army went about its chores and training, the two women chatted, and quickly seemed to understand each other. Within minutes, they were comfortable with each other, like friends of long standing, probably because there were so few women to talk with of their ken.

Eventually Christina asked Dianna how she met Thomas and the Templar.

"I was a spy for them in Aberdeen," offered Dianna as they walked. "I passed along to them anything concerning the castle or the English that I overheard at the Ram's Horn... the ale house where I worked."

"Ye did this for the Templars?"

"Aye," said Dianna sighing, "for *that* Templar!"

"Aye," replied Christina, smiling in understanding. They walked on in silence a moment before Dianna asked Christina a personal question.

"Ye the king's woman?"

"Nay," Christina replied, "... just his nurse."

"Oh, but I thought I saw a look in yer eye that..."

Christina cut her short. "Nurse!" she said emphatically, but Dianna knew from her expression that there was more to her relationship with the king, at least as far as Christina was concerned.

"Sorry," she whispered sympathetically.

"'Tis a'right," said Christina throwing the comment off more lightly than she felt. "Come! I will get ye a short sword for to carry at yer side," she changed the mood.

Dianna's eyebrows raised, "Are the men here'bouts that rowdy?"

Christina smiled. "We're surrounded by the enemy... who would take us by force and with delight and be rewarded for it in coin as well!" That knowledge put a chill into Dianna. She had not contemplated

343

such danger to herself as a woman when she rode away from Aberdeen with her Templar.

"Ne'er had need for a sword afore," said Dianna, soberly, "but if it weren't for this wee dagger, Milady..." she said hiking her skirt almost to her knee.

Christina smiled, "ye'll have need for a longer blade than that if ye stay here," advised Christina.

"Then a short sword, will I ha'e," Dianna replied.

• •

The next morning, before sunup, Edward Brus was the first to wake Robert.

"Dungal's English are movin' on us!" he reported, quietly.

Robert rolled over and sat on the ground for a moment, clearing his mind of dream stuff and moving to the reality of what his brother was trying to tell him. Then he asked, "How many?"

"The spy figured from a thousand to fifteen hundred," said Edward holding out his hand to help his brother stand.

"Does he know how to count?" asked the king.

"As well as any," replied Edward.

"That's more than we've got," said Robert, stretching the kinks out of his back in the cool morning air.

"They're camped downriver some, and on the other side. Reckon they'll be on the move soon," said Edward.

"We'll wait for them here," mused Robert. "They'll pay a heavy price just gettin' to us, comin' across the water."

Edward reflected a moment and made a suggestion. "How 'bout if I took, say... fifty knights on horse and headed downriver to cross in behind 'em?"

"Apt notion, Brother," said Robert, "Draw yer fifty and get goin'!"

Edward awoke his friend Walter of Ross first. "Ye want to come with me to kill some English?" he whispered.

Walter frowned and opened but one eye. "Afore light?"

"Just got to hunt 'em down," replied Edward.

Walter grunted and shook his head, but said, "Give me a minute."

"Wake Boyd and Haye!" ordered Edward, and left to get the others he wanted to go with him.

Within a half hour, Sir Edward Brus and his fifty knights were traveling south along the east bank of the River Cree, hoping to outflank the mostly English army of about fifteen hundred, led by Lord Dungal Macdouall and Sir Ingram de Umfraville.

Robert let the remainder of his men sleep in until after daylight. He wanted them rested and knew that the English were still at least three miles away. His pickets would give him plenty of warning, enabling him to hide most of his men in ambuscade while the others would act as "bait" and mill about as if they were not aware.

The fog lay thick and impenetrable to the eye beyond twenty feet, with no sign of dissipating, even as the early hours of morning wore on.

As they rode as quietly as they could manage along the riverbank some time later, Edward Brus whispered to Walter, "Reckon we're far 'nough to be behind them?"

"If we hain't," replied Walter, "we'll not be in time to help the king when they mount their attack!"

"Agree," said Edward. "This is about the last of the decent fords for miles, anyhow." He turned in his saddle and whispered to the men nearest him, "we'll water the horses here, and cross on over. Move slow and be quiet 'til we get on softer ground!" With that he guided his steed into the cold, clear river as it worked its way over and between the broad, flat stones that made up the riverbed. His men followed suit as they arrived.

Boyd and Haye took up positions with Edward and Walter about third of the way across. There, they allowed their horses to drink while others, their rough-hewn lances high, kept vigil as far as they could see in the dense fog.

As more of the fifty gathered in the stream, Edward and his three lieutenants ventured farther into the ford, until the water came almost to the horses' knee joints and they were totally enclosed in the fog, unable to see to either bank of the river.

"Ye know," said Haye, "this is passin' strange... like we're all alone in the world, or like what we can see... is all there is in the world."

"Aye, and all ye can hear is the sound of the water runnin' o'er the stones," agreed Walter. The words were hardly out of his mouth before the three heard a distant shout from the opposite shore.

"Ye hear that?" whispered Edward, holding up his hand for quiet, but they heard nothing more. Still, Edward asked, "Our lads are not ahead of us, are they?"

"Nay, they cannot be!" responded Boyd, looking back in the direction their men would be and seeing only vague figures on horseback coming toward them through the fog.

Edward was first to notice that the fog was growing thinner when he could see the edge of the far bank. "The fog's liftin'," he announced. "Walter, ride back to the others and tell them to be silent!"

"Aye," said Walter softly, and turned to move back to the knights.

The fog thinned more quickly than Edward thought possible, and in moments he saw a campfire lightly flickering in the whiteness beyond the river.

Edward pointed across the way. Their eyes widened.

The fog was dissipating by the second.

They could make out a campsite with smoke lazily coming from many fires. Walter could see it plainly as he returned.

Haye strained his eyes to read the flags and pennants. "'Tis Umfraville and his English!" he said.

"Umfraville! Why have they not moved upriver toward Robert ere now?" asked Edward, but no one spoke. The lesser knights were drawing nigh, and understood the danger they were in as soon as they saw the hazy figures moving amongst the fires.

"Foul luck!" said one, and he started to wheel his destrier, causing it to thrash the water.

"Stand still, Sir!" ordered Edward quietly.

It was too late for silence. The commotion of the horse attracted the attention of several English breaking camp near the riverbank, and they stood looking at the horsemen amidst the river, as surprised to see the Scottish knights as Edward's raiders had been to observe the English camp only yards away.

"Knights in the water!" mentioned one to his companion, and both continued to try to discern whose riders they were while more of the Scots moved closer, coming out of the mist.

"Brus!" said the one, a cold shiver traversing his spine. The second man simply dropped the burden he had just picked up and ran toward the tent of Lord Macdouall, his voice still until he almost reached his destination, and then he shouted loudly.

"The Brus! The Brus Milord! He is rising out of the water with his devils at his side! We are lost!"

Sir Ingram came out of his tent, sword in hand, to see the "devils" causing the excitement. Surely it could not be The Brus!

Impetuously, Edward Brus drew his broadsword and shouted, "Lances first, broadswords next!" The knights knew his meaning and were immediately arraying themselves.

"We might all drown in the river!" objected Walter, nevertheless pulling his blade.

"Not here!" Edward swore,, and after giving his renowned war whoop, yelled "CHARGE!" and kicked his spurs deep into his destrier's side.

Those men with lances soon pushed past Edward, eager to skewer some of Macdouall's fine English knights.

Lord Dungal's bodyguard, Gavin, had opened the flaps on his lord's tent at the first word of the men in the fog. "Sire, ye'd best arm yerself and get out here!" he shouted.

Dungal cleared the tent portal in time to see the Brus knights with lances mount the river bank and come to dry land.

The English nearest the bank grabbed their weapons but had no time to do anything with them but die, or run deeper into the camp.

Edward, Walter, Haye, and Boyd, along with about twenty others, were the next to bring destriers on to the shore.

Sir Ingram de Umfraville panicked and screamed orders at the top of his wind, but nobody paid any attention to him.

As fifteen hundred English warriors tried to get to their horses and weapons all at once, the scene was one of horror and calamity, to be sure, but also of bravery and even comedy.

Edward's fifty knights charging into the camp in which were nearly fifteen hundred of their enemies called for great courage. Those who had come ashore with wooden lances spent them readily, and quickly drew their blades. With broadswords and short swords busily swinging on either side of their mounts, they fairly galloped through the confusion unchallenged as the surprised and terrorized English had only seconds to make life or death decisions. Most only wanted to escape those large and deadly blades, but, alas, many were not able.

Ingram went to saddle his horse since his groom and his squire both fell wounded. In the excitement, the horses also panicked, and he soon gave up trying to catch even one.

During the melee Gavin managed to saddle Lord Dungal's horse. Dungal, dressed in only his blanket and boots and resembling nothing so much as an old Roman, climbed aboard his mount and swung his sword above his head, trying to rally his men, but no one was aware of his efforts.

"To horse! To horse!" screamed Umfraville vainly.

The few English knights who managed to get mounted were almost instantly bowled over by the forceful charge of the Scots. Most never rose again.

Once Edward's raiders reached the far side of the camp field, they wheeled their destriers around and looked at their results.

The camp turned killing field was a horrible sight to behold. Lying about everywhere were the dead and the near dead. The walking wounded stumbled out of the way of those who were still able to fight. Men dragged their fallen comrades out from under hoof while warriors and camp women alike were running to the river and splashing their way across. No more than eleven hundred still were viable fighters on the English side.

"Charge!" bellowed Edward again, and spurs bit to horseflesh as the Scots spread to cover the whole width of the field.

"Good God, they're fixin' to come at us again!" said Umfraville as another squire appeared leading a saddled horse. He grabbed the reins from the youth's grip and swung on the beast's back. "They're comin' back!" he shouted, looking around to determine what kind of contingent was mustered and ready for the fight.

The second swing through was not as easy as the first. Those English who were unscathed stood at the ready, sword in hand and determined that they would not share the fates of their comrades who had fallen in the Scots' first sweep through the camp.

Again, as the broadswords led the way, smaller blades, and even hammers, followed, completing the killing and maiming of those on the ground.

A few of the English knights managed to mount their steeds and charged the Scots line. The clash was swift and deadly and many fell on both sides.

Umfraville gathered about twenty-five mounted warriors to his side and charged the raiders, who were too loosely arrayed about the battlefield and had to be chased hither and thither to be engaged. Brave, but ill-fated, Umfraville was knocked from his horse and fell into the carnal mire, much as he had at Loudoun Hill.

Lord Dungal and Gavin rode across the field, their destriers ignoring bodies lying still, crushing the occasional wounded or dead with their enormous hooves. "Rise up ye goddamned heathen cowards!" Macdouall cursed as he rode over them.

Some of his knights on horse and about thirty infantry rallied around him and he charged by following in the wake of the attacking line of Brus Scots.

Men who had fallen as if harvested by a scythe through a field of ripe wheat encumbered the chargers, and Dungal's men could not mount a full run at their adversaries.

When Edward and his remaining forty-one got to the riverbank once again, they wheeled and almost immediately met with Dungal's near thirty.

Edward yelled and spurred his horse to the fore. His men followed without hesitation, and with blood fully on their weapons and spattered on their persons, they appeared so fearless and invincible that dread was immediately struck in the hearts of Dungal's men and they broke such ranks as they were in, and fled. Brus' men ran them down, cutting them to pieces as they were escaping.

Of the men who were with Lord Dungal, only he and Gavin got away unscathed, and the two of them hied through the woods toward Buittle.

Fewer and fewer warriors were willing to take on the Scots, and Edward's men made a final sweep across the field. They then went after the escapees with a vengeance, taking limbs and lives from at least two hundred more before Edward called a halt to the massacre.

"God has damned us! – God has damned us!" screamed Umfraville, seeing that in the time it would have taken for him to have his breakfast, his mighty army had melted away before his very eyes. He found an unmanned horse running loose in the field and commandeered it, after which he made his way toward Buittle by way of the river's edge.

That Lord Macdouall and Umfraville left the field and abandoned their troops was certainly not unnoticed by the hundreds of English infantry hiding in the wood. Cursing their failed commanders, they nevertheless followed their liege homeward.

"Where was the king?" asked the out-of-breath Walter of Ross after taking off his helmet and watching the last of the English army disappearing before them into the landscape.

Gilbert de la Haye and Robert Boyd also came to Edward's side, battle weary and covered with English blood.

"Did ye think that Robert was to be here?" replied Edward, leaning in exhaustion on his horse's neck.

"Aye! I thought we were to come from behind to pound them while Robert assaulted their front!" said Walter wrinkling his nose.

"Would have, if they had gone upriver. 'Tis our good fortune that they delayed their move and we caught 'em by surprise," admitted Edward.

"But we were only fifty!" cried Walter, unbelieving of their success.

"Against fifteen hundred," gainsaid Robert Boyd. Riding back through the battlefield impressed them with their victory even more.

Leaving Boyd, Graham, and Ross, and most of their surviving men as guards over the spoils of the field, Edward took three able knights and returned to Robert's camp. He truly realized how fortunate he had been to win the battle against such overwhelming odds and was anxious to report back to King Robert how the enemy's will to fight had been vanquished.

· ·

King Robert was still vigilant when, in early afternoon, his brother and the three elite knights came galloping into his camp, boisterous and loud.

Edward whooped loudly as they rode in, followed by his escort, whooping and rearing their mounts.

"Where in hell have ye been, Edward?" asked Robert angrily as Edward reared his horse right in front of him.

Edward smiled broadly. "We went to pay a call on Lord Dungal Macdouall and his English gang!" he broadly waved his hand back in the direction of the battle.

"Ye saw 'em?!" barked Robert. "How many? Are they near?"

"Saw 'em and killed most of 'em, Brother!" said Edward still high on his victory.

"Come off that horse and tell me about it," said Robert, aggravated that he was not getting straight, understandable answers.

"Send a party back down river to collect the armor and weapons, first," said Edward swinging his leg over the cantle and hopping to the ground. "The Boyd, Graham, and Ross... who's right good with a broadsword... and the rest are waitin'."

Robert looked at Thomas who knew what to do.

Thomas nodded and went about organizing a party of men, women, and pack animals to find and bring back their dead, and pick up weapons and armor from the site.

"Now," asked Robert, "to start...how many of them were there?"

"Must have been a full fifteen hundred," figured Edward, hardly exaggerating at all.

"A mighty lot for sure, for fifty knights to have killed!" said Robert skeptically.

"Hain't said we *killed* all fifteen hundred but we surprised them, we beat them, and chased them down, killin' most, scattered the rest.

"Thomas!" yelled the king.

"Aye, My King!"

"See that ye get a rough count of the bodies there'bouts!" he ordered.

Thomas mounted his horse and arranged for one of the knights that had returned with Sir Edward to guide them back to the battlefield. Later that afternoon, Thomas returned to confirm what Edward had said. Macdouall's army was all but obliterated by Edward and his two score and ten.

Proud of his brother's work at the battle, the king thought to leave him and Walter of Ross in the region with about three hundred men-at-arms to bring Galloway into submission while he moved to the north.

King Robert, realizing that his English foe in Galloway, under the guidance of Lord Dungal Macdouall had been all but destroyed, began to think about Argyll and the Lord of Lorne. The Brus had not forgotten the one to whom he owed much vengeance for the deaths of so many of his warriors, and the killing of his dog. The short-term treaty had long since expired. John of Argyll's winter respite was over. The piper must now be paid.

• •

It was almost dark when Sir Ingram de Umfraville finally made it back to Castle Buittle with about eighty straggling knights and foot soldiers in tow. They were soaking wet, worn, and gaunt, and plumb drained of fight.

Umfraville threw himself down on a bench seat in the great hall. The servants brought him wine, cheese and coarse bread. He looked up and saw that the secret peephole in Lord Dungal's solar was dark. That meant the lord was either blocking the light by keeping a fearful watch on the hall, or sitting in the blackness speaking in mumbles to his demons. Either way, it bode not well for Sir Ingram de Umfraville.

"You kill The Brus?" blurted out a voice from Ingram's right. He slowly turned to see Lord Aymer de Valence casually strolling to him, a flagon of ale in hand. Ingram knew that the earl had already heard a detailed version of the rout from Lord Dungal.

Ingram said naught and began peeling wet boots from his feet and placing them on the bench beside him.

Pembroke sat on the opposite side of the table. Ingram looked at the liege superior as he drank from his wine cup.

Pembroke cunningly smiled and drank.

Ingram unbuckled the dagger strapped to his shoulder and laid it on the table between him and Aymer.

"You should have known better," sagely said Pembroke.

"They are just men!" countered Ingram.

"Somehow… they are more," said Pembroke, his brow arched high.

Ingram was angry but had not the strength to challenge the older, stronger man. Still, he wondered and asked, "Why were ye not there leadin' yer men, Milord," he asked in his fading rough voice.

"The king wanted me to be an advisor," answered Aymer, "naught more."

Umfraville nodded that he understood. "And what advice do ye have for me?"

"Leave!"

There was silence between the two.

Umfraville then spoke, "Ye reckon I could go to Carrick right away, Milord Earl?"

"Achin' to be killed by The Brus, are you?" said Aymer. "You remember Percy?"

"Be blamed for this day's debacle if I stay," confided Ingram, on the verge of tears.

"I'm takin' what's left of the army and repairin' to Carlisle in two days," said Aymer, uncharacteristically feeling pity for Umfraville.

"Can ye protect me there, Sire?" whined Ingram.

"Better than here," was the reply.

Alexander Macdougall
Earl of Argyll

July 18th 1308
Castle Dunstaffnage in Argyll Scotland

"That damned Brus will be at our keep within a fortnight!" griped the young Lord of Lorne.

"Beg another six month truce," answered his father, Alexander, Earl of Argyll.

"He will not give it, nor will I ask," said John acidly as the two men were taking in a fresh breath of air atop Castle Dunstaffnage. John held firmly to the stone to steady his wobbly legs.

"He gathers vassals to him by speaking of 'freedom'!" groused John.

"I am not against bein' shed of England," countered the old man. "But I am against The Brus bein' the goddamned king!"

"I purely hate the bastard," cried John, curling his fingers into fists in frustration.

Lord Alexander watched his son's knuckles turn white in his rage, and sighed. He then looked northward, out over the water toward the small island just offshore. The scene was beautiful bathed in the light from the setting sun. He paused a moment and said quietly, but determinedly, "I have known this sight as familiar for more that thirty years. I have seen it in rain, sun, and snow. I have seen it at every hour of the day and night. Its moods elate me to rarified thought and sweep my fears away... and *I will not give it up to The Brus!*"

John looked across the loch at Eilean Mor and sighed. He too had spent time there. He had been born in Castle Dunstaffnage and spent many years of his youth there, but it mattered not so much to him as to his father.

Alexander quietly smiled at his scene.

John again pleaded his agenda. "Brus has lingered in Galloway and elsewhere, and his treaty time expired three months past," he explained, "He bides his time while we have tarried here, lo these wasted months, wringing our hands in worry... and feeding this multitude of warriors far too long."

"A fortnight... did ye say... and it will be finished?" questioned Alexander.

"I can't stand the wait!" John replied. "I'm sick... my shoulder aches me right regular and I shake to hold a weapon!" He paused, looking down at his withered legs. "My God, Father, I am *not* myself!"

"Balk against yer infirmities, Lad," encouraged Alexander stoically, "Ye can't fear when ye've got a war ye *must* fight!"

"I have met this man and his armies before, I *don't* fear him," argued John angrily, "but I don't know what to do... now!"

"Take a portion of these men ye have layin' about... and go *meet* him... set what trap ye can... kill him ere he kills us!" insisted the earl.

Lord John sighed as his father turned and strolled the wall walk... as if no conversation at all had taken place.

• •

Later that night young John summoned to his privy chamber one of his closest allies, the chieftain Rollo, who hated The Brus... perhaps even more than he.

"Brus lays about at Tyndrum gatherin' up more men by the day," groaned young John as he wrung the rag in a bowl of heated water and placed it gingerly on his shoulder wound that yet refused to heal entirely. He winced and kept his eyes closed for a full half minute absorbing the pain.

Rollo flopped into the large chair in front of John. "That hain't far from Dail Righ, where ye beat him year last," remarked Rollo, looking somber.

"Hain't the same!" responded John, still holding the heat to his shoulder.

"How many men-at-arms does Brus have, now?" asked Rollo almost casually.

"He's built up to near twelve hundred, with maybe more comin'," replied John.

"We've got more than three times that many," stated Rollo interlocking his fingers behind his head and raring deeper into the cushions. "What ye scared of?"

John's ire crackled, his angry eyes wide. "Goddamn yer skin!" he cursed.

Rollo stared into John's eyes with little compassion. "Ye fixin' to kill The Brus, or die on his blade?"

"We're killin' them all!" screamed John, shaking as much with weakness as with anger.

Rollo smiled. "Now, most likely, we can win," he said, satisfied his prodding had worked.

"And what about *yer* anger?" questioned John, pounding his fist hard on the chest where his pan of water jumped and sloshed out.

"My anger?" started Rollo sitting stark upright, and knitting his brows, showing his inner rage, "It lives in me every minute of every day... Him makin' me fetch that stinkin' dog hide." His fists, perched on the tops of the chair arms, tightened and his mouth twitched uncontrollably. "I gain comfort on seein' the dead eyes of The Brus staring back at me from the Devil's own fiery hell!"

"Then ye will help me plot his death?" asked John.

"Aye," replied Rollo, "I will, and I have a plan that will kill the bastard!"

July 22nd 1308
Castle Buittle

Lord Dungal lay quite alone in his solar. Lord Aymer had withdrawn many of the English troops to northern England and Castle Carlisle, the better to protect the border between the two warring nations.

Sir Ingram de Umfraville, fearful of Lord Dungal's temperament and concerned for his life, chose to accompany the earl and his retinue to Carlisle. The skeletal remains of the cadaver of Patrick the spy, hanging from the gatehouse wall, was certainly enough evidence for him to carry such worrisome thoughts.

"Umfraville!" screamed Dungal from his darkened bed.

The darkness yielded no answer.

Dungal got to his feet and went to his peephole overlooking the great hall. All was quiet except for an occasional servant passing within his vision.

He shivered, suddenly realizing that it was chilly in the dead of night, and crossed to the hearth to stir up the glowing embers in the fireplace. With the iron poker, he noisily uncovered the heart of the small fire, into which he tossed several small logs, and immediately heard an eerie, low moan across the room.

Dungal's head jerked round and his eyes widened, straining to see from where the mysterious emanation had come. As he blinked and tried to get his eyes to adjust to the darkness once again, he watched the covers on his bed rise upward from his pallet, animated by an unknown force. An apparition arose from where his own body had just lain. Poker in hand and ready to strike, he crept toward the shadowy figure, just as the cover dropped to expose a woman's head and her bare breasts.

When that groggy creature saw coming toward her the distorted face and form of the frightened lord illuminated in the firelight, she shrieked, threw back the light blanket, jumped from the bed, and ran out the door and down the corridor, totally bare and screaming all the way.

Every one of the guards in the halls along her route was given a quick glimpse of her fleeing, but knowing their lord, merely chuckled.

"Got to recollect to get rid of that lassie on the morn," Dungal grumped as he rolled his equally naked body into the recently evacuated bed.

Within a half minute he shouted, "Sentry!"

A large man appeared at the opened door, "Aye, Milord."

"Get me another lass!" he ordered. "One that hain't a screamer!" he added.

"Aye, Milord," said the guard and left to do as he was bade.

Dungal lay sprawled atop the covers. He was now feeling hot after the excitement of the "apparition." His only relief from the heat was to open the solar window. That provided a small volume of fresh air, and as he lay on his bed again, he could hear the night birds' songs in the neighborhood.

"Ye send for me, Milord?"

Dungal's eyes twinkled after he looked up to see a large woman dressed in a simple robe.

"Aye," he said, "I did send for ye!"

The woman, knowing the purpose for which she had been summoned, loosed her robe and let it slip to the floor.

Dungal sat on the edge of the bed and reached out to her with both hands. Pulling her to him, he buried his face in her soft flesh until she thought he was going to asphyxiate himself before he breathed his next.

Malcolm of Lennox

JULY 23RD 1308
TYNDRUM

King Robert had sent messengers to Moray to seek out Sir William Wiseman and his many highlanders, calling them to join him at Tyndrum.

At the same time, the king also sent for Sir Angus Macdonald of the Isles to muster warriors and galleys on the waters of Argyll. His intention was to finish what he had put off some nine months earlier, that being the taking of the lands of Argyll and Lorne from Lord John and his father, Lord Alexander, at Castle Dunstaffnage.

Restless from waiting for men and supplies to come together, the king took up a bow, and with a terse whistle, summoned Andrew to set off to a nearby wood to hunt for deer, thinking such would be a fine supper for his close retinue.

On foot, the pair stealthily made their way some three miles to the southeast, seeing no more than a single rabbit as game.

"Long way to drag a deer back, Sire" suggested Andrew.

"Hain't seen one anyhow," whispered Robert as he hunkered at the foot of a large tree.

Andrew followed suit and squatted beside his monarch. "We goin' to wait for them to pass this way, Sire?" he whispered.

Robert smiled and withdrew an arrow from his quiver.

Andrew sighed with boredom as Robert took the tip of the arrow and began doodling a map in the dirt before him.

"Yer wit on Argyll?" asked the squire.

Robert nodded. The hunt was to relieve him of the burden for a little while but, alas, he could not prevent the various plans and notions from coming into his mind.

Robert stared off through the woods. He thought of Elizabeth and again wondered if she were still alive. Somehow he had to believe she was.

Andrew gasped when he saw the big buck walking confidently through the trees, munching what vegetation pleased his never idle nose and tongue. The lad quietly and slowly pointed toward it.

Robert nodded slightly and nocked his arrow with slow deliberate moves. He started to crawl into a better position to make his shot; Andrew remained in place at the tree. Robert saw enough of a clearing to try for a kill. Drawing his bow, he was set to release his shaft when an arrow from another direction struck the large buck in the neck. It darted off but got only a few stumbling feet away before it fell.

Robert froze, not knowing the source of the deadly attack on the deer.

Behind him Andrew called out in a calm but warning voice, "My King!"

Robert turned, arrow nocked but bow relaxed.

Andrew pointed uphill where, in the woods, a long line of warriors had suddenly showed themselves.

Robert stood, holding the bow to his side. *I'll get at least one of them*, he thought.

Andrew, having only his dagger, stood so that he would not be in the king's way, knowing he would probably be second in line to his king to die. He was ready, but wished that he had some way of taking at least one of them to pay for his death.

"King Robert of Scotland!" called a voice from behind Robert, where the deer had fallen.

Puzzled, Robert turned to face the familiar voice at his back.

"My God, Robbie, Ye look poorly drawn!"

Robert smiled and replied, "Ye look ill treated yerself, Malcolm!"

The two men walked toward each other and embraced solidly.

"Thought ye were slain at Methven," said Robert with all enthusiasm, glad to find that Lord Malcolm had survived.

"Oh, I took a lot of those Pembroke men off yer trail by goin' south after that bloody brawl, but, I hain't got dead as yet," said the earl smiling.

"I can see ye hain't," replied Robert slapping his old friend on the back.

"Methven was more than two years ago... where have ye been in the meantime?" questioned Robert trying to put together the pieces.

"Wounded," said the earl patting his hip, which seemed to be the source of his distinctive limp, "... and hidin' out from the English!" He then added "Heard ye were lurkin' here'bouts and came a'lookin' for ye."

"Heard Little Edward gave yer earldom to Menteith, Malcolm."

"Aye, so I'm told, Sire."

"Well, far as I'm concerned, *ye* remain Earl of Lennox, and none other!"

"Thank ye, My Lord King," answered Malcolm, genuinely grateful.

"Why did ye shoot my supper?" asked Robert suddenly, in jest.

Lord Malcolm laughed heartily, "We'll all have that meat for our supper."

"These yer lads?" asked Robert as the warriors filtered down through the trees toward their leader.

"Got up this bunch just for the likes of ye, My King," said the earl bowing his head briefly in respect.

Robert again slapped Malcolm on the back and shook his arm vigorously, finding it hard to believe he yet lived.

"Nigh time ye get back into this fray!" said the king.

Andrew recognized the earl from Methven and was greatly relieved from the thought that this was to be his last day on the high road in Scotland.

The twelve-point buck was thrown across the saddle of the earl's horse, and Robert, Malcolm, and Andrew walked the three miles back to the camp at Tyndrum, the two men catching up to each other's events all the way. The warrior entourage following was a surprising and welcome addition to King Robert's troops.

Meeting up with Robert at the center of the campground, Christina teased him, "Ye go to fetch venison and ye bring back an army, My King!"

"Brought the meat as well, Milady," retorted Robert as he pointed out the destrier on which the deer was tied.

And we didn't have to drag it home! thought Andrew. He knew who it was who would have done most of the tugging.

· ·

Five days later, on July the twenty-eighth, William Wiseman arrived from Moray with nearly four hundred men from the high lands. Among them were Simon and Alexander Fraser.

Sir William had brought news that Reginald Cheyne and David de

Brechin had submitted to the king, and that Bishop de Murray had stayed in the north with his remaining army to keep the peace among the king's former enemies.

"Nigh onto fourteen hundred, we've got gathered up here'bouts, Robbie," said Wiseman as the meeting King Robert had called together started. In attendance were also Sir Robert Boyd, Sir James Douglas, Sir Thomas Randolph, Sir Gilbert de la Haye, and Sir Neil Campbell, who had brought with him about a hundred and fifty warriors from Kintyre.

"This is the most we've had together for battle since Methven," mentioned Robert glancing over toward Lord Malcolm.

"Except we hain't goin' to trust 'em to keep to their word, this time," answered Malcolm.

"Nay," agreed Robert, "we've got spies out for five miles."

"And the Macdougalls have spies out for more than five miles," put in Thomas as he withdrew his whetstone from his rabbit-fur pouch and began to sharpen the blade of his dagger.

"A few of our spies have met and dealt with a few of theirs," remarked Sir Neil.

"Get a message to them to not kill any more if they can help it!" ordered Robert.

"Ye want word to get back to Dunstaffnage, Sire?" asked Sir Gilbert, surprised.

"Aye," replied Robert, "surely, I do."

It was at that point that the gathered men knew their king had a notion to win over the lands of Argyll, and as he talked it out, his plan became their plan.

Oliver the Piper

AUGUST 2ND 1308
THE PASS OF BRANDER IN ARGYLL

Rising directly from the bottom of Loch Awe to its south, Ben Cruachan, that rugged and all but barren mountain of solid rock, peaked nearly two-thirds of a mile above the water. In the winter it was a snow and ice-capped behemoth looming above the stormy loch and the lower mounts and hills surrounding. In the warmer months, its lower reaches brought forth green, but were yet steeply treacherous, especially in the Pass of Brander, where some of the craggy walls descended nearly perpendicularly to the water. There, a careless step could result in a fall of hundreds of feet to the waters of Loch Awe.

The narrow pass, between Ben Cruachan and Creag an Aoineidh, was carved before time by excoriating glaciers and the northwest flow of the loch's waters heading inexorably for Airds Bay and Loch Etive. And where Loch Etive joined Loch Linnhe below the Falls of Lora... there was the home of the Lord of Lorne, Dunstaffnage Castle.

The Brus headed to Dunstaffnage as surely as the waters of Loch Awe.

Sending James Douglas and William Wiseman ahead with an army of about five hundred archers and men from the northern high lands, Robert and his larger force departed Tyndrum and traveled at a leisurely pace, finally camping near the headwaters of Loch Awe. He knew that his arrival so close to Brander Pass would be reported to and alarm Lord Lorne, awaiting Robert's coming for battle ever since their truce expired, these three months since.

He could wait a while longer.

King Robert sat calmly on the ground, across a chessboard from Christina. Both were solemnly focused on the game, taken from Castle Mortlach, when Christina suddenly and deftly moved her queen across the board and set it within two spaces of Robert's king.

"Check, My Lord King!" she said, victoriously smiling.

After running his eyes over his board positions, Robert laid his king on its side, acknowledging her win as he shook his head and smiled. "Perhaps I should make ye my first lieutenant!" he remarked. "Ye are a bold player."

"This is but a game, Milord," she countered. "No blood is spilt if misjudgments are made within these squares."

Robert again smiled and stood as he spoke, "Mistakes or naught, Milady, blood is always spilt... 'Tis war's nature."

Her smile gone, Christina gracefully bowed her head from where she sat and Robert left, while somewhere nearby, Marguerite played her harp, softly and sweetly.

Christina watched Robert walk across the peaceful clearing and mused, *It seems not at all like we are but one day from going up the Pass of Brander to certain battle.*

• •

"Our spy has reported that, this morn The Brus played chess with one of his women!" shouted the impatient John of Lorne. "Why does he not sally forth into our trap?!"

"He will... in good time," replied Rollo, holding tightly to the mast of the slowly rolling galley moored on the northwesterly end of Loch Awe.

"No sailor, are ye?" remarked John watching Rollo's face.

"I hate boats, Sire," replied the chieftain, feeling his stomach heaving to the galley's rhythm.

"Then get ye back to yer two thousand on the mountain," emphatically ordered Lord John. "They must surely come on the morn... Brus cannot play chess fore'er!"

When the seasick Rollo had left the galley, Sir John ordered the captain to rejoin the five other vessels in his fleet, anchored to the east on the south side of Loch Awe, in Brander Pass, from where he could watch the final destruction of the "Brus Rebellion."

• •

The last of the setting sun reflected a golden red on the shimmering loch below by the time Rollo reached his men, hiding on the rim of a crag a hundred feet and more above the water. He could easily see the six galleys aligned on the far side, their night candles barely visible in the shadowed sides of the vessels. Below him was the roadway along which The Brus and his army must file on their way to attack Dunstaffnage. Little more than a footpath, the ancient trail was so narrow in places that two men on horseback could not safely pass.

For almost a half mile, the Argyllsmen laid about in a fairly regular manner in the dips of the terrain and within sheltering bushes along the crag, remaining clandestine and waiting for the Brus army to traverse the pass below. Then they would spring their ambuscade.

"Ye see the lord?" asked the chieftain's second in command.

"I saw him," replied Rollo. "Said Brus was in no hurry to get at us." He laughed derisively.

"He's got to go through that pass sooner or later," said the chieftain, straightening his legs.

"Ye ready for 'im?" asked Rollo.

"Just as ye wanted, Sire," he said, leaning back against a large stone. "Reckon he knows we're waitin' for him here'bouts?"

Rollo shrugged. "Once he enters the pass, 'twill not matter."

The evening's warm colors were quickly losing their struggle against the darkness. The candle lanterns on the galleys were more clearly showing their glow, the brighter stars were beginning to come into sight in the east, and the waning moon, three days past full, was near to making its appearance as well.

"Tomorrow is the day we kill The Brus! I can feel it in my bones! Best get some sleep and arise ere dawn," suggested Rollo.

"Soon as I check on my pickets," said the older chieftain, rolling up on his knees and elbows before standing with much effort. "Layin' about up here for three days can stiffen ye up a mite," he griped. "The men are beginnin' to get testy, too. Wish The Brus would come on!"

• •

Early next morning, as the sky grew light above the Pass of Brander, the men on the crag overlooking the pass awoke to the distant skirl of a bagpipe, though they couldn't be sure they had heard it. At first it came and went with the wind, so that it was sometimes there, and sometimes not. As it grew louder, however, it was a steady tune that echoed off the sides of the pass and captured the attention of every man lying in wait for the army of The Brus. With haste they crawled out from their blankets and prepared themselves for the slaughter they would soon inflict.

Rollo and the chieftain watched the goat-path of a road at the bottom of the gorge. After listening to the pipes' approaching strains for a considerable length of time… or perhaps it merely seemed so in their anxiousness… they watched him finally come into their view. A solitary piper strode confidently along the narrow trail beside the tapering waterway. The men of Lorne silently held their positions.

A second figure followed after a bit, this one mounted and holding a staff flying the royal standard of Scotland's king, and Rollo's heart began beating faster. This was his day! The so-called King of Scots was riding into his trap!

Rollo and his men sat patiently as, one-by-one, more of Robert's men followed the piper into their lair… the next carried the blue and white saltire, the flag of St. Andrew… then came a string of mounted knights in chain mail, carrying shields and holding upturned lances decorated with colored pennants. They were followed by a nobleman on a coal-black Friesian stallion.

"Damn!" exclaimed Rollo in a whisper to the older chieftain, "I know that man! He's an earl, I think!" After a moment's thought more he added excitedly, "Lennox! He was the Earl of Lennox! We have him as well! My lord will be pleased to catch these two hares in the same noose!"

His grinning anticipation was that of a starving man suddenly beholding a feast.

They continued to watch more of Brus' knights parade before them. Loosely strung out on the confining roadway and seemingly oblivious to the peril into which they rode, they advanced toward the moment Rollo and his men would attack and destroy them.

At last, the knightly rider Rollo had anticipated came into view. Robert, King of Scots, dressed in chain mail hauberk and coif, and identified by the crown on his helm and the royal tabard that he wore, sat astride his great steed, carrying but a shield, a short sword, and an axe.

Rollo could hardly keep himself from ordering the attack at that very moment, but he knew that he must wait until Robert was completely within the trap and had no escape.

To go off the road on its far side was to perish in the loch, and it would be impossible for the king's horse to climb the steep hill toward Rollo and his two thousand men. Thus, once there were enough men before him and behind him that he could neither flee ahead nor go back… Rollo would get a handsome reward for the capture or death of the elusive "King of Scots"!

Finally, when Robert reached the narrowest section of roadway in the pass, Rollo stood and screamed his loudest, "ATTACK!" The shrill cry echoed back and forth across the loch and the men of Lorne rose, almost as one, to release arrows directly into the arrayed knights and to throw or push loose rocks down upon them.

"Make sure ye ride single file and keep yer distance twixt one another!" Lord Lennox had commanded as his knights prepared to take to the road. His reasoning was now evident as the knights maneuvered their animals deftly to avoid the projectiles from above so that few were struck, and fewer damaged, though there were several men lost.

An arrow pierced the chain mail armor of one of Sir Malcolm's knights who slumped in his saddle as a small boulder bounced downhill toward him. His destrier reared and whinnied but lost its footing on the edge of the roadway and went over into the cold water. Both mount and rider sank immediately beneath the surface and were seen no more.

Lord Lorne, on the deck of the galley anchored across the lake, saw the knight's fall and more stones hurtling down upon his enemy and smiled. A cheer went up from all six of his small vessels, for it appeared from across the loch that the army of King Robert was doomed in their trap.

Several other knights were painfully unmounted when solidly struck by large stones their attackers had dislodged from the crags and hurled down at them, but the mounted knights quickly wielded their shields to protect themselves and their mounts from the continuing barrage.

Rollo was pacing back and forth on his small piece of ground and observing the damage being inflicted, but it was not as severe as he had expected. The knights were not in close order as he had seen in his mind's eye, and were suffering few casualties.

The older chieftain beside him was shouting and throwing stones as far as he could fling them when he suddenly stood bolt upright... and fell headlong down the hill. Rollo could clearly see the arrow in his fellow chieftain's back. With knitted brows he turned his eyes uphill to see Sir James Douglas, and his men of the high lands, sending flight after flight into the line on which stood the men of Argyll.

Then, Douglas smiled and waved at him.

Rollo's hatred turned to jellied fear, then to rage in quick succession. "Archers... uphill!" he ordered as loudly as he could yell, but the din of battle allowed only the handful immediately around him to hear and understand the order. With arrows nocked they turned and loosed their shafts, mostly at Douglas, but he quickly dove for cover, only to stand and wave again.

The hillside above the Macdougalls fairly crawled with the Douglas' sturdy troops, who were used to making their way over such hillsides and whose early start from Tyndrum allowed them to claim the higher position.

In the midst of seeing his men cut down from behind, Rollo took a quick assessment and accurately estimated the numbers of Douglas' highland warriors to be far less than the men in his own command. He began to laugh.

"They hain't so many as are we!" he shouted over and over, and he drew his sword and started upward on the slope, urging as many as were in earshot to follow. They turned and followed him by the score, scrambling up the hillside and hurling rocks and arrows ahead of them.

But arrows rained on them in return, with The Brus' archers having the advantage of holding their positions while they fired. A heavy storm of shafts sailed into the Argyll lines and as many as followed Rollo were caught in the withering response.

Rollo himself stumbled and slid backward, one of the lucky ones who was not wounded or killed immediately. Recovering his footing, Rollo looked uphill to see The Black Douglas pointing at him with his sword while talking to two men with bows. A chill went down his spine as he realized he was being singled out by the Douglas.

James Douglas, however, was talking to Murdoch and MacKie differently than Rollo had suspected. Rather than singling him out for death, the Douglas wanted the brother archers to target anyone and everyone around Rollo, at least for the time being.

When a man approached Rollo to report anything or to ask something, an arrow from one of the two brothers unerringly found its mark and the man fell dead at his commander's feet. In response, Rollo would run or duck for cover, thinking he was the intended target, but after having lost a handful of his best lieutenants, Rollo grasped the idea that others were avoiding coming into his presence, considering it to be a sure invitation to die.

Indeed, that was the Douglas' intention.

After several others near him died in the same sudden fashion, Rollo found it difficult to organize or direct his men. And all the while the onslaught from above continued, with projectiles of every sort imaginable coming down on his line in great numbers. His harried warriors were suddenly being felled by the score.

A few of his archers ran downhill, toward the roadway, to get within closer range of the knights who had dismounted and now began to climb the mountain to engage them. The archers' bows were quickly abandoned in favor of the swords and daggers they wore at their waists.

Across the loch, John of Lorne was livid. He could see the men of Argyll struggling to get themselves out of the counter-trap, and he could see them falling in great numbers down the face of the incline. His legs grew unsteady from the effects of his continuing weakness and the ire he felt at the battle's decline, when he was unable to participate or even lend support.

Eventually, he was forced by his infirmity to lie on the deck and hold himself up by his arms on the gunnels to see the clash before him unfold. The veins in his forehead and neck bulged and he screamed, "If I were not thus shriveled…" all the while wishing it were not a hollow threat.

Sir Rollo, watching while his forces were decimated, and recognizing that he could not overpower the Brus forces when they were above and below him and attacking from both directions, thought to escape with the forces he had left and retreat to Dunstaffnage, where Lord Argyll would need the remaining warriors to withstand Brus' advance.

But, he needed to keep the Brus army occupied while he and the bulk of his troops retraced their steps and moved back down the mountain toward Dunstaffnage before The Brus blocked his way to the loch road.

Sending a sizable contingent to augment the archers who had attacked toward The Brus' men, Rollo then ordered the rest to extricate themselves and retreat to the west, along the track on which they had originally come. There, he even had some horses in reserve.

Douglas and Wiseman watched from their vantage point up the incline.

"He likes not bein' in the king's pincers," observed Sir James.

"He's goin' to flee, out toward Dunstaffnage," countered Wiseman.

"Reckon?" said Douglas.

"Aye. Look, he just sacrificed about a forth of his remainin' men... sendin' them against the king... to save the rest," said Wiseman using his sword to point to the various parts of the battlefield. "The rest are withdrawin' yonder. I'll wager he plans to reinforce Dunstaffnage."

"Lennox'll block the back way out!" stated Douglas as he moved to head off several Argyllsmen approaching from below.

"Nay, he cannot," replied Wiseman, "too busy with those comin' downhill on him, just as we cannot leave here!" He joined the Douglas as more of Lord John's men closed in. Between them, the two knights killed or chased off the lot.

Blade slamming against blade or shield, the groans of warriors hard at work and the screams of the wounded and the moans of the dying... all contributed to the cacophony on the hillside. The Argyllsmen were fierce warriors and plenty of men on both sides were dying, many pitching headlong down the steep hill, while others remained worrisome snags underfoot.

Sir David Graham, holding the high side of the mountain beyond the Macdougall warriors, saw Rollo's attempted escape, and taking twenty-three men with him, sought to assail those retreating men from the rear. Finding themselves under attack from a new source, the fleeing warriors swarmed to the aid of their weak flank and Graham and his men were instantly attacked, with Macdougalls all around them. The Templar and his men formed a knot with their backs to the center, but the Argyllsmen held their own with men falling quickly on both sides.

Robert Boyd, Neil Campbell, Gilbert de la Haye and Thomas Randolph stayed close to the king, who yet stood on the loch road astride his horse. They, and a small group of other mounted knights, held back to make sure none got to the road and survived long enough to reach the king. Macdougalls were all but leaping on top of one another to get to The Brus and his guard.

Catching a moment to breathe again, Wiseman and Douglas, spattered with blood and standing with men lying all about them, looked across the battlefield. As both gasped for air, Wiseman finally said, "Know what we can we do next for the king!?"

"Aye," said Douglas, "we can keep the Graham, yonder, and his men from dyin' for him!" Douglas nodded his head down the hill and westward to where James Graham and his band were still attacking the rear of Rollo's retreat.

"Then, let's go for them," said Wiseman, gritting his teeth.

Douglas smiled. "Just what I had in mind, Sir William. Pray, lead on!" With that Douglas gathered enough air and whistled to his men waving his sword toward Rollo's contingent trying desperately to escape with their leader to Dunstaffnage. As they could, the highland warriors disengaged from the individual battles they were in and moved in the direction Douglas indicated.

Murdoch released the arrow he had taut in his bow. It found a home in the neck of a Macdougall trying to make headway up the mountain toward him and his fellow archers, including MacKie.

Hearing Douglas' whistle, he and the other archers stood, and dropping their bows, gave screaming whoops, drew their swords, and made their way as fast as they could manage toward the fleeing Argyllsmen.

"Our men go ahead of us," remarked Douglas, watching the flood of Brus Scots hopping in side-step fashion down the mountainside. Though behind Douglas, the older knight kept up, slowing or stopping only to deal with the enemy.

Across the loch and fully aware of the desperation his men of Argyll were suffering at the hand of Brus and his minions, the galley-bound Lord John was his own worst enemy. He had thrashed about the deck so violently, with every ounce of energy he had in his body, that he now lay on the deck, depleted of strength and will and watching his grand trap for The Brus as it collapsed upon itself before his eyes.

"Milord," carefully said the captain of the vessel, "...perhaps if we go to the bridge over River Awe, we can destroy it before The Brus gets there."

"And what good will that do, pray... save hinder him a day or so!" replied John weakly, not taking his eyes off the ongoing battle on the mountainside.

"'Twill give yer father another day to prepare for the battle," returned the captain.

"My father can take care of himself!" retorted John angrily. He paused a moment and said, "Set sail for Inchchonnell!"

"Aye, Milord," answered the captain. He hesitated, hating to run from the fight and thinking Lord John would possibly change his mind.

"Set sail, goddamn it!" screamed John with the last of his resources.

The captain ordered the sailors to man the oars and set the sail, and passed the word to his counterparts on the other galleys to do likewise. They soon were headed south toward Castle Inchchonnell, on an island near the southeast coast of Loch Awe. The men and the galleys would be safe there until Lord John could figure what course to take beyond this grandiose debacle.

On the mountainside, the unfurled sails did not go unnoticed. In the midst of the hottest battle of his life, Rollo saw the galleys retreating to the south. His dead warriors were scattered across the face of the slope and all about him. Brus forces were coming at him from below and above. The men in the service of the departing Lord Lorne, battling to reach the king several hundred yards to the east of the dismayed Rollo, were dwindling fast neath the blades of the king's knights.

Amidst all the horror and fear, his mind reeled from indecision; his valor said stay and fight to the end of his men, his reason said to make a run for Dunstaffnage and save as many warriors as he could for use another day. It galled him to have to make such a decision, for he was losing the battle when he still had more able men upon the battlefield than The Brus!

Wiseman and Douglas, screaming their banshee-like whoops, were drawing fast upon him, making the decision more palatable and reasonable for the veteran warrior. "Retreat!" he barked loudly. He ran across the face of the hill, yelling at his men to leave the field, and they followed as topsy-turvy as they could manage along the ridge, toward the west end of the mountain.

Those warriors who were fighting to reach The Brus suddenly realized that the main body was leaving them, and saw the sails of their liege's galleys slipping silently toward the east. As the word spread among the battling men that both their lord and their commander had abandoned them, their anger raged even more.

From that second on the fury of the Argyll warriors was increased against King Robert. The blows were swifter and stronger. Robert's farmer army, unaccustomed to such a level of attack, were killed or maimed more frequently.

Robert quickly sent his knights to relieve the embattled foot soldiers. Seeing the experienced knights enter the conflict, many a Macdougall warrior lost his ire and took to his heels, though there were others who bravely, if wastefully, laid down their lives for Lord John on the blades of Randolph, Haye, Campbell, and Boyd, and their companions.

In the meantime, Wiseman and Douglas were vigorously chasing Rollo's retreating men, the leaders of whom had already reached their horses and were riding down the river road like the devil followed. Those on foot could not hope to keep up, but were running as fast as their nearly exhausted legs would carry them.

As they galloped by, on horse and on foot, they failed to notice a man who was missing three fingers on his right hand. He sat in the shade of a protruding boulder along the side of the mountain, and awaited his companions, who were to pass that way when heading to Dunstaffnage. Now, he knew, the army of Lord Argyll was in retreat and would make the ride to the river crossing in short order at the pace they had set.

He knew instantly how he could alert King Robert that the enemy was escaping, if the king only remembered songs from his youth. Tossing his bagpipe atop the boulder he had sat beside he climbed up with it. As quickly as he could, he brought the blowpipe to his mouth and filled the bag with air. Wrapping his three maimed fingers across the chanter, he began playing an old tune called *Eara*, about a lass by that name who waited on a river bridge for her lad to return.

After several miles at a dead gallop, Rollo came to the wooden bridge crossing River Awe and slowed not until he reached the southern end. Once there, he ordered that every man who made it across with a battleaxe must stay on the bridge and chop away the supports of the structure until it collapsed into the river.

He then ran to the north end of the bridge and held the next hundred or so warriors, ordering them to make a stand at that narrow crossing against the oncoming Brus until the axe-wielders had successfully completed their job.

Back on the hillside, Gilbert de la Haye and Robert Boyd stumbled out of the mass of bodies and gore at the base of the slope, exhausted and covered in blood. Other knights were battling the remaining Macdougalls to the finish, and would eventually join the king on the road.

The proud monarch had remained out of this battle, conserving his strength for Dunstaffnage, which would be, no doubt, the end of John of Lorne, or of Robert de Brus. Suddenly, he heard the faint strains of the piper's song. It was somewhat familiar to him, but he couldn't remember the words or the last time he heard it.

"Am I daft or is my piper playing?" he said to no one in particular, but he and Haye and Boyd all tried to listen.

"I hear it, too, Milord," said Haye.

"Aye," agreed Boyd, sitting on the side of the road.

"Well it must be intended for us to hear, else why would he be playin' with the battle still ragin'?" Robert listened.

"The tune is not familiar to me," Gilbert shook his weary head.

"I think I remember some of it," Boyd hummed a bit with the piper, and came up with the last line or so... "'the bonny lass Eara waits ... upon the bridge he'll cross to home...'" Before Boyd could recall more of the song the king had figured the code.

"The bridge!" he blurted. "They're after the river bridge!" He turned his white Cobb stallion west and called out to his knights, "We must cross the river bridge! 'Tis our only near way to Dunstaffnage!" He kicked his heels smartly into the stallion's flank and dashed away.

Baldred and Andrew, who had remained mounted and close by the king with their flags, looked at each other... then hied after Robert while Boyd and Haye ran to their chargers. Seeing the sudden activity on the road, Randolph called to Graham.

"Templar! Where ye reckon they be off to in such haste?"

The knight, wiping his face with his sleeve and leaving more blood smeared across his cheek than he removed, answered, "Cannot say... but must be of some import! Look! Lennox goes, and his men with him!"

At that, the two stalwarts hailed their fellow warriors and called and signaled them all to follow. Sheathing their crimson blades, they started down the steep incline, running, jumping, and sliding on their backsides until they reached the bottom. Those whose mounts still patiently stood on the road scrambled upon their backs and galloped away, followed by those less fortunate souls who ran on their own tired legs.

Eventually, all able bodied men in the army of Brus worked their way down the slanted killing field and followed where Robert led. By the time they reached the narrow road, their legs were stained red to the knees with the blood of the dead and the wounded they ran over and past.

Were there any men of Argyll left standing, or capable of it, they counted themselves fortunate and wended their way to the land of Lorne as best they could, hoping not to meet again with the men of Brus.

Robert, Malcolm, and their mounted knights and squires were approaching the bridge at a high gallop when the hundred left by Rollo to deny The Brus access to the span sent the first flight of arrows aloft. Released too soon, few actually reached their intended targets, but those that did caused several horses and men to go down, one into the river. Robert called a halt. Only then could he hear the sounds of the axes on the bridge supports.

"We cannot dally," said the king. "We must take the bridge from them or they will destroy it in a short time, judging by the way they are about it!" He looked at the tired, blood-stained men and said, "Man yer lances and shields, Lads! We are goin' across!" With that, he took up his own shield and his axe, and before anyone could stop him, Robert began the charge at the bridge with a war cry that would have curdled the blood of Lucifer himself.

His knights all followed his lead, and the men at the bridge were quickly faced with a full-blown charge by horsed men screaming at the tops of their voices, lances leveled, axes raised... the very same who had already killed and maimed most of their kind in Brander Pass. And after a half-hearted second flight of arrows were launched, several of the archers broke ranks and started to run, not across the bridge... for there was Rollo exhorting them to stand under threat of death from his own blade... but down the riverbank!

Once the few had fled the bottle was uncorked, and the remainder of the courage held within the archers began to flow out and carry along more and more of them until hardly a man was left at the bridge entrance by the time The Brus' horse clattered loudly across the structure's wooden floor.

The men working at downing the span held their places and their courage and feverishly chopped all the faster, in spite of the fact that The Brus and some of his knights were already across. If they could drop the bridge before the rest of his forces crossed, the King of Scots was surely undone. Some of the side braces were nearly ready to collapse and the water below carried away a constant rain of wooden chips from the flying axes.

Lennox also had darted across in Robert's wake and immediately slashed an oncoming Macdougall across the shoulder and into his chest, but another slid under the earl's horse and when he emerged on the other side, he hardly had time to get clear before the gutted horse fell to the ground, carrying the earl down and pinning his leg underneath. The horse whinnied only once before it died.

The Argyll warrior moved on to repeat his act only once more before one of Brus' men-at-arms saw him coming up from under the second unfortunate horse and struck him down with a single swift stroke of his battleaxe.

"Never mind me, remove the axemen from the bridge!" ordered the earl as several of his men tried to relieve him from the ton of horseflesh keeping him fast to the ground.

"Milord, we but follow the king's orders," said one of the men struggling with the dead charger.

Rollo, having tried to hold some semblance of a force at the exit from the bridge, saw his archers fleeing before the knights bearing down on them, and knowing further resistance was useless, turned and ran, his remaining toadies close on his heels.

The bridge, though damaged, was far from down, and seeing Rollo and his men running away and horsed knights in hot pursuit, the rest of the men of Argyll withdrew and ran up the road toward Castle Dunstaffnage.

"We shall run them down, Sire," said Thomas Randolph, after he and the others had crossed the bridge.

"Hold, Thomas!" said the king. "Let them return to Dunstaffnage and tell of the days events... 'twill give Lord Argyll something to think about ere we arrive at his gate!" Robert smiled. "Go instead and see to the bridge. We have more men coming who will want to cross it."

The king rode about the bridge, and seeing that his men were near exhaustion, ordered them to move into the glen across the way and rest. The men on foot began arriving after a while, and they, too, found places in the glen and were soon sound asleep.

"Oliver," said the king after sending for the piper when he saw him straggle in, "'twas a clever thing... playin' that tune to warn us about the bridge bein' in danger."

"Thank ye, Sire," said the man, amazed that he was actually being praised for his service. "I'm just thankful that ye remembered the tune... and the words."

"Oh, I didn't!" admitted Robert, shaking his head. "Ye will have to thank Lord Lennox for that... I had nothing in my head at hearing that tune that could have brought the words to my wit. My memory failed ye, but Lord Lennox did not!"

By nightfall Christina, Dianna, and the soldiers left behind to defend the camp at the head of Loch Awe, arrived, along with the camp followers bringing the army's victuals and the other necessities for pitching a camp in the glen.

There was much sorrow and mourning among the women in the train, for many were the lads who slept on the bloody high slope in Brander Pass that night, but miraculously, Robert still had an army. For the most part, the surviving men were in generally good shape, and there were none who would later die of their wounds. After some rest, some food, and some attention to their cuts and bruises, almost all the men would soon be fit again.

Later that evening, several of Robert's lieutenants sat around the fire talking with him about the day's action, and what was to come next. Christina brewed her medicinal tea for Robert, and as he sat talking with the other men and sipping his tea, she noticed that Dianna walked by and smiled at the Templar. Within a few moments, the Graham stood and stretched, said his goodnights, and left the group to go in the same dark direction Dianna had walked.

Christina stayed by the fire for a short time, then quietly rose, and leaving the men talking, went to her bed. They didn't notice she had left.

Baldred Airth

AUGUST 5TH 1308

THE LAND OF ARGYLL

King Robert set his camp in the wooded area near Airds Point, on Loch Etive in the land of Argyll, just two miles beyond the hard won bridge across River Awe, connecting Airds Bay to Loch Awe. Castle Dunstaffnage was yet six or seven miles more to the west, but the Scot was in no hurry to rush the bastion with his worn troops, knowing there were a'plenty more and fresh Argyllsmen waiting for him and itching to kill.

The fish seemed to be abundant, so he set some of his men to catching them. Men were also sent to forage for other foods, hopefully some that were, when dried or smoked, more stable for the longer period of time.

He sent two parties back across the bridge to the mountainside in Brander Pass, the one to bury the Brus dead, and the other to collect weapons and armor from warriors who would never again need them.

He then ordered the dead enemy soldiers' heads to be cut off and stacked, forming a pyramid on a flat spot on the ridge where they had waited in ambush for him and his men. He wanted to illustrate well their abject failure.

About midday, Robert came through the wooded campsite from a morning of hunting with his foragers. His prowess with a hunter's bow was equal to his ability with warrior's sword or axe, and was besides, as much recreation for him as it was necessity.

"I trust, My Lord, that the forests of Argyll are now sadly impoverished, at least in regards to deer?" gibed Christina when Robert strode into view.

"'Tis perhaps more so," he sighed. "It seems that even the deer and the hares of Argyll have abandoned the forests and crags around Dunstaffnage ahead of our arrival."

"Then I hope ye have an appetite for salmon, My King, for they have been right plentiful. Perhaps they had not heard that we were expected!" She smiled, trying to make light of the lack of provisions from the forest.

"Yer salmon would be a bonny substitute for venison at this point, provided there is enough. Our successes on the hunt were slight, not even enough to feed oursel's, and the men are near starved." He sounded tired and disgusted.

"We shall have ample for all, Sire, for the lake teems with fish and our pikemen have spent the whole mornin' at spearin' 'em." Christina was glad to relieve his worry, for she knew the feeding of his army was his paramount concern over the assault on Castle Dunstaffnage.

He took a deep breath and exhaled, and his spirits seemed higher already. "Then, perhaps ye had better have the cooks prepare a couple of 'em for me as well as some for the hunters, for we are hungry as wolves amid a flock of lambs!"

"A couple!" she was smiling. "Sire, the most of 'em are twenty or thirty pounds each, large enough to feed four or five men!"

"Then two should be enough for me!" he kept his countenance serious until he looked at her surprised face, then he laughed.

Christina laughed at his jest and said, "I'll have one of the cooks prepare two... large ones... for ye, Sire. She curtseyed slightly and left to do so, returning but a moment later. "Cook says, such large ones will take the rest of the afternoon to be dressed, filleted, and roasted, Milord!" but the smile on her lips betrayed her lie.

"And what am I supposed to do in the meantime?" Robert returned, going along with her joke.

Christina paused only the slightest bit before saying, "Would the king desire a rematch at chess?"

Robert teasingly grumbled and quickly walked away, but as he passed her by, he turned and almost imperceptibly motioned to her to follow him, which she did.

The two of them walked in near silence through the open woods to a northerly point jutting out into the loch, and sat for some time without word on the hillside that allowed an easy look in both directions up and down the loch.

He finally spoke in a soft tone, "Christina... what ye have done for me... for Scotland..." she put two of her fingers to his lips and smiled, knowing what he was trying to say, and as she did their eyes met. Her heart was thrilled and melancholy, all at the same time, and she glanced away suddenly, aware that the emotions then expressed would not do them any good. She averted the feelings by changing the subject.

"What do ye wait for, My King?" she asked.

Robert sighed deeply and sat straight up putting his back against the stout trunk of a tree. He picked up a twig from the ground and pointed westward, "Yonder's Dunstaffnage."

"Aye," said Christina, looking at the coastline that meandered toward the castle.

"'Tis nearly the last of the hard line against me," he said, again sighing deeply as if fear and excitement were intertwined in his heart.

"What about the Earl of Ross?" she asked.

He went to sit up straighter and his hand brushed against her leg on which she had her dagger strapped.

"What in the name of...!" he started feeling about the object neath her skirt, but she laughed, and reaching into the placket, withdrew her dagger. He was genuinely surprised.

"Ye e'er use that?" He took the blade from her hand and felt its well-honed edge.

"Aye." Remembering the killing of Eustace her face lost its look of amusement, which made him curious.

"To what purpose?" he pried.

"Sire... 'twas a long time ago..."

He nodded and returned the weapon to her. It was clear there were things about this gentle, clever woman of which he knew nothing.

She purposely avoided his gaze while she busily put the blade back in its sheath and straightened her skirt.

After a long, yearning look at her, he turned his eyes westward, scanning the loch while his thoughts wandered.

"The Macdonalds are here," he said quietly.

"Macdonalds?" She glanced about them.

"Yon sails..." he pointed to sea, "...the Macdonalds of the Isles."

The dark-haired woman looked out toward the galleys coming around the point about three miles west.

"How ye reckon they found us?" she asked.

"They hain't found us as yet, but they're fixin' to," he said smiling. "Besides, I told them where I'd be."

Christina shook her head and smiled, the thought of the killing the previous winter becoming a fading memory in her mind as she asked, "How'd *ye* know where ye'd be?"

"I knew I would be here... or on that hillside in Brander Pass," he said. He then pulled his hunting horn from around his shoulder and blew two short blasts on it several times.

"The king calls me," said Andrew to Baldred, and he scurried from the cook-fire following the sound of the horn.

"Ye want me, Sire?" asked Andrew when he found Robert.

"Andrew, sally down to the water's edge and wave yer flag so that those galleys see ye," he said by way of an answer.

Andrew yelled back as he started down the hill, "Aye, Sire!"

"Good lad," remarked Robert to Christina.

"That he is," he agreed. In only minutes, others from the camp arrived.

"What's afoot, Sire?" asked Sir Gilbert, eating a piece of deliciously aromatic roast salmon.

"The Macdonalds will be anchorin' off shore directly," said the king, his mouth watering.

Andrew ran and tumbled down the slope until he reached the water's edge. Scrambling to the top of some shoreline rocks, he pulled the yellow and red banner from within his tunic, and shaking it fully open, held it by the fly end and waved it as high as his arms would allow. The light wind pressed it out to its length and he waved it back and forth so the oncoming galleys could see.

Robert, his empty stomach growling, nevertheless returned his attention to the approaching galleys, waiting patiently to make sure that they saw his signal flag and sailed into the cove. There, they quickly set their anchors about thirty yards out.

Sir Angus Macdonald was the first out of the esquif as it pushed onto the sandy shore. Seeing the vessels anchor, Robert and Christina had led a procession of onlookers down the hill to the water's edge.

"Hail, My King!" shouted Angus from twenty yards offshore.

"Hail, Macdonald!" returned the king, "and welcome!"

Sir Angus dropped his heavy body onto the sand and bowed deeply. "Have near two hundred fighters and twelve galleys at yer service," he enumerated.

King Robert nodded. "We have fresh roasted salmon for ye and yer men, up yonder," he said pointing toward the midst of the camp. At that point, Christina hoped that the "plenty" she had earlier referred to would be enough for all to have something.

Noticing a second esquif pulling away from another galley and heading toward them, Robert asked about it.

"Sire, the fellow in the front of the boat is Sir Malcolm Maclaine, finest... *second* finest galleyman in all of Scotland!" Angus responded with a broad grin.

"I am well acquainted with Sir Malcolm! He is in fact, my kinsman, and right neighborly! I see one of his sons with him, do I not?"

"Aye, Milord! Iain Dubh by name!" answered the mildly surprised Angus.

"Ye see any other galleys on yer way up the loch, Angus?" asked Robert.

"Aye. Several… but they steered clear of us."

"They Macdougalls?"

"Best I could make out, they carried the banner of Macnab, My Lord King," answered Macdonald, as they waited for the Maclaine to land.

"How many men with 'em?" queried Robert.

"More than five hundred, I'd reckon… staggered in the wood … and the three galleys loaded well above the gunnels with stores, I saw."

"The Macnabs against us now?" said Gilbert.

"Always were," explained Robert. "Just ne'er showed their colors 'til now, I reckon."

"Aye? When did we fight the Macnabs?"

"Perhaps it was a Macnab that gave ye that shoulder wound at Dail Righ… ye remember?" replied the king.

Gilbert put his hand on his shoulder where it still ached on cold nights. For sure he remembered well the fellow that gave him that wound.

Robert turned to the now landed second galley and walked up to the Maclaines, then disembarking, and exclaimed, "Welcome, Uncle!"

The elder of the two Scots looked up at The Brus and broke into a grin, though it was barely visible behind his brownish-red beard that turned gray about halfway down its length. The fellow walked up to the king, and giving him a bear hug said, "Rob! What kind of a hornet's nest have he stirred up, now!"

"The biggest, Uncle!" the king replied. "Ye passed the nest as ye came into the loch from Ardmucknish Bay! We're goin' after Dunstaffnage!"

Patrick Macnab
Lord of Glendochart

AUGUST 10TH 1308
CASTLE DUNSTAFFNAGE

Patrick Macnab, like the proud Lord of Glendochart that he was, rode his large black Friesian to the base of the five stone steps in front of the main gate of Castle Dunstaffnage. Immediately behind him were twenty of his knights, and another hundred scattered themselves on the lawn leading up to the castle.

Situated on the peninsula guarding the entrance to Loch Etive, the Awe River, and upstream to Loch Awe, Dunstaffnage was a formidable gray stone fortress built by the Macdougalls on a great natural stone base some eighty to ninety years earlier. Of necessity, since the area of the stone base could not be exceeded, even the corner tower-houses were built to the inside of the curtain walls.

Alexander Macdougall, Earl of Argyll, peered over the stone battlements from the top of Dunstaffnage and watched the riders approach. "Rollo! Make fast the gate! We're bein' invaded by Macnabs! They now have joined the Brus!"

"Nay, Lord Alexander, they've come to help!" Rollo assured the earl as he also peered over the wall. "Ye must welcome Lord Patrick to the castle!"

The old man turned to see the mere chieftain who was giving him orders.

"They were invited here by yer son, Milord," explained Rollo hastily, referring to the Lord John.

"To what end?" asked the noble with eyebrows raised. He was immediately thinking of having to host and supply victuals to this Macnab horde at his doorstep.

"The Brus will be a'layin' siege to this castle... on any day he chooses, Milord," said Rollo. He knew that Alexander would simply ignore the thought, having withdrawn into a state of senility due to the unacceptable events of Brander Pass.

"Brus lurks not in this part of the country!" said Alexander forcefully. "This is Argyll, not Carrick or Galloway! He has no truck with us!" To prove his say he pointed to a small building a hundred yards away and added, "I went to yonder chapel this very morn, just as always. Saw nary a soul out of place!"

"Tomorrow, Milord, the ground where sits the chapel could be covered o'er with the Brus army!" said Rollo in his gruff voice, gritting his teeth.

"Where is my son?" asked the earl plaintively, suspecting that Rollo's words and actions were not in his best interest.

Rollo was yet enraged with John for having left him stranded at the Pass of Brander, and so clenched his fists to answer his liege in as rational a voice as possible. "Inchchonnell, Milord."

"Inchchonnell?" The earl frowned, confused.

"Aye, Milord."

"While we're bein' attacked by The Brus?"

"I am sure, Milord, that Inchchonnell is under attack as well," lied the chieftain.

"Oh, God!" said the earl, realization slipping into his mind like a fog rising on the meadow to reveal a sleeping monster about to awaken. He turned his back to the wall and slipped down it, squatting on the walk. He put his interlocked fingers over his face and began to weep softly.

Rollo sighed at the pitiful sight of this once proud soldier. His lord being unable, he leaned over the wall again to welcome Lord Patrick before an excessive lapse of time angered the lord's pride. If he returned to Glendochart, all would be lost.

On Sir Rollo's command, the gatehouse doors were opened wide and the portcullis raised for Lord Patrick and his immediate knights to enter.

The Macdougalls were tightly packed inside the citadel, as they had been for some weeks while awaiting the arrival of The Brus. The remaining six hundred and fifty three of the two thousand warriors who went to the Pass of Brander were among the many crowded into the relatively small castle. There was constant bickering and fist fighting, mostly among the soldiery. They needed for Robert the Brus to show up and give them a common enemy on whom to vent their frustrations.

As they entered the courtyard, Sir Rollo met the lord and his entourage and entreated them to join the earl and him in the great hall, and the visitors climbed down from their mounts, which were taken to the stable by several grooms.

There was much busyness within the hall, as the kitchen staff had not been warned of the impending guests. Flagons of wine were immediately served to placate the men until an appropriate meal could be prepared.

Rollo had managed to get Lord Alexander to his place at the table, and he assumed the next chair. Sir Patrick sat on the far side of the earl, his long blonde hair escaping his thrown-back mail coif. His four closest knights sat down table from him.

"I heard of yer "ambuscade" at Brander a few days past," said Lord Patrick to the earl, who sat in a stupor, staring straight ahead.

"Lord Alexander is not to himself, Milord," said Rollo, truthfully. "I beg yer forgiveness for his absence of awareness. He's been with a malady of late."

Patrick, his mouth full of wine, gulped and said, "He's *not* commandin' ye Macdougalls, I reckon!"

"I pray he will soon be returned to himself," replied Rollo. "Probably ere day's end. 'Tis but a temporary disorder at best, Milord."

"Macnabs hain't lurkin' here'bouts while Brus is layin' siege to these walls," growled Lord Patrick, adding, "We're here to help with the killin' of him and his ilk!" Then he bragged, "If need be, Macnabs alone can do the task without the Macdougalls!"

"Milord!" Rollo, seething, objected, "...ye'll be hard put to lay off our Macdougalls as slackers against Brus!"

Patrick paused a moment and then apologized. "I meant no offense, Sir. I watched ye and yer brave Macdougalls in the fight at Dail Righ."

"Aye! From neath the trees, where ye *stayed* if I recollect rightly, Milord!" countered Rollo.

The Macnab knew he had struck a nerve, and tried to assuage Rollo's ire. "Some of our lads joined ye, but we could see that ye were managin' the skirmish wi'out our help. And we wanted to see if them Argyll men wearin' nothin' but their boots lived up to the testament of their reported mettle."

Rollo narrowed his eyes and flared his nostrils but held his temper, when he asked bluntly, "Where ye fixin' to be for the *skirmish*... this time, 'round?"

"Yonder wood," replied Patrick, determined not to escalate the situation. "While he's busy with the castle, we'll come at him from the wood side." He kept his eyes down and avoided provoking the chieftain further.

The two sat quietly sipping their wine and saying nothing more for a while and eventually Rollo's concern turned to more current matters. "My Lord, we are desperate for additional stores, bein' holed up for this long spell. Can ye get us victuals?"

"Aye… with our galleys… on the morrow," said the Lord of Glendochart, drinking more wine from his cup and refilling it from the table flagon.

"I am sure the earl will be most appreciative, once he has recovered," spoke Rollo to Patrick around the head of the earl, who remained torpid, only to sigh, occasionally.

"Have ye sent out foragers?" asked Patrick, slurring his words slightly from drinking so much wine on an empty stomach.

"Aye, so much so that almost all game has been kilt for miles around," said Rollo.

"And that young, impetuous, Lord of Lorne, where keeps he his arse?" sneered Sir Patrick.

"Inchchonnell, at present, Milord," returned Rollo, "Raisin' more army to help us defend Dunstaffnage, I would reckon," came back Rollo knowing the say to be false but vaguely hoping it to be true.

"Best not tarry," replied the lord. "I hear tell Brus is near fixed to make his move!"

"Who said such?!" asked Rollo.

"Spies." That was the one word that ostensibly separated information from gossip.

Rollo nodded worriedly.

The smells wafting from the trays of food entering the hall filled the nostrils of the company and the thought of defending the castle and killing The Brus was lost to satisfying their more immediate gratifications. Though plain fare, there seemed to be enough for all, and they ate and drank until they had to be put to bed… or, if no bed was offered one instinctively found himself a corner in which to sleep. Lord Alexander was helped to bed having eaten nothing.

AUGUST 11TH 1308
CASTLE DUNSTAFFNAGE

Early next morn, when a twig under Murdoch's foot snapped, it made a sound loud enough for the startled Macnab picket to turn quickly toward him. Murdoch's arrow was swift, but not deadly; though the shaft left his bow at the instant of the noise, it missed its primary mark when the man spun around. The picket yelped with surprise and ran, Murdoch and MacKie following in quickstep. They and about thirty other archers had been combing the wood for guards on watch around Dunstaffnage.

The wounded picket, voicing his pain and fright, ran all the way up the gentle slope to the open field in front of the castle, where his squalling alarmed a hundred Macnab knights awaiting the exit of their lord from the castle. The sting of arrows followed immediately and took their toll on the hundred in painful wounds. The victims could not tell the size of the attacking force or how close upon them it might be because of the rising sun's glare, directly behind their attackers.

"To horse! To horse!" loudly ordered the lieutenant in charge. He squinted through gloved fingers into the sunny tops of the trees, attempting to see the approaching enemy.

Another knight cried out, "The horses have been scattered!"

"Hie for the castle!" said a third, making his way to the independently standing chapel nestled in the midst of several ancient oak trees.

King Robert sounded a signal on his horn and the archers withdrew into the wood as quickly and unceremoniously as they had come to the field.

"What ye reckon they're afixin' to do?" asked the Macnab knight from his spot behind the chapel wall.

The field was suddenly as near silent as if naught had occurred. A scattering of songbirds chirped in the trees, and a few knights were heard cursing and begging their mounts to mind their orders as they attempted to round them up.

"'Tis the stillness ere a terrible storm," whispered one, breathless and wide-eyed from the sudden, brief incursion.

"Maybe it's done," hoped another.

"Ye damned fools!" berated their leader upon riding to the abruptly dispersed men. "Get to yer horses and we'll run 'em down!"

Knights and squires hastily put saddles and bridles on caught destriers, while others, seeing no immediate enemy, felt no need to rush to their possible deaths. The most seriously wounded walked or limped south toward their main bivouac for assistance. One rider was sent ahead to the camp to warn the Macnabs of the unexpected... and of a possibly impending... attack. A second hied to the castle to report to the earl.

Robert sat atop his white steed just inside the tree line and watched the confused commotion that he had purposely caused on the castle's kitchen garden field, and was fully aware that where he wanted to attack was well beyond the effective range of the archers on the wall.

He slowly slipped his helmet over his head and settled it comfortably in place. Thomas, Gilbert, Neil, and Boyd were close on his sides; James Douglas held the right flank and Wiseman the left. David Graham was in the rear with the remaining total of Lord Malcolm's knights and some of Robert's as well. Behind the knights were the foot soldiers, who were to remain within the line of trees until called upon.

Alarm horns and bells were sounded frantically on the wall of the castle.

"Reckon the inmates are comin' alive," remarked Robert in a near whisper. Boyd was the only one who was close enough to hear his remark, and he smiled slightly at the irony of the statement, since many would soon be dead... in his estimation.

Robert drew his battleaxe from its saddle-loop, propping the butt-end of the handle on the top of his thigh and grasping the weapon loosely, hand just below its head. His men knew that stance to be their signal and drew to hand their own blades and maces and flails.

The king then nodded to the waiting piper. Oliver puffed air into his bag through the mouthpiece, and as the drones started their hum, began to play a melody. The tune filled those on the field with a mixture of fear and bravado. Even the early morning dew seemed to be quaking with its vibrations.

"My God!" prayed the Macnab lieutenant when he heard the piper's skirl, and yelled, "Get yer goddamned horses under ye, and be quick about it!!"

Robert made his way through the remaining ten feet of woods. His knights followed and hastily lined the edge of the copse. The sun was still at their backs in the tops of the trees, but the movement at their bases left no doubt to the Macnabs that an army of Brus knights was about to fall on them... how many, they could not assess.

Inside the castle, the heavy headed Lord of Glendochart heard the horns blowing and the bells sounding, and the screams of excitement outside his doorway. When it came to him what it all represented, he sat bolt upright in his bed. His closest knight, still in a heavy drunken slumber, lay on the floor next to him. Another sprawled on the cold hearth at the other end of the small room.

"Come alive! -Come alive! -Come alive!" he screamed. One knight jerked and rubbed his nose, but remained asleep.

Patrick Macnab jumped to his feet and kicked his companion hard on the leg, allowing pain to bring his knight from the realm of Morpheus to the reality of his own.

At that moment, Robert whooped his war cry and jabbed his spurs deep into his destrier's flanks. His knights followed his example, and yelling fearsomely, all started across the field at the Macnab warriors, no more than eighty yards away, who yet milled about in confusion. Some managed to get on horseback, and some were still on foot, but all knew The Brus was rapidly bearing down upon them.

Oliver the piper, calmly crossing the field on foot, was quickly passed by the king and his mounted warriors, and walked in their wake playing as loudly and as dearly as he possibly could, all the while knowing he was as much a target on the battlefield as those for whom he played.

"Toward the castle!" bellowed one of the Macnab knights to his fellows. He realized that the attacking cavalry would have to change course to follow them, and would thus no longer have the sun behind them... but it was too late. Robert's axe had drawn first blood.

Hearing the hoofbeats charging across the garden, the Macnabs' commander, having dressed hurriedly and arrived in the courtyard, cursed and shouted, "Open that goddamned gate!" His saddled destrier was brought to him by one of the ten Macnab knights fastened inside Dunstaffnage with him.

"Milord!" pleaded Rollo, "For God's sake! If we open the gate, The

Brus will enter!"

"It'll matter not to ye!" screamed Patrick, his long hair flailing the air and getting twisted in his beard for lack of a helm. After climbing aboard his horse he looked down on Rollo and finished his threat, "... for ye will be cold dead... by my hand if ye do not order it opened!"

His knights swung up and seated themselves upon their destriers as best they could.

"Bar the gate!" defiantly ordered Rollo to his Macdougall guards.

"Ye've made a poor choice, Chieftain," barked Patrick, drawing his sword and holding it straight up and over his head, prepared to strike.

Rollo stood his ground, his feet wide apart, his eyes daring the Macnab to bring down the blade. He was in control, here. His Macdougall men instantly began to jostle the lord and his knights. No blood was yet spilt, though both sides were armed with drawn weapons of various sorts. The mounted Macnab knights and their horses were in danger of being gutted by the crowding Macdougalls at any moment, while outside the battle for Dunstaffnage was underway.

Tension on both sides had every warrior prepared to kill, and the archers on the wall walk fairly itched to loose their arrows into the Macnabs, if just to test their prowess.

"Open the gate!" boomed a loud voice from two-thirds of the way up the stairs of the wall walk.

All the heads in the bailey turned toward the strong and once familiar voice of Lord Alexander. He was dressed for war, the sun peeking over the wall just enough to glint off the small flat plates on his leather chest armor and helmet. He was splendid, the knight like whom every knight wanted to be.

"Open the gate to our friends!" repeated the old warrior, forcefully.

The gatekeepers obeyed, lifting the huge beam and swinging wide the doors. Patrick Macnab stood in his stirrups and held his sword high and gave his war cry in salute to the Earl of Argyll.

The old man did come around after all, thought Patrick as his stallion reared and whinnied. The Macdougalls standing in the way of him and his contingent swiftly moved back to permit their passage onto the front field, where his hundred knights were doing their best to withstand The Brus and his army.

The Brus archers were positioned within arrow range of the castle so that they could add flights of deadly shafts to the assault on the stronghold. In order to provide themselves with shelter from the castle, Murdoch and his archers had quietly drawn ashore three of the Macdougall galleys from their anchorage in the small cove near the castle, and turning them on their sides, created a redoubt for themselves in the early hours before dawn.

After the initial attack, they had retreated there, to pick off enemy soldiers as they exited the castle in their counter-attack on the king and his forces. They got only two volleys off before the charging Macnabs were out of range, and Murdoch was disgusted that only one horseman was hit badly enough to fall from his mount.

Thomas Randolph caught sight of Patrick Macnab and his men riding at them full tilt from the castle gate and shouted to warn the archers, "More comin'!" This time the archers assailed the men as they turned south toward Robert's flank, culling several of the last ones through the egress and wounding two others.

Rather than having a straight run into the king's right flank, Patrick saw that he was about to run afoul of an established "hedgehog" position of forty men, commanded by The Black Douglas. Guiding his men away from the vicious trap, the Macnab took them west around the chapel and then south to join his own knights.

"Stay here!" yelled Randolph to Douglas, "Could be more a'comin' from inside!"

Douglas agreed by nodding his head, and Thomas called forth the reserved soldiers of foot, dividing them into two groups by pointing with his sword.

"Ye foot follow me!" shouted Thomas at the group he wanted to advance with him. To try and outflank Macnab's forces, he led the foot soldiers to the north of Douglas' pikemen, and turning between them and the chapel to follow Patrick.

A certain amount of confusion still disturbed the Macnabs' main body, under heavy attack from Robert's mounted troops. The king was in the thick of the melee, drawing Macnab blood at every swing of his battleaxe.

Three of the Macnabs' horsed knights attempted to hit The Brus with their lances in a concerted effort to bring him down. Charging directly for Robert, two had their lances aimed at his horse, and the third, at Robert's chest.

Neil Campbell saw what was afoot and struck his heels into his horse's side, slamming his destrier hard against the closest charging knight, throwing him and his mount off balance and sending them under the hooves of the second. From the back of his injured horse, Campbell swung his sword at the second knight with such force that the man's arm was fully severed, and he went down.

The third managed to get through the defense lines to Robert, who looked up just in time to see the third Macnab's lance pierce the white destrier's chest. Reacting instantly, the king kicked off his stirrup and rolled off the horse as it collapsed, before the animal's considerable weight fell on him and pinned him to the ground.

Seeing Robert on foot, Patrick Macnab shouted loudly, "*Kill The*

Brus!–Kill The Brus!" He tried valiantly to get free of the fight he was in so that he might perform the deed, but was surrounded by the king's Scots.

Gilbert Haye and Robert Boyd also had seen Robert's predicament and moved to form a barrier for their king's protection. Neil dismounted his injured stallion and came to the king's side to fight off the flocking Macnabs trying to follow Patrick's order. The number of men who responded and were trying to get their weapons at some vital part of Robert's person found that they were so packed around him that most could accomplish little. Meanwhile, Robert and Neil, their backs protected by Haye and Boyd, were free to take on any who approached too near.

Thomas was having some luck flanking Patrick on the north, and the Lord of Glendochart could no longer ignore Thomas' success.

Patrick's hundred and ten knights had been reduced by nearly half, which lent to his decision to withdraw when Lord Lennox and his fresh mounted troops intervened, breaking Patrick's southern flank and quickly making their bloody way toward the center.

From the castle ramparts Lord Argyll watched the battle raging below. "The Macnabs are gettin' whipped!" he said, his eyes following the movements of the fighting.

"Should we not help, Milord?" asked an anxious Rollo.

"Bide a wee, Chieftain!" cautioned the earl, and he pointed to the archers poised behind the galleys. "Yonder, they have set a trap for us... which we will not fall into. More wait there... in the wood, as well."

The chieftain was stoically quiet whilst the jeers and yelps of his men filled the air. He did not agree with the old earl, but would abide by his word. He was sorely mournful that he could not be on the field below with his sword, flailing at King Robert. On the other hand, his hatred for The Brus was not so strong that it would hasten his wit to be overtaken by stupidity. He could, after all, see that men were waiting in the wood, and behind the galleys.

• •

Thomas came to Robert on horseback. "What is yer command, My King?!" he asked.

"Bring me another horse," said Robert, "and form up, from the chapel to the wood!"

"Aye, Uncle," said Thomas, bowing his head slightly.

David Graham rode to the king trailing a good highland horse by the reins.

Robert smiled as the Templar leaned down to offer it, and he didn't hesitate to mount the steed and see how he responded to rein. Finally, he wheeled the nimble beast around toward Thomas and shouted,

"Ne'ermind the horse!"

Thomas playfully shook his fist at his friend Sir David, who let out a light chortle.

From every single inch of ramparts on the top of Dunstaffnage came a unified roar from the wild and angry Argyllsmen. They hurled sticks, arrows, and stones from the walls of the castle at the Brus warriors, but all fell woefully short.

The king rode about checking on his troops and their leaders. As he approached Lord Lennox, the earl pulled his water skin from around his shoulder and offered it to Robert, who put it to his lips and drank a much needed refreshment, then handed the skin back to Malcolm, who also drank.

"The Macnabs will be returnin' with their full force," said Robert.

"We are already outnumbered, just by those in the castle," replied Malcolm sagely.

"They do make a grand hoot," observed Robert turning toward the ramparts from whence flowed the roar of many hundreds of voices.

"Why are they not out here?" asked Malcolm.

"They will be directly, and the Macnabs will return at our backs," said the king cocking one eyebrow toward his companion in arms. "They have an army of about five hundred landed away to the south, to be brought up as needed."

"To crush us betwixt 'em," nodded Malcolm.

"If we stand this ground," said Robert, heaving a great sigh.

"We have lost many men in this last hour for naught more than the takin' of this wee bit of sod," Lennox lamented, watching the dead warriors being separated from the wounded and laid side-by-side next to the chapel wall.

•   •

"Sails!" shouted Rollo from the ramparts and pointing southwest across the water at the twenty vessels coming their way, "Macnab Sails!"

Cheers were renewed on the ramparts, for all knew the Macnab galleys brought fresh stores.

Out on the water, Angus Macdonald and Malcolm Maclaine were prepared for battle. Two nights earlier, under black sails and darkened moon and the orders of King Robert, they had sailed their galleys west on Loch Etive and secreted them northwest of Eilean Mor, the island only a few score yards to the north of Dunstaffnage. Out of sight of the castle, Macdonald and Maclaine had dropped anchor and waited.

Having placed a lookout on the southern tip of the island, they now watched the signal being given. The Macnab supply galleys were coming north along the coast toward Dunstaffnage.

"Aweigh yer anchors!" shouted Angus to the fleet. The men on the various boats, not being content to hide, were excited to have some action at last.

They hove the anchors aboard and hoisted their sails; this time the sheets were bright yellow. Fortunately, they had a good steady wind and strong backs at the oars.

Sir Angus, as fleet captain, was eager to be at sea and fingered the hilt of his sword incessantly. "Bloodthirsty bitch," he murmured to the weapon as he imagined the use to which he was about to put it.

Like lightening, they came around from the north side of the island and headed straight for the Macnab vessels, every oarsman pulling with all his might to intercept.

The crowd of warriors on the castle wall soon grew hushed as their attention was refocused on the yellow sails sweeping out of the north.

"Yonder's more come to join them!" happily observed Lord Alexander, sighting the galleys coming around Eilean Mor. "We'll have a'plenty to fight for us!"

Sir Rollo leaned as far out as he could over the wall and strained to see.

"Hain't they more?... How many?" asked the old earl.

"Plenty more a'right," spoke Rollo, "but hain't of use to us, Sire!"

"What say?!" queried Alexander, his hand cupped behind his ear, almost completely baffled.

"Yellow sails... Sire. They are Macdonalds," the chieftain said almost whispering.

"Macdonalds are sons of Somerled same as we are... they hain't against us!" insisted the earl.

"They're aligned with The Brus, Milord," Rollo contradicted with a heavy sigh.

Alexander's face went from delighted child to dour old man within the time it took to say those words.

The news traveled the circle of men quickly, and they again began to shout and jeer and demanded to be let out from their castle cage to fight The Brus as they had at Dail Righ... in a fearsome charge for which they were widely famed.

Lord Alexander saw the Brus army on his citadel's grounds, so defiant, so evil to want his castle, and yet, he could not give the order to turn his hordes upon them.

"We must be released, Milord!" demanded Rollo pushing his face near the earl's to assure his being heard above the crowd. "If ye will not lead them into battle, Sire, then I will!"

"Cease yer prattle and mind yer place, Chieftain!" scolded the earl, "We will attack when we see the Macnabs on land comin' from the south."

"As ye wish, Milord," he acquiesced. Rollo withdrew from the earl's face, satisfied with the answer but still wondering about the state of the wit of his liege.

. .

The Macnab fleet saw the Macdonald and Maclaine galleys suddenly coming from around the islet. The captain of the lead vessel thought they could yet deliver their warriors and supplies to Dunstaffnage before the enemy could do them any damage.

But, the wind was against him, costing him time, while the hard muscled Macdonald-Maclaine oarsmen were vigorously assisting the following wind in their sails.

"On ye bastards!... Row, goddamn it! Row!" commanded Angus as the combined fleet made its way toward the Macnabs. Oarsmen in each galley strained against the water as hard as possible, with each coordinated stroke causing their vessel to leap forward. The warriors, standing with sword and shield, ready to do battle, moved to the sterns of their vessels and held tightly to anything sturdy as they went faster with every stroke.

"They're fixin' to ram us, Milord!" screamed a Macnab sailor to his captain.

The captain, standing tall to get the best look at the oncoming boats, realized the sailor was right.

Warriors in all of the Macdonald and Maclaine galleys set up a roar and began to slap their swords on their shields, as the Romans of old had done to strike fear into the hearts of their enemies.

The Macnab vessels pulled their steer boards inward, trying to meet the challenge head on, but it was too late for some. The bow of Sir Angus' lead galley crashed into the foremost Macnab galley before it was halfway into its turn, toppling warriors and sailors alike into the cold water of the bay.

Angus pitched forward on top of some of his oarsmen. Warriors in the stern were no less shaken and struggled to their feet to make their way forward, where they were to jump onto the Macnab galley and wreak devastation on all they met.

Water was already coming into the Macdonald galley; the oarsmen reached for their bailing pots, and rags to seal the broken and separated boards as they had done many times before. Angus scrambled to his feet shouting over the voices of others and the screams of wounded and dying men.

Those suffering in the chilly water wondered if there was anything they could do to salvage their sinking galley, or if it would be better to try the two hundred yard swim to the shore of the peninsula.

The Macnab vessel's sail was half immersed in the water when the Macdonalds reached the bow, ready to fight. Against them was only one very defiant, very large, albeit wobbly-legged, warrior in chain mail, swinging his sword around his head as he stood on the sinking larboard gunnels, until a sudden twist of the hull threw him, as well, into the water with his comrades.

Angus quickly turned his attention to the remainder of his fleet, ordering the captain to steer for the next pair of galleys locked in combat some thirty yards away.

"To yer places!" ordered the captain to his winded oarsmen, who took their oars in hand and began to row, but the men in the water hung tight to the blades of the oars in a vain attempt to stay afloat.

Sir Angus hung over the bow with his sword, hacking at the drowning Macnabs and trying to keep them from grabbing at the oars as they struggled to live. Suddenly, from beneath the roiling water, the warrior who had stood on the gunnels of the sinking Macnab boat rose up and grabbed Angus' sword arm. With one deft jerk he pulled the rotund Angus into the water with him.

"The Lord's o'erboard!" yelled the captain in a panic.

The Macnab sailors on either side of the boat let up a cheer when they realized what had happened, in spite of the fact that some among them were themselves drowning.

Two Macdonald warriors made their way forward to see if there was anything they could do. Peering over the bow, they saw nothing except a string of small bubbles that had escaped from the lungs of at least one of the men.

"Lord Angus is gone!" shouted the one, while the other hastily removed his surcoat and chain mail, grabbed his broadsword by the handle, and slung the sheath away as he went overboard in an attempt to save his lord.

Under the water he saw Angus struggling to free himself from the large Macnab warrior holding him from the back in a bear hold and determined to outlive his prey in the life and death struggle.

The Macnab saw the rescuer coming for him and loosened his grip on Angus in order to draw his dagger. Angus kicked and struck at the fellow as hard as he could and still could not break free, but in the struggle he turned his great assailant around so that his back was to the approaching swimmer.

Holding Angus with one arm and his blade in his other hand, the Macnab tried to right himself to defend against the looming attack, but it was too late. The Macdonald warrior reached the man and pushed his blade into the fellow's great throat. Struggling to hold to his quarry, the Macnab made several quick stabs at his attacker though his lifeblood poured into the surrounding water from his wound.

The water became clouded with ruddy billows and when last the Macdonald warrior saw the other two, they were still engaged in their life-or-death struggle. Unable to see to strike at the Macnab or to aid Angus, the man surrendered to his burning lungs and swam to the surface and a welcome breath of air. He twisted about to see if Lord Angus had managed to get free before he drowned, but nowhere did he see the head of Sir Angus.

"I have failed!" he sorrowfully shouted to his companion on the bow of the boat.

The comrade dropped his head at the news, when he heard a great gasp no more than a few feet away. Turning toward the sound he saw Angus' head bobbing in the water, coughing and choking and trying to clear his airways.

"Tis Sir Angus!" the warrior on the bow shouted to his friend and he cheerfully offered his hand to the thankful, corpulent knight.

Sir Angus and his savior were both pulled aboard shivering, and the sailors' blankets were fetched to warm them.

With their master back aboard and the galley's oarsmen having wrested their oars from the desperate men in the water, the ship's captain ordered the vessel to re-enter the fray in which the other Macdonald and Maclaine galleys were still engaged against the Macnab fleet. Directed in their efforts by Malcolm Maclaine, they seemed to be wreaking heavy damage on the enemy, though their vessels were greatly outnumbered.

"Sir Angus! Shouted a nearby warrior, "Ye are wounded!"

Angus looked about his person, finding a red splotch on his blanket. Throwing back the heavy cloth, he found a freely bleeding wound in his left arm. He had been so cold that he had not felt the gash, not when it happened, and not when it was found.

"Damn the whoreson!" cursed Angus. "Goddamned baseborn knave caught me with his blade after all!"

Rags were hastily tied about the Macdonald's dagger wound, and after he ceased being angry at the accursed villain, he realized how dreadfully close he came to death and was openly thanking God for having survived. Then his consciousness returned to normal and he recalled what he had been doing before being pulled overboard.

"My sword!" he remembered. "Where be my sword?!"

A sturdy oarsman immediately in front of him indicated he had no knowledge.

"Let me have yers," demanded Angus.

"Can't, Sire," said the fellow.

"Why not?!"

"Hain't got one," said the oarsman rhythmically rotating his oar handle with the others as the galley raced to the fight.

"Reckon yers was lost when ye were pulled o'erboard, Sire," suggested the warrior who had saved him.

"I reckon," moped Angus. As he looked around to see the disposition of his fleet in the ongoing battle, he turned and caused the first pain to his wounded arm, severe enough to make him wince.

· ·

On the castle ramparts the roar of the Macdougall warriors, wanting to get into the fracas, increased steadily. "Ye must turn us loose, Milord!" screamed the chieftain into Lord Alexander's ear over the roiling of the men.

"Mind yer tongue, Chieftain! We venture out on *my* word!" commanded the earl with grit and growl in the timbre of his voice. He grunted and looked back over the water watching the severe victory of the Macdonald galleys over those of the Macnabs. He was angry and frustrated as his men, but fear tingled his backbone as well.

He knew that his men were hungry for more than foodstuffs. They had watched as their Macnab allies were soundly trounced in the field in the early hours of the morning, and again, at sea, while they were forestalled from taking part. The loss at sea had been like setting a blazing torch in a haystack. The men were growing more ungovernable, and he knew he had only moments to choose between allowing his warriors to join the fight, or facing mutiny.

At that instant, a shout caught his ear.

"The Macnabs!"

He turned to look south, into the wood beyond the long expanse of now ruined farm fields where the battle of the knights had taken place only a short time earlier. There were the Macnab reinforcements.

"How's The Brus arrayed!?" the earl suddenly asked.

"We know not, Sire. They withdrew into the wood, yonder," said a near knight who had been keeping an eye on the field.

"Just when we were fixed to trap 'em," groused the earl. He looked at Rollo, whose countenance wore a definite frown.

"We a'goin'a let the Macnabs get whipped again, Milord?" challenged Rollo gritting his teeth. The crowd of warriors was still louder as the men recognized the conflict between their two leaders. It was then the earl made his choice.

"To horse! To arms!" decided the earl with a loud shout, drawing his sword and holding it high into the air above the ramparts. A great cheer went up from his cooped up warriors. Now they would fight The Brus.

When the Earl of Argyll mounted his destrier, the gates swung open before him. The hoots and screams from the Macdougalls mounted to a continual roar.

"Onward!" shouted the old earl as he rode out through the gate, down the several stone steps to the lawn and onto the battlefield. He swished past the overturned galleys near the shoreline, half expecting the Brus archers to stand and fill the air with deadly barbs, but there was no sign of them. He reined up at the chapel area where Lord Patrick sat his destrier and waited for his sometimes ally, the Macdougalls, to join him.

"Where's Brus?" asked Alexander brusquely, establishing his dominance.

"Ye've certainly come more alive since last we met, Milord," remarked Patrick.

"Collywobbles," remarked the earl. "Bellyache is all! Where is Brus!?"

Patrick smiled deferentially. "Yonder wood, Lord Argyll," he carefully watched the old man's face to see if he had the will to prosecute the battle to the end. "Let me take yer warriors and go rout The Brus," suggested Patrick.

"Mind yer place, Macnab!" snapped the earl, eyes flashing.

Patrick smiled and nodded compliance. "The woods are full of wild vermin, Sire," he said. He held out his hand as if to show the way to the natural labyrinth that his dreaded enemy was using for cover.

"Ye'd think they'd come to the open and fight on fair terms!" squirmed Alexander.

"Would ye?" replied Lord Patrick with a smirk.

The old man glared at the Macnab and wheeled his destrier south, toward the trees. Raising his broadsword over his head, he whooped his loudest and kicked his horse hard. Rollo and the other mounted knights followed, with the Macdougall warriors fast behind and scattering thick and wide through the wooded hillside, knowing that King Robert The Brus had some kind of trap laid for them.

"Ye! Take a hundred men south until ye leave the woods, then cut around east far enough to get in behind Brus!" Patrick ordered one of his knights, who left immediately. He next waved his hand and the remainder ambled with him, down the slight slope, into the woods, behind the loudly screaming Macdougalls.

This time, Macdougalls, ye shall do the dyin', he thought to himself and smiled.

· ·

Deep in the woods, the archer Murdoch whispered, "I hear 'em a'comin', MacKie!"

"We're ready for them," replied his brother, and quietly passed the word to the others.

"Aye, as long as the arrows hold out," murmured Murdoch, and he nocked his first shaft onto his bowstring.

Not far from the archers, King Robert and his mounted knights waited.

"Ye recollect Dail Righ, My King?" asked Andrew in a soft voice. Waiting next to the king, the squire sat astride his horse, the royal banner draped across his saddle.

Robert turned to the young man. "Aye," he replied, "I recollect our defeat at the hands of the Macdougalls!" The taste of the words were bitter on his tongue.

"We will win, this time, Sire, will we not?"

"Aye, Lad," the king answered. "This time we *must* win!"

• •

Murdoch and MacKie, standing side-by-side, witnessed the last of the wild Macdougalls coming through the trees. Beginning with the hindmost, the brothers dropped many with well-placed arrows, while those in the front, unable to hear the wails of those who were struck over the loud voices and cries of warriors on both sides, continued their sally unawares.

Once the mob had gone beyond the range of Murdoch and MacKie's longbows, other archers down the line took up the tactic, thinning the numbers of Macdougalls before they reached King Robert and his forces. At that point, MacKie tried to convince Murdoch to pull back, but he refused.

"We still have arrows… we'll stay," said Murdoch pulling a shaft from his quiver and nocking it into his bow. As the two archers hugged close to the larger trees and continued to wait, the clopping of hooves on random rock grew louder.

• •

Just east of the woods, The Brus and most of his men stood, quietly sweating from the midday heat and the anxiety of facing death. When the earl and his Macdougalls arrived they would be met first with a schiltrom.

The second line consisted of Robert and his horsed knights, his best, most highly trained warriors, having a score to settle with the Macdougalls and the Macnabs for past, hard-fought battles. They stood on a rise to the southwest of the schiltrom, with weapons of all descriptions… lances, pikes, maces, axes, flails, and blades from daggers to broad swords… at the ready.

To the northeast of the schiltrom, the Earl of Lennox arrayed his horsed knights along the crest of another hillock, and with the Templar, David Graham, formed the third line. If the Macdougall-Macnab forces got by or through them, there was nothing left but the wounded and camp followers, mostly women, including Christina and Dianna.

The plan was in place. It was now up to their enemies.

"Here they come!" hollered Randolph, keeping his eyes toward the edge of the woods.

"I see," replied Robert. He winced at how many were yet left after his archers had thinned the pack. The archers were not finished, however, and would fall in behind the onrushing Macdougalls and pick off stragglers and still dangerous wounded.

As the amassed men's voices reached a frenetic crescendo, one of the men in the schiltrom broke ranks and charged the enemy, screaming at the top of his voice. Every one of the others wanted to do the same.

"Hold steady!" ordered Robert in a loud voice, but the schiltrom members could not hear his command, and his warning was in vain. Three more broke and rushed forward the same as the first.

The first one got by a mounted knight's mace, but waiting Macdougall warriors made short work of him. The other three never slowed, and their fellows in the phalanx derided their foes all the louder when the three reached the line of charging Macdougalls and were immediately swallowed in death.

Angry and roaring, the remainder still seemed prepared to hold for the moment and Robert was thankful for it.

The Brus' knights were not in the forefront as traditionally positioned, and when Alexander Macdougall saw the king's oddly arrayed forces, he reined in his mount, as did many of his knights. However, there was no holding his charging foot soldiers. The deaths of the four hotheads from The Brus' line had stirred the blood on both sides of the conflict.

There was a terrible, sickening clash as the Macdougall warriors ran headlong into the spears of the Brus schiltrom. No man standing near the center of the field escaped the splatter of blood as the men in the rear of the frenzied mob ran over the backs of their dying comrades to leap upon their enemies.

Robert lifted and slipped on his old-style helmet... as worn by the Vikings, with a vertical nose protector... and drew his axe. He was ready for his knights' charge against those of Argyll.

· ·

Patrick and his Macnab knights, picking their way through the wood in the wake of the Macdougalls, came upon the first of Murdoch's archers' kills.

The Lord of Glendochart drew rein and looked about warily. His dog, traveling at the heels of his horse, sniffed the air as well as the ground.

Murdoch and MacKie held stone still, knowing that they had no chance against such a force of well-armored knights. The brothers were the last archers there, the others having gone ahead behind the Macdougalls, to kill any that fled from the battle.

The woods were silent, only an occasional snort from a horse was heard, when the dog caught a whiff of the hiding brothers, and barking incessantly, began to run straight for their hiding place behind the large trees.

"Run MacKie!" shouted Murdoch as he drew his bow and loosed his shaft into the charging dog's chest, killing it instantly. MacKie, shaken, obeyed his brother and ran away through the woods as fast as his legs would carry him.

"On him!" cried Patrick, and three of his knights wheeled and dug their spurs deep.

Murdoch set another arrow on the string and let it go at the foremost of the knights chasing his brother. It stuck upright in the side of the knight's leather chest armor. The Macnab knocked it out with a swift stroke of his mail-covered elbow, suffering barely a scratch.

The archer shot again, trying to give MacKie as much time as possible to get away. This time he struck the knight in the throat, above the chest armor. As he went down, his foot caught awkwardly in the stirrup and the horse dragged him along the ground at a gallop until the dead knight's body smashed against a tree. The foot tore loose from the leg, and remained in the stirrup as the horse continued to run.

MacKie, worried about Murdoch, turned back.

In quick succession, Murdoch loosed another three arrows at the charging knights, this time aiming for the necks of the horses. The first shaft struck true and the horse tumbled, spilling its rider onto the ground and killing him. The next went to fell the mount of the third knight and he, too, was thrown to the ground.

"Three knights to get two damned bowmen!?" roared Patrick Macnab in disbelief. He motioned for three more knights to go after the pair, and he and the remaining men continued on toward the battle raging ahead of them.

Murdoch pulled out one of the last two arrows in his quiver and turned to run. Seeing MacKie waving to him from no more than twenty yards away, he yelled and waved his arm for his brother to go back. "My God, MacKie... RUN!"

Amazed that his brother was angry with him, MacKie obediently turned and again ran frantically away. Murdoch, wanting to lead a trail away from MacKie, ran in another direction.

The Macnabs, seeking revenge for Murdoch's bringing down three of their comrades, stayed on his trail, as Murdoch had hoped, and paid no mind to MacKie. Both brothers were running as fast as they could manage.

The destriers had little trouble catching up to the wind-starved Murdoch, and as he turned to release the set arrow, his face was met dead-on by a morningstar mace, its two-inch spikes piercing his skull and ripping it open. His lifeless body tumbled backward and landed hard on the quiver holding his last arrow, his coveted longbow still in his hand.

•   •

South of Dunstaffnage Bay, along the eastern edge of the woods, the air was filled with screams of agony and wails of despair.

Sir Patrick and his men arrived after the Macdougalls had emerged from the woods and charged into the schiltrom, leaving slaughtered horses and knights, as well as enemy soldiers in their wake as they drove a wedge through to the heart of Brus' phalanx. As he watched, The Brus and his knights swept off the rise and into the hapless Macdougalls on Argyll's right flank.

Thus, he decided to wait and watch. The men he had sent over the hill to outflank Brus would soon return to the field behind the king. He would then attack, with The Brus caught between his two forces... and the Macdougalls taking the worst of it in the meantime.

King Robert, Thomas Randolph, and Robert Boyd pushed through the phalanx that was disintegrating by the minute. After the initial shock of the Macdougall charge, the spearmen began to pick the opponent closest to them to fight. Many held only the stub of the spear they had wielded, but nevertheless applied them with daring and enthusiasm.

Bravery and death were everywhere and on both sides.

Rollo and other Macdougalls were holding their own against a contingent of Brus' men as they worked their way toward Lord Alexander, who was getting winded, fast. In the frustration that his body would not go beyond its limitations and obey his will, the old earl screamed and shook his sword uncontrollably.

Even so, the superior Macdougall numbers were paying off.

• •

The company sent by Patrick Macnab to outflank the king's forces were making their way northeast. Having marched several miles around the forces of Brus, they were sure they had skirted the fray for they could hear it off to the northwest.

"Sounds like they have The Brus caught," said one of the leaders.

"Aye, or The Brus has them!" replied another.

"How far ye reckon 'tis from here?" asked the first, taking a swig from his water skin.

"Can't be more'n a mile or so, don't ye think?" asked the second of a third.

"I see people millin' about!" he answered.

"Don't be silly, ye mooncalf! Ye can't see that far!"

"Nay, not there!" he shook his head and pointed off to the east, "down yonder!" The several knights sat their horses and looked where he had pointed.

"That hain't no battle."

"No, but there's people movin' 'round."

"Reckon it's Brus' reserves?"

"If so, we should head 'em off, don't ye reckon?"

"We'll see," replied the first, "Ye two come with me, the rest, stay here!"

Down the hill they sauntered their horses, uneasily aware that they could be attacked at any moment.

In the camp below, Christina was carrying some water from the nearby burn when she saw three figures on horseback riding slowly down the hill. She continued on her way until she got out of sight of the three, then set the water bucket down and whispered to Dianna, "Three men up the hill!"

"Who ye reckon they be?!" asked Dianna excitedly and almost out loud. She dropped her mending and stood.

"Knights, it seems, and don't look like ours! Macdougalls or Macnabs, they're not goin' to leave them wounded layin' about in camp, nor us," Christina still spoke softly.

"How can we stop them?" asked Dianna, trying to see the approaching trio without herself being seen.

Christina, looking about at the lives soon to be taken and realizing that nothing would save them but their own mounting of a defense, suddenly ran out into the middle of camp and yelled at the cooks, the wounded, the men and the women tending their mundane chores and shouted, "All who can hold a blade... put hand to yer weapons... the enemy is nigh upon us!"

Rapidly the camp came alive as all who could took up something with which they could defend themselves and their camp mates, while a few of the women took the younger children and tried to hide them from the coming enemy.

Some of the wounded, unable even to stand much less fight, simply lay on their pallets and awaited their deaths. They knew that the approaching knights would be impossible to stop with the warriors gone from camp.

Hearing the commotion rising from the scene ahead, the three Macnab knights pulled their swords and continued, though one turned back to those left behind, and whistling loudly, motioned for them to join the raid.

When the other riders and soldiers of foot came into view, Christina turned to Dianna, "Ye must go find the army and tell the king, or the Templar... Douglas... any of them, that the enemy is fixed to come on them from behind!"

"Aye, Milady, but..." Dianna started to ask a question.

"Go! I know a Macnab flag when I see one! And stay out of sight of the bastards as much as ye can!"

Dianna said not another word, but turned and ran.

Christina put her hand through the open pocket in her dress and drew her dagger from her leg scabbard.

Gelis had found a sword and came to stand with Christina. Soon there were about fifty such women and older boys standing ready to fight, along with about thirty-five wounded men, some of whom could barely stand.

One of the forward Macnab knights caught sight of Dianna and pointed her out, "Yonder goes one to warn The Brus!"

Another kicked his horse hard and charged down the gentle slope in her direction.

"Ye needn't tax yer horse, so…Lord Patrick might have kilt them all by now," said the first, but the knight continued at a fast gallop.

Dianna ran on, the knight on horseback closing quickly.

"Huh!" he muttered with delight when he realized that she was a bonny wench.

Dianna moved through the trees swiftly and traversed the thickest of them to give the knight's horse an indirect route to follow.

"If ye stop, I won't kill ye," teased the knight, putting his sword in its sheath.

"In a pig's eye," she said under her breath, now coming in deep gulps and her side was beginning to ache. It seemed she could feel the horse's breath on the back of her neck. The Macnab knight was taunting her, calling her names and telling her what he would do when he caught her, since she wouldn't stop.

She struggled to stay ahead of her horsed pursuer, growing more and more desperate, finally screaming as loud as she could, in hopes that perhaps someone would hear her.

The knight had lost the idea of returning to battle and chose instead to indulge his lust. Watching her run, her skirts held high off her ankles, her ample breasts lifting and falling… aye… he would have that one ere she died.

She had run out of the protective trees, and he rode up beside her and struck her in the back with his stirruped foot, sending her sprawling down into the grass.

Stunned, she lay moaning and catching her breath as he dismounted. She was unable to run away.

"Yer screams'll not be heard o'er the noise of battle, Lassie," he said, putting his foot on the end of her skirt so she could not bolt. He grinned and removed his mail coif, revealing a finely formed head and curly blonde hair, dripping sweat that ran down his grinning face.

"And ye," said Dianna, still gasping for air, "reckon to have me for yerself, do ye?"

"Aye, Sweet One," he replied.

"Then have at it," said she, and laid her head back into the meadow grass.

She did not struggle as he loosed the front opening of his trews, and coming down on his knees, straddled her, pushing her skirt out of his way.

"Ye'll ne'er forget this time," bragged the knight, lowering himself on top of her.

"Ye ne'er will, yerself," she replied, still panting heavily.

Suddenly the man's eyes opened wide and he groaned weakly. The cold, bloody point of Sir David's broadsword pricked the skin on the back of his neck. The fellow started gasping for air, and suddenly went limp, his full weight bearing down on Dianna.

"Get this heavy whoreson off me!" she howled.

"Ye heard the lady! Get up!" said David sternly.

The man did not move.

Dianna maneuvered her arm, and with a great growl, rolled the man off her. He went to his back easily.

David winced when he saw the dying man's very bloody groin.

"Were ye fixin' to kill him, My Love?" she asked as she stood and looked down at her scarlet soaked skirt. "Damn him!" she cursed.

"I think ye be quicker with a blade than the likes of me," said the Templar in amazement.

She held up the dagger with which she had sliced open her attacker's groin, saying, "It's a little notion I learned from Lady Christina," and she slipped the dagger back into the scabbard on her leg.

They both turned and walked away from the permanently unconscious man.

"Watch yer manners in my bed from now on, ye will?" she said smiling and with one brow arched.

"Aye," said David a slight smile playing within his beard.

"Oh God,!" said she, suddenly recalling her mission, "Macnabs are at the camp!"

"Take the knight's horse and go to Lord Malcolm, yonder, on a steep hill," the Templar said, pointing in the direction of the battle.

He swung himself onto his horse and quickly rode off in the direction of the camp.

When Dianna caught up to Lord Malcolm, he, on the orders of the king, still held his knights in reserve as the last wave. He immediately told twenty of them to go back to the camp with her.

As she left, Dianna could not help seeing the battle raging no more than fifty yards away. The ground was littered with the dead serving as stumbling traps for those remaining upright and fighting. King Robert was in the thick of the battle exhorting his men to fight on, and killing those who came within the range of his deftly wielded axe.

She could barely distinguish the men on the far side of the battle who simply stood and watched. *Perhaps they are the last wave reserve for the Macdougalls*, she thought. There seemed to be so many more of the wild warriors than there were of King Robert's men.

• •

Haye and Douglas had fought their way close to Lord Alexander, but were unable to break through the inner circle. Rollo and the other horsed knights had the earl well surrounded near the center of the battle. As the Macdougalls arced their swords around their heads, they continually blazed a grand swath, slashing any who ventured within the blades' range. It proved too dangerous, even for their own Macdougall warriors, who tried to duck under the swings to reach The Brus' knights.

Getting to the hub of the fight is not going to be possible, thought Gilbert.

"The earl must retire from battle!" shouted Rollo to the Macdougall knights. One of the closest of them turned and nudged his horse to the rear of the Macdougall line. Rollo and another knight held the worn earl in his saddle as they retreated.

"Givin' up the fight?" asked Lord Patrick mockingly as the small, retreating contingent came by him.

"The earl is worn to tatters, Milord," answered Rollo. Alexander, who could barely sit his mount, glared at the impertinence of Patrick but did not have the strength to speak his mind.

"Surely, Milord," spoke Rollo sarcastically, "ye will take advantage of the missing leadership of our army and come to the forefront of this battle. Ye could win against The Brus… and be our savior!"

Lord Patrick knew he was being scorned and challenged, but did not want to fall prey to the provocateur. His destrier danced as Patrick held tight its reins. The Macnab knights awaited a positive answer from their lord as, from the beginning of the battle, Patrick was calculating when his men would arrive to attack the Brus army from the rear.

"I will be most pleased to fight at yer side, Milord," offered Rollo.

Patrick knew he could wait no longer and still save face. He drew his broadsword and whooped, and dug his spurs deep. The beast on which he rode bolted and Lord Patrick made a direct line for King Robert. Rollo, true to his word, kept pace even though he was far from being as fresh as Lord Patrick.

• •

The first Macnab knight who had thought to lead his fighters down the hill to The Brus' campsite and destroy it said, "These are just the *wee folk!*"

"Aye, and Lord Patrick awaits our arrival at the battle, Sire," suggested the second knight, his line of men already formed to charge against Christina's camp followers who were prepared to do battle to the death with the hardened Macnab knights and foot soldiers.

"We can take them later," said the first, thinking it best if they followed the orders of their lord.

The decision was taken from them by one swift command.

"CHARGE!" yelled Christina at her loudest.

The entire group of mostly untrained women rushed the astounded Macnabs. The horsed nights and trained soldiers of foot could not believe they were being attacked and none took the situation seriously until they felt the sting of a farm tool turned weapon cutting into or bruising their skin. This was certainly not what the Macnabs bargained for, but they finally began to fight back. They had wanted only to get unencumbered from the mob and go the aid of their lord.

Neither side had a clear direction as to their behavior, and the fight was more like a brawl than a battle. Driven by the idea that they were protecting their men and their camp friends, the women were fierce and uninhibited in their actions.

Sir David drew rein hard when he arrived on the scene. Taking a quick assessment of the battle, he went for the mounted knights, who were doing the most damage to those least likely to return harm to them. The Templar's sword was at the ready, and reaching the fray he caught the first knight by surprise, felling him in little time or effort. Seeing a more able foe, the second knight turned from his easy kills and charged the Templar full force. The swords clashed and within a minute he, too, was dead on the ground. Several of the other knights saw the large ruddy cross of the feared brotherhood on the Templar's surcoat, and either yielded or hied away to avoid fighting him.

Lord Malcolm's knights' appearance on the horizon left little starch in the backbones of the remaining Macnabs and they dispersed as fast as they could flee, hoping those barbaric wenches and lads would not follow.

The Templar wheeled to greet the newcomers to the scene, telling them, "Ye knights hie back to the battle… the king needs ye more than these warriors here."

The commanding knight looked around. "Women whipped the Macnabs!?"

"Whipped these," answered Sir David with a broad grin. He turned to Christina, still hot for the idea of pursuing the Macnabs. "Saints be praised! Have we Boadicea come again in our midst?"

"Not likely," replied Christina, stoically, resenting being teased.

The Templar laughed and kicked his horse to return to the main battle. When he passed Dianna, who was just riding into camp, he winked and smiled and went on. She knew he was pleased with her and it made her feel warm all over.

· ·

"Here comes that Macnab and his horde, Robbie," shouted Thomas Randolph.

"I see him," barked Robert, checking the disposition of his men and realizing they were scattered too much to form any kind of phalanx. Robert shook his head and with determined lips he commanded, "Charge the sorry blaggards!"

Thomas Randolph nodded in agreement and turned to have his destrier kick the life out of an attacker trying to get to him.

Robert looked toward Lennox and his reserves, still waiting faithfully. The king gave a long blast on his horn, and turned back to the fighting near him, for his signal had been heard.

"For King Robert and Scotland!" shouted the earl, and he took off down the hill ahead of his troops. The air filled with their cheers and blood-freezing war cries, drowning out Robert's steadfast piper's melody as they followed, for they had been itching to get into the battle since it began.

Lord Malcolm and his reserves charged headlong into the oncoming mounted knights of the Lord of Glendochart, causing the foot soldiers on both sides to scatter, thus avoiding the horrific clash of the two fresh armies and their great destriers.

Patrick had come with an eye to attacking the king. He knew that Robert was the one knight on whose shoulders the whole of the rebellion rested, and he determined to cut him down.

Reaching proximity to his target, he swung his broadsword at Robert who deflected it off his yellow and red shield, and immediately struck back with an axe blow. The Macnab was just as quick to parry the king's axe with his shield.

As the battle raged all about them, the two continued exchanging blows, each trying to catch the other off balance or unprepared, but neither managed to inflict a wound on the other.

Knowing that the king had been fighting non-stop since the battle started, Malcolm tried to intervene, to allow the king a respite. He directed his destrier between the combatants and tried to shield Robert and take Patrick on, but Robert was not about to allow the earl, no matter how well intentioned, to keep him apart from this Macnab.

"Choose another, Malcolm!" he ordered brusquely, and Malcolm instantly obeyed. The Brus took up the fight again.

"Ne'er will ye be king of the Macnabs, Robert Brus!" grunted Patrick between blows.

"Ye will be either vassal... or dead by the end of this day!" answered Robert confidently, striking back at every opportunity.

"Lest... I best... ye!" continued Patrick.

Robert slammed his axe heavily against Patrick's shield, and Patrick heard the leather-wrapped wooden device crack. He countered with a strong slam against Robert's shield, pushing Robert off balance momentarily. Patrick smiled with delight; the great Brus grew tired.

Robert shook his head to relieve his stunned wit and before he could straighten himself in the saddle, Patrick repeated the sword stroke. The blow glanced off his shield and struck the king on the left side of his face, leaving a crimson gash from his brow down across his cheek, breaking the bone. Robert cried out in pain and blood ran into his left eye, blurring his vision. Only his helmet had kept the blow from being deadly.

Seeing the king at such a disadvantage, Patrick swiftly moved in for the kill, but Robert regained his seat and blocked the lord's next swing with his axe. He saw Douglas and Boyd trying to come to his aid, but he shook his head and again raised his battleaxe.

"Stand away!" he ordered, blood trickling from the wound and forcing him to close his left eye.

"But, My King!" protested Boyd as Malcolm held Patrick at a few feet distance.

"*My fight!*" insisted Robert.

The knights moved back as ordered, and the warriors near to them stopped fighting and watched the duel between the two men.

Patrick again smiled to see the tired and wounded king demanding that he, Lord of Glendochart, chieftain of the Macnabs, be allowed to be his executioner.

Robert drew himself up by the saddlebow, as tall as he could manage. He wiped the blood from his left eye as best he could with his leather gauntlet.

"Ye fixed to die?!" shouted Patrick for all to hear.

"Are ye?!" said Robert with great calm.

Patrick smiled. Robert didn't.

Patrick kicked his horse hard and the animal bolted toward the lone figure sitting his horse.

Robert's fingers tightened around the reins, pulling them slightly taut, and his highland horse sensed the tension and stood ready as Lord Patrick neared them.

David Graham arrived in time to see Patrick's maneuver. All knew that this would surely spell the end to the battle, and the complete rout of the losing side.

Patrick swung his sword, the blade already stained with Robert's blood, again hitting the king's shield with a resounding whack.

The king quickly turned his more nimble horse, and with one deft movement was behind Patrick and slung his axe to the back of Patrick's neck... but seeing movement out of the corner of his eye, the Macnab pulled up his shield, preventing Robert from landing a lethal blow. Still, The Brus' blade drew blood and struck bone.

Stunned, Patrick hit the ground with a thud.

A cheer arose from the Brus army. Robert raised his hand to call for a cessation to the cheers.

Patrick, red oozing down the back of his surcoat, staggered to his feet in great pain.

"Are ye ready to come to the king's peace?" asked Robert calmly.

Patrick said nothing, but with effort picked his sword handle up from the ground. With his other hand, he held his aching head for a moment, great tears of pain rolling down his face. Suddenly, he moved his bloodied hand from the back of his head to the hilt of his sword, and raising the heavy two-handed blade with great effort, charged toward Robert.

The Brus easily wheeled and could just as easily have killed Patrick who, exhausted, fell sprawling to the turf. The back of his surcoat was nearly all scarlet.

Robert dismounted and threw his helmet to the ground. Blinded in the left eye with his own blood, he found the helm's nose guard to be too obstructing of his remaining sight.

Patrick forced himself to stand, and picking up his shield, raised his sword and again started for the king, who stood ready with shield and axe, but it was clear that Robert would have no need to defend himself, as the Macnab's limbs were failing in their strength. He was no longer able to maintain hold on his shield and let it drop. His sword point was trailing in the dirt, and before he could reach to strike at his enemy, he fell at Robert's feet.

A hush came over both armies as they realized the battle was finished. All stood looking at the wounded king and the dead lord.

Across the circle of warriors, an astounded Rollo looked at the two men and his disappointed anger flared. He let out a yell and kicked his horse toward King Robert.

David Graham perceived the man making his move even before Rollo's spurs reached his horse's flanks, and with no word of warning the Templar and his great steed burst past the Lennox knights and headed straight for Rollo.

Douglas too, set a course to intercept the charging Macdougall.

Robert, his axe and shield at the ready, awaited the attack.

Rollo was almost upon the king, his sword poised for the kill that was denied Patrick.

David passed the king by only a few feet when he clashed sword-to-sword with Rollo, altering the Macdougall's course. Douglas' arrival was almost at the same instant, and as he passed Rollo on the other side, the stroke he intended for the chieftain struck instead the chieftain's mount. Though the injured beast skidded to the ground, Rollo showed his horsemanship by riding it down without injury.

David wheeled his horse ready to do battle with Rollo, but seeing him afoot, drew rein and dismounted, and stood holding his weapon with two hands, offering a duel.

Rollo smiled and approached the Graham without reserve.

It was he who struck the first blow, hard and quick, followed by two others like it. Graham parried, but was impressed with the man's ability and strength, which brought a voice to the crowd formed by the two armies.

Douglas remained mounted and close to the king, who would not permit Andrew to tend his wound while the two men fought, though his blood yet dripped onto his royal tabard.

Graham retaliated with several sharp hits aimed at Rollo's head, but the chieftain deflected them off to one side and festinately brought his blade around toward David's leg.

Though the Templar blocked the blow, he lost about half his foible in the process, leaving him with a shortened blade and at a disadvantage.

He therefore went on the attack with a series of strikes and counterstrikes that left both men breathing heavily and studying each other out more closely. In that brief pause, Douglas threw his sword to land upright near Graham, and the knight in the cross-blazoned surcoat retrieved it with one swift turn.

Immediately, Rollo laid on with heavy, jolting blows that rang throughout the glen as a hammer striking an anvil, but Graham parried them all. It was then the Macdougall's eyes betrayed him, foretelling his next blow.

David Graham stepped aside, avoiding the arcing strike and countering with one of his own. The Templar turned and threw his whole weight behind his blade, severing the Macdougall's trunk completely, the shoulders and head thrusting on forward with the momentum of his swing and landing a good six feet beyond his lower extremities.

Exhausted, David nevertheless held his sword at the ready in case some other Macdougall stalwart wished to try his luck and add his own blood to that of Rollo's on the Templar's blade, but the others had no fight left.

Leaderless, they turned and ran or walked away in every direction before the king had them all executed. Their war was ended and the forces of The Brus had won.

"Get after them!" commanded Lord Lennox to his knights.

"Nay, Malcolm! Let them go!" countermanded Robert, his left eye almost swollen shut from the wound.

"They will gather to attack us again," argued Malcolm, but Robert disagreed.

"The Macnabs will go home and lick their wounds, and be grateful they were not among the dead," he prophesied. "Tomorrow we will take Dunstaffnage from Lord Alexander!"

ARGYLL

It was a night of weeping and revelry in the camp of The Brus as they mourned their dead and celebrated their survival. Horsemeat was the main course in their one course repast, which gave them a short break from their recent diet of smoked salmon and pike. Pickets were placed several deep around the campsite to maintain the army's safety, but no band of any kind tried to penetrate the defenses that night.

Christina tended Robert's face wound and prayed it would not fester as she packed it with herbs and mud to draw it closed. His cheekbone was shattered and agonizingly painful, with lesser wounds above his eye and below on his jaw.

Even so, the next morning his men were roused before dawn, again. They mustered in parallel lines and prepared to march to Dunstaffnage two abreast. Robert planned to take the narrow pathway along the water in order to avoid the battleground of yesterday.

Sir Angus had been ordered to take his and the captured Macnab galleys, with as many warriors as they would carry, around to the far side of the peninsula. Again, Robert would utilize his forces' closing in from both sides... if the Macdougalls, and perhaps even the Macnabs, awaited on the battle-stirred ground in front of the castle.

This day, the fighting will be much different, thought Robert. His cheek ached abominably despite the medicine pack Christina had applied, yet he led his highland warhorse along the tree-lined path with the army following. The sun, rising at his back, was not yet above the horizon, but it would matter little for the clouds made the day even darker.

"Sire!" Douglas rode up the line to speak to Robert.

"Aye, Jemmy," the king answered.

"A man has come out of yon trees to speak with ye." Robert stopped.

"What does he want?" asked the woeful king. Every step his horse took pounded in his skull.

"He says he has news."

Riding behind Robert, Andrew recognized the man and said, "'Tis yer spy, Milord!"

The king looked toward where Andrew pointed, and with his one good eye, recognized him as well and waved the man to come forward. When he arrived, he bowed.

"Yer report," snapped Robert impatiently.

"Sire!" huffed the out-of-breath spy. "The Macnabs ran off this morn!"

"Ran off?! Where? When did they leave?" he asked rapidly and with a modicum of emotion.

The spy raised his brows to indicate he did not know.

Robert took a deep breath then said, "Go find out! When ye know where they're goin', come back and tell me!"

"Aye, My King," said the fellow, and bowed deeply once again before turning and trotting off to disappear back into the wood.

Robert gently shook his head in disbelief and turned, resting his weight on the cantle of the saddle, signaled Thomas to come to his side.

"Ride ahead and see what awaits us," he ordered.

"Aye, Uncle," Thomas said and dug his heels into his horse, to lope off toward Dunstaffnage. Robert sent Douglas, with six knights, uphill to keep watch over the army and to direct his spies and pickets, spread out through the woods. He then continued his column at a pace suited to his aching head and the quick step of his many walking troops.

Within a quarter of a mile he saw Thomas riding back down the path toward him, and five Macdougalls riding behind him.

Robert halted his column and waited for Thomas to come near enough to talk in confidence, leaving the others some distance back.

Thomas said, "Sire, I bring an ambassador from Lord Alexander!"

"Ambassador?" asked the king, disbelieving. "A trick?" Robert looked about as widely as he could without further distressing his pounding head.

"Nay, Sire. I think not. Will we receive him?"

Robert agreed and Thomas snapped his fingers toward the foremost Macdougall, motioning him to approach the king.

The leader of the delegation dismounted and walked to the side of Robert's horse. He bowed slightly and handed a waxsealed letter to the king. Robert motioned him back to his horse, then opened and read the document stoically.

"Says Argyll wants to give up the fight, just wants safe passage for his men!" quietly related Robert to Thomas with a deep sigh.

Thomas smiled. "Ye takin' it?"

Robert raised his hand to Thomas to show he wanted no more questions in front of the Macdougall. "Tell yer liege, I will meet him in the great hall at Dunstaffnage within the hour," he said sufficiently loud for the fellow to hear from where he stood.

"But, Sire..." objected the ambassador, then quickly swallowed the rest.

"Within the hour!" Thomas insisted as he approached the man, threatening with merely his close presence.

The Macdougall again bowed, saying not another word. Mounting his palfrey, he wheeled, and the whole of the retinue took off at a canter for Dunstaffnage.

The news of the potential surrender traveled fast through the hardened, battle-weary soldiers of Robert's army. Soon the whole hillside was bathed in whispers of "praise be to God!"

Christina worked her way through the disciplined, but celebratory throng to Robert. She took his hand and he turned to her.

"'Tis for sooth?" she asked, hopefully.

"'Ppears, so," said Robert smiling as broadly as he could, considering.

• •

Within the hour, Robert's men were strewn thick over the grounds and the interior of Castle Dunstaffnage. The Macnabs had, indeed, left to return home with their dead knights, including the body of Lord Patrick.

Many of the Macdougalls, holed up in the castle for the last several months, had slipped away as well, and scattered to at least three of the four points of the compass, across Lorne and beyond with only a few of the king's out-posted spies to see them leave.

In the great hall, Robert accepted Lord Alexander's capitulation. In return, he promised safe passage for the men of Argyll who had already left, and no harm to those still lurking about... if they struck not first... but the king had one more demand for the earl's personal release and safety, perhaps one of the oddest demands ever.

Before he was allowed to retire from Dunstaffnage, it was required of the earl that he, himself, pull down the elegant Macdougall family tapestry above the fireplace in the great hall, and drop it to the flagstone floor.

After the defeated old man had reluctantly done as he was bade, Robert brought forth the scarred pelt of his faithful yellow-gray hunting dog, so viciously tortured and killed by Alexander's son John. The poor creature's hide was then hung in that place of honor, with instructions that it was never to be taken down as long as he lived and was king.

Christina, standing in the shadows, smiled at the ironic justice of the gesture.

Thomas Randolph watched and remembered transporting the dog, from Lord Pembroke in Aberdeen to John Macdougall in Argyll, to aid in the hunt for Robert. He often regretted that he had not thought to kill the dog on the trail so that it could not be used against his uncle. *But alas, the past cannot be changed,* he mused, taking another long swig of his ale as the dog pelt was nailed to the wall.

The humiliated earl was afterward put on a galley and sent to Castle Inchchonnell, there to warn his son John, Lord of Lorne, that henceforth neither of their English titles were valid, and that both of them were to surrender to the Scottish king's peace or leave the country empty-handed. The old earl was not about to leave his beloved Argyll.

MacKie sadly took Murdoch's body home to their heartbroken

mother. Many were the bitter tears she cried for her son for the rest of her days, but she was consoled somewhat by the knowledge that in giving his life, he had given Scots back their country.

Murdoch's bairn, a lad of only five years, received his father's longbow and quiver, still containing a single arrow.

Sir Angus Macdonald returned to the Isles, excited to take up his "trading" business once again, this time without the English breathing so near to his purse.

Sir David Graham, the Templar, accompanied Sir Angus back to Dunaverty, where he would arrange transport from the Orkneys of unspecified goods belonging to the ill-treated French Templars, to be sent from there to the diverse Isles under the command of Sir Angus, for various purposes and disbursements. Dianna accompanied the Templar, who did not put up much of a fuss.

As for Dunstaffnage... it was one castle The Brus did not raze. Further, due to the persuasion of Sir Neil, who had always served well his brother-in-law king, Robert turned the castle over to the Campbells, charging them with maintaining the king's peace and interests within that region of Scotland. In less than a fortnight the chieftains of the Campbells arrived to take on the duties bestowed upon them.

Robert sent a message to his brother, Edward, in Galloway for the release of Walter de Ross, that he might go home to his father and tell him to prepare for war... or for peace... the choice would be his.

With the word of the King Robert's success against Dunstaffnage quickly spreading, he was having no trouble bringing in volunteers of every kind. He knew that, by the time he reached Ross, his army would be of sufficient strength to take on any army that the earl could pit against him. In his heart he felt revenge against the earl would be sweet... but in his mind, he knew an ally in that region would bring the greater part of Scotland to his peace.

James "The Black" Douglas was sent back to the southeast with his army... to continue to harass the English strongholds in Roxburgh and Jedburgh, and to join forces with Sir Edward de Brus against the castles of Galloway... when needed.

Within the next month the king made his way east to the lands around Perth, where the English still held castles but feared to sally forth and attack him and his army. He went to Inchmahome and Dunkeld. And he began drafting instruments of a government for the kingdom.

But, there remained the question of Ross.

Thus, he moved his army northwest, toward Sutherland.

September 25th 1308

Aberdeen

A lone figure stood before Castle Aberdeen.

He remembered times when he had been an honored guest within, but now it was as cold as the autumn wind that blew through his disguise of "ordinary citizen." He pulled the woolen hood tighter to his lightly gray bearded face, as much to hide his features as for warmth. The Scots were in command of the town, and he wanted them not to know that he was about.

This was a personal pilgrimage he was making, one he neither understood himself, nor would speak of to another living soul. His entourage of six mounted knights and his destrier he left on the other side of the River Cree to await his return.

He feigned a hobbling walk through the streets as the final glow of day sank into starless night, when he at last arrived at the Red Lion and entered. He chose a small table in the far corner, where even the newly lit candles denied their light and a man could sit unnoticed by other patrons.

After a while, however, the innkeeper's wife saw the customer sitting in the corner and came to his table.

"Ale," he uttered in the coarse rumble of a large man, his hood still well covering his face.

The alewife hesitated a moment, thinking she recognized the voice, but decided otherwise and went her way to get the traveler his ale.

She returned in a moment and set the flagon of brew and a pewter cup in front of him. He spoke not a word as he pushed an eighth-penny piece toward the wife. She chattered her usual prate to make her guests feel welcome, then she took the money and left.

For a span of about a half-hour the man sat and sipped his ale and watched.

Lela came to the tavern floor from her living quarters in the back, finishing tying her long red hair in a knot at the back of her head. The man's pulse quickened when he saw her, but he made no move to attract her attention.

Moments later her sister emerged from the back with her arms full of two squirming bairns. She went to her mother to ask a question and the man choked with desire. He wanted to go to the family and hold the little ones himself... but he dared not. Instead he sat and watched the small girls as their grandmother took one and held her, and the other played with her mother's red curls while the women talked.

No one saw him leave. He disappeared as mysteriously as he had arrived. His pilgrimage had been accomplished.

The alewife noticed his absence after a while and went to the table where he had sat. As she picked up his half-emptied flagon, she saw a small leather pouch on the table. She looked around the room as she picked it up, but he was nowhere to be seen. She opened it and poured out a handful of coins.

"God in Heaven!" she uttered aloud and crossed herself as she stared at the fortune.

Lela ran to her side thinking something must be wrong. When she, too, saw what was in her mother's hand, she gasped and looked around the room for the large man who had left an additional five English pounds to pay for his ale.

October 31st 1308
Auldearn near Nairn in Scotland

"The Earl of Ross has arrived, My King," the Steward of Castle Auldearn informed Robert and his retinue.

"We'll be down directly," instructed Robert Boyd, gently pushing the nosy steward back through the door. "Tell yer master to make all ready for the ceremony."

Small in comparison to many of the others in the region, the castle at Auldearn had a stockade curtain wall of about ten feet in height, with a two-story rectangular donjon and a single-story structure that served as both entrance gatehouse and stable. The chapel was on the far end of the bailey.

Taken by the forces of Bishop David Murray only months earlier, the castle overlooked the small village and castle of Nairn and beyond, to the broad waters of Moray Firth. The water was a beautiful blue on this autumn day of almost cloudless sun, contrasted with the gently rolling hills beneath their winter coat.

The Earl of Ross and his two sons, along with their entourage of knights and remaining servile following, arrived in Nairn by galley, and with borrowed horses for the nobles and knights from the badly damaged castle at Nairn, made their way up the hill to Auldearn where waited King Robert.

Colorful flags and banners waved in the light but cold breeze coming over the firth from the north. King Robert already had an agreement with Lord William, but demanded that he present himself before him personally, with all the pomp that could be generated considering the dire circumstances of the surrounding country.

Sir Hugh de Ross, the earl's first-born son and heir, was also to swear fealty. Sir Walter de Ross, who had been fighting alongside The Brus through the previous winter and summer, was to give permanent oath, having sworn temporary allegiance to The Brus earlier.

The Bishop of Moray and the Bishop of Ross would act as sureties for the ceremony, to see to it that Lord William would honor the words he would mouth before God and the gathered assemblage. The earl was greatly relieved that the two bishops agreed to stand as sureties, for he had a nagging fear that King Robert would kill him on the spot when he showed up in Auldearn, and that Moray, alone, might let him!

As the earl and his attendants slowly mounted the hill, Bishop David Murray, dressed in his vestments, stood squarely in the path and watched them patiently. Soon, the Earl of Ross could go no further without running the bishop under the hooves of his borrowed horse.

Almost serenely, the bishop reached for the reins close under the chin of the earl's mount and stood looking up at him.

"Yer want?" barked Ross.

"And a good day to ye, My Lord Earl," the bishop chided the earl's lack of proper and respectful manners. The earl said nothing.

"Ye remember yer say at Skelbo, winter last?" asked Murray, pleasantly.

"Aye," replied the earl.

"My lands have not been returned to their original condition, as ye agreed they would be," said Murray.

"In due time, Bishop, I swear," he returned.

"In due time, I shall have ye excommunicated, My Son," said Murray, smiling over clenched teeth but remaining low voiced.

"I remind ye, once again, that ye and all the Brus army are already excommunicated by the Holy See in Rome, My Bishop," smiled Ross, thinking he had gainsaid.

"As ye also will be, when ye swear yer fealty to King Robert this day, Milord?" asked Murray, smiling.

The earl's mouth fell agape. He had not considered that he, too, would be excommunicated when he gave oath to The Brus.

"I will be able to reinstate ye with yer Lord God," returned the bishop holding the cross that hung from the chain around his neck.

"Stand aside, Bishop!" he growled. "I'll have yer lands restored plenty good by spring plantin'!"

"Fair enough, My Son," he replied. He made the sign of the cross in the air to bless them, and stood back from the earl's horse to let the line pass without further hampering.

"Seems like Father is havin' to keep more agreements this day than he reckoned on," laughed Sir Walter.

"The Brus will have the whole of our teeth ere it's done, I fear," countered his brother Hugh with a quiet chortle.

Waiting squires received the mounts of the arriving earl and accompanying party as they reached the gatehouse and dismounted. In the small bailey, the chickens constantly clucked around the feet of the meandering villeins as Oliver inflated the bladder of his pipes and began to play.

Robert's knights lined up four rows deep along the front of the two-story donjon, their rough manner not being overlooked by the earl as he was directed to the small chapel.

By the time the whole of the earl's entourage entered the bailey, and the king's retinue came forth from their tents and village houses, the bailey was fairly packed with bodies wanting to see and hear whatever there was to see and hear.

Lord William entered the castle's small kirk and came forward to the altar where the two bishops stood awaiting the honored guests. Sir Walter and Sir Hugh followed closely. Bishop de Murray held up his hand slightly, giving the signal to the earl and his party to halt their approach. The area closer to the altar was for the king and his attendants.

"Make way for the king! Make way for the king!" those at the front of the crowd in the bailey began to shout when Andrew emerged carrying the king's standard through the front door of the two-story donjon. Baldred walked to his left with the Saint Andrew's flag fluttering.

The crowd parted to see the two proud lads take the three steps to the ground level of the bailey. Oliver piped his tunes once again, and all the louder.

King Robert stepped out resplendent in brightly polished chain mail and a newly made surcoat with the red lion rampant on its chest. On his head he wore a new leather helm to which was attached the thin, much abused gold band used at his coronation. Neath his mail jerkin he wore the silver and gold decorated chest armor given to him by his kinswoman, Christina of the Isles. Had she not gilded and otherwise supplied his early efforts, Robert knew, the English king would still be riding roughshod over Scotland.

The whole of the body within the bailey, and villeins standing beyond, cheered to the tops of their lungs in jubilation, and plunged their weapons into the crisp wintry air above their heads.

Robert smiled and waved toward the cheering throng. They were heartened all the more, incessantly shouting "The Brus! The Brus!"

He took the steps to the bailey floor and began to make his way through the crowd, mostly made up of men who had fought by his side.

Robert was followed down the stairs by Malcolm, Earl of Lennox, Sir Thomas Randolph, Sir Robert Boyd, Sir Neil Campbell, Sir Gilbert de la Haye, Sir Alexander Fraser, Sir Simon Fraser, Sir William Wiseman, Sir David de Barclay, and lastly, by Sir Henry Sinclair. He had come from Aberdeen to give the king a report on the trade beginning to take place between independent Scotland and the rest of the world.

Christina and the king's youngest sister, Matilda, watched the procession from an open upper story window.

"Good God!" exclaimed the Earl of Ross as he listened to the ruckus in the bailey.

"I told ye Father," said Sir Walter, "they are mad with eagerness for the king."

"Aye," agreed William, "and I fear him e'en more!"

"Ye hold yer word and he will hold his, Father," assured Walter.

"I think Walter advises ye well, Father," added Sir Hugh. "He lived and fought with them for some months."

"Ye will be the inheritor of whate'er happens here today, Hugh," warned William "for ill or for good!"

"Today, we will live… to see what tomorrow brings," wisely added Hugh.

Lord William grew silent, reflecting on the actions he planned for this day's swearing of fealty. King Edward of England had certainly not come to his defense as he had promised, and the earl was thus twice glad he had not broken his word, though Sir Reginald Cheyne had tried to persuade him to join against King Robert.

That family's power had certainly eroded.

Lord David of Strathbogie had come to the king's peace, falling within a hair's breadth of losing his earldom.

Cheyne and Brechin both lost many of their estates.

John Comyn and his brother, Alexander, lost all their property, and the earl, remaining in England, grew weaker in body by the day.

Lord Mowbray, having sworn that one day he would have revenge on King Robert, went almost weekly to the tower of London to beg King Edward for troops to do so.

The flags of king and saint were dipped to get through the doorway of the chapel. Robert was close behind them and he, too, stooped to enter, one hand on the pommel of his broadsword. He strode directly to the altar behind his flag bearers, his close lieutenants trailing tight behind.

The doors closed and the cheering subsided in the bailey. It was almost as quiet as a tomb except for the strings of the harp being quietly plucked from a far corner.

While the bishops performed their part of the ceremony, Robert rolled back and forth on the balls of his feet. Looking at the earl, he could not help thinking of his dear, sweet Elizabeth and of the fact that, if it were not for this man standing solemnly before him, ready to bend his knee, that Elizabeth would be at his side. He secretly swore, in that moment as in many others, to find her… if she yet were alive.

Robert suddenly realized that Ross was moving toward him with head bowed low, his two sons close behind. The earl knelt as Robert had envisioned only a moment earlier, and Robert seethed.

The Earl of Ross began softly, "Because the magnificent prince, Sir Robert by the Grace of God King of Scots, My Lord, out of his natural goodness, desire, clemency and special grace…" he paused and looked up at the towering figure before him, swallowed hard, and continued as he had rehearsed, "…has forgiven me… *sincerely*… the rancor of his mind and relaxed and condoned to me all transgressions or offenses against him and his by me and mine…" Ross again looked up at the king half expecting Robert's axe, strapped to the king's side, to find the back of his neck. Robert simply stared straight over their heads and the earl continued, "… and has graciously granted me my lands and tenements and has caused me also to be heritably enfeoffed in the lands of Dingwall and Ferncrosky in the sheriffdom of Sutherland of his benign liberality..." he paused again with a long nervous sigh, "...I, taking heed of the great benevolence of such a prince and because of so many gracious deeds to me... do surrender and bind me and my heirs and all my men to the said lord my King..."

The earl's one knee was about given out, and with a signal, he asked his eldest son to help him get the other knee on the floor. Sir Hugh stood and with his supporting his father's arm the man managed to get to both knees. Within a moment he was comfortable enough to continue.

"...and we will be of a surety faithful to him and his heirs and we will render him faithful service assistance and counsel against all men and women who live or die. And in token of this, I, William, for myself, my heirs and all my men to the said lord my King have made homage freely and have sworn on the Gospel of God."

Ross paused and again looked up to indicate that he was finished.

Robert looked down at the earl and waved his hand to allow him to rise from his shaking knees, which he managed with Sir Hugh's help. At that moment, Robert knew that he must put thoughts of revenge behind him, for his Scotland needed Lord William, and he believed the earl to be sincere in his oath of fealty.

Within moments Sir Hugh had taken his father's place before Robert, and on one knee, swore fealty to the king and briefly reiterated his father's say, assuring Robert that the peace would be continued when the earldom fell to him.

Sir Walter was next, smiling at the king as he approached. Robert returned his smile as the young man, determined to return to Galloway to fight with Sir Edward, went to his knee. He too swore his fealty, "fore'er and e'er."

The harp again began to play as Andrew and Baldred turned, and holding the flags high and dipping them only to clear the doorway of the sanctuary, led King Robert and his faithful knights forward. Ross, his sons, and his knights then followed in queue.

As the king came through the door into the bright sunlight, all who were within the bailey gave a grand spontaneous ovation, shouting, "The Brus! The Brus!" again and again. Oliver's pipes played cheerfully.

Food of all kinds was placed on tables. The king retired within the donjon to get away from the throng of people. His cheekbone yet ached, especially in the cold, and the great scar down his countenance yet burned and itched in its healing, making him unpleasant to be around. Besides, pomp was not his bliss, though he knew it to be necessary.

In the bailey with his brother, Sir Hugh saw what he thought was "the most beautiful young lady" wandering about through the milling crowd. Her grace and poise struck him as being a genuine statement of perfection.

"Ye know this one?" he asked of Walter.

"Aye," replied Walter, "She is the king's sister."

"Introduce me, Brother," urged Hugh with almost an adolescent eagerness.

Walter weaved his way through the crowd toward Matilda with Hugh in his wake, while Christina observed from a window on the second floor of the donjon.

"Ah, ah, ah..." she cautioned lightly, "'ppears young Hugh of Ross has taken an interest in yer baby sister," she commented.

"That so?" returned Robert, doffing his boots and sinking deep into an over-pillowed couch.

"I reckon the interest is mutual between 'em," she said as she turned toward Robert, lying with his eyes closed. She knew then that his wound was paining him, and closed the heavy curtains to ease his eyes. She crossed the room and put her warm hand on his scar. They sat just so for a long enough time that she thought he was asleep and started to leave.

"Word came this morning that Castle Rutherglen, in Galloway, has fallen to Edward and Douglas," said he.

"That *is* good news, Sire," she replied. She then realized with a sudden jolt that his eyes, his beautiful eyes, were looking at her. The longing that they felt for each other was sometimes greater than either could bear alone, but they had an understanding that nothing must happen between them. She first broke the spell, this time.

"I ken Ross will not take ye astray," she said trying to force her mind in another direction.

"Fear makes good vassals," said Robert, throwing his stocking feet on the couch.

"Love makes good vassals as well, Robert," she said, sitting on the sliver of the couch allowed her by his large frame and looking deep into his eyes.

Robert smiled. He wanted to reach out to her and take her into his arms.

She sighed as if her heart would break and bravely said, "Ye seem right fit of body now."

Robert sensed her agenda. "I still need ye about, Christina," he said. A hint of desperate pleading tinged his voice.

"Ye... dear Robert... have fought against the greatest of odds... against the most mighty English... against the Comyn clans, north and south... and have won them all! And besides my other... feelings for ye… I am proud to have ye as my friend…"

"But there is far more to be done, this is but the beginning!"

She shook her head. "Not for me, Robbie. 'Tis time for me to get back to our children," she said quietly. "They need me more than ye, and with the winter settin' in…" She spoke no more, but felt the tears rolling down her cheeks and wiped them away with her fingers.

Since Dunstaffnage he had dreaded hearing these words, and knew they would be too soon in coming.

"Aye," was all that he could get from beyond the lump in his throat to his lips. His heart saddened at her say.

"I shall leave on the morrow." She wiped tears off his face, too, and laughed softly. "I shall take Agnes with me, if she will go. I asked if she would go for a visit and she didn't say no. Her healing is well begun, and she is even speakin' to me, though to no other, save yerself."

"Take with ye yer survivin' highlanders, as well. If they want to return to me when once ye are safely to yer kith, they are welcome. Ne'er have I seen more fierce fighters."

"They fought for us… we all fought for us… for Scotland, My King," said she, tears again welling in her eyes. "If e'er ye need me, my Robert, I will come, and willin'ly, but for now the greatest har'ships are behind us all."

How could they have foreseen Bannok Burn…

Bibliography

Barbour, John *The Bruce.* (with translation and notes by A.A.M Duncan) Edinburgh, Scotland, UK: Canongate Books, Inc., 1997

Barron, Evan Macleod *The Scottish War of Independence.* First published 1914 Current publisher New York, New York, USA: Barnes & Noble, Inc., 1997

Barrow, G.W.S. *Robert Bruce and the Community of the Realm of Scotland.* London, England, UK: Eyere & Spottiswood, 1965

Bingham, Caroline *Robert the Bruce.* First published 1998 Current publisher London, England, UK: Constable and Company Limited, 1999

Boutell, Charles (translated from the French of M.P. Lacombe, and with a Preface, Notes, and One Additional Chapter on Arms and Armour in England) Arms and *Armour in Antiquity and the Middle Ages* First published 1907 Current publisher Conshohocken, Pennsylvania, USA: Combined Books Inc., 1996

Campbell of Airds, Alastair *A History of Clan Campbell Volume I, From Origins to Flodden.* Edinburgh, Scotland, UK: Edinburgh University Press Ltd., 2000

Cosman, Madeleine Pelner *Fabulous Feasts.* First published 1976 Current publisher New York, New York, USA: George Braziller, Inc., 1998

Crome, Sarah *Scotland's First War of Independence.* Alford, Lincolnshire, UK: Auch Books, 1999

LaCroix, Paul and Meller, Walter Clifford *The Medieval Warrior.* San Francisco, California, USA: BCL Press/Book Creation, LLC, 2002

McNamee, Colm The Wars of the Bruces. East Lothian, Scotland, UK: Tuckwell Press Ltd. 1997

Oakeshott, Ewart *A Knight in Battle.* First published 1971 Current publisher Chester Springs, Pennsylvania USA: Dufour Editions, Inc., 1998

Robinson, John J. *Born in Blood: the lost secrets of freemasonry.* New York, New York,
USA: M. Evans and Company, Inc., 1989

Scott, Ronald McNair *Robert the Bruce King of Scots.* First published 1982 Current publisher New York, New York USA: Barnes & Noble, Inc., 1993

Scottish Fairy Tales. Compiled Senate Press Limited 1994 Current publisher Edinburgh, Scotland, UK: Lomond Books 1998

Tabraham Chris *Scotland's Castles.* New York, New York, USA: Barnes & Noble, Inc., 1997

Made in the USA
Middletown, DE
22 September 2016